THE FOLLOWING STORM

PETER A. MOSCOVITA

D1065818

Copyright: 2020. Peter A. Moscovita.

No part of this publication may be reproduced, stored in a retrieval system, transmitted in any form or by any means, electronic, mechanical, photocopying, recording, or otherwise without prior written permission of the author/illustrator.

This book is mostly fictional; however, it is based on historic events commencing in 1936. Characters in this book are fictitious. Any similarity to real persons, living or deceased, is coincidental and not intended by the author.

For information regarding permissions, contact the author at: *peteramoscovita@aol.com*

ISBN: 978-1-7346839-1-2

Credits:

- E-book Formatting Fairies
- Ashley Lopez. Graphic Design
- Martine Moscovita
- Mary Storsteen

This book would not have been possible without the generosity and guidance from the team at Formatting Fairies.

To my wife Martine, for the many hours she spent proofing and assisting me, thank you will never be enough.

To Mary Storsteen and Carole Clark, my thanks for the friendship and encouragement you both took in reading the draft copies of this book.

CONTENTS

Dedicated to the Memory
of my father
Amilcari Moscovita

This book is mostly fictional; it is inspired by actual historical events leading up to the start of World War II.

For over twenty-five years, my wonderful wife Martine and close friends encouraged me to write this book, based on the prewar life of my father, his time in the merchant service, and later his career in the British Intelligence Service. My wife Martine was also the inspiration for the added spice (sorry, Dad).

*The title, **The Following Storm**, portrays a man having to cope with staying ahead of a world spinning out of control.*

FOREWORD

The inspiration to write the Following Storm was based on events that led up to the start of World War II and forever changed the life of my father, Amilcari Moscovita.

Throughout my childhood and early adult years, I would listen to the stories of my father's life, living and working in Vienna, Austria, as a structural engineer. Later, he entered the maritime academy, eventually rising to the position of first officer on a fast cargo-passenger ship regis-tered to a German shipping company. These stories I kept in various notebooks but mainly in the archives of my mind. His friends in the military and maritime services were a great source of information, more so than my father, who really did not volunteer too much about his past. Over the years, this story has always been close, but I needed a push to start writing and make it happen. Thanks to my wife, Martine, I started writing in December of 2018. Connecting the tales gave me the perfect outline to create my fictional character, Karl Vita, and this story, The Following Storm.

These fascinating tales were the backbone and ideas to write a prewar story that would portray the tensions building in Europe before the Second World War. Although this book is based on my father's life, it's by no means an actual account of his private life.

My aim was to create a fictional character and a believable story that portrayed a world spinning out of control.

Goodbye to the *Tristian*

T he dawn crept up onto the horizon. It was a new day for the Langstaff Shipping Company's *Tristian,* heading for Marseille, France, at ten knots.

Karl Vita lay half-asleep in his cabin, watching the light of day illuminating the small cabin. Then, a loud rap on the door brought him to full consciousness. His steward entered with a raspy, "Good morning, sir, did you sleep well?"

Karl answered, "Yes, thank you, Arnold. Can you get me a bun or something and deliver it to the bridge?"

He washed and brushed his teeth, then dressed quickly in a warm turtleneck sweater and his dark blue officer's uniform. Sitting on the corner of the bunk, he pulled on heavy, warm socks and boots, stood up, and reached for his officer's cap, placing it on his head.

He then faced the mirror to make sure it was tilted to one side to give him that old salt look; he was now ready to assume his watch.

Heading along the companionway, he stopped briefly to look

at the notice board located by the door that led to the ship's bridge. There at the top were the watch assignments for the day,

First Officer Karl Vita 0700 hours till 1300 hours. He loved his rank being next in line to the captain.

His thoughts drifted momentarily to the storm that was brewing that had nothing to do with the weather or sea conditions and everything to do with this last voyage on the *Tristian*. Shaking his head brought him back to his duties as the watch officer.

He entered the bridge, saluting the current watch officer and his bridge crew, who had skillfully steered this three-year-old freighter for the last five hours. "Morning, Lieutenant Wieseman, I'm assuming the watch," Karl barked out to the junior officer, followed by, "Any reports that I need to be aware of?"

"All's quiet; no problems, the ship is on course at thirteen knots making good headway for an on-time arrival in Marseille at approximately 1300 hours," replied Lieutenant Wieseman.

With that, the officer handed the bridge binoculars over to Karl and headed to the bridge door.

The incoming watch crew took their places and waited for Karl's new orders. "Carry on steady on course three, three, zero." The bridge crew enjoyed reporting to this officer. He always had a kind and cheerful manner. Today, though, his manner was more solemn with a stern look on his face. *What could be bothering him today?*

The sun was rising, coming in and out behind fast-moving clouds. The seas, however, remained calm. Karl was saddened by the realization that today would be his last day on the *Tristian*, a ship he had the privilege of sailing from its christening three years prior to this last voyage. How he would miss her. What would happen to her once the dark clouds of war erupted?

The plan, his plan, had formulated in his mind over six months earlier. War was inevitable. The German chancellor was crazed with dominance over Europe and maybe the world. How could good German people follow such a disruptive dictator as Hitler?

"Sir, landfall two points off the bow," brought him back to his duty.

"Very well, make the entry in the log. Sighted mainland France at 0940 hours. Maintain course and speed." After docking in Marseille, the plan would be to leave the ship without belongings or luggage, nothing that would give him away except for all the cash he had accumulated. This, he would hide inside the jacket and trousers of his uniform, attaching the bundles and securing them by adhesive tape. Whatever else he owned would remain in his cabin.

Orders had come down that all crew members should remain on board through this refueling and cargo stop. The company was concerned that the French members of the crew might try to jump ship.

As the First Officer, Karl would be responsible for coordinating the paperwork and manifest at the company offices located outside the dockyards. This process frequently took up to four hours or more to complete, enough time to leave Marseille and his career as a merchant seaman forever.

"Stand by to take the harbor pilot on board. Reduce revolutions and maintain five knots. Escort the pilot up to the bridge once he has boarded." The pilot was a middle-aged Frenchman with a rugged, sea-beaten face, usually friendlier than today's meeting.

The winds of war were probably responsible for this attitude change. Karl ordered the helmsman to take further course and speed directions from the harbor pilot.

Two tugs stood by as the *Tristian* slowly edged her way toward her assigned dock. Seamen at the bow and stern cast off feeder lines to the tugs, followed by the heavy dock lines attached to the feeders. Once the lines were secured, the winches pulled the dock lines tight as the tugs maneuvered the big ship toward her berth. "Done with engines. Secure the helm." Karl had just given his last command. With that, he dismissed the watch crew, making his last entry into the log. The ship was now secure. He looked around, making a mental farewell, then left the bridge for the last time.

Back in his cabin, Karl took off his uniform and hung it up in the wardrobe. Reaching down, he removed his suitcase, which he always kept locked, due to the sizable amount of cash it contained. Karl removed the bundles, neatly tied together with string in varying denominations of French, German, and Austrian currencies, then quickly taped these bundles to his thighs, lower limbs, and waist. Moving to the wardrobe, he reached for the new uniform along with a fresh, starched white shirt and black tie that had the company logo embroidered on it. He put his company identity card and passport into the left inside pocket, then an envelope of ready cash into the right inside pocket. The new loose-fitting uniform he'd had made in Livorno, Italy, had been hanging in his wardrobe ready for this day.

He prayed the bundles of cash taped to his body would not be noticeable under this loose-fitting uniform. He made sure his pocket compass was in his briefcase. Stepping out into the corridor, he stopped, turned, and took one last look at the small cabin that had been home for so long.

He felt uncomfortable and self-conscious as he made his way toward the office to pick up the manifest, along with other ship's documents that were to go to the company port offices. He was worried that someone would notice the difference in the uniform; fortunately, this did not happen.

The captain sat at his desk, reviewing the documents before turning them over to Karl. "Karl, I believe all is in order. Make sure you wait for the new manifest and fuel numbers before returning to the ship. Sorry, you will have to wait probably two or more hours. There's nothing I can do about that."

Karl smiled to himself. This is what he was banking on. "Not a problem, Captain. I'll get some coffee while I'm waiting. Thank you, sir."

So far, so good—he adjusted his officer's cap to one side, confidently proceeded to the gangway, saluted the sailor guarding the only exit from the ship, then started down to the pier below. Halfway down, a pulling feeling made him stop; turning around, he took a last look at the *Tristian.* A lump in his throat made him realize he was violating the trust of his captain, a man he so admired and now would betray.

2

_____

Getting Away from Marseille

Karl walked briskly along the dock toward the main gate, which would take him approximately six minutes to reach. With the ship's documents in his briefcase, he pulled out both his company identification card and passport and presented them to the guard. Out onto the boulevard, he turned left and headed toward the offices located on the Boulevard Du Littoral. The distance took only ten minutes to walk. Today, he would do it in less time as he was in a hurry.

The traffic for that time of day was light; this surprised him for a weekday. Could it be that the locals knew war could be close at hand?

The Langstaff Shipping Company offices were located on the second floor of a large commercial building that, on the outside, looked run down and dirty. Inside, it was quite different, with brightly colored walls and comfy couches lining the hallway. The attractive receptionist logged him in, then informed him that the elevator was out of order. He thanked her in French, then asked if there was a bathroom close by: "Yes, down the hall to the left."

In the bathroom, he removed the bundles of cash that right now were sliding down his legs, irritating his skin. He placed the money into his briefcase, then returned to the hallway. The stairs were back near the entrance. He climbed them two at a time; he was, after all, in a hurry.

Karl addressed the receptionist. His French was textbook perfect. "First Officer Karl Vita of the *Tristian* here to transfer the ship's documents. I will return in a few hours to pick up the new manifest if that's alright with you." The receptionist smiled and asked him to take a seat while she located the office manager.

Karl became concerned, in fact, a little nervous, hearing this. Like the times before, he thought he would simply drop off the documents, then leave. A door opened, and a well-dressed gentleman came out of the office, smiled at Karl, and extended his hand in friendship. Karl started to relax. Helmut Gourts, speaking in German, explained it would take at least three hours or maybe even longer due to additional cargo being added.

"Not a problem, Mr. Gourts. I have a few errands to take care of in town, so this will work just fine." Karl headed downstairs and out onto the boulevard. The last time the *Tristian* was in Marseille, several months back, Karl had made a street map on the back of an envelope that would lead him to the garage where he had given a deposit for a used Opel Kadett automobile. He was still uncomfortable with the plan he had confided to *Claude*, the French garage owner; however, he needed a reliable car to make the long road trip to Vienna, so he reluctantly gave the deposit to hold the car till his return to Marseille.

As part of the purchase, Karl made a stipulation that four jerrycans of benzine (petrol) would be included in the final payment. He had explained that his ship would return in eight weeks, give or take a day or two, at which time he would take delivery of the car. Karl also asked that any service the car may require be performed prior to his return as the drive to Vienna would be long. This little car would play a big part in his plans to get his mother, sister, and nephew out of Austria and Europe altogether for an indefinite time. With war on the horizon, this car had to make it to Ostend in Belgium.

He now followed his map, taking a right turn on the Rue Du Refuge, and following that for seven blocks until he reached the narrow alleyway that led to the garage at its far end. As he walked down the alley, he thought back to that time several months ago when his trusted friend, Carri an Austrian friend living in the suburbs of Marseille, had introduced him to Claude Guinevere, a rough-looking Frenchman that owned a small garage nearby. They had met in the Le Genou Des Navires, a tavern close to the harbor. After several glasses of red wine and meaningless small talk, Claude described the Opel Kadett he could provide, and, of course, what he would be willing to sell it for.

Now, as he approached the end of the alleyway, an old sign that was barely visible over the door read Auto Services. Near the garage doors lay rusting car and truck parts that were strewn around on both sides of the alley. Karl started to worry whether the Opel Kadett would be reliable enough to make the long road trip be was about to embark on. He continued standing in front of the door, not ready to enter it just yet. He thought back once again to that first meeting when he listened astutely to the details of the little German car. He though more about the price they had settled on; had he been too eager to accept it? He started to think of how Claude had smiled as they shook hands, and Karl had said, "You realize this is all conditional to an inspection and a road test."

He smiled again, thinking of Claude's response, "You're the one that needs a reliable car, so let's go try out that little German car, shall we?"

Leaving the tavern, the two friends followed Claude to his garage to inspect the car. Karl and Carri looked at each other as they walked along the Rue Du Refuge, thinking but not saying how old and rundown this part of town appeared. Entering the garage from the side street, they saw the dark brown Opel in front of the garage doors. Walking around it, they visually examined the tires as well as gave the car a thorough inspection. When they were satisfied, Karl slid behind the wheel and started the little 1,076 cc engine, which fired up immediately. He tried the clutch and brake pedals, then cycled through the three-speed gearbox. Satisfied that everything was in working order, they took the little car for a road test. Claude was accommodating by opening the garage doors; then he jumped into the passenger seat; Carri sat in the back. Karl selected the first gear, then drove out into the sunshine and down the street.

Satisfied with the car's performance, Karl drove back into the garage, got out, and went over to a workbench where he produced an envelope, counted out the deposit in French francs, then handed the cash over to Claude. "I will get you a receipt—one moment, please," said Claude.

"Before you do that, there is a sensitive question I would like you to consider before we go any further." Karl was about to put himself in a dangerous position, but he knew it had to be done. Karl leaned against the workbench, his head lowered. After a few minutes, he looked up, "Claude, all is good with the car. I will pay you the balance in French francs, but I need your help by providing me with a lease agreement for this car. It may make things easier for me to cross the borders with French number plates." Karl further confided he would change the registration once in Wien. Driving in other parts of Europe would require another registration to reach his destination. He was careful only to mention Vienna (Wien) and no further details for the onward journey to Ostend in Belgium.

"Claude, once I have arrived at my destination, I will post a letter to you, which will only say thank you for your help. When you receive this letter, inform the authorities that the car was not returned, so you need to report it stolen. Claude, my destiny is now in your hands. Will you do this for me?"

Claude reached over, taking both his hands, and said in a calming tone, "If this will help you, it will be my pleasure to do so."

Now, as he stood in front of the side door to the garage, he was ready to close the deal and get on the road. Opening the door, the same nagging thoughts were spinning in his head, *would this car make it to Wien? More importantly, would it be in the same condition as when he saw it last?* There was only one way to find out!

Inside the garage, a single lightbulb dimly illuminated the space around the Opel Kadett—so far, so good. Karl, not seeing anyone, called out, "Hello, is there anyone here?"

The familiar rugged face of Claude popped up from behind a workbench. "Sorry, I was working on a truck engine. Everything you requested is ready for you, sir." Karl inspected the car again and found it all in order. In fact, it was cleaner than when he first saw it. Encouraging, he thought.

Two of the jerrycans had been placed in the boot with the other two roped to the roof rack, tightly covered with a tarpaulin. "Do you mind if I make sure the cans are full of benzine?" asked Karl.

"Of course not. Go right ahead. Let me take the tarp off for you."

This Frenchman was turning out to be an upstanding individual, which eased Karl's apprehension. Claude could have turned him over to the authorities, in which case he would probably be in the hands of the gendarmes right now. "Now, let's go for another brief drive around the block to be sure everything is in order before we complete the transaction, shall we?" asked a much happier Karl.

"Of course. Let me open the doors," replied Claude.

Satisfied with the test drive, Karl and his little Opel Kadett were ready to start the long journey to Vienna (Wien). Back at the garage, Karl gave the balance of the payment to Claude and received a bill of sale along with the rental agreement. In addition, he received other documents he may need to present as he crossed over borders along his trip home to Wien.

Claude took out a large brown paper bag from his old wooden desk that contained road maps for virtually every country in Europe. Karl examined the ones he would need to reach his destination in Austria before thanking Claude again.

Karl was running against the clock and in a hurry to put kilometers between himself and Marseille. Claude, however, felt they should take a few minutes to review the route options together over a cup of coffee. The route Claude felt would be safest would be to travel northeast in France in the general direction of Lyon, then over secondary roads toward Bourg, crossing the border into Switzerland east of Lausanne.

The crossing, Claude explained, was not well guarded, and no one was likely to question Karl about why he was driving a French registered car into Switzerland; the rental agreement should take care of that, along with his well-rehearsed story. As agreed, Claude would only report the car stolen when he received Karl's letter.

At every border, Karl would have to explain that his mother in Vienna was sick and did not have long to live. Renting a car in Marseille was the most expedient way to get home. Karl started to feel guilty about his first opinion of this rough-looking but genuine Frenchman. *Never judge a book by its cover* came to mind.

Claude's wife, Martine, entered the garage, carrying a thermos of coffee along with a large paper bag containing a large flask of water and slices of homemade bread with cheese wrapped in a cotton napkin. She also had included a couple of apples. "For your trip, monsieur, I thought you would like some refreshments to take with you. Sorry it could not be more. We will be praying for you." With that, she left the garage.

Time was running out. "Claude, thank you so much, but I must be on my way. I will remember you always for making this happen." Karl removed his cap and blazer, putting them neatly on the passenger seat; turning back to Claude, he wrapped his strong arms around this man, giving him a big hug.

Tears now appeared in both men's eyes. Karl slid behind the steering wheel, started the engine of the Opel, and drove out through the garage doors. At the end of the alley, Karl turned right onto the Rue Du Refuge and headed out of Marseille and the life he once knew and loved.

3

The Long Road Home to Wien (Vienna)

Following the route Martine had neatly printed for him because Claude's printing was illegible, Karl drove the little Opel along secondary roads toward Lyon, approximately 320 kilometers north of Marseille. *This would be a long drive*, Karl realized. He needed to relax as much as he could as he intended to drive straight through to Wien. Removing his black tie and unbuttoning his top button would help to make him less conspicuous. He started to feel more comfortable, even enjoying the little Opel.

Claude had told him the Opel was economical on benzine (petrol) and should take him approximately 170 kilometers before needing to be refueled. Claude advised Karl that even though the four jerrycans would hold an additional fifty-five liters of fuel, he should top off the fuel tank whenever he came across a benzine filling station. Fuel was not always readily available.

Driving along the narrow roads, Karl could not get enough of this serene countryside that was so pleasing to the eye. The straight rows of tall trees equally spaced on either side of the road felt like driving in a green tunnel. Karl started to remember from history classes that the French roads are incredibly straight, originating back to Roman days when getting from point A to B quickly was the objective. Now, intrigued by this, he thought back to other reasons why the French roads were so inviting to travel.

Most of these tall, straight trees were called plane trees, originating from Persia and brought to France by Romans and Greeks. Other trees lining the road were stone pines, ash, and a few chestnut trees.

Napoleon also saw the advantage of these straight roads to move troops and armaments quickly without congestion. Could it be that these same practices would be used again if a war started?

Shaking his head brought him back to concentrating on his driving. He also noticed that the car kept pulling to the right, a result of a camber in the road. Not to worry, the little Opel was running smoothly.

It was now getting late in the day. It was still sunny and quite warm, though. Checking his Jaeger watch Karl noticed it had been more than six hours since he walked down the gangway of the *Tristian*.

The staff of the Langstaff Shipping Company began wondering where Commander Vita could be. It was almost closing time, and he had not yet returned. What could have happened to him? The office manager decided to call the dock office and have someone go to the ship and inquire if he had returned. The attendant said he would call back with a status. Climbing the gangway, the attendant asked the seaman guarding the entrance to the ship, "I have been asked by the company office manager to find out if First Officer Karl Vita is on board. The ship's manifest has still not been picked up."

"Please wait here a moment. I'll see if he has reported back on board."

After about six minutes, an officer approached the attendant. "It appears the First Officer never returned to the ship. The captain assumed he was still waiting for the return documents. "We will send someone else to retrieve the documents while we try to find Commander Vita."

Captain Giovanni Sauvé crossed his hands and bowed his head. "Karl, Karl, what have you done? You, above all others, I thought I could trust." The bond between these two officers was genuine and strong. They regularly talked openly about their families and what would happen to them if war started in Europe.

Like a bolt of lightning, Captain Sauvé sat up straight in his chair, realizing what his friend Karl had decided to do. As much as he admired Karl's brave action to save and protect his family, he, as the captain, would have to report this action as desertion of duties to the company and the police in Marseille.

Returning to the bridge, he gave instructions that as soon as the new manifest and other documents were safely back on board, they would depart Marseille and set a course to their next destination of Genoa, Italy.

He turned solemnly and made his way to the office to make an entry into the ship's log as well as draft a telegram to the main office that First Officer Karl Vita had not returned to the ship. "Let me know when the dock police arrive," commanded the captain.

Two police officers entered the captain's cabin along with the acting first officer. "Will this take long?" asked Captain Sauvé. "We are scheduled to sail on the evening tide."

One of the police officers explained that desertions these days at the docks were becoming quite commonplace. Sailors from transient ships worried about their families, and loved ones were taking advantage of Marseilles' access to many parts of Europe and had left without a trace.

"As far as we're concerned, it's another sailor heading home." With that, they completed their report and left the ship.

4

_____

First Night on the Road

Nighttime was rapidly taking over from the warm, sunny day. Karl looked at the fuel gauge, which was down to a little over a quarter of a tank. At the next town or village, he would try to find a garage that had benzine available.

Luck was still on his side as he passed through a small village.

He spotted a garage on the opposite side of the road with trucks lined up on the side of the building in front of a small café. It had to be a rest stop, and hopefully, they would have fuel available.

Two pumps had large trucks in front of them. Karl swung the car around to line up behind the outside truck and waited his turn. The attendant asked Karl how much benzine he should pump. "Can you fill it up, please?" The attendant asked how far he would be traveling, as fuel was becoming hard to get. "Into Austria," Karl replied.

"In that case, I will fill the tank for you."

Karl asked if fuel would be a problem as he traveled toward the Swiss border. "We are the main fuel stop for southbound trucks. Our allocation for the next shipment is not for another four days. More and more big trucks are heading toward Marseille. That is why we are getting low. You should be okay, though."

After filling the tank, Karl looked at the café and decided to get some hot food, keeping the supplies Martine had given him for later during the night when the strong coffee would keep him alert.

Locking the Opel under a light pole, he walked toward the café and was surprised to see only a few seats taken at the bar. Only one of the small tables was occupied. Karl said to the waitress behind the bar, "With all those trucks outside, I expected to find all the seats taken."

The pretty waitress told him the drivers usually come in to eat, then return to their trucks for a few hours of sleep before getting back on the road. The first mug of coffee went down quickly, followed by another that he sipped slowly. The waitress said the beef was popular today. Karl said, "In that case, I would like to order that. What is your name, young lady?"

"Monica," she replied. "Have you worked here long?" asked Karl.

"About two years now—I was glad to find a job so quickly after leaving Paris." It was obvious Monica was blushing at the attention the handsome, dark-haired gentleman was giving her. Karl chuckled quietly to himself, realizing this was the first time in days he was starting to let his guard down and relax.

Monica came back with his supper. *Good choice*, he thought. It smelled so enticing. "Can I get you anything else?" she asked, blushing again, realizing what she had said. "To eat or drink," she added quickly. "You know, most of our customers are truck drivers. We almost never see well-dressed, educated gentlemen in here. What made you stop tonight?"

"Well, Monica, I heard you were working today." At this, they both laughed.

18

"No, seriously, why did you stop?" she asked again.

"I'm in transit to Austria to see my family. That's why. Also, I needed to fill my car with benzine."

They talked for more than thirty minutes. While Karl devoured his meal, Monica kept topping off his cup with piping-hot coffee. When it was time to leave, Karl paid the bill and gave Monica a generous tip. He made her blush one more time, "Monica, I would love to spend more time with you. You are a charming lady. Another time, maybe, we could have made it a longer evening, but today I'm only passing through."

"Will you be coming back this way soon or ever again?" Monica asked, hoping that this handsome man could make a difference in her dull life.

"Sadly, no, I will not, and that is a big pity for both of us."

Before leaving, he kissed the back of her hand, then stood up from the barstool, walked toward the door, and turned back. Monica was smiling a long last farewell.

BACK IN THE CAR, Karl decided he would take a power nap before continuing. Maybe one or two hours would help him drive on to the border of Switzerland.

Karl woke suddenly. A loud knock on the car window brought him back from the deep sleep he had fallen into. It was Monica. "Sorry that I scared you. I wanted to make sure you were alright."

"Well," Karl replied, "I thought a few hours' sleep would do me good before driving on again. That obviously is not happening."

Monica had just finished her shift. Seeing Karl's head against the window of his car sent her senses whirling, *what am I doing acting like a schoolgirl chasing a man I met only a few hours ago.* "Do you have time for a drink before you push on?" Monica asked.

Karl now realized he had to let this girl down softly. There was no room for complications on this trip. "Monica, another

time I would like that very much, but not tonight. I'm sorry."
With that, he got out of the car, drew her toward him, and held
her tightly. He could feel her back arch toward him as her
nervous tension built. Slowly, he turned her head toward his and
lightly kissed her on the lips. Monica was now totally aroused by
this handsome gentleman.

"Please, could you stay just a little longer? I live only two
streets away."

Karl realized he was making things worse by allowing this to
continue. Climbing behind the wheel, he said a final goodbye,
started the engine and turned around in the parking area.
Monica looked longingly at the departing car. With war coming,
the chances of meeting him again would be slim indeed, or would
they?

Back on the road, Karl grew angry with himself. How could
he have let his guard down like that? All these months of deceit,
self-control, and planning lost to a few minutes of escape. He
wished he could turn the car around and go back to apologize to
Monica for leading her on that way, especially on his first day
away from the ship.

As he drove, he willed himself to think of anything other than
Monica. His mind focused on times gone by, the dashing
maritime officer with pretty ladies so ready to be on his arm in
almost every port the *Tristian* docked in, so many adventures that
were becoming faraway memories placed in the corner of his
mind, gone but never forgotten.

5

Crossing the Border into Switzerland

T he mountain roads were becoming narrow and dark. The headlamps on the Opel were not bright. Even with the high beams on, they were dim. One good thing was early morning traffic was almost nonexistent.

He drove on till he saw a sign that read last fuel stop before the Swiss border. *I'd try to top the benzine off again*: Claude's recommendation rang like a bell in his head.

Pulling up to the fuel pump, he thought, *I believe they could be closed*, even though a dim pole light illuminated the pump. To his surprise, an older gentleman came out of the office and asked him if he needed benzine. Karl replied, "I would like the tank filled, please."

The old man removed the fuel cap and started pumping the benzine. "How far to the Swiss border?" asked Karl.

"About thirty-five kilometers," the old man replied. "Is that where you're heading?"

"Traveling through Switzerland to Austria," Karl replied. The old man cleaned the windshield and wished Karl a safe trip. Back on the road, the hills kept getting steeper with more curves to negotiate. The road was barely passable for two vehicles. *I'm sure this will slow me down. What is my next landmark on this road?* he thought.

Referring to the route Martine had made, he realized what Claude had intended. Staying off the main roads would make his trip more challenging; however, the risks would be minimized by doing so.

Driving along, he started seeing signs in both French and German that read five kilometers to the border. He should be prepared to stop. Karl began to get anxious as the frontier got closer. In his mind, he went through the story he and Claude had put together should he be challenged.

Another sign read: "You are approaching the French border. Be prepared to stop." Ahead, the brightly illuminated guardhouse had a white barrier with red stripes across the top, blocking the road.

Two guards waved at him to stop in front of the barrier. One of the uniformed guards approached the car. "Your passport, driving papers, and the documentation for this car, please. Do you have anything that needs to be declared?"

"No, I don't." Karl handed the documents to the guard, who looked at them quickly, then turned and entered the guardhouse. The other guard, in the meantime, walked around the car, stopping at the front number plate before looking up at Karl.

"Is this your car?" he asked.

"No, I'm renting it from a garage in Marseille."

"Do you have a rental agreement or something that gives you permission to drive this car over the border?"

"Yes, I have the agreement here."

The guard took out his flashlight, looked the document over, then looked at Karl. "If you are going to Vienna, why did you not take the train instead of driving?"

"Well, I did look at the train schedules but decided I needed to leave right away. I felt it would be much quicker driving."

The other guard returned with the vehicle documentation. "It all looks in order, but the car is registered to a Claude Guinevere in Marseille. What is that document you have in your hand?" asked the guard of the other guard.

"It's a rental agreement to Karl Vita from the Guinevere fellow."

The two guards stepped back from the car, speaking quietly, so Karl could not hear them. One of the guards returned to the car. "When are you returning to Marseille with this car?"

Karl spoke clearly in his best French accent. "I'm not sure. I would expect no longer than two weeks, or it could be sooner if my mother passes away."

The guards looked at Karl, sympathy in their eyes. "We are sorry that you are having to make this bereavement trip. We wish you a safe trip and hope you get to your mother in time. To help you cross the borders quicker and make the rest of the trip go smoother, we are issuing a temporary travel pass for you and this car. It is dated for today with an expiration date thirty days from today. That should give you the time you need. Show this document at the Swiss, then the Austrian border."

Karl thanked the guards for their kindness and started the engine. "Proceed to the Swiss guardhouse about one and a half kilometers straight ahead on this road." With that, they lifted the barrier and waved Karl through.

Karl sighed with relief as he quickly covered the distance to the Swiss border crossing. Pulling up to the barrier, a single guard approached the car. Speaking in French, he asked Karl for his passport and the car's documentation. The guard looked at the cover document, then saluted in a relaxed manner and told him to proceed through the barrier.

That's it? Karl thought, *what on earth is in that travel pass?*

6

_____

Switzerland

He was now in Switzerland. It felt good to be over this first of many hurdles. About three kilometers further up the narrow road, Karl pulled over into the entrance of a field. He reached for the paper bag, removed the thermos of coffee Martine had made for him, then took a slice of the bread and broke off a chunk of cheese. Sitting back in his driver's seat, he sighed again. His good fortune was holding up, thanks to Claude and Martine. *Without your help, I would already be in trouble.*

Referring once again to his route, he studied the mountain roads that would take him through Switzerland to the border of Austria.

Right now, I need some sleep—maybe an hour or so. I can't take the risk of falling asleep at the wheel. He pushed his driver's seat back as far as it would go, retrieved his uniform blazer from the back seat, and wedged it against the window pillar. His head had barely touched the blazer before he drifted into a deep sleep.

A loud noise made him sit straight up. *They have found me* was the first thought that came to him as he struggled with waking.

24

Looking out the window, he saw a farm tractor was waiting for him to move his car. The driver was waving for him to move to the left side of the gate. Starting the engine, he pulled away from the gate. The farmer jumped down from the tractor, opened the gate, then walked back to the car. "Are you alright?" he asked.

"Much better now," Karl replied, "got tired after driving all night."

"Where are you heading today? Can I help with directions? You are driving on narrow mountain roads. Wouldn't you be better on the main trunk roads?"

"Thanks, but I wanted to enjoy this road trip away from the busy main roads. This countryside is so beautiful, so I decided to drive all night to get into Switzerland. I only have a few days off to enjoy this." *Great story*, Karl thought as he returned to the car.

Karl started the engine, then looked down at his watch. *My God, I've been sleeping for over two and a half hours. No wonder it's so bright and sunny.* Honking the car's horn, he waved farewell to the pleasant farmer. He drove back to the road, then quickly checked his brass pocket compass, bought for him as a graduation gift by his parents. It still pointed NNE. *Heading in the right direction*, he thought.

After about three hours negotiating the many steep curves, he came upon a small village nestled in a beautiful valley. The road continued down the hill through the central main street. Looking at his fuel gauge, he decided to stop at a garage he saw on the left side of the hill. Going into the village, an old fuel pump was located to one side of the entrance. Waiting in the car for a few minutes, he looked to see if anyone was going to come out to serve him. Just as he was about to drive off, a younger man in greasy overalls came out and asked him if he needed fuel.

"Can you fill the tank? And check the oil and water as well, please."

"If you drive over to the garage after the fill-up, I'll check the tire pressure for you." *Really nice people up here in the mountains*, he thought. *Pity I couldn't stay here till the war is over, or better still, I hope war never starts.*

After the attendant checked the tires, Karl asked him if there was a café open. "Yes, drive down about a kilometer and look for a large chalet on the left. It's back away from the road to one side. You will see the café." Karl asked the attendant if he preferred French francs or German marks. "It does not matter. If you have plenty of francs, I would prefer those."

Karl drove slowly down the road until he found the chalet, and there on the side was the café. Inside, Karl found a window table and sat facing out, keeping an eye on the little Opel. Low varnished beams adorned the interior of the café. Lots of brass ornaments and a variety of beer mugs hanging from either side of the beams made the atmosphere so warm and enticing. Brightly colored tablecloths and matching curtains added to the charm of this café.

An older woman in her early sixties came over with a menu. Karl noticed she was wearing a traditional dirndl dress—more Austrian than Swiss. "Can I get you something to drink, and will you be ordering anything to eat?" she asked politely in a pronounced Austrian accent.

Karl spoke back to her in the same dialect of Austrian German.

"You sound like a Wiener, are you?"

"Yes, I am. Sounds like you are too. Are you?"

"Of course," she replied, smiling, "married a Swiss national, and now I've been living here for almost twenty years. As much as I love living in Switzerland, I always miss Wien. Are you heading home?"

"Yes, I am. Should be there by tomorrow. Now, how is the pork and speckle?"

"Wonderful choice. Now, what would you like to drink?"

"A large soda water, please."

Shortly, his meal came out, smelling so delicious that Karl

attacked it, realizing he was quite hungry. With fresh bread in hand, he wiped the plate clean.

After a hot cup of coffee, he asked to have his thermos filled, with added milk and some sugar, along with a refill of his water flask. "Can I also please order two rolls with salami and tomatoes to take along with me?" asked Karl.

"Of course, would you care for anything else while I'm here?" she asked.

"No, I think that will keep me going till I'm over the border."

Back in the car, Karl mapped out his route toward Liech and the Austrian border. *So far, so good, and I have not had to use any of the spare fuel. Hope this luck holds out for me!*

The weather was so inviting. *Mountain air is always this way,* he thought as he drove up and over the many curves, making his way through the mountains. His arm rested on the open window of the driver's door while Karl took in the fresh air and recharged his spirit.

As he rounded another steep curve that led down to a straight stretch of road, the hair on the back of his neck stood on end. *What is this in front of me?* A roadblock with two police cars formed a barrier across the road.

What can this be? Surely, nothing to do with me, he thought as he waited his turn to be waved through the barrier.

"What is your final destination?" asked one of the four police officers.

"Vienna," replied Karl. "Do you need to see my documents?"

"No," replied the officer, "we are looking for two escaped prisoners who are thought to be hiding in this area. If you stop, make sure it's in a built-up area and not on the side of the road. Also, do not stop for hitchhikers or anyone trying to flag you down. If you see any suspicious-looking men, stop at the next village and let the local police know, or anyone who can call our barracks with the location." Karl could feel himself relaxing as he listened to the officer. "Pass on through, and remember, do not stop for any strangers."

"Thank you, Officer. I hope you are successful in apprehending those prisoners."

Through the barrier and now making up for lost time, the little Opel was straining at each curve and incline. Karl felt confident that his little car would get him all the way to Wien and then on through Germany to Ostend, Belgium.

The need to continually change gears as he negotiated each curve and hill was keeping his speed down, something he knew would happen. But looking at the route also showed he was making good time toward the border. After about two hours, as he crested another steep hill, he got an amazing panoramic view of the lowlands of Switzerland and his first sight of his homeland, Austria. Giddy with excitement, Karl started humming a traditional Austrian folk song, *Wien, Wien, a Do Allein*.

It would not be long now before Karl crossed into Austria, then there would be no more stops other than fuel till he pulled into Mama's house in Churnin Platz.

Driving along now at a much faster pace, closing the distance to the border, Karl started thinking of what had to be done once he arrived home—so much to do and so little time to get it all done.

On his last visit to Wien, over five months earlier, he had met with his old and trusted school friend, Paddy Grunter. Paddy owned and operated a service of used car facilities close to Karl's mother's house. The two had spent time discussing how to get across Germany into Belgium in a car with French number plates. This would be a problem, and Karl needed Paddy's help to obtain a set of Austrian number plates and registration and a logbook to get him across Germany. Karl explained to Paddy that he intended to purchase a used car in Marseille with the help of another old school friend, Carri.

The problem would be the French registration. There was no

way around this. Asked Karl, "Can I get a set of plates and registration through your contacts once I arrive home? I'm not sure yet what type of car it will be, but keeping in mind the present tensions in Europe, I will try to buy one that is not made in France."

Paddy thought hard for a moment, then said, "Karl, wait a minute. I have a damaged Opel Kadett behind the garage. I've had it quite a while now. It's beyond repair, so we kept it for parts. Better still, I have never surrendered the plates or logbook. I could never find the time to fix it up. I'm glad now that I didn't. If possible, try to buy one similar, then we can make the switch once you are home. The Opel Kadett is popular all over Europe, so I'm sure you will have no problem locating one. Better still, get word to Carri to start looking for one in Marseille."

Karl liked what he was hearing. *Once the plates have been changed, I can hide the French plates and registration under the tool kit below the rubber mat in the boot.*

With that out of the way, the two friends headed to the guest house for a large mug of beer.

"But what do I do once I'm close to the Belgium border?" asked Karl.

"Well, you will need to find an area where you can change the plates back to the original French ones and hide—or better still, destroy—the Austrian ones. I think it will be safer if you cross over on the original plates. Don't you?"

"Agreed. Now, let's drink."

Karl snapped back to his driving—must stop wandering off all the time. Signposts for Liech and border crossings started appearing on the side of the road. He was getting close. The knot in his stomach started acting up again as he closed the final five kilometers.

A big sign across the road read in German and French: "Approaching the border, be prepared to stop." The traffic was heavier than any of the other border crossings he had passed through. *This could be a blessing in disguise*, he thought.

Ready to explain his story once again, Karl got his documents together and placed them on the passenger seat with the transit document on top.

A guard waved the Opel to the barrier, then put his hand straight up to stop the car.

The guard approached and asked for Karl's driving license, passport, and the logbook for the car. Karl handed over the documents, saying nothing.

The guard looked up and said in a kind voice, "Hope you arrive home safely." Then, he returned the documents. "Show this again at the Austrian border, three kilometers down this road."

Entering Austria will be the hardest challenge, thought Karl, as he covered the distance to the Austrian border. Above the building, a red-white-red flag proudly swayed in the breeze. Karl was coming home.

As he approached the barrier, two guards pointed to a parking place on the left. "Park your car, then come into the office with your documentation."

Different procedures at this border, thought Karl as he walked toward the guardhouse.

Inside, the line had about four people in front of him, which did not look too bad. A truck driver in front of him asked, "Are you returning home or just visiting Austria?"

"On my way home to Wien," he replied with a broad smile.

After about ten minutes, it was Karl's turn. "Passport, driving license, and documentation for the vehicle, please. Is that the car in the third lane?" asked the officer behind the desk.

"Yes, it is, sir," replied Karl.

"After I review these documents, you can show me the contents of the boot. What is under that tarp on the roof rack? Do you have anything else to declare?" added the border guard.

"I am carrying extra fuel in case I cannot find filling stations that have fuel available."

"Smart move. Now, let's go look at your car," replied the officer.

Satisfied that the tarp, in fact, covered two jerrycans of fuel along with the two in the boot, the officer looked again at the documentation. "So, you are in transit from Marseille to Wien. Is this correct? Will you be returning to Marseille in this rental car using this same route?"

"That is correct," Karl replied, wondering where this line of questioning was leading.

"You do realize this transit document is only good for thirty days, don't you?" asked the officer. "Well, if time permits, I may go back through Italy to visit relatives. Chances are, it could be a long time before I see them again."

"That's fine but remember the term of the transit document. I wish you good luck with your mother. Do you need any help with directions?"

"Only one—do you think I can make it home by tomorrow?"

"I would say you will be there by tomorrow's nightfall if you stay over someplace tonight," replied the officer.

Karl thought, *okay, enough of the small talk. Let's get back on the road.*

7

Annie Lourie

Karl started to think about this last leg of the route, and what should he do about tonight—stay over or drive through? The worst was over. He was back in Austria.

If I can make it to Innsbruck before it gets too late, I could look up Annie Lourie. I have not seen her in over nine months. I wonder if she is home. The main roads allowed Karl to cover the distance efficiently, arriving in Innsbruck just after dark. The town seemed quiet. There was not much activity to be seen. Karl knew the way to Annie's parents' home on Kerber Street. *I hope she is home,* he kept thinking.

He parked the car in the driveway and walked to the front door. A curtain on the second-floor window moved to one side, allowing light to shine down on the driveway. Karl used the brass doorknocker to announce his arrival.

The door flew open, followed by Annie's arms around his neck, taking Karl's breath away momentarily, "Karl, you are here. You are here. I can't believe it."

Inside the spacious first floor of Annie's parents' summer

home, Annie led him to the beautifully appointed living room, which he knew so well. "Darling, please, sit down. What can I get you to drink? Are you hungry?" she asked.

"Just a glass of wine, maybe. I left the ship in Marseille; it's been a long trip so far. Before arriving back at Mama's house, I thought I'd take a chance and see you here in Innsbruck before driving on."

"Well, you are in luck. I'm leaving tomorrow to return to Wien. One day later, and you would have missed me."

A bell went off in Karl's head. "Annie, if you are going home tomorrow, why don't you travel back with me? I would enjoy the company."

"Oh, Karl, that would be wonderful. I will have to go to the train station to cancel my ticket. Maybe we could do that first, then go downtown for some supper if you are up to it."

"I would love that, but first, can I take a bath and have a shave? I have not had a chance since leaving the ship."

The hot water felt so invigorating against his skin that he could have easily laid there for an hour or more, but a beautiful lady was waiting for him downstairs. Annie cracked the bathroom door open and, in a low voice, said, "I have laid some of my brother's clothes out in the bedroom next door. Yours are way overdue for a cleaning."

After canceling the train ticket, they drove to the town center and parked the car in front of a local restaurant that Annie frequented. *So Austrian*, Karl thought as they walked through the door.

An older gentleman in traditional lederhosen trousers and a checkered shirt escorted them to a window seat. "Would you like this one?" he asked.

"That will be fine. Thank you," replied Annie.

Karl decided he would sit next to Annie instead of across the table from her. The broad smile on her face told him she was pleased with this move. The waiter took their order for a bottle of white wine, leaving the menus on the corner of the table.

Annie turned to Karl, taking his hand in hers, "I have missed you so much, Karl. I was starting to think I would never see you again."

"Annie, you are so wrong. Being at sea for so long doesn't allow too much time to keep in touch. Nevertheless, I should not make excuses. I'm sorry. Will you forgive me?"

Hearing this, Annie moved closer and kissed him intensely, sending him a message that he would not get too much sleep tonight.

The waiter brought the wine with two glasses, placing them between them. "Excuse me, are you ready to order dinner?"

"Give us a few minutes to decide," replied Annie.

"Have you been seeing anyone, Annie, while I have been away?" asked Karl, searching her face for an answer.

"No, Karl, I have not. Don't you know what you mean to me? I always thought you would return to me. The sea may have you for now, but not forever."

Karl, hearing this, thought hard about confiding in her the real reason he was returning to Wien. He had been careful to this point, only giving that information to people he had to confide in to make the plan work. Should he now include the beautiful Annie?

"There is something I need to share with you—why I'm returning to Wien. I cannot, in all fairness, deceive you by letting you believe this is just a visit to see the family. I need you to make me a firm promise that what I'm about to tell you will not go any further. Can I trust you completely?"

"Karl, do you really need to ask me? Of course, you can trust me."

"Some six months ago, when I last visited Wien, I had lunch with an old classmate of mine who now has a high-level position in the government. He confided in me that in the not too distant future, maybe a year or less, Austria will more than likely be annexed by Germany."

Annie looked at Karl; the expression on his face said it all. Austria was in danger. She lowered her head momentarily, then took both Karl's hands in hers.

Karl continued, "We, as a nation, have virtually no military; furthermore, Adolf Hitler, being an Austrian himself, is determined to have Austria become a puppet state for Germany. There is no way we can resist."

Karl went on to explain that he was telling Annie all this because of her mother's Czechoslovakian background and her father's surname.

"Should you still be in Wien when Germany overruns it, your family could be in grave danger. My friend closed by saying, 'Take this advice and act on it quickly. Get your family out of Wien and out of Europe.'"

Karl paused and asked, "Do you intend to stay in Wien?"

"No, Karl, I will not."

"I am moving my family to England within the next several months, and I'm glad you're thinking along the same lines."

"Karl, you are moving your family out of Wien?" asked Annie, her hopes now looking shattered for Karl to eventually leave the merchant service and return to her.

"The danger is too high not to," he replied.

"Where will you go? And Karl, what about us?"

"I decided it would not be right to keep you in the dark, especially after thinking I had left you. As for the route I have planned and the exact destination, I prefer to keep that to myself, but I promise you this. As soon as the family is safe, I will contact you. Will you wait for me? It could be a long wait," said Karl, not expecting a good answer.

"I've waited for you till now, haven't I?" Annie now had tears in her eyes.

Taking Annie into his confidence had lifted a tremendous

weight from his shoulders. With that behind them, he turned all his attention back to the beautiful lady now sitting even closer to him.

"Karl, I'm so happy that we can be together for these few days. Let's make the best of them. What do you say?"

Their dinner finally arrived. "I'm quite hungry. Are you?" asked Annie.

"Yes, I am. Shall we order another bottle of wine?" During dinner, the conversion turned once again to what would happen to their families if Germany controlled Austria. "Annie, your family has two factories and substantial real estate holdings in Wien. What will happen to those, or will they try to continue under the new regime? Have they made any plans yet?" asked Karl.

"I'm not sure. My father and brothers believe that they are in good standing as citizens of Austria. There is so much at stake here—employees who rely on my family for their livelihoods, customers. And quite honestly, how could they sell their business with German control looming over their heads?"

"We have a similar situation. However, my father and two brothers are committed to remaining in Wien to protect the business. My third brother is moving shortly to Italy, which I believe is a bad move with the dictator Benito Mussolini flexing his muscles and rattling his saber along with his pal, Herr Hitler. They're both wild men."

"What will your sister do?" asked Annie, being careful not to sound too inquisitive.

"She and her baby will travel with my mother and me. Remember, she is married to a Royal Air Force officer and travels on a British passport. Annie, maybe you should consider leaving as well."

Annie looked away and said quietly, "We are." Now, sitting straight up on the bench, she continued, "It's me now that must confide in you, and Karl, that is the reason we all came together here in Innsbruck. My mother and I will be leaving. My father and brothers refuse to go but insisted that my mother and I move for safety reasons to Switzerland; her sister lives outside of Bern. It's not easy for us, is it, Karl? How can we plan a future together with both of us moving farther away from each other?" Annie was now becoming very emotional.

"We will find a way, Annie. I promise you."

"Drink up, sailor. We're going home to an empty house, and I have some loving to catch up on," said Annie, changing the topic of discussion.

"Is that right? Sounds like a plan. Let's get the bill," answered the very happy sailor.

Barely through the front door, Annie spun around and wrapped her right arm around Karl's neck. With her left hand, she started to unbutton his shirt. Her mouth found his, and the two locked together in a passionate kiss. Annie's tongue found his, moaning with the sensation. She guided them both to the couch nearby in the living room.

Annie slipped out of her skirt and helped Karl remove his trousers. Karl's breath was taken away as he looked at this sensuous woman standing in front of him in black lingerie. "Remember this, sailor?" asked Annie giggling. "Karl, I have dreamed about this for so long; show me now how much you have missed me." They locked together again, Annie reeling with passion as their lovemaking gathered intensity. There was no holding back. Annie begged Karl to climax with her.

She wanted to feel him explode inside her. Their climax was so intense that Annie cried out loudly in ecstasy.

Laying, quivering together, it was not long before Annie started kissing him again, madly urging him on to another erection. Encouraging him further, she slid down the couch and took his member into her mouth. That changed everything, with Karl responding immediately and thinking, *she's never done this before. God, it feels so good.* "Don't stop doing that, Annie. It's so good."

A little chuckle from Annie drove him on to his second climax, which she loved. She wanted to please him so much.

Karl lay on the couch, while Annie poured them a glass of port, then joined him. "So, did you enjoy that, sailor?"

"I did. Let's toast to a time when we can be together for more than a day or two." Karl was thinking, *that could be a long time, if ever.*

"Let's make it an early night if we are going to reach Wien, which is a 485-kilometer drive. With all going well, we should be there by early evening," said Annie.

As Karl climbed into bed alongside Annie, he drifted back to putting the next part of his plan into action. Sadly, those plans did not include Annie. Maybe one day, that would be different.

The alarm clock woke them up at 6:00 a.m. Neither one was in a rush to get up. Annie put on her bathrobe, telling Karl she would make coffee, while he used the bathroom and got dressed. "Use my brother's clothes today. You can get your uniform cleaned once we are back to Wien. I can't believe you didn't take any other clothes when you left the ship."

Karl thought, *Guess I should have told her how I left the ship.*

"Annie, what about the house? Should we clean up and make the bed?" asked Karl as he put on his shoes.

"That's okay, darling. Greta and her husband always take care of the house when the family leaves to return to Wien. When they come in, they cover all the furniture and shut off the water, so don't worry about the house."

After a traditional Austrian sweet roll and strong coffee for breakfast, Karl placed Annie's bags on the back seat of the Opel.

"Why don't you put them in the boot?" asked Annie.

"Can't do that, my dear. It has two jerrycans of benzine in it."

Annie had made sandwiches for the trip, filled the thermos with hot coffee, and refilled the water flask. "Okay, we are ready. Let's get on the road."

Driving east, the road continued over steep hills and many

curves. *This will be a long day*, thought Karl. However, with Annie's company, it would be more enjoyable than the trip so far. Neither of them said much for the first few hours. They were both thinking of what would happen to their relationship once they arrived home in Wien. The road entered a small village, and the traffic backed up at a four-way stop sign. Karl turned his gaze to Annie; the expression on her face told him everything.

"Annie, I cannot promise you anything. I'm sure you realize that, but I promise to stay in touch by mail so long as the mail gets through. I need to get your aunt's address in Bern, Switzerland before we part later today."

"Yes, I was thinking that also, but Karl, I have no way of writing to you. Your sister has an English husband, can I write to her address?"

"Annie, please, you know too much all ready. Again, I promise to send you all the contact information once I arrive at my destination. You must trust me. People are relying on me for their safety."

Reaching for her handbag behind the seat, she retrieved a small writing case and pen. "Here is my aunt's address. My father maintains an office in Bern, so I'll give you that address as well."

The traffic started moving again. Soon, they were away from the built-up area in the center of the village and back onto the country roads, winding their way through the beautiful Austrian countryside.

"Karl, how long will you stay in Wein before leaving again?"

"Maybe three days. I have some things that need my attention before making that decision."

"Darling, will we have any time at all while you are home?" Annie asked, fully expecting a negative answer.

"Maybe a few hours to say goodbye. Annie, it is imperative you tell no one of my plans and why I'm really in Wien, not even your family. As far as they are concerned, I'm here on leave from the ship. Promise me now, so I need not worry about the real reason leaking out."

Annie reached over and put her arm around Karl's neck. "My sweet Karl, you can rely on me to keep your secret. I, too, have a lot to lose as well, and that is you."

"Look, Annie, we are passing the signpost for Bischof-shofen. The next landmark will be Weiner Neustadt, then Baden." Seeing this familiar sign cheered them both up. "Let's find a place to stop and have our coffee and sand-wiches, then find a garage and top off the fuel tank," said Karl.

About six kilometers later, they came across a filling station. Getting in line, Karl took his time to clean the windshield and stretch his legs.

Annie got out as well and walked to the garage to find a lava-tory. "I'll wait for you over by that pole," Karl said as he moved the car up to the pump. "Fill it up and check the oil and water, please."

"German car with French plates," the attendant observed.

"It's a rental. I'm home on leave to see my family and girlfriend."

"Oh, you are an Austrian then."

"A Wiener, my friend," said Karl, laughing. To this, the atten-dant broke out laughing in agreement.

"You know, we rarely see French people or cars around this part anymore. The political tension is getting pretty bad." Like a bell sounding off in his head, Karl could not wait to change these French plates for the Austrian ones waiting for him at Paddy's garage.

After paying the attendant for the fuel and oil, he drove across the parking area and parked the car under the telephone pole. As soon as Annie returned, he excused himself and headed for the lavatory behind the garage. When he returned, he saw two young men leaning on the side of the car door. Annie was speaking to them with anger in her voice, "Please, get off the car and go away."

"You are Austrian. Why then are you in a French car? Must have a French sugar daddy around here somewhere," sneered one of the men.

"Right behind you," Karl barked as he approached the two.

One of the men pushed at Karl's chest. It was not a good idea to do that to a muscular merchant sailor who was used to dealing with young, big-mouthed men. One lightning swing and the man was flat on the ground. "Would you like some of the same?" Karl said to the other man.

"No, we are sorry. We were just having some fun. Please don't hit me," he screamed too late. A steel hammer of a fist caught his jaw and sent him sprawling to the ground. Both men now scrambled to their feet and ran away. One turned and yelled, "Go back to France. We don't want you in our country!"

"Karl, what on earth made you hit those boys so hard?" Annie said.

Karl, with anger in his voice, replied, "Herr Hitler will be recruiting young men like that sooner than you think, and there is nothing we can do to stop this from happening. That's why." Sliding back into the car, they decided it would be better to drive on and find a quieter place to have their sandwiches and coffee.

Driving through the beautiful countryside had a calming effect on them both. Karl reached over, taking Annie's hand, and said quietly, "I'm sorry for that outburst back there. I guess all the bad things that are going in Europe have been building up inside me. Sorry again."

Annie stopped him midsentence, "Karl, look, there's a layby with a picnic table. That's our stop."

Sitting at the picnic table, eating their sandwiches and sipping coffee, was beautiful. The clean, crisp air and sunny skies recharged their batteries. Annie, without looking at Karl, asked, "Darling, I was wondering if you will return to the sea once you have gotten the family to safety. Would you consider serving on a warship, if asked?"

"I have no idea what the future holds for me, but yes, I would love to return to the sea, probably back in the merchant fleet if I can. It's time to move, darling. Are you ready?" asked Karl.

"Whenever you are," Annie responded. Back in the car, neither said much other than a passing comment on what lay on either side of the road. Annie studied the map, then said, happily, "We are almost to the outskirts of Wien. Are we going straight to my parents' house first? If so, will you have time to say a quick hello to them? You know they would love to see you after so long."

"Of course, I will. They are wonderful people. Then, I must drive on to my family's home. They will be wondering where I am."

"Karl, tell me now; will I see you at all tomorrow?"

"Tomorrow, I have things of importance to attend to. Once that is done, I will try to stop by in the late morning to return your brother's clothes. Annie, that will probably the last time we see each other for a long time," Karl said, trying to find the right words to answer her.

Annie moved over to Karl, putting her arms around his neck and crying softly. "My darling, Karl, how can I let you go again? It's not fair at all."

"One way or another, we will find a way to be together again. I promise you. Annie, if you keep distracting my driving, we might not get home at all." They both laughed at this with Annie saying sorry.

Up ahead, familiar sights of Wien made them happier as well as sad. They were on an emotional roller coaster. The traffic was not bad for this time of day. The late sun was still high in the sky, and the summer temperatures felt comfortable.

People were rushing along the sidewalks on their way home

from work. Wien, however, did not seem its usual happy self. What would 1938 bring for this city and its people?

"Here we are," said Karl, pulling up to the gate of Annie's family's home.

"Wait. I'll open the gates for you," said Annie as she got out of the car and swung the big iron gates open. Karl drove in and around the circular driveway, stopping at the front door.

The front door opened, and Annie's mother and father came out, smiling, so pleased to see their daughter and her dashing sailor boyfriend.

"Karl, thank you so much for driving Annie home from Innsbruck. We hope you two had a pleasant drive. Did you have any problems driving with French plates?" asked Helmut, Annie's father.

Annie answered before Karl could. "Not really, Father. I'll tell you all about it later."

Annie looked at Karl as he retrieved her luggage from the back seat with a look to reassure him his secret was safe with her.

Annie's mother had always liked Karl. She walked over and gave the handsome maritime officer a big hug. "Karl, so glad to see you again. It's been quite some time. How long is your leave?" she asked.

"Unfortunately, Madam Lourie, it will be short. I'm lucky to get leave at all."

"Karl has to leave. May we have some time alone?" Annie asked her parents.

"Of course. I hope to see you again before you return to the ship," said Helmut, turning toward the front door and carrying Annie's luggage into the house.

Karl now turned his attention back to Annie, holding her in his arms with her head on his shoulder. "These have been the best two days I've had in so long. Now that we both know what's ahead, it will be so much more tolerable to bear. Remember this always, Annie. I love you so much, and your love will remain in my heart."

They held each tightly for what seemed like an eternity.

"Now, I must go, Annie."

Annie cut him off. "Karl, I know this is the last time I will see you. I understand your urgency to leave Wien as soon as possible. You don't have to hide it anymore. I've known since Innsbruck. When you drive out those gates, it will be a long time before we can hold each other once again."

Karl looked her in the eyes, tears falling freely from her cheeks.

"I tried to hide the truth yet again. I must apologize for leading you on this way. I am so sorry, darling." Karl found himself feeling terrible about misleading her again.

"Karl, I understand. I really do. Please don't turn around when you leave. I can't bear to have you see me cry. Let me keep the image of you in your uniform in my mind for as long as it takes."

Returning to the car, Karl slid behind the wheel, started the engine, and drove slowly down the driveway. He did not turn around, as requested by Annie. However, he did look at her through the rearview mirror. She was standing in the driveway with her head in her hands, crying. Her mother, seeing this, came out of the house to comfort her daughter. She must have sensed that this would be a difficult goodbye. As Karl turned the corner, he said softly, "Goodbye, my sweet Annie. May God keep you safe."

8

Wien (Vienna)

K arl drove the last twenty or so minutes to his parents'
house, his heart aching after leaving Annie. The winds of
war were not making it easier to part or, someday, to reunite.

As he turned into the courtyard of his parents' home, he
recognized his old car, which he had given to his older brother
before leaving for his last tour with the ship, pulling alongside.
He shut the engine down, thinking, *Done with engine. Secure the
helm.*

From the boot, he retrieved the briefcase he had hidden
behind the jerrycans along with his uniform from the back seat
and walked to the front door. Before he got close, the door
swung open, and out came Mama, his sister, Freida, carrying the
baby, and his oldest brother Mino. "You are home. We have been
worrying about you out there on your own," cried his mother as
she held her son.

"Karl, my boy, is safely home. Thank God. You must be
hungry after that long drive?" she asked as they walked arm in
arm toward the front door.

"For your cooking, always," answered Karl. At the kitchen table, they sat. While his mother prepared him dinner, his brother eagerly asked a string of questions about the trip and how he got off the ship without being caught.

Over the next hour or so, Karl told his story, after which he said, "Now, let's talk about the plan to leave Wien and what Papa, Mino, Ardi, and Ello will do once we have left."

Mino looked down, his hands clasped together, "We will stay here, although, I have sent my wife and son away to our relatives in southern Italy. However, the four of us will stay to protect the family business. There is no other way around this unless we simply flee the city, and that we cannot do. There are too many employees that rely on us for their livelihoods."

Karl argued, "Mino, staying in Wien, or, in fact, anywhere in Austria, is too dangerous. Is there any way we could place the company in the hands of the general manager until this is over?"

Mino snapped back, an angry tone to his voice, "No, that would not work. He has been with us for over twenty years. He's trustworthy and reliable. However, what will happen to that reliability should Herr Hitler start to nationalize Austrian businesses?"

"Well, if that happens, you will have put yourselves in danger for nothing," protested Karl.

"Karl, this is our problem. You never took an interest in the business. Your interest was the sea and probably will be again once you get Mama, Freida, and baby Franchot to England. That's assuming you make it that far."

After dinner, they all sat at the kitchen table, going over other plans that needed addressing. Midnight came quickly. Karl, feeling weary, told the family he had to get some sleep. It had been a long day.

0600 hours found Karl staring at the ceiling, mapping out all that needed to be accomplished today. "First things first, I need to go to Paddy's garage and make the registration switch. I will walk there or use my brother's car. Keeping the Opel out of sight will be prudent right now. I will ask my brother to drop off Annie's brother's clothes sometime this week. I cannot put her through another meeting."

Mama was busy in the kitchen, making breakfast for the family.

"Karl, you are up. I was going to let you sleep in this morning."

"Mama, there is so much to be done, and we only have today and tomorrow to get everything accomplished before leaving. I hope you remember what I said last night. We need to limit your luggage to one small bag each."

After breakfast, Karl had a nice hot bath, then a close shave. He put on a fresh shirt, pants, and a pullover from his bureau. From the chair, he gathered his uniform, stuffed it into a canvas bag, then returned to the kitchen.

Everybody was now up and pleased to see their baby brother.

"More coffee?" asked Freida.

"Mama, what time does the cleaners open?" asked Karl.

"At 9:00 a.m. Do you want me to drop off your uniform and the clothes you arrived in?" asked Mama.

"Please, could you? And tell them we must have the uniform back no later than tomorrow afternoon. The other items can be picked up later in the week. Mino, would you do me a favor? Could you drop off Annie's brother's stuff at her parents' house after you pick it up from the cleaners?" Karl's officer discipline had taken charge.

"Of course. Is there anything else you need me to do before or after you leave?"

"Yes, pray really hard. Can I use your car this morning? I don't want to use the Opel till it's time to leave."

"The keys are hanging on a hook next to the front door," replied Mino.

The Amilcar seemed like an old friend as Karl started the engine and backed out of the courtyard. It took only ten minutes

47

to get to Paddy's garage. He pulled into the back lot and parked close to the wrecked black Opel. *This will work*, he thought as he got out of the car.

He walked to the front door, which was still locked. He pressed the big brass doorbell, smiling at the loud tone. Paddy's familiar face looked around the corner of the divider at the back of the showroom. Smiling, Paddy unlocked and swung open the heavy door, "Karl, so good to see you. I was worried about you driving all this way. Did you park in the back lot? If you did, you must have seen the wrecked Opel."

"Yes, I did. Other than it being black, it's the same as mine. So, how are we going to do this switch?" Karl was hurrying things along and realized his friend was not in the same rush.

"Slow down, my dear friend. Let's have some coffee before we get started. Are you in your car?"

"No, I'm in the Amilcar. I didn't want to drive here in daylight in the Opel, so I thought I would collect the plates and logbook this morning, then change them once I get home. Is that okay with you?"

"Well, I thought we would make the switch here in the parking lot. But taking the plates with you will also work well. Maybe it's a better plan, now that I think about it."

Karl looked at his friend and said in a concerned tone, "Am I putting you in a dangerous position by doing this switch?"

"There is always a level of risk doing something like this; however, I think the plan will work to our advantage," replied Paddy.

"The car out back belongs to me. My story is that I intend to rebuild it one of these days. Once I know you are safely out of the country, I will contact the department of transportation and report those plates stolen."

"Now, once you are at the German-Belgian border, I'm assuming that will be at Aachen, you must find a place that is secure enough for you to switch the plates back to the original French ones.

Then, bury these Austrian plates along with the logbook. Also, try to cross the border at night."

"Paddy, what will you do if that madman enters Austria? Do you have a plan? Will you stay here in the city?" asked Karl.

"I'm not sure. This is home to my family and me. Where would we go? No, Karl, we will stay and carry on with this business. Although buying a new car will probably be a thing of the past. God willing, the repair work will probably keep us going."

The two friends embraced each other, both thinking but not saying this may be the last time they would see each other. They parted by wishing each other safety from the storm that was advancing toward Austria and the beautiful city of Wien.

"Goodbye, Paddy. How can I repay your kindness?" Karl said, becoming quite emotional.

"By getting this letter back to me. Please, please, make sure you post this once you are in Belgium. It simply says. 'How are you, Paddy? Hope to see you again soon.' Once I receive this letter, I will report the plates and logbook as stolen," Paddy said, trying to hold back the tears as his friend left the showroom probably for the last time.

On the way home, Karl stopped at a flower shop to buy his mother some flowers that she would not see wilt because she, Freida, Franchot, and Karl would be long gone.

Freida had picked up Karl's uniform, along with Annie's brother's shirt and pants, which were also ready. Karl packed his belonging. In a few hours, they would be gone into the night.

9

_____

On the Road Again

Once the daylight had turned to night, Karl and Mino changed the number plates, hiding the French set along with the logbook below the rubber mat in the boot. Next, they placed the luggage under the tarp on the roof rack and squeezed the smaller hand luggage into the cramped space of the boot. The left side of the rear seat was already piled quite high with other items going with them.

For the long journey, Freida and Mama had made a stack of sandwiches along with pickles, biscuits, some sliced cake, and plenty of fruit. Two thermoses of coffee and water flasks made up the supplies for the entire trip. Freida made room for them in the left rear seat, rearranging some of the items to make everything fit.

Karl made sure his mother and Freida did not overpack.

The plan was to drive through the night, putting as much distance as possible between the family home and sweet Annie— all left behind in Wien.

Now, it was time to say goodbye. The brothers stood by the

front door, tears flowing freely. Mama and Freida could not contain their sorrow, almost to the point of hysteria as they both leaned through the open car window. Mama's parting words were, "Please, stay safe, and don't take unnecessary chances. Kiss Papa for us when he returns home and tell him I love him dearly."

Karl turned the Opel around in the courtyard. Through the open windows, they waved their final farewells, not knowing when they would meet again, if ever!

Driving out of the city was mostly uneventful. The traffic was moving without concern for the gathering storm coming from the Germans.

The mountains that surrounded Wien were steep. The little Opel felt sluggish, struggling with the grade at every turn as they drove over the Kahlenberg Mountain Range, concerning Karl somewhat.

The distance to the Belgium border was 985 kilometers. Karl figured if they could drive six hundred or more kilometers each day, they would need less than two days to cross Germany before reaching the Belgium border, not an encouraging thought, considering the present climate sweeping across the German countryside.

Their route took them close to Linz, then on to the border crossing at Passau, Germany. Karl made sure they rehearsed their story. There could not be any mistakes. Their story would be that they were taking their mother to Aachen to see her sister, who was terminally ill and expected not to last more than a few weeks.

"Mama, you must look distraught when questioned by the border guards, and Freida, you must look like you are comforting Mama. Getting sympathy from the border guards will be important. Are we all on the same page?" Karl said, reinforcing their plan.

The kilometers clicked by. Other than a couple of stops for

food and benzine, the trip was uneventful. No one wanted to talk; their thoughts were back in Wien.

Late the following day, the signs for Passau started to appear on the side of the road. "Not long now," said Karl.

Further along the road, a big illuminated sign read, "Last exit before the border."

Another crossing thought Karl. *God, please get us through.*

Approaching the Austrian side of the border, a line of trucks stretched back like a long train. They were on the left side of the barrier. Karl realized he could go to the right side of the line, which was meant for cars only, and drive to the barrier with only three cars ahead of him. "Mama, give me those documents in my briefcase on the left side of your seat, please." Karl opened the file, making sure all three passports, along with the Austrian logbook and the new bill of sale for the car were there. Karl thought, *Thank you, Paddy.* The car was now ready for inspection. The guard signaled him to park on the right side near the guardhouse.

This, Karl did, then opened the door to get out of the car. The guard, in a loud voice, told Karl to stay in the car until they were ready for him.

"This is different from the other crossing," Karl said, looking at Mama and Freida. About ten minutes passed as they waited their turn. Mama asked several times, "Are we okay, Karl?"

"I think so, Mama. They must be busy with all those trucks to the left." Thirty minutes came and went with no further contact from the border guards.

Karl was just about to get out when a tall heavy-set guard approached the driver's side of the car, "Sorry, folks, for the wait. Too many trucks crossing over tonight. We are overwhelmed. Your papers and passports, please. What is your reason for leaving Austria to enter Germany tonight?"

Karl answered before anyone else could, "We have a medical

emergency. My mother's sister is extremely ill and probably will not last too much longer."

At this, Mama started crying, her head bent into a handkerchief. Freida leaned forward over the front seat to console her. "Where does your mother's sister reside in Germany? I assume it's in Germany," asked the guard, now speaking in a much lower tone, aware of the older woman's distress.

Mama answered, cutting Karl off before he could speak, "Aachen, my daughter and son have been kind enough to drive me there. My husband is away on business. He could not return to Wien in time to drive me. This all happened so quickly. I'm sorry for the crying episode. That's not at all like me."

Karl sat quietly while his mother explained their journey to the guard. *God, she is good. Almost got me crying as well. I think he is buying the story.*

The guard continued to examine the documents, then said, "I will be back in a moment."

Karl and Freida both looked at Mama. "Where did that come from?" asked Freida.

"Your mother may not say much, but when challenged, I can still put on a show if I have to," Mama said, smiling.

Karl, with a big grin on his face, leaned over and kissed his mother on the cheek, "You never cease to amaze me, Mama. We all love you so very much. Thank you."

The guard returned to the car and said, "Here are your passports and automobile documentation—one question for you, Herr Vita. The logbook states this car is black. It looks more like dark brown to me. Please, explain."

"Well," said Karl, "when I bought the car, the paint was quite bad, so I had it painted when I was in Wien. An old friend said he could repaint the car for me. However, he did not have any black paint. To avoid having to buy new paint, he painted it with a dark brown, which he had available and was close to the original black. In a moment of weakness, I told him to use the dark brown paint. Getting the car painted at no charge had a shortfall, I guess. It does not look that great, does it?"

The guard laughed as he returned the documents, "When you return to Wien, young man, make sure the logbook is updated with the new color. Madam Vita, I hope your journey to see your sister brings comfort to both of you. Drive safely, and remember, Austria may be changing soon, so consider making a quick return should this happen. Drive on; God be with you."

Karl started the engine, backed out of the parking lane, waved at the guard, and reentered the traffic toward the German border, only two kilometers farther down the road.

Once again, they entered the line of traffic to go through customs control, feeling a little more confident that, this time, their story would get them into Germany without problems. After about fifteen minutes, their turn came. "Car papers and passports for all three of you."

No please or thank you with these people, Karl thought as he handed the German officer the documents. *How Austria will change with these jack-booted people dictating our futures. The carefree spirit of Austria's people will dim; the laughter and music will be no more.* Once more, they told their story. Only this time, they received a curt response from the customs officer, "Wait here while I process your documents."

He returned, saying, "Are you aware your logbook states this car is black?"

Once again, Karl told his story. The guard stood by the open car window with a frown on his face. "Under normal circumstances, I would have to detain you until we could verify this is your car and logbook." Karl's heart sank into the pit of his stomach.

As Karl opened his mouth to speak, the guard cut him off, "We are busy tonight, and you have a mother who needs to be with her sister, so I'm letting you cross. When you return, you need to take care of this logbook right away. Not all guards are as considerate as I am. I am adding a note to the logbook, just in case you are stopped en route."

"Thank you so much, Officer. We are truly appreciative of your kindness." The border guard stepped back, allowing Karl to drive on.

"My God, that was close," Freida said.

Karl and Mama replied simultaneously, "Too close."

With that behind them, they drove on for about an hour. Suddenly, Mama pointed to the side of the road, "There is a layby. Let's stop and have one of the sandwiches. I could use a toilet about now as well."

A dirty latrine toilet, more like a shed, was the only option for toilet needs. "Freida, hand me that blue and grey sack. There should be toilet paper in there." Karl let out a contagious belly laugh. It was the medicine they all needed after the long, strenuous day.

"Mama, you think of everything. Don't you?"

After eating, Karl took the opportunity to add fuel from one of the jerrycans on the roof rack. Now, they would be ready to drive through the night, heading northwest toward Aachen. Karl explained that it would be best to drive through the night, find a roadside hotel to stay at till early afternoon, then continue to the border.

The traffic had started thinning out as the hours ticked by, turning night into early morning. No one had spoken in more than two hours. Mama was sleeping with her head against the window, her coat acting as a pillow.

Freida was holding the baby while looking out the window, her thoughts on the family left behind and the life she would have in England with her husband Ronny serving in the Royal Air Force.

Karl spoke up, and Mama awoke. "We are all tired, so let's find a place to sleep for a while." After fourteen kilometers, they saw a sign on the side of the road, "Pension rooms available."

They turned and drove slowly down the unpaved lane.

Farmworkers were busy in the fields as they drove by. Up ahead, a weather-beaten three-story building had a sign on the front door, Pension Entrance. "Guess this is it," said Karl.

Mama and Karl entered the front door. A desk in the corner had a large bell with a sign over it: "Please ring for attention."

An older woman, Frau Reid, walked out from what must have been the kitchen and asked, "Can I help you, please?"

"We would like two rooms for today. We will be driving on in the early evening if that is acceptable to you."

"Driving long distance, are we?" asked the woman.

"We are traveling to Aachen to see my sister," said Mama. Karl brought a few things in for Mama and Freida, along with a toilet kit for himself, including his briefcase.

The woman asked Karl if he would like to park his car in the barn.

He thanked her, saying, "We will only be here today, so if you don't mind, I'll leave it close to the front door."

The only bathroom was at the end of the hall. Mama said she would bathe first, then Freida with the baby. Hopefully, there would still be enough hot water for Karl.

After his warm bath, Karl set his travel alarm clock for 5:00 p.m., climbed into the comfortable bed, and fell into a deep sleep almost immediately.

The alarm clock woke Karl like a gunshot, making him sit upright in bed. Dressing quickly, he put on a clean white shirt and the pants from his uniform. He put his officer blazer and tie on a hanger, packed the clothes he had traveled in from Wien into his valise, then left the room and tapped on the door next door to make sure his mother and sister were up and ready to go. Karl took their luggage and returned to the car. Then, he went back upstairs to collect his valise, carrying the baby under his right arm.

At the bottom of the stairs, Frau Reid came out of the kitchen, a big smile across her face, and announced, "I have made you some supper. Please, come into the kitchen."

They looked at each other with surprise, "That is so thoughtful of you, madam," said Freida. In the kitchen, fresh ham, eggs, boiled potatoes, and homemade bread were laid out on the table on a beautifully embroidered blue and white tablecloth.

Frau Reid gave them a woven basket to take the remainder of the food they did not eat. "For the road," she said, smiling once again.

Karl paid the bill along with a generous tip, walked to Frau Reich, and gave her a big hug, whispering, "God bless you, madam; this country could with do more with people like you."

Before leaving, he topped off the benzine in the tank from the second jerrycan on the roof rack. He returned the hand luggage they'd taken out earlier, carefully hung his uniform blazer on the hook above the rear seat, then placed his cap on top of the luggage on the back seat. Karl turned to Frau Reich and asked, "Could your husband use this empty jerrycan?"

"Oh, yes, that would be nice. We store fuel in the barn for the farm equipment."

"Goodbye, and thank you for all your kindness," said Mama as she and Freida climbed into the car. Karl started the engine and turned around in front of the pension, waving as they drove up the lane leading to the main road.

As Karl returned to the main road, he said out loud, "Oh, my God, where did all this traffic come from? I hope we do not run into traffic delays. Hopefully, it will get lighter as the evening progresses." *The mood is much better now than earlier today*, thought Karl as he urged the little Opel on to one hundred kilometers an hour, overtaking a steady line of trucks going much slower as they struggled with the incline.

What was left of the daylight started fading into twilight.

Soon, we'll be out of Germany, thought Karl. "New story, ladies, for the border. Let's go over it while we are driving and you're still awake. At the German side, we will tell them that Mama's sister, living in Belgium, is in failing health. I was in Wien, on leave from my ship, when she received the news, so it made sense to drive my mother to Leuven before driving on to Marseille and returning the rental car before meeting my next ship, the *Global Star*.

"Freida, your story is that you decided to accompany your mother to help her for a few weeks before returning to England. You should show your English passport on the Belgium side, even though you have been using your Austrian one so far on this trip—best to be on the safe side." Karl was once again tense, thinking about the border crossing.

"Before the German-Belgian border, we can look for a quiet, safe place to change the license plates back to the French set and bury the Austrian set. No need to chance it." Finding a secluded area off the road, Karl dug a hole, using the left front wheel hub cap, then put both plates and the logbook into the hole, pushing the soil back into the hole, and finally covered the area with dead branches.

Another hour and forty minutes passed in silence before Karl said, "Now, ladies, do you need to make a toilet stop before we go across the border?" About forty minutes later, they found a road-side truck stop. "Great, we can get coffee here and top off the tank," said Karl, reaching for a piece of Frau Reid's delicious cake. "Mama, this is the last hurdle. Once we're into Belgium, we will only be about 230 kilometers away from the port in *Ostend*.

"Once we get there, we will have to find a ship to get passage to any port in England. Luckily, I know the port harbor adminis-trator, so we will go to his office first to see if he will help us."

The tension was building once again as the lights from the German border crossing illuminated the road ahead of them. "Are you ready, ladies? You are becoming pros at this game," Karl said, trying to keep the atmosphere as upbeat as possible by laughing.

Like before, a guard waved them to a parking lane, following them with a flashlight pointed at the license plate. Karl wound down his window, turning in his seat to face the guard. "Your passports and car papers, please. Where is your destination tonight?"

Showtime thought Karl as he started his well-rehearsed story. The guard cautiously listened to Karl's response to his question, then lowered his head to look at Freida. "Madam, do you live in England, and is that your final destination?"

"Yes, that is correct. My husband will meet me when the ship docks."

"Wait here in the car while I process your documents."

"That went well, I think," Karl said in a low voice.

The guard returned about eight minutes later. "Madam Vita, how do you intend to return to Wien?" asked the guard.

"Probably by train. If my stay is longer than two weeks, one of my other sons or even my husband will probably pick me up in their car."

"The reason I am asking this, madam, is there is building tension between Germany, Belgium, and France that could cause travel delays, so if they can drive you back to Wien, that may be the smarter option. I'm so sorry for the inconvenience. You are cleared to exit Germany. Please proceed to the Belgium barrier. Goodbye and good luck," were the parting remarks from the German border guard.

Very polite, thought Karl as he backed the car out of the parking lane. "One more border, Mama, then we are on our way to Ostend."

10

Ostend, Belgium

A big Belgium flag flew over the guardhouse as they slowly approached the barrier. Once again, they waited their turn to be processed, staying in the car with the documents on Karl's lap.

The guard approached, and, like the other crossings before, asked for the documents and the reason for entering Belgium, "Do you have anything to declare?" he asked.

Funny, thought Karl, only one other border guard asked that question. "No," replied Karl as the guard walked to the office.

The guard returned, "What is under that tarp on the roof rack? And what is in the boot?"

These questions were only asked once before at a border crossing. "Some larger luggage pieces and a jerrycan of benzine are on the roof. In the boot, there are two more jerrycans. We did not want to run the risk of running out of fuel on this trip."

"Please, uncover the tarp and open the boot for me."

"Glad to," Karl replied.

After satisfying his search, the guard told Karl to tie the tarp down again on the roof rack and close the boot. "Move on, please, and welcome to Belgium," said the guard as he waved his arm for them to reenter the road.

"Not home free yet, but damn close now. Let's have another one of Frau Reid's sandwiches. First, we need to find a layby."

The mood now was noticeably upbeat. "Only fifty kilometers left now, Mama," Karl gleefully said as he willed the little Opel on to the coast. Somewhere in the back of his brain, a feeling of sadness started to nag at him. This little Opel had been so reliable throughout the entire journey. It had taken him over borders, mountains, and so, so many kilometers. The painful memories of the time spent driving to Wien with Annie would always be linked to this little car.

He would say goodbye to his little Opel Kadett in Ostend, probably selling it to some dealer, or use it as a bargaining chip to get passage.

The road was becoming congested with early morning traffic heading to the terminal. As they got within a few kilometers, Karl pulled over to the side of the road and asked Freida to hand him his uniform jacket, which he put on after fixing his black tie, feeling a little nostalgic as he did so.

"We need to head toward the west gate and park near the harbor master's office. If Olivier is still there, he will give me advice and maybe some help on how to obtain passage on any ship that is leaving for England. Hopefully, it will not be days."

Karl got out of the car, placed his officer's cap to one side on his head, and buttoned up his jacket, saying, "How does this old sea dog look, ladies?"

They both answered, "So, handsome."

"Stay right here, try not to talk to anyone, and keep the doors locked." Walking through the front door felt so familiar to Karl, as he had been here so many times before. The smells of a working port building filled his nostrils. He missed this life.

On the second floor, he walked down the hall to an office that said "Port Authority" on its frosted-glass door. On the inside, a secretary named Madeline was sitting behind an old wooden desk. She looked up with amazement, "Olivier, it's Commander Karl Vita."

With that, a short, balding man looked around from an office door and repeated, "My God, Karl, it's really you. Your ship is not due in Ostend till next month."

"Well, right now, I'm not with the ship, or, in fact, any ship at this point." Over the next twenty minutes or so, Karl explained the whole story to Olivier and told him that he now needed his help to get on any ship leaving for England.

"That could be a real problem. There is not one ship you can buy passage on right now. Every ship is leaving completely full," explained Olivier.

Karl looked at his friend, "Come, look out the window with me. See that brown Opel down there in front of the office? Well, my mother and sister and her baby are down there waiting for me to find a way to get passage. Olivier, what is it going to take to get you to help us out?"

"What are you going to do with that Opel? If you do get on a ship, there's no way you can take it with you," remarked Olivier, loading his next question. "Karl, would you sell it to me?"

"Sell it? No damn way. Get me on a ship right away, and I will give it to you free and clear." Karl had played his best hand and now stood staring at Olivier, not blinking or making a move.

"Well, now, that is an enticing offer. Let me do this. Go get your family. They will be much more comfortable in here instead of sitting in the car, and I will start making some calls. Could you be ready to leave this evening? If yes, I think we could arrange a berth on the *Clyde Princess* sailing tonight. She will be making a stop in Dover tomorrow morning. Go get your family."

Karl walked to the car with a big smile across his face. "No promises, but my old friend is hard at work right now, shuffling bookings around for a berth on a ship called the *Clyde Princess*. We are going upstairs to wait in his office."

"How much will this cost?" asked Mama.

"That cost, Mama, was paid for the day I bought the Opel in Marseille," replied Karl.

Upstairs in the office, Madeline made them comfortable on the couch, bringing them hot, fresh coffee and pastries. Karl sat at a spare desk, writing a bill of sale for his Opel Kadett.

By late morning, Olivier had made all the arrangements to board Karl and his family on the *Clyde Princess*.

Olivier had begged the local company representative to make an exception for a fellow maritime officer, as well as a personal favor to him by getting this officer and family on the *Clyde Princess*. Olivier further explained that a medical emergency meant there was little time left to get them to England.

This fellow is putting me to shame with this story. Hope it works, thought Karl as he sat quietly in front Olivier.

"It worked. The company agent here at the port agreed to issue a VIP cabin, usually reserved for company officials. Okay, we are in luck, and way better off than if you tried this yourselves."

Olivier hoped this justified the gift of the Opel. "This is what we are going to do. First, come with me, Karl, and bring your passports. We will go right to the customs office down the hall. They all know me, so getting the passports stamped will not be a problem. Then, we will walk over to the shipping agent's office in the next building and collect the VIP tickets and boarding passes. When that is all done, you can provide me with the bill of sale and the logbook for the Opel. I will drive it home tonight, then re-register the car here in Belgium sometime in the next few weeks. I may run into some problems because of the French registration, but we know enough people to make it happen. Do you want me to send the license plates back to France or not bother?"

"No, best to let them disappear," said Karl, thinking of Claude as he spoke.

"When we return to my office, you and the family can follow Madeline and me in the Opel to dock C-3. There, we will remove all your luggage and give it to the officer and steward, who will be waiting for you at the boarding gangway," said Olivier, excited at the thought of acquiring a car for nothing more than a few telephone calls. "Once that is all done, Madeline will follow me back to my house in my car, and I will drive the Opel. I live close, so we will be back in the office in no time.

"By the way, there are two jerrycans full of fuel still in the boot, a parting gift to you from me," Karl said sarcastically. They both laughed at this comment. "There are two more requests I need to ask of you. First, would you post these two letters for me? It is imperative they get posted once we have sailed."

Olivier looked at the addresses and the two countries on the envelopes then looked up at Karl and said, "These are important; I can see. Madeline, make sure they go out in tonight's mail."

Karl looked at his friend, thinking, *I would be willing to bet he knows what is in those letters.* "Secondly, I need to make a telephone call to my sister's husband in England with the sailing information."

"Karl, that is expensive. The company frowns on personal use of the telephone," Olivier said, objecting to the request.

"Really?" said Karl, "I just gave you an Opel for assisting us, for which I'm truly grateful. However, this is the last request, and it's important to let my brother-in-law know we will be in Dover tomorrow morning."

"Understood, but make it quick," answered Olivier.

"Will do, and thank you." Karl gave Madeline the number to place the call.

"It's ringing," she said as she handed Karl the telephone receiver.

At the other end, a secretary's voice came on, asking, "Can I help you, and who is calling, please?"

"Lieutenant Ronny Whiting, please. This is Commander Karl Vita. Can you get him quickly? I'm his brother-in-law calling from Ostend, Belgium."

"One moment. I'll get him right away; he has been expecting your call," replied the secretary.

Almost immediately, Ronny picked up the receiver, "Karl, I have been so worried about all of you."

"Ronny, write this information down quickly. I don't have long. We are arriving on the *Clyde Princess* tomorrow morning in Dover. You need to get yourself down there to meet Freida, Franchot, and Mama. I'm not sure what will happen with me, so you must be there to meet them. Is that clear?"

"On my way," replied Ronny. "One other thing, Karl, thank you for what you have done and all you have gone through to get our family to safety."

"They're my family too, Ronny. You would have done the same for me. See you tomorrow." Returning the receiver to Madeline, he looked at Mama and Freida, thinking to himself, *Almost out of harm's way.*

Olivier observed the eye-play among them. He could feel the tremendous sorrow they had been carrying. Seeing this tension, he walked over to his friend and placed his arms on the shoulders of this brave sailor. "My friend, shall we now make that drive down to the pier? You have a ship to board."

"Yes," replied Karl, now with visible tears in his eyes. The anticlimax of all that had happened during the last ten days was now being released from his usual controlled self.

11

Farewell to Europe

Back in the Opel for the last time, they followed the port authority van to the pier and got waved through the guarded gate and out onto the dock. Olivier waved Karl to park close to the boarding ramp, where a ship's officer and a steward stood waiting for them.

Karl got out of the car, saluting the officer of the day, and asked in English, "Good afternoon, is it you that I give the boarding passes to, or should I give them to the seaman over there at the boarding ramp?"

"I will take them from you, sir, and I will be escorting you and your family members to your cabin once you are ready to board."

With that, he directed the steward to unload the luggage and help the ladies out of the car. Olivier spoke briefly to the officer, "May I have a few minutes alone with Commander Vita?"

"Of course, take your time," replied the officer.

"Karl, from here, you are on your own. I'm glad I could do this for you." Laughing, he added, "And I got an Opel Kadett for my efforts. Do you want to give me the keys now?" he asked, holding the envelope containing the bill of sale and logbook in his left hand.

Karl, at hearing this, laughed as well, replying, "That little car has been the best car I have ever owned. Take good care of her." He took a quick look inside the car and boot to make sure every-thing was accounted for. "She is now all yours. Thank you again for making this happen."

Karl stood watching as Olivier slid behind the wheel, started the engine, and turned around in front of Madeline, waiting for him in the company van. As they drove off, Olivier waved and yelled, "Good luck, old friend. May God be with you."

With that, the little Opel was gone, passing through the secu-rity gate, turning left, disappearing forever.

Karl turned to the officer, saying, "We are ready now. Thank you for waiting."

"This way, please," replied the officer. "Your luggage is being delivered to your stateroom. When you have settled in, the captain would like to invite you to the bridge if you're up to it."

"I would like that very much," replied Karl, carrying Franchot as they walked up the steep boarding ramp.

Karl could not shake the feeling that had been with him since Marseille, a sense of being very much alone with no direction in his life. *I have got to shake this depressing feeling that is in my gut. Maybe once we have slipped our dock lines, I will feel better.*

"Here is your stateroom," said the officer as he opened the door. "The crossing will be reasonably quick. However, our sailing time is not till nine o'clock tonight, so you will have time to relax and get caught up on some overdue sleep. We will be laying off Dover during the early morning hours until our pilot and tugs pick us up around 0700 hours. After you have settled your family in, come up to the bridge, and please, take your time."

The stateroom was quite roomy for this cargo-passenger ship.

Two single beds were on the left side under a porthole window, and a couch and two side chairs were on the opposite wall with a bathroom to the right of the entrance. The steward had placed the luggage, unopened, in the generous closet. Almost immediately, Mama and Freida lay down on the beds, totally exhausted. Franchot was already fast asleep.

Karl locked the stateroom door, then proceeded down the corridor toward the bridge. He was right at home, navigating his way around the ship. He entered the bridge, saying, "Permission to enter the bridge."

"Permission granted," came the response. The bridge looked very much like the *Tristian's*; only the *Tristian* was so much newer.

"So pleased you could join us, Commander Vita," said the captain, who was sitting in his high swivel chair, drinking a mug of steaming tea.

"Can we get you something to drink?" asked the officer on duty.

"Coffee would be nice if you have some," answered Karl.

The two senior officers moved to a chart table that had two comfortable chairs in front of it. "Your ship was the *Tristian*, I believe. Is that true?"

"Yes," replied Karl, not sure where this line of questioning was heading.

"We were docked close by to her in Alexandria, Egypt, a year or so ago. She is a magnificent vessel. I'm sure you will miss her." The captain looked Karl right in the eyes, waiting for him to continue this conversation.

"Your line of questioning is correct. I left the ship in Marseille without prior approval. For this, I will be forever saddened, as I let my captain down by leaving. Captain, let me set your concerns straight about what has transpired since I left the *Tristian*.

"My family lives in Vienna. It's only a matter of time before

68

the Germans and that madman, Hitler, overrun it. Austria has only a small military to defend itself. He is an Austrian himself and has been making overtures for some time about making Austria a part of the German empire.

"So, I knew it would be up to me to get my mother and sister with her baby out of the country while the borders were still open."

Captain McKinley listened without taking his attention from Karl's face, looking for any hint that this story could be false. Karl continued, "Once they are safely in England, I intend to seek asylum for myself. My sister lives in England with her husband, a lieutenant in the Royal Air Force. My mother will be staying with them. By the way, my brother-in-law will be waiting for them when we dock in Dover.

"I realize my actions may forever keep me from my love of the sea and the career I enjoyed as a maritime officer. Given a choice, I would make the same decisions all over again. My family will always come first with me."

They both sat quietly for what seemed an eternity to Karl, then Captain James McKinley reached over and took Karl's upper arm, "Young man, what you have done is a true act of unselfish courage. Putting your family first above any thought for your own safety or future is a decision I would have taken myself. Would you join me in my day cabin for a glass of sherry? I think you could be ready for one about now."

"I would love that and thank you for your understanding. I did not like the thought of going over to England in leg irons."

"Austrian sense of humor," said the captain, laughing as he opened the door for him and Karl to leave the bridge.

The two officers sat in the day cabin for about forty-five minutes, talking about a host of topics, including the shortage of qualified officers for the expanding maritime fleet, "Karl, do not give up on your chances of returning to sea duty just yet."

With that, they shook hands, Karl feeling like another weight had been taken off his shoulders as he returned to the stateroom. Opening the stateroom door quietly, Karl found Mama playing with Franchot on one of the beds. Freida was sitting, reading a book she had been carrying with her from Wien.

"What say we go down to the dining room and get a nice, hot meal? You both must be hungry by now."

"Yes, we are," said Mama. "It is going to be nice to sit at a table instead of having sandwiches on our laps."

Dinner was typical English overcooked meat, potatoes, and some vegetables topped with hot gravy. When you're hungry, everything tastes good.

Returning to the stateroom, Karl said, "If you don't mind, ladies, I'm going to get some shut-eye before we depart at nine o'clock tonight."

"Freida, I will use the couch, so could you move over to the bed?"

"Will do," replied Freida.

As a seasoned maritime officer, any changes to the sounds and movement of the ship would wake him immediately. A clanging sound on the dock did just that. The evening sky brought a yellow glow from the dock lights through the porthole window. "I'm going up on deck to watch us cast off. I'll be back soon."

Even though Karl had an open invitation to observe the departure from the bridge, he elected to go to the stern instead. He needed to be alone. Standing by the rail, he watched the dock stevedores single up the dock lines, standing by for the next command to cast off the main lines. Two tugs moved into position to push the ship away from the dock once all lines were cast off.

In his mind, he was giving maneuvering commands, thinking, *will I ever do this again?*

As he stood there, he felt a hand on his shoulder.

70

It was his sister, Freida, "What is going through that mind of yours, sailor?" she asked as Karl put his arm around her waist.

"I was thinking this may be the last time we see Europe for a long time."

"I know. I was thinking that also," Freida said with a sad tone to her voice. "Karl, what is happening to the life we had, and why are the German people allowing Herr Hitler to take their independence away from them?"

"Very easy, Freida. He has convinced them he will restore their dignity, their prosperity, and give them a higher standard of living. He says he'll return Germany to a world power; that's why. I'm also concerned that, as we sail tonight to England and out of harm's way, we leave behind family members and close friends that are right now directly in harm's way! Can Papa keep his opinions to himself and not be outspoken when addressing the new German masters of Austria? All of these things are going through my mind right now," Karl said, speaking softly to his sister, his hand holding up her head toward his as he spoke.

Freida, hearing Karl talk like this, put both arms around her brother, trying to console some of the pain he was carrying inside.

"Karl, what will your options be if you ask for asylum? Do you know, or will you try to find another ship that is not German or Italian registered?"

"Freida, I don't know. This ship's Captain McKinley told me there is a shortage of licensed maritime officers, so maybe that's the approach I'll take."

The ship, now under its own power, was turning toward the breakwater and out to the open sea. As they stood at the stern, the sea air filled their lungs, "We have made it," Karl said without moving.

Freida squeezed him tighter and raised her head to kiss his cheek, now wet with tears, "Yes, we have."

Back in the stateroom, they found Mama asleep with Franchot in her arms. Freida put her finger across her lips as a sign to keep quiet and let them sleep.

Karl removed his cap, jacket, tie, and shoes and curled up on the couch, sleep coming almost immediately. Freida did the same, only on a much more comfortable bed.

12

England

Karl woke to a change in the ship's propeller revolutions. *We are slowing down to a stop for the remainder of the early morning hours.*

Might as well try to get some more sleep. It will get quite hectic later in the morning. I need my wits about me for what is coming, he thought.

Karl had asked the steward to wake him at 0545 hours. A quiet knock got Karl up immediately. He opened the door to the aroma of hot coffee on a tray that the steward was carrying. "Thank you so much. That smells so good," Karl remarked.

"I brought some rolls, butter, and jam as well. That should hold you over for a while," whispered the good-natured steward. "The captain also sends his compliments. You should join him on the bridge to watch as we enter Dover and the docking procedures."

"Thank the captain and inform him I'll be along shortly," Karl said, taking the tray and closing the door.

Mama and Freida were now sitting up in bed, looking so

much better than the day before. "If you don't mind, I'll use the bathroom first. The captain has invited me to the bridge. You two should go down to the dining room and have a hearty breakfast; it will be a long day today. Don't worry about me. I'll get something on the bridge. By the way, the steward gave me these tags for the luggage. They will pick them up about seven o'clock. Just leave them outside the door. I will collect you once we have entered the harbor."

Dawn was now rising fast to a perfect morning, not that much different to the last morning on the *Tristian*. "Permission to enter the bridge," Karl asked in an authoritative voice.

"Permission granted," came the reply.

"Good morning, Commander. Did you have a pleasant evening?" asked the captain, smiling from his swivel chair. His greeting was echoed by the others who made up the bridge crew.

"I did; thank you very much."

"Last night, I contacted the company and explained we had a fellow maritime officer aboard from a German shipping company, traveling with members of his family. I have requested on your behalf an early disembarkation to meet with customs officials. I further explained that Commander Vita would be seeking asylum in England."

"Captain, once again, I find myself thanking you for looking after us," said Karl.

"It was my pleasure to help in a small way, Commander," replied the captain. "Stand by to board the pilot," came the next command from Captain McKinley. "Number One, prepare your docking crews fore and aft, and please have commander Vita's family moved to my day cabin. They may wish to view the docking in Dover."

"How are we doing, Commander?" Captain McKinley said to Karl, laughing.

That got a roar from the rest of the bridge crew.

"I don't think I could improve on it so far, except, I think having hot coffee available on the bridge as well as tea would give me hope for the future." To this, everyone started to laugh again, loudly.

"The pilot is now on board. Ready to proceed to the tug rendezvous pick-up point," said Number One. "Make your revolutions for five knots. Bring the pilot up to the bridge once he has his tea or maybe coffee." The captain was in a jovial mood this morning.

The door to the bridge opened. In came Mama; Freida elected to stay in the day cabin as she was worried about Franchot disturbing the crew during the docking procedure. "Good morning, Captain, nice to meet you," said Mama in very broken English, then sat down at the desk.

"May I get you some tea or maybe some coffee?" asked one of the seamen.

"That would be nice, coffee if you please," replied Mama.

Over the next sixty-five minutes, the ship was positioned and led into the harbor by the tugs that shepherded their charge to its assigned berth. The last command spoken by the captain, and so familiar to Karl, was simultaneously repeated by Karl in his mind: *Done with engine. Lock the helm.*

Now that the docking procedure was complete, the captain turned to Karl, saying, "We need to get you together with the customs officers and the authorities once they have boarded."

"Captain, the boarding ramp is now attached. Will you meet the customs officers in your day cabin or here on the bridge?"

"In my day cabin," came the captain's reply.

Two uniformed customs agents and two plain-clothes intelligence officers were already in the day cabin as the captain, Karl, and Mama entered. Freida sat with Franchot and now Mama in two chairs on either side of the small desk. "Good day, gentlemen. I hope we didn't keep you waiting too long," said the captain.

"Not at all," came a response from one of the customs officers.

75

"I'm assuming from the uniform you are the Austrian officer seeking asylum. Is that correct?" asked the senior intelligence officer.

"That is correct," answered Karl, extending his hand to the officer.

"Captain, I suggest Commander Vita and his family accompany us off the ship and allow these customs chaps to proceed with their task of clearing the ship if that is alright with you."

"My sentiments entirely," replied the captain as he turned to face Karl. "Commander, we have been together such a short time. I sincerely hope our paths will cross again. Please, keep this someplace safe. It's my home address in *Edinburgh*. Please stay in touch, Karl, and always remember, if I can help you in any way, it would be my pleasure to do so."

The captain took one step back and saluted in a sign of respect to the younger commander. Karl responded in the same manner.

One of the intelligence officers held the door for Karl and his family to exit the day cabin, then led them to the boarding ramp.

As they walked down the ramp, Karl thought, *I'm leaving another ship—only this time with permission.* Something made him stop and look back toward the ship.

There at the rail was Captain McKinley, watching them. He moved his hand in a gesture of professional respect and friendship by touching the peak of his cap in a casual salute. Karl did the same, silently saying thank you. A nod from the captain made Karl nod back.

All is well.

In the customs hall, the intelligence officer addressed them, "If you two ladies would like to collect your luggage, this porter will assist you. Then take it to the customs line over there; they will process you through, after which you can wait on the opposite side of that barrier. I'm not sure how long we will detain Commander Vita; however, if it looks like it will be an extended period, then I will have someone update you on what is planned for your son. I've been told your husband is waiting for you. Is that correct?"

"Yes, he is," replied Freida.

"Can you make him out in that crowd over there behind the barrier?" asked the officer.

"Yes, he's the one in the RAF uniform."

"Good, wait here. I'm going to bring him over to help you with the luggage and baby."

"Oh, thank you so much," answered Freida.

Ronny, once the barrier was opened, ran over to Freida and Franchot, holding them close. He wrapped his other arm around Mama, "God, it's so good to have you all safely home again. Where is Karl? Did they tell you what will happen to him?"

The intelligence officer spoke before anyone else could. "I've just been informed he will be detained for two to three days in a military camp not far from here, after which numerous avenues may determine his future. Although it's against normal customs regulations, wait here, and I will bring him out to say his goodbyes."

Mama, hearing this, broke out in tears, "My boy, my boy, what will they do to him?"

"Madam, please do not alarm yourself. Right now, he is in the best of hands; this I can assure you," said one of the officers.

They waited for what seemed like an eternity before Karl came out into the customs hall. Two uniformed military police guards accompanied him to the barrier. "Please, be quick; this is not usually allowed by the customs department. I, however, do not work for the customs department," said the senior intelligence officer with a little sarcasm in his tone.

"Mama, promise me you will not worry about me. I expected something like this when I asked for asylum," Karl said, holding his mother close.

Ronny cut in by asking, "Karl, is there anything I can do right now for you?"

"Not really, but if it looks like I'm going to be out of touch for a while, I have been assured by these intelligence chaps that you will be kept abreast to the extent security will allow."

"Sir, we must be going. The customs people are waving at us to stop. Please, say your goodbyes," said one of the military police guards nervously.

"Ronny, they are in your care now. Thank you for being here to meet them." With that, Karl turned without looking back and walked through the door that said *No Admittance Security Personnel Only* and was gone.

Ronny took Mama's arm; Freida with Franchot followed behind with the porter. When they reached the car, Freida asked Ronny, "This is a military car; how did you get it?"

"Well, my commanding officer is a golfing friend of mine. When I explained Karl's telephone call, he asked how I would fit three people, a baby, and luggage into my small Austin 8 car and told me to use his staff car. The drive back to Baldock is going to take about five to six hours, so try and get some rest." Ronny started the Humber's big engine, thinking, *Thank God I'm not paying for the petrol.*

"Once we get home to the bungalow, I'll run out to the corner shop to pick up some groceries until you can go shopping tomorrow. Is that alright with you two?"

"That will be fine. Remember to buy coffee," Freida replied.

Karl, feeling quite alone now, sat at a table drinking instant coffee. *Just awful*, he thought, as he forced the next mouthful down.

The office was small, with no windows. A single light fixture provided a minimum amount of light. The two intelligence officers returned, one carrying a ham and cheese sandwich for their new charge.

"By the way, it was so hectic this morning that we never properly introduced ourselves; sorry for appearing so rude. My name is Major Clive Knight, and this is Captain William Lowes. We are both with the office of Central Intelligence. Let me officially welcome you, Commander Vita, to England."

As they talked, a loud ship's horn signaled the departure of the *Clyde Princess* from Dover. *Godspeed, Captain McKinley. Stay safe,* thought Karl.

"Well, Major, what will happen to me now?" asked Karl, not sure of himself as he faced both men.

"From what we have accumulated so far, it would appear that you have a lot to offer, if, in fact, you are serious about asylum in England. Over the next few days, we will find out if there is a fit for you here. Right now, you have five options to consider.

"One is to be immediately deported back to mainland Europe. I cannot believe after all you have gone through that is the option for you.

"Two is to accept internment without a term limit; that would appear to be a waste of your abilities.

"Three is to join the Free European Brigade that is being formed right now; this includes the free Germans, Italians, Poles, and others from countries in Europe.

"Four, you may also be considered for a position in the British Maritime Service. God knows we need qualified officers like yourself about now.

"The fifth and last option open to you is by far the most important reason to meet you at the ship. Our current needs are for Europeans that are multilingual with a strong maritime background, both of which you score very highly in.

"Assuming we are satisfied with the outcome of the interrogation phase, and, of course, meeting our requirements, you may be given an opportunity to join a branch of the British Intelligence Service."

There it is, thought Karl, *my opportunity to strike back. I hope they ask me to join.*

Major Knight went on to say, "We are not expecting an answer right now, but we need you to consider these options carefully before meeting the panel of officers that will conduct your interrogation hearing tomorrow. From here, Captain Lowes and I will be escorting you to a holding center not too far away. You should be prepared for a grueling and extensive interrogation, after which the committee will assess the viability of you joining a branch of one of these services that we have outlined for you, so we want you to think about that carefully. Are you ready to leave, Commander? Do you have any other luggage to collect?" asked Major Knight.

"No, just this one case," replied Karl. "I do have one request to make before leaving if you could help me. I have some German marks, a little in French francs, some Austrian shillings, and a few Swiss francs. Is there some way to exchange these before we leave? This way, I will have some British sterling on hand."

"Not a problem. If you give that currency to me, I will get it exchanged before we leave. Do you have the exact amounts handy? If not, count it out now. Would you like the exchange rates as well?" asked the major.

"Not really, I did not expect to land here with that much in my case," answered Karl.

Shortly, the major returned with Karl's passport and an envelope with a sizable amount of British sterling in it.

"Shall we leave now? I would like to get you processed today, so we can start early tomorrow morning."

"Sounds good to me. I hope I can get a bath once we get to wherever we are going," answered Karl.

"Most certainly, you can, Karl. May we start calling you by your first name instead of all this formality?" asked Clive.

"Well," said Karl, "can I also do the same?"

At this, both intelligence offices chuckled, "Of course."

In the car, Clive turned to speak to Karl, "Let me give you a heads-up on what to expect once we reach the processing center. You don't need to get overly concerned about the procedures we follow to create a file for new arrivals. The file we started in Dover will be given to a uniformed clerical person on our arrival. He or she will issue you an identification number and badge. Once that is done, you will be escorted by an officer to the quartermaster's office, then to the cafeteria for a meal. Now, Karl, don't expect too much from the food they serve. I personally would rather not touch the stuff, but at least it's hot."

A little after lunchtime, the staff car entered a long driveway with a guardhouse painted in white with a red barrier across the entrance. Four armed soldiers stood on either side of the barrier, while two smartly dressed military policemen approached the car, "Identifications, please." Both Clive and Bill showed their ID's and immediately received a salute from the guards.

"We are escorting a new arrival to the detention center," said Clive, putting his ID back in his inside pocket.

"Thank you, Major. Please proceed through the barrier."

Karl gave a little chuckle as they passed through, saying, "They never saluted me like that when I went through the border crossing."

"Well, Karl, maybe we can work on that," replied Bill, looking at Karl. They all laughed, which made Karl feel good.

The driver pulled the big staff car up in front of the main entrance.

"Are you ready, Karl?" said Clive.

"Yes, as ready as I'll ever be," replied Karl.

The army driver opened the car doors, saluting to all three as they exited the staff car. "Follow me, Karl. The driver will take your suitcase." The three walked down a narrow hallway to a set of double doors at the end. The sign next to the doors said "Processing" in bold, red letters. Once inside, Karl saw rows of desks with pretty army (Auxiliary Territorial Service) women, better known as the ATS.

"These ladies provided all the clerical and secretarial duties for this center," said Bill.

Lieutenant Kitty Johnson approach the trio, "Major Knight, so nice to see you again. It's been a month or more; has it not?"

"Yes, we have been busy processing new detainees, you know," said Clive, looking somewhat embarrassed.

"And, Captain Lowes, you look so handsome in your civilian attire."

Blushing, Bill said, "Well, tomorrow, I'll be back in my plain, boring captain's uniform."

"Oh, you always look smashing in that uniform—my kind of man."

Kitty was a flirt, alright.

"That's enough, Kitty. You've embarrassed me enough. Please, let me introduce you to Commander Karl Vita. He will be staying with us for a while."

Kitty eyed the handsome maritime officer up and down before saying, "Now, that's what you call a well-made uniform, Commander. Pity, you will not be wearing it anymore starting tomorrow. My girls would be following you everywhere if they allowed you to continue wearing it." Kitty was making Karl feel easier about being the center of attention. "What is the schedule for the commander tomorrow morning?" asked Kitty.

"Please, will you call me Karl, as I'm not an acting commander at this point?"

"Be glad to, Karl. We're going to become the best of friends. You'll see," Kitty remarked, a twinkle in her pretty brown eyes.

Both Clive and Bill did not miss the eye play.

She better behave herself. We have plans for this young man, thought Clive, a little hurt that he was not the center of Kitty's attention.

"Before we get you some food in the cafeteria, I will escort you to the quartermaster's store. He will issue you a khaki uniform, boots, shirt and tie, and other things like underwear, socks, and so on. All detainees at the center are required to wear these. They are not flattering by any means and bear no markings except the country you are from, worn on the left shoulder. Depending on how long you will be with us, you will be issued other items of clothing as required," explained Kitty as they walked to the next building. "If you are wondering why there are armed soldiers on every corridor, that's self-explanatory; although you are not a prisoner, you are, however, a detainee. In addition, we lock each building during the evening hours, so, Karl, if you decide you don't like us anymore, too bad, you can't leave. Is that perfectly clear?" said Kitty with a slight sound of sarcasm in her voice.

"Yes, it is Kitty. Although, it's unfortunate, as I had hoped you could join me some evening for a cup of tea or something," said Karl, throwing it right back at Kitty.

Kitty surprised him with a quick answer, "Well, Commander Vita, there is always a way, isn't there!

"Now, let's take you to your quarters. You will have a private room due your rank. After you have dropped off your new Savile Row uniform, we can go to the cafeteria for that cup of tea over an early dinner."

Kitty smiled, looking right back into Karl's eyes.

"Our first dinner date," remarked Karl, openly flirting with the shapely, pretty lieutenant.

"Why, you handsome fellow, are you flirting with me?" said Kitty, thoroughly enjoying the attention.

"But of course," replied Karl.

After eating a God-knows-what meal, Kitty momentarily lost her smile. Placing both hands together on the table with her head lowered, she sat quietly for a few minutes before speaking, reiterating once again, "Tomorrow will be a stressful day, Karl. Take the time tonight to consider the options that were outlined earlier. The answer you give will change your life here in Great

Britain and could endanger your life sometime in the future. Am I making myself clear?"

Karl now saw the cooler professional side of Lieutenant Johnson.

"I will do that, Lieutenant Johnson. Thank you for reminding me why I am here."

Kitty stood up and extended her hand, "I hope you have a peaceful evening, Commander. A guard will wake you at 0530 hours. After you have bathed and had breakfast, you will be escorted at 0730 hours to Interrogation Room #5, so again, consider your options carefully."

"Have I done something to offend you?" Karl asked as they stood.

"No, Karl, I briefly forgot for a moment why we are all here. The last couple of hours have reminded me I'm a woman as well as an intelligence officer, so, no, you have not offended me. Karl, thank you for making today a little brighter."

With that, Lieutenant Johnson turned and marched out of the cafeteria. Kitty entered the main building, walked down the hall, and stopped in front of the door that had a sign: Authorized Personnel Only. She knocked and entered immediately.

"Kitty come in and have a seat," said Major Knight. "What's your impression so far? Do you think Karl will be a viable candidate for this department? You were coming on a little strong earlier today, and he appeared to respond to that approach very well."

"He does like to flirt; that's for sure. However, that's as far as it goes. About anything of importance, he remained close-lipped. He did, however, tell me how he planned to get his mother and sister out of Vienna. It's quite a story; make sure he tells you about it. I would say he plots every detail very carefully before putting it into any type of final plan. He is very organized, never out of control, and always a gentleman; he is the type of agent we need in the BIS," concluded Kitty, covering up that she enjoyed every minute of the brief flirtation.

Bill asked, "Do you think maybe he was on to you and was playing with you, leading you on to see how you would react?"

Wish he would have, thought Kitty.

"We must be sure he is legit and not a mole sent here by the Germans. He is one smooth character, that Austrian. We need to watch him carefully," Clive remarked as he closed Karl's folder.

In his small room, Karl lay on his bed, allowing his mind to once again focus on giving these English intelligence boys an answer to the options mapped out for him earlier. *I need to know much more information before giving them any type of commitment. One thing is certain; I am not going back to Europe.*

Karl looked at his watch and decided he would take a shower tonight. That way, in the morning, all he would have to do is shave and clean his teeth. Getting up from the bed, he crossed the room to the small wardrobe and found, to his surprise, a striped bathrobe, worn but clean. His shoes were by the door; he put them on without tying the laces.

The bathroom facilities were down the hall to the right. Opening the door, he was surprised to find lockers on the left, followed by individual toilets. On the opposite wall were the sinks. The shower stalls faced him at the back of the bathroom. Green shower curtains provided some privacy to the users. *Not too bad,* thought Karl.

These English are okay.

13

The Interrogation

Promptly at 0530 hours, a sergeant knocked loudly on the door.

"Time to get up, sir."

"Thank you," Karl replied. After shaving and brushing his teeth, Karl took out the English uniform from the wardrobe, laying it on the bed. His first thought was how coarse the wool material felt to the touch. He looked at the underwear provided for him, saying, "There is no way I will wear these. I will use a pair of my own from my suitcase. God knows how this shirt will fit."

Once he had dressed, he took another look into the mirror above the sink. "My God, is this what is in store for me? Looking like this?" Now, he took a hard look at the boots supplied with the uniform. Once again, he repeated out loud, "I refuse to wear these big, ugly things. My dress shoes will do quite nicely. Thank you."

The cafeteria was quite crowded for this early morning hour. *Now, what am I supposed to do?* Karl thought. A detainee, seeing

Karl's dilemma, walked up to him, speaking in German, "Stay with me. It was also confusing to me at first. My name is Gunther, and you're?"

"Karl, from that dialect, I would venture to say you're from the Hamburg area. Is that correct?"

"My God, you are right. How did you know that?"

Karl almost slipped by telling him about his father being a professor of languages at the University of Wien. Instead, he answered by saying, "I used to work with people from that region. It's a distinctive accent."

Karl followed Gunther to the sign-in registry, "Just enter your ID number and time, then proceed to the food tray line. Don't be too disappointed. This food will not grow on you, but it will stop you from having hunger pains."

Karl pushed his tray along, looking at the breakfast selections. "I can't believe people eat this stuff. Any suggestions?" Karl asked Gunther. They looked at each other and broke out laughing. It must have been contagious because all the other detainees started to laugh as well. In just a few moments, Karl had made new friends.

He ate his breakfast with his five new friends. They all had so much in common, even though they divulged very little. Looking at his watch, he said, "Gentlemen, I must leave you. I have a session at 0730. I do not want to be late for the first meeting."

Simultaneously, they said, "Good luck. See you later today."

Walking through the compound, he thought about how he would be treated; would they pressure him to decide, or would they simply get information from him, then kick him out of the country?

One thing was for certain. He would not be intimidated or treated as a second-class citizen: *Could that be why I'm wearing this God-awful uniform?*

"Good morning, sir," the guard at the entrance door said as he opened the door for him.

At the door marked I-5, another guard asked for his ID card and name. "Karl Vita. I was told to report here at 0730 hours for a meeting."

Returning the ID card, the guard opened the door, allowing Karl to view the room and the body of uniformed men standing around drinking tea and talking about who knew what. The door closed behind him. He stood, waiting for direction from someone in the group. One of the officers turned. It was Major Knight. "Karl, good morning. Did you sleep well?"

"Yes, Sir, thank you."

"Can we get you some tea? No, I believe you would prefer coffee before we start. Is that correct?"

"Coffee would be nice. Thank you." Karl was now on his best behavior.

Major Knight, in an elevated tone, said, "Gentlemen, please join me in welcoming Commander Karl Vita to this hearing." With that, he led Karl by the arm to meet each of the committee members.

Not as stuffy as I expected, thought Karl as he shook hands with each officer. To his surprise, they were giving him the same respect as someone with equal rank status. "Commander, if you would take your place at this table, we can start."

His small table faced the committee's horseshoe-arranged tables. This way, Karl could address each member directly. Major Knight now stood, saying, "Gentlemen, I will now call this preliminary interrogation hearing to order. Will the clerk please call and log each officer as his name is called?

"For the record, and for those of you who have not had a chance to review the current status file on Commander Vita, let me provide a condensed overview of what we have presently. I would also ask the commander if it would be acceptable to him if we all address him by his Christian name of Karl during this hearing?"

"That will be perfectly expectable, Major," replied Karl.

"Karl, I will now ask you a series of questions. Please, answer *yes* or *no*. Please, do not add additional comments as the clerk is recording every word being spoken. Is that clear? Do you understand this directive?" asked Major Knight.

"Yes, I do, Major," replied Karl.

"Karl, up until several weeks ago, were you the First officer of the *Tristian*, registered to the German Langstaff Shipping Company?"

"Yes."

"Did you deliberately leave that ship without prior permission from the captain or the Langstaff Shipping Company?"

"Yes."

"Karl, did you three days ago board the RMS *Clyde Princess* with your mother, sister, and nephew in the port of Ostend Belgium?"

"Yes."

"Karl, did you disclose to the captain of that ship you would seek asylum once you disembarked in Dover, England?"

"Yes."

"Karl, once the ship was docked in Dover, did you meet with two British customs officers as well as two officers of the British Intelligence Service before you disembarked?"

"Yes."

"Karl, were you given numerous options to consider, including being refused permanent entry into England?"

"Yes."

"Karl, I will now ask you those same options once again. If, during these hearings, it is proven that you are acting indecisively or exhibit signs that could prove detrimental to the security of this nation, do you understand we will deport you as an undesirable back to the port you came from?"

"Yes."

"How say you to being interned should war be declared between England and Germany?"

"No."

"How say you to joining the free European Brigade?"

"No."

Would you entertain a position with the British Maritime Service?

"No."

"How say you to going through an extended evaluation and training, after which you may be asked to become an operative for the British Intelligence Service? Before answering that, Karl, let me ask you once again, have you thoroughly considered the hardship and danger that could be associated with excepting a position such as this?"

"Yes."

"Karl, thank you for cooperating with us on those questions. I hope you understand we must be extremely careful about individuals entering England under false pretenses as German informants. Gentlemen, before we move on, do any of you have additional questions you wish to ask of Karl?"

The committee members looked at each other with Colonel Jacks answering for all, "We think we should move forward and reserve any questioning till later in the session."

Over the next four hours, the committee heard Karl's whole story again, with many questions being asked at each step by various members of the committee. Major Knight called a recess a little after lunchtime. Karl was looking tired and maybe a little tense.

As the committee members wandered over to the lunch buffet, Clive approached Karl, still sitting at his table, "How are you holding up, old man? Sorry we had to be so formal and a little hard on you at the beginning. It's standard procedure. I hope you understand we are sensitive to German operatives entering England. Are you ready for some lunch? You must be famished by now." Clive now showed his kinder side to Karl. It was obvious they both liked each other.

The door opened and in walked Lieutenant Johnson. "Hope you don't mind. I asked Lieutenant Johnson to join us for lunch. You have been around male officers too long this morning."

"You said it. Not me," replied Karl, now smiling at seeing Kitty.

"Well, Karl, you're still standing on your first morning. How do you like your new uniform?" asked Kitty.

"Wrong question to ask me right now. How on earth can anyone wear this uniform made of such scratchy material?"

"Sorry about that," remarked Clive, feeling sorry for his new friend.

"Is it possible for me to wear my civilian clothes?" pleaded Karl.

"Not during these hearings, Karl. You must be patient. It's only for a few more days till we decide what to do with you." Clive felt bad and agreed with Karl that these uniforms were not necessary.

The three sat down at an empty table, limiting the conversation to anything not associated with the hearing. The roast beef sandwich and potato salad were acceptable but a far cry from what Karl was used to on the *Tristian* or at his mother's house.

"Karl is there anything you need right now?" asked Kitty.

"Actually, Kitty there is. I need to call my sister Freida. Is there any way I could telephone her? She and my mother must be worried about me right now. They have not seen or heard from me since the two military policemen escorted me away at the docks in Dover."

"Well, Major, can I set that call up for Karl?" came the request from Kitty.

"I think we could set something up. It will have to be censored through our security people. Kitty inform them that I will be accepting full responsibility, and Karl, you will not make any mention of this location or its function. There will be no mention of what these meetings pertain to, and finally, if asked by your mother if you will be staying in England and when you will be joining them, you will simply say it may be a while and that you are treated well. Is that understood? I'm allowing this because there is a high degree of confidence from all of us here that you are an honorable and trustworthy officer," said Clive, looking at both with a stern look on his face.

"Also, you must keep this call to yourself. None of the other detainees have been given this privilege; is that clear?" interjected Kitty.

"Thank you so much. When can I make that call?"

"How about 1645 hours today, right after we adjourn for the day? Meet me at my office. Do you remember how to get there?" asked Kitty.

"How could I forget our first meeting, Lieutenant?" Karl now had that smile back on his face, and Kitty was blushing bright red.

She knew exactly what those piercing eyes were implying.

"So, I'll see you there about 1645, alright?"

"Gentlemen, shall we reconvene?" Colonel Jacks was getting everyone's attention to return to their places. "Are you ready to continue, Karl?" the colonel asked as he sat down at the middle of the table.

"Yes, Colonel, I am," replied Karl with a definite change to his tone.

The rest of the afternoon was spent questioning Karl on every aspect of his upbringing: schooling, professional training, his early carrier as a midshipman on a German training (tall-masted sailing ship) barque.

How did he manage to work his way up to become the First Officer of the *Tristian* in such a short period?

Other areas of questioning were centered around his knowledge of European ports. Had he seen ships of the German Kriegsmarine, especially the new battleships, in and around Kiel and Hamburg?

Karl was getting tired as the same questions seemed to be repeated over again by different officers.

At 1620, Major Knight called for an adjournment with a continuation at 0730 the next morning. Clive walked over to Karl, saying, "Well done, Karl. I believe you have suitably impressed the committee for today anyway. You look tired; get to bed early tonight. Tomorrow, we will start in on how we can work together."

"Does that mean I'm not being thrown out?" asked Karl, laughing openly. Other officers, hearing Karl's comment and laughter, joined in. The wall of trust between them was starting to build.

WALKING along the path to the main building, he decided to stop for a few minutes at the bench near the beautiful flower beds to collect his thoughts before meeting up with Kitty. *I wonder what they are saying behind my back right now.*

Outside building number #5, the air felt cooler and sweeter to Karl's nostrils as he headed over to meet with Kitty. He was starting to feel so much better about this camp and more confident that making this journey to England was absolutely the right thing to do.

I wonder how Papa and my brothers are doing in Wien. *It must be difficult right now. How can I get a message to them that we are all doing alright? I'll ask Kitty for her help.*

As he approached the main entrance, he was met by Kitty, who could not contain the news that was giving her a big smile.

"Kitty, you look like a Cheshire cat that just caught a really big mouse. It must be everything is going in the right direction for you today."

Kitty answered, saying, "You're the good news, Mr. Vita. Although, I shouldn't be telling you this right now, I wanted to be the first to tell you the good news. I also know you can keep a secret if given one."

"Okay, you have my attention. What's the big secret for this afternoon?"

"Major Knight, Clive to you, called me to let me know the committee will be asking you tomorrow to stay in England and will ask you to consider joining the British Maritime Service as a senior officer or maybe a captain. Don't be surprised if they also ask you to consider joining the Intelligence Service. Your knowledge of languages and dialects is of major interest to us right now." Kitty was so excited to tell him this.

"And what else is of interest to them?" asked Karl, feeling there was an underlying interrogation coming.

Kitty looked at him and said, "I was asked not to mention this part yet; however, I feel you should be given adequate time to consider this carefully. Karl, because of your maritime position, you have firsthand knowledge of German ports, as well as other ports and military installations on the western approaches of Europe. That's one area they will focus on tomorrow, and the other interest is recent sightings of ships of the German Navy. Earlier today, you talked about your time first as a cadet then sailing as an ensign on several German training ships. This firsthand knowledge and familiarization of naval units in places such as Kiel and Hamburg could be invaluable to our intelligence people." Kitty, sitting on a bench near the door, studied Karl's reaction to what she had told him.

"So, if I read between the lines, what they are interested in is how much I know about German heavy units and maybe how much more I could find out for them. Is that correct, Kitty?" asked Karl, sitting on the bench next to her.

"I would say you're on the right track, sailor. Let's go make that telephone call, shall we?"

Kitty felt relieved about telling him what was happening, but sad she could not divulge that she was told to leak this information to him in advance of tomorrow's questioning. Clive and the panel wanted to make sure he had tonight to consider the risks he could potentially be facing should he agree to cooperate with them.

In Kitty's office, she said, "Karl, give me your sister's telephone number, and I'll place the call."

After four or five rings, a voice at the other end said, "Baldock 3607. Who's calling?"

"Freida, it's me, Karl."

"Oh, my God, Karl, we have been so worried about you. The last news we received was from someone who called Ronny at his office to let us know you were well and being taken care of."

"That is true, Freida. I am being treated well. I just needed to hear your voices. I miss you all so much. Have you received any news about Papa and our brothers yet?"

"Yes, Karl, it looks like Papa will not cooperate with the authorities in Wien. You know Papa. He can be so stubborn. He has already made enemies by refusing to become a manufacturer of uniforms for the German military. His belligerence will get him thrown into prison or something far worse."

Freida knew more than she was letting on, but at least she told him how grave the situation was. "Karl, where are you? When can you come home?"

"Freida, I'm not at liberty to discuss my location or what I'm doing. I will let you know as soon as I'm able to. Can you write a letter to Papa and the boys for me, telling them I'm alright and not to worry?"

Kitty slipped a note in front of Karl. It read: you are being given a five-day leave starting next week, so you can spend time with your family.

Karl's face lit up at reading the note. "Freida, I have just been told I can come home next week for five days. This is wonderful news; see you next week. Big kisses to all. Oh, and please make

95

sure you have coffee at home." Karl hung up the phone as did the security officer at the other end of the office.

"Kitty, why did you not tell me before we made the call?"

"Well, Karl, you could say I've broken the rules again. Major Knight was going to inform you of this after tomorrow's session. I decided to take it upon myself to make your call that much more meaningful."

"Thank you so much, Kitty. I am truly grateful." Karl was all smiles as he said this.

"I have a little time left before I go home. Would you care to join me in the officer's lounge for some tea and scones? I believe you may even be able to get some camp coffee if you prefer," said Kitty, hoping he would say yes.

"Am I allowed?" asked Karl, not knowing the rules and limitations of his expanding freedoms.

The officer's lounge was large with dark wood paneling and pictures of officers on horseback and other pictures that portrayed famous battle scenes. Round tables with leather chair were placed in the center of the lounge. Some armchairs and long couches were at the far end of the room. The bar was small but well-stocked with liquors and beer selections.

"Well, this looks so much nicer than the cafeteria across the way," Karl said, feeling more like what he was used to aboard ship.

"Let's take these two armchairs in the corner; it will be quieter than being close to the bar," said Kitty.

"Sounds good to me. Won't the other officers mind a detainee uniform in here?" asked Karl.

"Not at all. Right now, you are very much the center of attention," said a beaming Kitty.

Karl looked around at the officers sitting at the tables and others standing at the bar. They all appeared to be looking toward them, smiling and raising their glasses in a sign of acceptance.

"Kitty, only this morning, I felt so alone, even displaced, and here we are sitting among your fellow officers who are accepting me. Why?"

"Perhaps it's because you are quickly becoming an important person of interest to all of us. That's why," Kitty replied with a confident smile.

Clive approached and asked if he could join them.

"Absolutely, it's your lounge, after all." Karl's spirits were once again displaying the cocky officer he had been only a few weeks ago.

"Today was a little rough on you, old man. Had to be done, though," Clive's tone was softer now than in room #5.

"Clive, I understand completely. For all you know, I could be a spy, which, let me assure you, I'm not," Karl said, laughing as he spoke.

"That's funny because, if you were, I would have had you shot." Now, Clive was laughing, but he meant every word.

These two are getting a little silly, thought Kitty. *Here, I thought I would get him all to myself for a while.*

"Strictly against the rules, old man, but may we buy you a drink? Bet it's been quite a while since you've had one, right?" said Clive as he turned to walk to the bar.

"That would be nice of you," replied Karl.

"Kitty, will you have one, too?" asked Clive.

"So much for tea," replied Kitty.

Before too long, Bill and another officer had pulled up chairs, listening to the numerous stories that were being told.

About 1900 hours, Kitty interjected that Karl needed to be back at his barracks and that she would escort him there.

The officers around the table eyeballed each other. They were all thinking the same thing.

Walking back across the compound, Kitty stopped by the big oak tree and asked Karl to join her on the bench. "The night air is so sweet and warm. It's way too nice not to sit and enjoy it for a while; wouldn't you say?" Kitty sat, patting the bench for Karl to sit next to her.

"Sounds like a good idea." Karl could sense that she was acting differently tonight, not so sharp, not so much the military professional. She was showing her softer side, allowing more of her femininity to show through.

"Karl, you have been here only a few days; although, to you, it must feel like an eternity. You have no idea how much you are impressing people at this detention center, especially me." Kitty moved closer, reaching for his hand, then she turned toward him. Her eyes looked so big and sparkling in the fading light of day. "I have a habit of breaking the rules around here. Tonight, I think I'm breaking a real big one."

With that, Kitty moved in, giving Karl a warm, moist kiss that seemed to last longer than it did. "Wow, I did not see that coming," said Karl, looking into her eyes.

"You liar," came the response from Kitty.

"The likelihood of a war between England and Germany is growing more likely with each passing day. What will happen to all of us in the Intelligence Service is so uncertain. Taking chances when opportunity arises is becoming a new way of life for me. I hope I did not offend you by kissing you just now," remarked Kitty.

"Not at all. However, it did not last as long as I would have liked."

Karl's reply was now melting any barrier that was between them.

Kitty giggled at his response, "There's only one way to correct that," she replied as she moved back to him, her mouth opening to accept his eager tongue.

Karl could feel her tense up, her chest moving with nervous energy. His mind started to drift back to someone else who had reacted in much the same way, Annie Lourie.

Karl drew back from Kitty. The thought of what he was doing

so far away from Annie made him withdraw and turn inward, back to his protected self. "Karl, are you alright?" asked Kitty, now wondering if she had crossed the line. "You are thinking of someone else. I can tell by the look on your face. Have I made you do something that has violated the trust of someone else?"

Kitty held his hand again, saying, "Why don't you tell me about her? Talking with a stranger might help you right now."

"Her name is Annie. We have been seeing each other on and off for years. However, due to my maritime career, we did not get to spend that much time together. My shore leaves were very infrequent, sometimes six months or more between visits. Last month, on my way to Vienna to pick up my mother and sister, I met up with Annie in Innsbruck. We had a wonderful evening before I asked her to join me in completing the remainder of the road trip to Vienna together, which she thought was a great idea. That was the last time I saw her, crying on the steps of her parents' home in Vienna. With any luck, she is now living with her mother in Bern, Switzerland, and out of harm's way. Will I ever see her again? I can't say. You probably know more about my future than I do at this point."

"Yes, I do. Sometimes, this Intelligence Service can be a burden. I, too, have a boyfriend who is somewhere out at sea. It's been more than five months since we said goodbye at the pier. I should not have been so forward with you, but Karl, sometimes I feel so lonely hiding behind this uniform. The warmth and tenderness of being held is such a comfort that it made me take the liberty of kissing you. Does any of this make sense to you?" Kitty asked, facing Karl.

"Yes, yes, it does, Kitty. We are ships that are passing in the dark, maybe never to meet again. You have made me look at things so much differently right now."

His strong arms wrapped around her waist and pulled her to him, her head on his shoulder.

He heard a quiet whimper, then felt her tears of relief start.

Karl did not release the hold on Kitty. Instead, he continued to comfort her, hoping that some of the guilt and pain would go away.

Kitty turned her face back to him, saying, "See what you started?" while trying hard to smile. "You have a definite effect on the ladies around here." Kitty tried to make light of her emotions.

"Well, we can't have that, Lieutenant, can we? Kitty, would you mind if I kissed you again? It is so nice to be able to escape, even if it's only in a kiss."

"Be glad to oblige, so long as those hands stay behind my back and north of my belt line." Karl rolled back in a fit of laughter, followed by Kitty before they came together again in a meaningful, passionate kiss that meant so much more than the first one.

Kitty walked him to the entrance, saying, "Good night, Karl. I hope you sleep peacefully, and I'll see you tomorrow morning."

With that, she turned and marched to the main office building. Karl could see she had a new spring in her step. *I wonder why?*

Returning to his room, Karl lay awake, thinking of all that had transpired during the day, drifting to thoughts of Annie, and finally to Kitty, who he was becoming quite fond of. Pangs of guilt kept intervening every time he came back to this complex attractive English lieutenant.

The following morning, Karl was awakened again at 0530. It was still dark outside as he got himself ready. Following the same routine as yesterday, he walked to the cafeteria for breakfast.

There, he met with his new friends, all chatting in German. "Gentlemen, why don't we start speaking in English? We will be speaking it for what appears to be a long time," said Karl.

"Good idea," said Gunther as he started speaking in English with a German accent. "Let's get some egg break fasting with a plate on top of bread." This was way too funny, and they all started laughing. Gunther enjoyed seeing his friends laughing in high spirits at making fun of his rusty English; little did they really know, Gunther was indeed fluent in English.

Dan, another Austrian detainee, stood up and said, "Why don't we have Karl give us lessons after supper each night in conversational English?"

"Great idea," replied Gunther, speaking again in German.

"Maybe I can ask for help from some of the camp officers. I will ask for a blackboard as well," said Bruno.

"Well, shall we all get some eggs over easy before leaving for the interrogation center?" said Karl, laughing with the group.

Karl entered Interrogation Room #5. Most of the panel members were already standing, having their morning tea. "Good morning, gentlemen," said Karl, thinking this was a little different today.

The room had a new arrangement. Instead of a table with one chair facing the panel, there was now a longer table with four chairs. *Hmmm*, thought Karl, *looks like we are going to do something different here.* Clive and Bill walked up to him, Bill saying, "Your coffee is on its way, old man. Kitty and I will be joining you at the table today. You looked too lonely by yourself yesterday," said Clive.

"That's funny this early in the morning, Bill." Karl's old sarcastic self was back, and they all loved it.

14

The Offer

"Gentlemen, shall we all be seated? Good morning to you, Commander," said Colonel Jacks as he sat in the middle of the head table.

As Karl approach his seat, his nostrils sensed a charming fragrance coming from behind him. It was Kitty; of course, it was!

"Kitty, good morning. Glad you will be joining us today," said Clive as he turned to sit down. "Lieutenant, this is the segment you will play a major part in, so welcome."

"Thank you, sir, and good morning to everyone." Kitty sat down, facing the panel.

"Does that include me?" said Karl with a big smile on his face.

"Especially to you, Commander," said Kitty with a different look to her smile.

Clive looked at Bill, both thinking, *is there something we don't know?*

Clive stood and, in an authoritative tone, said, "Will the steward take the roll call before we start? First on the agenda this morning, is a summary of where we left off yesterday. Commander Vita, let me first, on behalf of this committee, commend you for an outstanding display of confidence and the thorough way in which you addressed all those difficult questions yesterday. "Do you have any questions or concerns for us at this time before we move forward?"

"Yes, I do; however, it has no direct association with this hearing."

"Well, alright, then, what is it?" asked Colonel Jacks.

"Before you scramble my brains into sauerkraut, I would like to tell you all about a conversation the detainees had over breakfast this morning. I have noticed a lack of understanding or ability to speak English, which I'm assuming would include writing abilities. Is there a way we could get a blackboard and the assistance of some officers or other personnel to help us learn English correctly?

"We all are reconciled to the fact that we will be in this country for a long time, so being able to converse would prove to be a win-win for all concerned." Karl stood, facing the panel, displaying his strong leadership capabilities.

"Thank you, Karl," said Clive, "that is scheduled for later in our acceptance program, once we have decided on those who will stay and those who will be deported. However, if you are all anxious to get a head start, I think everyone here would love to arrange some training after hours in your cafeteria. I will make those arrangements. We have quite a few in our ranks who have teaching backgrounds," he added, shifting his gaze toward Kitty.

"Now, let's direct this hearing to how we can work together, shall we?" said Colonel Jacks.

"We are still gathering background information on you, Commander. You understand that, as much as we all like you, we must be certain there is no hidden agenda to your seeking asylum in England.

"So, during your stay here, and until the security issue is a closed case, we will move forward with the clear understanding that we will not disclose all our long-range plans that could include your involvement. Is that clear?" reiterated Colonel Jacks.

"Absolutely, sir. I would expect nothing less. How long before you will be at that point?"

"Our chaps in the back room work quickly. I would venture to say by the time you arrive back from your leave, we can continue. Is that fair?" replied Colonel Jacks. "Can we now discuss your maritime career? I'm led to believe you were highly thought of while serving with the Langstaff Shipping Company, and from the information we now have, you would have been the replacement for the *Tristan*'s Captain Sauve when and if he retires." Colonel Jacks surprised Karl with this statement.

How the hell did they know that so quickly? thought Karl. *It's only been a few weeks, although it feels like months and years.*

Another officer, Captain John Benson, asked, "I have a few questions for you, Commander, or can I also call you Karl?"

"Of course, you can," said Karl.

"With such a distinguished record as a senior maritime office, why on Earth are you not asking this committee to assign you to His Majesty's Maritime Service? God knows we are desperately short of qualified senior officers."

Karl, hearing this, put his hands together, lowered his head, and thought hard for a short moment before answering this question.

"Captain Benson, you are asking me a question I ask myself daily. My love for the sea and all it entails pulls at my heartstrings constantly. Let me answer this way. In a perfect world, I would never think of leaving the maritime service. It's part of me forever.

"However, today, we are facing a crisis in Europe, and more specifically, the capitulation of my homeland of Austria. We will be overrun shortly. My father and two of my brothers still remain in Vienna."

"Excuse me for butting in, but I have a question to ask you," Captain Butler, a maritime officer on the panel, interrupted. "Are you sure about their present situation? When did you last get some sort of an update?"

"Their fate is questionable at this point, and from what I now know, my father is already defying any form of cooperation with the authorities about producing uniforms for the German military."

Karl looked more stressed at this line of questioning.

"I'm truly sorry for asking that question, Karl. I'm only trying to sense how grave the situation is."

Captain Butler realized that might not have been the most pertinent question to ask an already stressed detainee.

"Captain Butler, it was a fair question to ask me. Now, if I may be allowed to continue, my hope is that the English authorities will see the value of my knowledge of German ports and building facilities.

"My understanding of shipping in and out of those ports, especially naval units based there, could be invaluable to your assessment of their strength, and let's not overlook the new units being built.

"I see my contribution in assessing your enemy's ability to expand its naval strengths in numbers and technologically advanced vessels that could well be superior to those of the Royal Navy.

"Now, back to my family and business in Vienna. The factory is run by my brothers, with minimum involvement from my father. What you may not know is my father is a professor of languages at the University of Vienna. Other than speaking nine languages, his specialty is understanding their dialects and the origins of surnames.

"I, myself, speak and write seven languages, including their various dialects. To conclude, I see myself being an asset to this intelligence service by providing an accurate location of where an enemy combatant or person of interest may be from during an interrogation. Further, it would be easy for me to provide invaluable and accurate information on enemy ports and shipping activities.

"Yes, God only knows how I love the sea, but right now, there is a maniac on the loose in Europe, and there is no clear plan of how to stop his conquest of all the countries of Europe. Gentlemen, you cannot trust anything he says. You will be on Hitler's list sooner rather than later. With that, I thank you for your time." Karl sat, getting a pat on the back from Clive.

Colonel Jacks asked for a brief adjournment, asking only the committee members to remain. "If you would be so kind as to wait in the officer's lounge, we will send word for your return. Lieutenant Johnson, would you please escort Commander Vita to the lounge and stay with him until called back to this session?"

"Yes, sir, are you ready, Commander?" asked Kitty.

"Yes, I believe I am," replied Karl as he stood to face the panel, saluting them out of respect, then turned, following Kitty to the door at the back of the room.

An armed military police guard held the door open for them to pass through, then closed it again before reassuming his position.

"Well, Karl, that was quite a performance you put on back there," said Kitty.

The answer she got back was as cold as ice, "Kitty, every word I spoke in there was the truth and hopefully conveyed there is no waiting for a satisfactory conclusion to this conflict in Europe. One way or another, it is going to happen! My family may forever be separated. It's the not knowing that gives me such pain. Let's get some coffee and change the subject for a while. Does that sound good to you, young lady?" Karl said, now feeling sorry for snapping at Kitty.

Walking slowly back to the officer's lounge, they commented on the beautiful weather and how warm it was for this time of year, deliberately staying away from anything to do with the hearing.

"Kitty, what do you do with your free time? Do you get any time off like weekends, or is it only one day off a week?" asked Karl, trying to break the silence.

"Funny you should ask me that, Karl. I haven't had a day off in a fortnight; I'm way overdue for time off. I'm going to ask Clive if it's at all possible for me to show you around the town one day next week before you go on leave. Would you like that?" Kitty's heart missed a beat at the thought of being alone with Karl.

"Yes, I would! I have not seen anything in the area since arriving here. It would be even better with you." Karl was also feeling good about the prospect of being alone with Kitty.

"Well," said Kitty, "I am going to work on that."

To their surprise, the lounge was completely empty. "How nice is this?" said Kitty as she guided Karl to the armchairs in the corner. "I am going to join you for a cup of coffee. How do you like the Camp coffee we serve?

What is Camp coffee" asked Karl.

"It's a bottled liquid coffee with Charisse added for flavoring."

"Never heard of it before. Must be an English thing." Kitty smiled at his answer.

"So, what are the chances of getting that pass for a day?" asked Karl.

"Not sure, but I can tell you this. The confidence being shown by this inquiry board is encouraging, so I would say excellent. The weekend is coming up, so let's ask for Saturday, shall we?"

Kitty had already made up her mind on this date.

The military policeman returned to escort Karl and Kitty back to the investigation room. The panel of officers returned, taking their places.

Colonel Jacks walked to the center of the group, addressing everyone. "This committee, being aware we cannot linger too long on this case, has reviewed the file that has been gathered on you so far. Commander Vita, we still must complete our due diligence on your prior history and political affiliations. We must also tread carefully by not making decisions that could turn out to be damaging to the British Empire.

"With that said, let me now jump to our interest. Commander Vita, we find your maritime experience to be uniquely positioned in assisting us in acquiring data on the German naval and military buildup. While you were out of the room, I called the war department and the foreign office about how best to handle this case. Based on their response and the directive given to me and this committee, we would like you to consider joining the British Intelligence Service as an assignee from the Free Nations of Europe.

"Furthermore, speaking so many languages and the ability to pinpoint where someone comes from by listening to his or her dialect is unique and could be key to our overall effectiveness in interrogating methods. Before I continue, does anyone else from the panel wish to add to this?" Colonel Jacks looked at the row of officers seated behind their tables.

"I have a question to ask if you don't mind, Colonel Jacks. Is there a way we could see a live demonstration of Commander Vita's language and dialect abilities before we adjourn today?" asked Captain Watts, a regular army officer who up to now had not addressed Karl or added to any of the questioning fielded during the hearing so far.

"Karl are you up to this challenge once I finish?" said Colonel Jacks, obviously annoyed by this question so late in the interrogation.

"I will be glad to accommodate the good captain," came a stinging response from Karl.

"Now, gentlemen, may I continue?" said Colonel Jacks.

"Time, Karl, is not on our side. We all know that a conflict with Germany is close at hand, and for this, we must be prepared. This hearing is far from complete. It will go on for another few weeks, but we cannot wait. We need to know whether you are prepared to join us. I must stress, we cannot waste time. Are you prepared to give us a conditional commitment today, Karl?"

Although Colonel Jacks suspected Karl's eagerness, he wanted to give him time to reflect on his decision. "While you are considering this, Karl, maybe we should take the time to have some detainees brought over to give Captain Watts a live demonstration, shall we?

"Major Knight, will you have someone get three or more detainees at double-quick time?"

Colonel Jacks was looking to shut this Watts chap up without wasting any more time; the look on his face gave him away.

Three detainees from three different parts of Europe marched into the room, coming to attention, facing the panel, not aware of why they were there. Clive asked the three detainees whether they had spoken to or met Karl Vita before this meeting.

The answer came back, "No."

Karl stood, straightened his uniform, then walked to the detainees, asking different questions of each one. To the amazement of all present, Karl proceeded to speak to each detainee in his native language, then, after hearing them speak, he answered in their local dialect. He concluded by telling the panel the precise region of Europe each one originated from.

Karl was not aware that Gunther was standing at the back of the room, beaming a big smile.

Karl thanked the three men, then walked back slowly to his seat without taking his eyes off Captain Watts.

"Will that satisfy your distrust in my language ability, Captain Watts, or do you need to see more?" Karl's tone held a cold sting.

"I am more than satisfied, Karl. I hope you understand that we all needed to see for ourselves that you can deliver."

Colonel Jacks once again stood, addressing the room, "We will take a recess break, so Karl can make up his mind about the BIS; we will reconvene in twenty minutes. Please, take this time,

Karl, before we return to consider your position. Let me
encourage you to ask as many questions as you like. You need to
be comfortable with the decision you are about to make."

Karl, sitting at his own table, sipped a cup of coffee. He
needed no time to ponder an answer; that decision was made
yesterday.

When everyone returned, Karl slowly walked around the
table and stood next to Colonel Jacks, facing the committee.
Deliberately lowering his head, he stood there quietly for a long
minute while he gathered his thoughts. Lifting his head, Karl
began his response, "Sirs, in only a few short days, I have come to
respect and admire the few English people I have met here at this
camp.

"Because I believe this country is committed to doing the
right and honorable thing when it comes to standing firm against
German aggression, let me now give you my answer, Colonel
Jacks, to your question.

"It would be my honor to accept your invitation to become an
operative for the British Intelligence Service. Thank you for your
confidence."

Captain Watts was the first to stand. Walking around the
table, he extended his hand, saying, "On behalf of all of us here,
welcome." Stepping back, he came to attention, saluting Karl and
Colonel Jacks.

Clive, Kitty, Bill, and Gunther stood at the back of the room,
Clive quietly saying, "In all my time here, I don't think I have ever
witnessed something like this."

The strain for Karl was over. It was like a heavy weight had
been lifted from his shoulders. He was no longer a ship without a
rudder. He was about to enter a new phase of his career.

His ship was back on course.

Colonel Jacks turned to Karl, saying, "Let me congratulate
you, Karl; I did not expect that from the Watts fellow, did you? I
know it has not been an easy time for you. I'm so pleased to

know you are joining us, Karl. We need all the men we can get like yourself about now. Is there anything you need from me before we all go get a pint at the lounge?"

"Well, now that you are offering, I do need a day off, perhaps to see the local sights, town, and pubs. This Saturday would be nice if you will authorize it for me," asked Karl, knowing full-well the colonel would not say no.

"You will have to be escorted, you know. Let's ask Lieutenant Johnson if she can accompany you, shall we?" Colonel Jacks was now laughing out loud with his hand on Karl's shoulder.

The colonel moved to the table still occupied by Clive, Bill, and Kitty. Gunther had slipped out so as not to be noticed. "Lieutenant Johnson, I have a big favor to ask of you for this Saturday. I know it's your day off, but we need to show Karl here some English hospitality. Could you please take on this responsibility for me?

"I would be most appreciative. My staff car will be available to you, and I will authorize the paymaster to give you an advance so you can buy Karl a nice lunch and dinner. Are you willing to do that for me?" Colonel Jacks continued to smile as he waited for Kitty's answer.

"Sir, I did have plans, but I'm sure they can be rescheduled."

Kitty was looking at Karl while she was answering the colonel, thinking, *how did you pull this one off, sailor?*

Karl stood, holding his arms across his chest with a big smile that clearly gave away his intentions.

"Saturday it is, then. Tomorrow, you chaps will meet with three naval intelligence officers I have invited to join us. We need to know more about those big battlewagons the Germans are hiding away up the Kiel Canal," said Colonel Jacks as he walked to the door, followed by most members of the committee, all heading to the lounge.

Clive and Bill both shook Karl's hand, saying, "Welcome aboard. See you in the lounge. Don't be long."

Kitty turned to Karl, "What on Earth did you say to make Colonel Jacks allow us to take this Saturday off?"

"Just asked; that's all. It was his idea to ask you to be my chaperone," Karl answered with a huge smile across his face.

"Did he know or suspect something?" asked Kitty. "If we have the day off with a staff car, let's make it a fun day. Do you have civilian clothes with you?" asked Kitty.

"Of course. What a treat not to have to wear that horrible uniform again." Karl openly showed his distaste to having to wear such an outfit.

"Oh, on that note, Karl, Clive slipped me a note during your summary, saying: Tell Karl he will be issued a new uniform befitting an officer on your return to the camp Saturday. Kitty was beaming as she showed Karl the note.

Monday, you will be sworn in, wearing your new uniform, then moved to regular officers' quarters, followed by a visit to the paymaster's office to set up your pay book. In addition, a permanent visa is being issued tomorrow; it will be here before you leave for Baldock, so things are moving rapidly for you, sailor."

Kitty was enjoying this.

Your Monday afternoon is booked solid with meetings with various departments. Tuesday morning, I will be taking you to the train station for your five-day leave to visit your family. I will call them myself to give them the train's arrival time in Baldock. Now, let's go celebrate you becoming one of us."

Walking to the officer's lounge, Kitty explained, "Saturday will be an out of uniform day for both of us. We're on a date, and I, for one, need to let my hair down."

"Kitty, I am so looking forward to seeing you in civilian clothes with that beautiful hair of yours flowing freely around your shoulders. You're not going to wear those horrible army-issue stockings, are you?" Karl was playing with Kitty.

"Of course not. I intend to be a dolled-up lady in nylons. Is that okay with you, sailor?"

"Yes, it most certainly is, but remember, I've been locked up in here for the last couple of days. There's no telling what I'm capable of doing." Karl was back in flirtation mode.

"That's okay, Karl. I have a big bang handgun in my handbag in case you decide to throw your anchor into my ocean." They both laughed at the tennis match they were playing.

15

Friday with Naval Intelligence

Karl opened the door to the officer's lounge for Kitty, then followed her in. Everyone there turned and clapped as they entered, totally stunned at the reception they were being given.

Clive spoke first, "Karl, it may be a little premature at this time to extend our congratulations, but occasionally, someone comes to us who gives new meaning to trust and honesty, doing the right thing for the right reasons."

"Thank you all so very much for trusting in me. I will do my best to live up to your expectations. May I be permitted to buy the first round for all you gentlemen?" asked Karl.

"Absolutely not," came the reply from Colonel Jacks.

"Tonight, it's all on us. Just remember, tomorrow is still a workday, and you need to be sharp as a tack for those navy chaps."

With that said, the beer and glasses of whiskey started to flow.

Later in the evening, Clive guided Karl away from the bar and

asked him to sit with him for a while, as he needed to brief Karl
on the following day's questioning.

"These navy types are a good bunch. They have been patiently
waiting to question you on your current knowledge of the
changes you have observed in certain German ports. They most
certainly will question you on any additions you may have seen
with Germany's naval buildup," explained Clive.

"Understood," replied Karl, swigging down another whiskey.

"Now, about your quarters in barrack #36. Friday night will
be your last there. When you leave Saturday morning, leave all
your gear on the bed. Your new steward, Corporal Neil Brown-
ing, will move it into your new quarters in building #9.

Your quarters, by the way, is B-13.

As for that pesky uniform you dislike so much, leave it in the
room when you leave tomorrow. Friday will be informal, so plan
on coming in your civilian gear," explained Clive.

"On Saturday, when you return from your day off, go directly
to your new quarters, where you will find your new uniform
hanging in the wardrobe. Please, try it on prior to Monday's
committee meeting in case it does not fit correctly. We must have
you look your best for the swearing-in ceremony."

Should let me wear my maritime uniform then, thought Karl, not
letting on what he was thinking.

"As for the rest of your new gear, it will be in the room when
you return. Is that all clear?"

"Yes, it is, Clive. Do I retain my present ID number and badge,
or will I be issued new ones?" inquired Karl.

"Not right now. They will be issued in a couple of weeks,
along with the permanent visa for the United Kingdom, which
replaces the temporary one Kitty told you about. Okay, enough
of business, Lieutenant Vita," said Clive as he guided Karl back to
his new drinking friends.

"What?" said Karl. "Where did that come from? Nobody said
anything about a rank to me."

"I thought you should know before the swearing-in ceremony, and by the way, that commission came directly from War Office earlier today."

"Who else knows about this?" asked Karl, still shocked at how fast everything was moving.

"Everyone," replied Clive as he put his arm on the shoulder of his new friend.

Back at the barracks, Karl went into the recreational area. There, sitting at a round table, he found his European friends being schooled in the English language by two noncommissioned officers (NCOs) and Kitty, standing next to the blackboard.

"Why, Karl Vita, it's so nice of you to join us for this first introduction to conversational English. Please, pull up a chair," said Kitty with a smile.

Karl found an empty chair, then placed it next to Gunther, who welcomed him, saying, "Congratulations, Lieutenant Vita."

How on Earth did he know about my commission? thought Karl. "News travels quickly. How or who told you that I'm joining the BIS?" asked Karl.

"Soon, you and I will be working together. Let's find a quiet place to talk after this session ends. If we are going to work together, we always need to be on the same page," said Gunther, quietly whispering into Karl's left ear.

"Agreed," replied Karl.

After the lesson, Kitty walked over to Karl and Gunther, smiling at both, "You two seemed to be on a different agenda during our attempt to teach you the basics of speaking English."

"Sorry," they both replied.

"We did not mean to distract you like that," said Gunther.

Karl nodded in agreement.

"So, Lieutenant, are you ready for that day off on Saturday?"

"I thought I was to keep that quiet," said Karl, somewhat shocked at Kitty for saying that in front of Gunther.

"That's alright, Karl. Gunther knows a lot more than you do

right now," replied Kitty. "Gunther is part of my team, which you will also be part of after this coming Monday.

"Right now, I must leave you two, as today's work is still far from over. Don't forget the naval session tomorrow morning, 0730 sharp," said Kitty as she left them to carry on their discussion.

"The two of you?" asked Karl with a puzzled look on his face.

"That is correct, and this is why I thought we should talk privately before the meeting tomorrow morning," answered Gunther.

"I'm listening," replied Karl, a little on the defensive side.

"Karl, you know I'm from Hamburg, Germany. What you don't know is that I was a major in the regular German Army until nine months ago, when I deserted to come to England.

"Like you, I did not like what was happening to my country and the army that I was so proud to be part of. I decided to make a break for it before leaving would become impossible.

"I have extensive knowledge of the German military buildup; moreover, I also know what Herr Hitler intends to do with those forces and where he intended to use them. The Spanish Civil War started in July 1936, and what better place to find combat conditions for the fledgling Condor Legion named for Luftwaffe to hone their flying and killing skills? My job was to coordinate many of these deployments. I quickly realized that all I was doing was helping train these forces for a much bigger offensive that would inevitably sweep Europe in the coming years, and that's when I knew I must leave.

"In addition, I need you to know that I was part of the investigation carried out on you from when you first arrived here. This is also a good time to apologize for the deceit used on you by attempting to get you to tell too much in the cafeteria when you first arrived. I also told the intelligence people you had an uncanny way of detecting where someone originated from by listening to his or her dialect. That capability is going to be important in the coming years. So, now you know who I am and how I got here.

"Karl, we are on the same team, and we will be training and operating together over the next year and probably way beyond that." Gunther stopped speaking, waiting for Karl to respond.

Karl sat quietly with his hands clasped together as he looked at the floor. Another surprise had just been thrown at him. How many more will there be?

Gunther, recognizing that he had just dumped another big surprise on Karl, waited patiently for him to process all that he had just heard. After a few minutes, Karl sat up in his chair and asked in a calm, controlled voice, "So on the first day, you were trying to get me to tell you how I could associate dialects with where someone came from. Is that right?"

"That is correct, and you skillfully managed that, didn't you?" Gunther now felt that Karl had processed the course of events that had brought them to this table.

"Are there any more surprises you need to disclose before we go to the lounge, which I have full confidence in you frequenting when I'm not around?" asked Karl as he stood up, reaching for Gunther's hand in a new show of friendship.

Gunther now smiled, saying, "Thank God I don't have to leave by the side door anymore each time you come into the lounge. I was getting tired of doing that."

As they walked across the compound, they continued to talk about events they might be a part of in the coming months and years. Without any notice to Gunther, Karl stopped and said, "Gunther, you know my surname, but I do not know yours."

"It's Gunther H. Fischer," replied Gunther, now looking straight into Karl's face. "Does that surprise you, Karl? You must be aware I know about your mother's background. The staff officers felt we would be more effective together as we both have some Jewish blood running through our veins," he explained.

"Why did you not tell me if you already had information on

my family background?" asked Karl, showing signs of aggrava-
tion about yet another surprise.

"In this facility, it's all about secrets and cautious movements.
That's why. Now, to answer your next question. How did a Jew
rise to the rank of major in the German Army without being
thrown out? Well, when I joined the army as an officer candidate,
my identification papers and birth certificate had Fisher, not
Fischer, on them, that's why. My parents made that happen
before my christening. My mother was a Catholic. They felt
Fisher would create fewer problems for me growing up in
Germany. I did not find out until I was a commissioned Ober-
leutnant.

"Now, let me tell you something else, of course, in confidence,
over half the detainees in our barracks, and most of the regular
European Brigade have Jewish backgrounds. They, like us, do not
like what is happening in Europe.

"There is no safe place for anyone who is not of total Aryan
descent in the new Germany. More recruits are joining us daily."
Gunther stared at Karl, waiting for his response.

"So why did I get all that attention?" asked Karl.

"Karl don't be so naïve. You and everyone in our barracks has
some sort of special skills, either military, governmental, or engineering related. That is why. Please, don't ask me stupid questions like that again. We all got the same treatment. Each one of
us can play a vital part in undermining the advancement of the
German Nazi Party. Is that clear enough?

"Now that you have got my anger up, the first and second
rounds will be on you." Gunther had lost his composure, and this
he regretted. Like the professional he was, he recovered quickly.

"I'm so sorry, Gunther. I did not mean it in a way that makes
me look superior or special. It's that every time I turn around, I
get a piece of a story or plan that is already in play. I guess I'm
getting tired of all the games these English are playing." Karl was
now feeling stupid for his last remarks.

119

"Karl, I understand your frustration. It's a case of being sure that each candidate for the BIS is screened repeatedly until they are truly satisfied,they can be trusted with highly confidential information."

Gunther was back to his controlled self and a little sad he had lashed out at his new friend, Karl.

The lounge was packed with off-duty army and intelligence types.

No one particularly paid too much attention to the two chaps entering, other than an acknowledgment of their presence.

"So, what is it to be?" asked Karl.

"Let's start with beer and a whiskey chaser," said Gunther as they found a place at the bar.

"Good start. Guess we will be here till closing time," replied Karl.

Last call came too quickly. "Gentlemen, last call, if you please," called the steward behind the bar.

"Are we doing one for the road?" asked Karl.

"One short whiskey on me, then off to bed. Must be sharp for tomorrow's meeting," said Gunther.

Walking back across the compound, Karl asked Gunther if he knew about the move to new quarters. "Yes, I do, Karl. Your interrogation period is almost over. Your new life is about to start, so enjoy your day out with the lovely Kitty. Next week, you will also be enjoying some well-deserved time off with your family. I look forward to meeting them one day very soon, if you invite me, that is. Well, Karl, here we are. Sleep well.

"See you in the cafeteria at 0630, and if asked by any of the detainees about being in civilian clothes, tell them you were given the option, and leave it at that. As for moving barracks, no one knows about that, so let's keep it that way, okay?" explained Gunther.

"Good night, Gunther. Sorry again for being a pig head earlier."

"Don't worry about that, Karl. I think you and I will be long-term friends, so don't worry. All is good. Good night." Gunther turned and walked down the path toward building #36.

He's done it to me again, thought Karl. Only this time, he burst out laughing. Gunther could hear Karl laughing. With a big smile on his face, Gunther kept walking, waving without turning around.

Friday morning, Karl got ready, wearing a white shirt, grey trousers, and a bottle-green V-neck pullover. Sitting on the edge of the bed, he pulled a pair of green and grey socks on, then put on his polished black shoes. "Now, I feel good again." Next, he packed his suitcase and placed it in the wardrobe, ready for tomorrow when he would leave this room for the last time. Walking down the hall toward the cafeteria, he had a new spring in his step. He had a purpose and reason to get up each morning. He was an officer in the BIS.

"Good morning, all," said Karl as he signed in, knowing full-well all eyes were upon him.

"Karl, is there something we don't know?" asked Herman sarcastically.

"My uniform has a tear in the trousers, so that's why. Now, can we talk about something else?"

Gunther sat at the opposite end of the long table in his civilian attire, quietly eating his breakfast of scrambled eggs and buttered toast, not wishing to be pulled into this discussion. *Karl is a true professional*, he thought, sipping his coffee. *He will handle himself well under scrutiny.*

After breakfast, all the detainees dispersed, some to meetings, some to training sessions, and a few had the day off to linger.

Gunther and Karl stepped out into the bright sunshine, walking away from the barracks and out of earshot. Karl said in a low tone, "Building #36, why am I not surprised?" Karl tried hard not to smile or laugh.

Gunther was ready for him, "I was wondering how long it

121

would take for you to comment on my departure last night. Now you know that secret too." Gunther reached out to take Karl's arm.

It was so obvious that their friendship was becoming so much more, now that they both knew they shared similar family histories.

Entering the now-familiar Interrogation Room #5, they were surprised to find that the only attendee was Clive, who was wearing an army jumper and dark trousers. *English Army casual* thought Karl. "Morning, you two. Looks like you are getting on famously. Got all those obstacles out the way, right?" Clive was probing each of their faces, looking for any sign of tension between them.

Good, he thought, *our plan worked. They are becoming good friends. They will make great team members.*

"The navy types will be here shortly. They are driving here from a local hotel. While we are waiting, let's get some tea and go over what to expect. Remember, this will be an informal meeting.

"Their interest will be in your knowledge of harbors along the western seaboard and any changes you have observed that look like new naval installations. Karl, you will be best to address these questions.

"Any insight you can provide on naval shipbuilding will also be a big help to them. Gunther, your direct involvement as a German officer in planning and supply logistics, especially how they pertain to the Spanish Civil War, will be invaluable to how quickly the German war machine can respond to a major buildup.

"Let's keep it pretty general unless they ask for more specific information, right?" concluded Clive.

At 0835, four casually dressed naval officers entered the interrogation room. They all appeared to be quite jovial for this time of the morning. Clive walked over to them, his hand outstretched to welcome them, "Gentlemen, welcome to this early morning gathering. Before we get down to business, can we offer you some tea and a buttered roll? We also have some pastries if you prefer."

"Admiral idea," said Captain Roy Adams. The senior officer walked to the breakfast table with Clive. "Let me first introduce my officers assigned to this detail." One by one, each officer introduced himself and the area of his expertise.

When the last one got to Karl, he said, "Nice to meet you again, Commander Vita. It's been more than two years since I met you in Montevideo, Uruguay!"

"Your name, sir?" Karl asked, confused at not recognizing the tall, handsome officer holding his hand in a firm grip.

"Martin Dupree. From the look on your face, I would say you can't remember meeting me. Well, your ship was quite new back then. Your captain had invited some senior Royal Navy chaps on board on a courtesy inspection, with, let me say, some marvelous food."

"Now, I remember you. You were a lieutenant back then. I remember your comments on the tour of our ship."

"Yes, what a stylish vessel the *Tristian* was."

"And still is," replied Karl.

"I stand corrected—not the right thing to say to the former First officer of that vessel."

Karl smiled and nodded his acceptance.

Clive stood at the head of the U-arranged table and asked everyone to be seated. "Today, gentlemen, we are fortunate to have with us two officers who will share with us their overview and current information on the military buildup in Nazi Germany.

"Major Gunther Fisher, formerly of the German Army, will give us insight into supply and delivery in the German military.

"With him is Commander Karl Vita, former officer with the German Langstaff Shipping Company, and, let me add, until very recently was the First officer on the fast passenger-cargo vessel the *Tristian*."

"His knowledge of European ports and growing naval construction will be key to understanding what we already know to be true—that the new vessels currently on the way could be superior in many ways to any ship presently in the Royal Navy fleet.

"Although our own navy is a much larger force, these new vessels appear to be superior in design and firepower.

"Gentlemen, we need to be a match in every way as we move forward. Gunther, why don't you start this meeting by bringing us up to date with your involvement in directing the buildup of military forces and supply activities for the Germany military?

"These fellows, I know, are anxious to hear any insight you could provide to the extent of German intervention in the Spanish Civil War. If you could hold your questions until Gunther has finished, I'm sure it will keep this meeting flowing smoother." Karl sat quietly listening to Clive, thinking, *this will be a long day.*

For the next eight hours, Karl and Gunther shared everything they had accumulated about the German war machine. The navy people had so many questions that the five-hour meeting ran over and could have easily gone on much longer if it was not for Clive calling for an adjournment a little after 1700 hours.

Clive thanked everyone for making this such a productive meeting, closing by saying, "Gentlemen, with the information we have already gathered, and the additional information supplied by these gentlemen, we need a station in and around these German ports, especially those that have shipbuilding capabilities.

"This branch of the Intelligence Service is being formed to continuously monitor all the ports we have discussed here today.

"Gentlemen, it is imperative to our survival that we obtain

firsthand knowledge of the rapid buildup in Germany's ship-building.

"In two weeks, these two officers will go through an extensive training course in Scotland with the understanding that they will be sent back into Germany to head up an intelligence force made up of members of the Free European Brigade and members of the Royal Navy. The direction for this operation will be controlled from this center. I, along with my staff, will be your interface. The code name for this operation was used by Karl early in his interrogation session. 'Following Storm' is appropriate; don't you agree?

"And, of course, it is to be kept in the strictest confidence from here on," Clive said, now concluding the session.

Karl looked at Gunther and said in a low tone, "Should be more careful about phrases I use."

"I kind of like it," replied Gunther, looking at Clive and waiting for approval.

"Now, if you navy types would like to join us in our lounge, the BIS would like to extend our hospitality by buying you all a pint," Clive said.

"Hear, hear," was the loud response from the four navy officers. "Only rum would go down much easier."

"Totally agree with you on that," said Karl, laughing.

In the lounge, Clive briefly pulled Gunther and Karl aside to thank them for a well-orchestrated meeting, even though Clive could see traces of guilt on both their faces.

Changing the subject, Karl asked, "So, when were you going to tell us, or should I say tell me about Scotland? I'm assuming Gunther has already been briefed on this training?"

Gunther looked at Clive before answering, "We originally were planning on disclosing all of this on Monday. However, today seemed to be the perfect time to announce our intentions. I hope you're not too rattled, old man? We didn't want to overload you with too much more before your day off on Saturday. Sorry for that, Karl," Clive said, answering for Gunther.

"Well, now, I know, so please, let's not dwell on this any further," said Karl, downing the rest of the rum in his glass.

After a couple more drinks, Karl said goodnight, then turned to leave the merrymaking. Saturday was coming fast, and he wanted to be fresh and full of energy.

16

Saturday with Kitty

The alarm went off at 0530. Karl was already awake, lying in the dark. His mind was trying to process everything that had happened in just a few short weeks.

Turning the light on, he cleared his head, grabbed his dressing gown, and headed down the hallway to the bathroom. Today's weather should be warm, so he put on a clean blue and white striped shirt, grey trousers, black shoes and socks, and a dark blue cardigan.

After dressing, he finished packing his things, placed his suit-case on the bed, then carefully placed his maritime uniform on a wooden hanger alongside his case. His soft bag contained his shoes and toilet accessories; these were the last items to be packed. "That's it; I'm ready to leave this room and thank God, I will never see that English uniform hanging in the wardrobe again."

From his locked suitcase, he removed a small leather pouch, then counted out thirty-five pounds in British sterling. He then placed his ID card behind the money, securing it with a blue rubber band and walked into the hallway, closing the door quietly behind him.

As he entered the cafeteria, he noticed there were a few of his friends sitting at the tables. *Must be too early for the rest of them—it is Saturday morning, after all,* thought Karl to himself.

He ate some scrambled eggs, toast, and black coffee. He thought, *I don't need to be at the main entrance till nine o'clock, so I have about an hour and a half to kill.*

Might as well read some more of the documentation Clive gave me to review. I'll retrieve it from my luggage in my old room along with the day pass I nearly forgot as well. It should be quiet in the lounge, considering it's Saturday, so I'll find a nice corner in which to study.

With the folder under his arm and his day pass in his pocket, he walked outside into the morning air. Karl felt good; his ship was sailing on silver waters.

In the lounge, Karl poured a fresh cup of coffee from the thermos on the counter. Looking around, he spotted a big leather armchair and walked over and flopped into it. He placed his coffee mug on a side table and started to read from the material Clive had given him.

After about an hour, a steward came up to him, saying, "Sir, the guardhouse has informed me that Lieutenant Johnson just passed through control and will wait for you in front of the main door."

"Oh, thank you, Parson."

Karl looked around to see who else was in the lounge. Bill Lowes was sitting with some other officers. Karl approached the group, saying, "Excuse me for interrupting your breakfast, but I need to speak with Captain Lowes for a moment."

"Not at all, Karl, what can I do for you?"

"I'm off on a day pass. Is there any way you could lock up this file for me, then give it to me on Monday? Will that be alright?"

"Not a problem, old boy. Have yourself a wonderful day. Just remember to be back before 2230," replied Bill.

"Thanks, Bill," answered Karl as he headed for the exit.

Karl don't act like a schoolboy today, even though you really want to. Old habits die hard, I guess. Just remember Annie before you start something.

Karl's mind was racing with mixed thoughts and emotions. However, he could not stop wondering about how Kitty would look today!

17

Kitty, my new love

The guard at the main door asked for his ID card and day pass, then opened the door for him, saluting as he walked through.

Outside, the walkway was clear of vehicles except one, a large Humber military staff car. *That must be Kitty*, thought Karl as he walked toward the car.

The Humber door opened, and out stepped a stunning Kitty in a flared floral summer frock with a matching wide belt, her shapely legs shown off by bronze nylons and white closed shoes. Her long, fair hair now flowed freely over her shoulders, completing the transformation of Lieutenant Johnson.

"My God, I cannot believe how different you look in civilian clothes, Kitty," said Karl, still walking to her.

"Well, sailor, I told you that I intended to surprise you, did I not?" Kitty enjoyed the attention Karl was showering upon her.

"Climb in, and we will be off. Ready for a nice day, aren't we?"

Kitty was so bubbly that she did not resemble the military officer Karl knew and admired so much.

130

"I thought we would start our day by driving through the back roads, so you can see the area, then head for Aldershot, our local town; we can park the car in the town center, then walk around for a while. There is a wonderful inn at the end of the High Street. They make a nice plowman's lunch. After that, I thought we could drive down to the Blackwater River. It's a beautiful day, so I thought we could enjoy the afternoon sitting on a blanket, watching the rowboats go by. I have wine and glasses in the boot along with some munchies," said Kitty.

"Sounds to me like you have thought of everything," said Karl as he watched Kitty maneuver the big car down the drive that led to the guardhouse. "Not everything, Karl. Some things I'm still working on. I'll let you know how they turn out later." Kitty had a devilish look on her face. *What did she have on her mind?*

As they drove along the narrow, hedge-lined lanes, Karl saw how beautiful this part of England truly was in the midday sun.

They eventually came to an intersection with a black and white signpost pointing left; it read: Aldershot 10 miles. Kitty put on the left signal indicator and turned the car onto a much wider road than the lanes they had been driving through so far.

Entering the town, Kitty parked the car on the High Street. "Let's get that Plowman's lunch, shall we?" she suggested as they walked to the Red Lion Brewery, with Karl smiling at how friendly the local people on the street were.

The inn was large with white walls, black trim, and a beautifully maintained thatched roof. On every window, flower boxes with chrysanthemums created the perfect picture.

"Kitty, how nice it looks, is this one of the regular places you visit?"

"Yes, Karl, one of them," replied Kitty as they entered the front door. The inside was so charming with its low beams and brightly decorated walls with old paintings on them. Beer mugs of all shapes and sizes lined the shelves and even more hung over the large mantel above the big fireplace.

A middle-aged man behind the bar gave Kitty a big smile, saying, "Good day to you, Lieutenant Johnson. How nice to see you, and let me say how charming you look today. What's your pleasure?"

"Well, Jim, I thought we would have a plowman's lunch with a pint of mild and bitter if you please."

"Pint of mild and bitter," Karl said, wondering, "What is this drink?"

"Well," replied Kitty, smiling at the look on Karl's face, "it's a beer drink made up of two different flavors, half a pint of mild and half a pint of bitter. You can get something else if you don't like it."

Kitty told Jim they would sit at the table in the bay window.

The sun shone warmly on the table and Kitty's back, which she really enjoyed. Jim brought out the two mugs of frothy beer and placed them on beer mats, "I'll be back in a few minutes with your lunch, alright?" Karl looked at his mug of beer, then gingerly took a sip.

"What do you think?" asked Kitty.

"Well, it's like you English say, bloody marvelous," replied Karl with a big ring of foam around his upper lip.

Kitty clinked her glass against Karl's, then looked out the window, saying, "I must admit, Karl, that this day is the medicine I've needed for quite some time. I told you that the other night, but today, it means so much more because we are away from the camp with no other military types around. I hope you feel the same," Kitty said, looking right into Karl's eyes for approval.

"Yes, I do, more than you know, Kitty. My life is changing so fast that sometimes at night, I get anxious. My family is divided and not knowing where they are is killing me. As for my career as a sailor, that's done as well, and now I find myself in the English Army. You wonder why I get headaches." Karl was feeling very different today, but not really knowing why.

Kitty listened in silence, her face showing sadness at seeing and hearing the pain that Karl was wrestling with behind his smile.

There is so much more he is holding back or hiding, she kept thinking.

Jim brought over the plowman's lunch, "How about another mild and bitter?"

"Why not?" answered Karl, snapping out of his sadness.

"Tuesday, you get to spend time with your family in Baldock. I'm sure that will cheer you up. Monday, while you are in your meeting, I will call your brother-in-law Ronny and give him the arrival time of the train. This visit will be good for you, so let's drink to that, shall we?" said Kitty, holding Karl's hand.

He looked at her face and with his other hand, cupped her cheek, leaned over and kissed her tenderly on the lips, after which he sat back and thanked her for listening to him.

Just like that, he snapped back into his jovial self. "Now, Miss Kitty, you have my undivided attention for the rest of the day. Let's eat up and head for that river. What do you say?"

"Sounds like a good plan, ready to go?" came Kitty's reply.

Leaving the Red Lion, they walked hand in hand back to the car, not saying much. They were both thinking the same thoughts.

Karl opened the driver's door for Kitty. As she slid into the driver's seat, he could not help but admire her beautiful upper thighs.

"And what is it you are looking at, Mr. Vita?" smirked Kitty.

"I would be lying if I did not admit to admiring your beautiful legs, Kitty," remarked Karl.

"That's funny, Karl. I swear to God that your vision was way north of my knees." Kitty and Karl were sparring once again.

This will be a wonderful afternoon! The drive to the river would take about twenty minutes or so. The traffic was light, which made the drive through the tree-lined road enjoyable and reminded Karl of driving the little Opel in France.

"You are enjoying this drive, aren't you?" asked Kitty.

"Yes, I am. What could be better than this area, a beautiful sunny day, and an absolutely beautiful chauffeur driving me?"

Karl was sitting sideways in his seat, his eyes darting between Kitty's face and her magnificent legs.

Kitty's heart was pounding, knowing this handsome man was lusting over her, making her feel so like a desirable woman. She decided to take advantage of this by making the view so much more enticing. With her left hand on the wheel, she reached down and slowly moved the hem of her dress up high on her thighs, saying, "So, how do you like my stocking tops, sailor? High enough for you?"

Karl could not take his gaze off the vision Kitty was giving him, so he slid across the bench seat close to her so that he could feel her excitement building while she concentrated on her driving.

"Kitty, I want you to keep both hands on the wheel at all times, alright?" Karl said in a very controlled voice.

"That depends on what it is you're planning to do," replied Kitty, a slight tremor in her voice.

About a minute or more passed without Karl making a move. He sat close, his eyes burning into her. *Oh, God, what is he doing? How can I continue to drive like this?* Kitty had started something that Karl would now finish, and she knew it.

Slowly, his hand lightly touched her thigh. This took her breath away. Karl could sense her cocky sarcasm was quickly changing to a lady who was burning with desire. Not one word left her lips as Karl's hand worked his way high on her thigh. "Don't take your hands off that wheel, and keep your eyes on the road, alright?"

"Karl, you're driving me crazy. Please, let me pull over, please," Kitty pleaded with him but to no avail. He again repeated, "Hands on the wheel, and don't think about what I'm doing."

Kitty knew she was putty in his hands, and trying to resist

would only spur him on, so she kept both hands on the wheel and her eyes on the road. Whatever happened next was going to happen. In a tremoring voice, Kitty said, "We are almost there."

"That's really good, Kitty." His hand now moved above her suspender belt and stopped close to her underwear. He could feel her damp heat on his fingertips.

"Oh, my God, Karl, what are you doing to me?" She turned into a lane that stopped at the river's edge. Reaching over, she shut the car's engine off, then pulled the hand brake up between them. This motion moved Karl's hand right on top of her wet mound. With a lurching shudder, she had an orgasm on Karl's hand, her body spasming as she repeated this with a second orgasm. Kitty's pent-up sexual anxiety had been satisfied while she was driving, and the seductive plans she had for the afternoon were usurped by this suave Austrian sailor.

Sitting in the car with the windows down, Kitty was spent. She lay back, breathing heavily, holding Karl's hand and arm to stop him from repeating what had just happened.

"Karl, I swear to God; you are a devil. You wrecked my plans for seducing you on the blanket. I had this romantic notion that being here alone together, I could take your pain away for a short while by enjoying each other."

"And who said we are finished?" asked Karl.

"What are you thinking about doing? You're making me nervous," said Kitty, trying to second-guess his next move.

"Nothing. I'll get the blanket and the basket out of the boot."

The spot Kitty had parked in was secluded with big oak trees lining the riverbank. *What a great place to have a romantic afternoon. Hope Kitty is up to it*, thought Karl as he spread the blanket out on the grass.

Somewhere in the back of his brain, an image was being suppressed—one that he could not bring himself to think about right now.

Kitty was still lying back in the driver's seat with her eyes closed. Karl opened the door and scooped her up from the seat. Kitty kept smiling at Karl in a new way as he laid her down on the blanket. "Now that you wrecked my plan, sailor, are you ready for round two, or is your hand too tired?"

"Tired of what?" snapped Karl with a grin on his face.

"Let me give you an idea," said Kitty as she lifted her dress high, revealing her garter belt and light blue panties.

God, this woman is a tease. I guess I will have to silence her again, thought Karl, lying down beside Kitty.

Kitty turned into Karl, unbuttoning the front of her dress and removing her belt. "Darling, no need to rush. We have all afternoon, and I want this to be special for both of us, alright?" Kitty was showing her tender side.

"Of course, Kitty, you are a real temptress in that outfit, though."

A few minutes went by as they embraced with long, tender kisses, then Karl slid his hand under Kitty's panties, arousing her once again. "Wait, Karl, let me take care of you. I want to. Up to now, it's been all me, and I need desperately to have you inside me but not just yet."

With that said, Kitty sat up and opened Karl's trousers. His member was erect and throbbing. She made deep sounds in her throat.

They were sounds of joy. Placing her hand around Karl's erection, she stroked it softly before the building desire was too much for her.

She lowered her head, allowing her hair to fall around Karl, then opened her mouth to surround him, with her tongue doing its job at making Karl arch his back and make sounds of total joy.

Karl's hand started massaging Kitty's wet mound then entered an index finger into her well-lubricated vagina. This drove her into a frenzy of excitement, her mouth sucking stronger with faster motions as she slid up and down his shaft.

"Oh, my God, Karl, I'm coming again. Don't stop. Please,

please, don't stop; I beg you." Hearing this, Karl could not hold back either.

They both came together. Kitty buried Karl's member way down in her throat.

Spent, they both lay on the blanket; Karl had undone Kitty's bra and was fondling her breasts softly. "God, that was intense," Kitty said as she held his head against her breast. "If you think you're getting more, sailor, think again. I'm shot." Kitty could see that devilish look on his face.

"Well, there is one thing left to do while we are here, Kitty," said Karl quietly.

"No, there is not," said Kitty again.

"Wrong, lady." Karl bent over her, removing her panties and his trousers.

"Oh, Karl, you are such a romantic. Of course, we need to make love. I can't deny you anything." With that, Karl slid inside her, and the love-making started all over again.

Kitty felt Karl go deep inside her. *I can't get enough of this man. He can do whatever he likes to me,* and with that, she let out a scream of pleasure as she came yet again.

Lying back on the blanket, Karl reached for the bottle of wine, then uncorked it with a corkscrew that read "Property of the British Army" engraved on the handle. Karl laughed at this, saying, "British Army, what else says that? The basket, I suppose."

"Well, I'm property of the army if you want to think about it, and as of Monday, you will be too," replied Kitty.

"Guess you're right on that one. You know, Kitty, I was thinking about what we had heard aboard ship and in many ports of call, which is that English women tend to be cold as fishes. I can tell you they are so wrong because you are a tigress when you get going."

At this, they both laughed out loud, followed by Kitty telling Karl, "Mr. Vita, you are an Austrian, and Austrians are Anglo Saxons just like the English. Ever thought of it that way?"

The sun was nice and warm and felt good as they lay quietly, sipping their wine and holding hands.

This was the best of days for them both.

Emptying the wine, Kitty returned the glasses to the basket, then they both drifted into a relaxing sleep.

Kitty woke first and looked at her watch, "Oh, my God, it's nearly 1800 hours. Guess we both needed that afternoon naptime before to head back to town, Karl. Up and at 'em," said Kitty as she pushed him off the blanket.

Returning to the car, Kitty stopped in front of him as he held the door open for her, "Karl, I may sound like a romantic fool by saying this, but I think you realized since you got to the camp that I was taken by you from the first time we met.

"I have no claim on you, nor do I want you to think that today gave me any further hold over you. There is an obvious history that you keep locked away from anyone who gets too close to you.

"This, I will always respect. However, while we are working together, we can take comfort in each other's company when off-duty, and I mean off-duty, which I'm sure will not be too often. Are you alright with that?" Kitty, holding him by his arms, continued by saying, "Karl, as your superior officer, I must insist that personal feelings and time together be kept separate from our professional duties. If this creates a problem or a liability to our duties, I will stop it dead like the cold English fish I can be. Are we clear on this issue?"

Karl faced her for a few minutes before answering, "Kitty, I believe it will be hard not to stroke your backside in meetings or in the upcoming training in Scotland. However, like you, I am a professional who knows how to behave and can be straight-faced when the need arises. When called upon to concentrate and focus on whatever the task may be, I too can be as you have reminded me, a cold-hearted Anglo Saxon. So, understood."

Closing the driver's door, Karl walked around to the passenger side, getting in with a big grin on his face.

"Kitty, seeing as we are still on personal time, how about we have a repeat performance of early today while you were driving?"

"No, you will not. Now, take that devilish look off your face. This body of mine can't take any more of your trickery. Anglo Saxon be damned; you're really an Italian. You think I didn't know that before today? And Karl, you can take your hand off my thigh right now." Kitty could not stop laughing.

She knew he was ready to send her head spinning once again. *I need to control this wild man I'm dating or try to.*

Kitty once again pulled the car into the Red Lion parking area, opened the car door, and swiftly swung her legs out before that devil Karl could come around to her side of the car.

Can't be too careful with this bloke; he's capable of doing something like putting his hand up my dress in the parking lot. I must admit, it's like being a teenager all over again. This is so much fun, though.

"The colonel gave me money for lunch and dinner, so let's get something to eat before heading back to the camp, shall we?" said Kitty, reaching for Karl's hand.

The Red Lion was full of locals, many of which Kitty knew, greeting them as they made their way to the counter. "Jim, we are here for dinner. Any way we can have that bay window again?"

Jim looked over to see if the table was free and asked them to wait a minute while he cleaned it off and set it up.

"What's on the menu tonight, Jim?" asked Kitty.

"If you want something quick, try the shepherd's pie. It's made fresh every day."

"What is shepherd's pie?" asked Karl.

Jim looked at Karl with a surprised look. "From the Continent, I presume."

"Correct," said Kitty, not providing any other information.

"What I would like," said Karl, "is two pints of mild and bitter for Miss Kitty and myself."

After an excellent dinner, they made small talk until Kitty said, "Time to head back, Karl. Are you ready?"

"Not really, but I guess we can say we had a wonderful day. Didn't we?"

Kitty drove through the guardhouse and pulled up in front of the main door, "You know you can't kiss me here, don't you, Karl?"

"Yes, I know that, but can I maybe do something else to say good night?"

"No, you don't, Karl. We are back inside the camp, and I meant what I told you. I will lock down this relationship at the first sign you are crossing the line and violating my trust." Kitty acted nervous as she spoke.

"Kitty, I just want to hold your hand and thank you for making me feel so special today," replied Karl as he opened the door to leave.

"Karl, wait a minute. I should not have reacted that way; I'm concerned that people will get the wrong impression about our day out. I'm so sorry. Please, don't leave like this," Kitty begged, feeling angry with herself for reacting that way.

"It's alright, Kitty. You are absolutely correct. We are now back in our other world. See you Monday morning."

Karl smiled, closed the car door, and walked to building #36, his new home in room B-13. Kitty sat in the car and watched him till he went inside.

She started the car and headed back out through the guard-house. On the way home, tears began rolling down her face as she thought, *I'll never have this man for all my life. I'm a fill-in date for someone else far away, maybe in Austria.*

Karl opened the door to his new room, turned on the light, and walked in. The room was small, with a nice-looking bed and wardrobe. A chest of drawers had a large mirror behind it on the wall.

His belongings were neatly laid out on the bed. In the wardrobe, he found his maritime uniform, and alongside it was his new English officer's uniform. On the right shoulder, a patch identified him as a member of the Free Austrian Brigade.

Karl removed the trousers and tried them on; they fit perfectly.

Next, he tried the jacket, which also fit perfectly. He could feel a big difference in the material. "Now this, I can wear," he spoke his approval out loud.

Next, Karl tried his new officer's forage cap, thinking, *this is so different from my maritime cap, so new to me, so I guess I'll get used to it.* The last item he inspected was the wide leather belt, which had a shoulder strap that crossed his chest and attached to the belt on the left side. Placing the uniform back in the wardrobe, he decided to have a long, hot bath before retiring for the night.

Sunday morning, Karl woke early, had a shave, brushed his teeth, then put on a white shirt and casual trousers. He sat on the corner of the bed, slipped on a pair of brown shoes, brushed his hair, and headed for the door.

Entering the officer lounge, he made himself a hot cup of coffee at the kitchen window, then found an empty table, sat down, and looked around. *I wish Bill were here. I need my files to review before Monday. I should have mentioned that to him on Friday.*

Karl approached the steward behind the bar, "Do you know if Captain Lowes is due to be here today?"

"Yes, sir, he is in his office," said the steward. "Would you like me to ring him for you?"

"Oh, please, I did not realize he would already be here."

"I served him tea and a crumpet at 0700, sir."

"Captain Lowes, this is Albert in the lounge. I have Lieutenant Vita here; he asked if you could bring his file over, or would you like me to pick it up? Thank you, sir. I will let him know."

"Captain Lowes sent his compliments and said he would bring it over and join you for a cup of tea."

"Thank you, Albert, I will be over there in the corner," replied Karl.

Bill walked in with Karl's file under his arm, "There you are, old boy. You're lucky I had work today, or you would have waited till Monday." After some small talk and a pot of tea, Bill excused himself and left the lounge.

Karl ordered a sandwich with coffee, then opened his file, thinking, *there is so much for me to memorize. It's good I have this day to study.*

Later that afternoon, Albert approached his table, "Excuse me, sir. Sorry for disturbing you, but we close the lounge on Sundays at 1500. Is there anything I can get you before closing the bar?"

"Thank you, Albert. I will take a bottle of lemonade with me if you can get me one."

The rest of the day, Karl sat outside the barracks in a deck chair, studying, the sun feeling warm against his skin. As hard as he tried to concentrate, his eyes kept crossing, and he eventually gave in to a long and restful sleep.

A gentle tug on his arm brought him back quickly to full consciousness. "Oh, I must have dozed off," said Karl to Gunther.

"You have been out for over two hours, my friend. I think you needed that time to relax in the sun. Are you ready to join me for some supper?" asked Gunther.

"I am famished. Glad you woke me." Over dinner, the two talked extensively about the following day, what to expect, and more of how their futures in the BIS would affect their reliance and trust in each other.

"Remember this. Kitty is the leader of our intelligence cell. Her word is absolute and something you need to remember, no matter if you disagree with her.

"There may come a time in the future when you, in fact, disagree with her judgment or direction. If this happens, voice your concern constructively, or bring it to me, and Karl, for the record, I'm her number two. Are we clear on that?" said Gunther, looking Karl squarely in the eyes.

"Gunther, you and Kitty can rely on me. You know that, don't you?" replied Karl.

"Yes, I do, and that's the answer I needed to hear from you." Gunther wished Karl a pleasant evening as he walked away.

Karl returned to his room. *I need to continue with my homework. I must be ready for Monday*, he thought as he spread the documents over the bed.

Monday came early to Karl. He walked to the bathroom and found it completely empty. *Either I'm too early, or maybe just too late for everyone else*, he thought.

He had a nice, hot shower, shaved, and brushed his teeth. In his room, he put the new light-colored khaki shirt, then the new khaki trousers, followed by the khaki woven tie.

The English support their trousers with elasticated braces, which Karl did not like. He preferred a matching belt like his maritime uniform had. *Oh, well*, he thought, *not in the merchant service anymore*. The last items were his jacket and shoulder belt before he donned the new brown leather shoes. *The English always did make the best shoes*, he thought as he laced them.

Turning to the mirror, Karl said in a jovial tone, "Not bad, not bad at all. Oh, forgot to put my new forage cap on. Now, let's see how I look." In the jacket side pocket, he found a bill from the paymaster for all the items that made up his new uniform. What a nerve, thought Karl, reviewing the total that would be deducted from his pay over the next six pay packets.

Karl entered the lounge to find it almost full of high-ranking officers from all branches of the English military and other uniforms he recognized from other countries in Europe, including members of the Free European Brigade.

Clive and Bill were at a table with Colonel Jacks, Kitty, and some naval types. "Over here, Lieutenant Vita," called Clive. "We will make room for you."

It sounded strange to be called by his new rank. "Thank you, gentlemen, and a good morning to you, Lieutenant Johnson," he said as he sat down in between Colonel Jacks and Kitty.

"Karl, I have spoken to your brother-in-law. I gave him the arrival time of the train in Baldock. He will pick you up when you arrive tomorrow," said a reserved Kitty.

"Thank you, Lieutenant; I am so looking forward to reuniting with the family, even though my father and brothers are still in Austria. The short time we have together will do me a world of good."

Karl felt a certain strangeness coming from Kitty.

Gunther was the last to join the group. "My," remarked Karl, looking at the Free European Brigade Uniform, "I did not know you had the rank of captain."

"Well, Karl, as I said to you before, some things are kept quiet till needed. Good to see you in yours today as well."

After breakfast was served, the colonel spoke to all at the table, "Today we will be swearing in different groups that are joining the Free European Brigade.

"Some are joining the Infantry, some are joining the Artillery, some will join the Royal Air Force, which is in desperate need of qualified pilots, and a few of you are joining the BIS. Gentlemen, we need all the help we can get."

Karl spoke up, "And what about the Royal Navy and Merchant Service? Don't they need men as well?"

"Good question," said the colonel. "These branches are handled by another branch and not part of our recruitment efforts."

That's funny, thought Karl, *I should have given that more thought, but then again, this branch needs me more right now.*

The group headed out, walking to the main building to meet

the other groups that would join them in this strange ceremony of Europeans. Outside, all the officers put on their caps.

Colonel Jacks walked alongside Karl and said in a low voice, "Karl, I know you maritime chaps wear your caps to one side of your heads, but here in the British military, we wear them squarely on our heads. Be a nice chap and straighten yours for me." The colonel, with his hand on Karl's shoulder, had a big grin on his face.

"Will do, sir. How does that look now?" Karl was having fun with the colonel.

"Marvelous, simply marvelous, young man, we will straighten you out yet," Colonel Jacks said as he glanced over at Kitty for her approval.

Inside the large meeting room, the tables were arranged in two columns with a wide aisle in the middle. Each table had a label on it, designating what group it was assigned to. "Here's our table," said Gunther as he pointed to the third table back on the left side of the room.

The ceremony started with the base commander, Colonel Malcolm Ward, addressing the assembly.

"Welcome to all of you who are in attendance today. Each one of you has a story to tell of what you have seen in your own countries.

"As a result, you have elected to leave those countries for political and religious reasons; we commend you for your courage and the actions you are taking to stop further aggression by the National Socialist Party in Germany. We salute your brave decision and now welcome you here to England.

"Soon, you will become part of a growing combined military force that will stand ready to stop further advancements by the Nazis in Europe. In approximately two weeks, your intense training will start, so in a fashion, this swearing-in ceremony is premature. I recognize you must feel like you are being rushed; well, gentlemen, you are.

"Most of you arrived here only a few weeks ago, yet here today, you are gathered together wearing the uniform of the Free European Brigade. All of us pray and hope a war will never start; we must, however, prepare for one that may commence sooner rather than later. Gentlemen, time is not on our side. Again, and to repeat, all of us here salute the brave actions you have taken. Thank you again. May God keep you safe. God save the King."

Rousing applause came from the English officers in attendance.

The swearing-in ceremony concluded by all in attendance taking an oath of allegiance to the Free European Brigade and its host country, Great Britain.

"From here, you will break off into your groups to start the indoctrination. Proceed to the designated area assigned to your group," said Colonel Ward, leaving the stage.

Colonel Jacks spoke to his group, "Today, you will start to work together as a team. I will not be with you during this, but Major Knight will keep me abreast. Please, remember, time is not on our side." With that, he headed out the door.

Kitty now addressed the group, "In seven days, we will travel to our training site in Scotland. Before leaving, we will inform you about the skills in which you will need to become proficient. Remember, for your own safety and those who rely on your actions, these skills could mean the difference between success or failure, life or death. Do not allow your mind to wander at any time for any reason. I cannot stress this enough." Kitty glanced at Karl as she said this.

"I need you to understand that the materials we have provided are only as good as your ability to understand and memorize them. You will need to be proficient with their content before we arrive at the camp in Scotland, is that perfectly clear to all of you?

"For those of you in English classes, you will continue this afternoon. Now, if you will follow me, we will set you up with the paymaster," commanded Kitty as she marched toward the administration building.

Karl noticed Gunther did not follow them. He walked swiftly through the compound to a waiting Jeep, joining three other military types. Once onboard, they drove to the main gate.

I have a feeling my new friend is not so new to what goes on around here. Must be another one of those secrets!

When Karl's turn came to sign the registry and pay documents, he noticed that the first payment for his uniform had been deducted.

What nerve, he thought as he signed.

Back outside, Kitty spoke to Karl in a hushed voice, "There is no need for you to attend the English class this afternoon, so take the time to study some more. Get your things together this afternoon, so you'll be ready to go on leave tomorrow. I will pick you up about 0830, alright?

"I have a packet here that contains your train tickets both ways. Remember, the train from here pulls into Paddington Station; from there, take the underground to Victoria Station.

"When the train stops at Letchworth Station, your stop, Baldock, will be the next one, so be ready to get off the train. Also, in this package is your first pay in cash, alright? Do not lose your travel and leave passes. Always keep them with your military identification card," Kitty said as she looked at him, her heart aching. "One last thing, my darling, I am already missing you." Kitty looked at him with longing in her eyes.

"I thought because we are on military time, I would not tell you that I am hoping you pick me up from the station on my return; I will need to kiss you so very much by then," said Karl.

As Kitty handed him the package, their hands touched, and Kitty squeezed his arm, saying, "Hurry back to me, Karl. You know by now that I'm head over heels in love with you, don't you?"

"Yes, I do, and hearing you say that makes me realize that I too have fallen for you." Karl stepped back and came to attention, then saluted his commanding officer. Kitty saluted back before returning to the main building to meet up with her class for the afternoon.

Walking slowly back to his barracks, Karl's head swam. His mind was saying, *What on Earth are you doing again and again? When will you realize you cannot go through life breaking hearts and falling in love with every woman you make love to? You have a responsibility to your family. Think about Annie, who loves you very much. God knows where she is presently, and now Kitty. Karl, you need to decide soon what you are doing and where it is you are going.*

Approaching the bench where he and Kitty first spoke openly, he sat down quietly for what seemed like a lifetime.

He lowered his head and scorned himself for being such a romantic idiot. *I have allowed myself to wander once more like a ship without a rudder. Starting today, I am going to grow up and take responsibility for the damage I have done.*

As he sat thinking about the mess he had created, he felt a hand touch his shoulder. It was Gunther.

"Karl, you look like you have the world on your shoulders. Are you alright?"

"Yes, and no," replied Karl. "It's too complicated to explain right now."

"Try me. I'm older than you and have probably been through similar situations myself. As a commanding officer in the German Army, I have sat with many a troubled soldier who has lost his way and turned to similar escapes to get comfort," said Gunther in a consoling voice.

The two friends sat on the bench together for well over ninety minutes, Karl pouring his heart out about everything that had transpired since leaving the ship and now the mess with his love life.

"Karl, as I told you a few minutes ago, the distractions you have fabricated for yourself are no more than diversionary means for escaping from the burden and the pain you have been carrying. I understand where you are right now."

"Gunther, how do I go about correcting this mess?" asked Karl.

"My advice to you at this point is to take charge by putting your priorities in order. When you were on a ship, you were in control, knowing what each day would require of you. Since you have been here, I have watched you, and quite honestly, I have concerns about how you will be once we go undercover in Europe as operatives for the English."

Gunther spoke with concern in his voice, then went on to say, "My job over the last eight months has been to evaluate the stability of each detainee who passes through this facility. When you came along, I told my commanding officer, which, by the way, is not Kitty, that you would be the perfect person for me to travel back into Europe with. Your knowledge of ships and port facilities has been something we have been missing for quite a long time. Karl, will you be someone I can count on to be there for me when that happens? Are you the partner I can count on?" Gunther asked.

Karl sat upright as if someone had given him a jolt and that someone had been Gunther. "I have made a real mess of things, Gunther. I'm not sure how to proceed, but this I will promise you: when the time comes for us to return to Europe, I will cover your back as you will cover mine. I mean that, Gunther. Are we clear on that?" asked Karl.

"That was the answer I have been looking for. Now, my friend, you need to organize the mess you have created. In the matter of Kitty, you must know she is very much in love with you...to the point that she has confided in me that she will be seeking another assignment on our return from Scotland. Karl, you should not take this the wrong way. Her concern is that your relationship may cloud her vision sometime in the future when we are operating in the field. That's all."

"Is there anything else you're holding back?" Karl asked Gunther with a restrained look.

"Let's see. Did you know Kitty taught languages at the university level before being recruited by the BIS?" explained Gunther.

"No, I did not know. What languages does she speak other than English?" asked Karl.

"She is fluent in French and German and has a passable understanding of Italian. How's that?" replied Gunther.

"I'll be dammed," said Karl. "There is never an end to the secrets in this BIS, is there?"

"No, there is not. I keep finding out new things every day myself," Gunther replied as he put his hand on Karl's shoulder and continued by saying, "Remember, only you can correct the mischief you have done. See you at the end of the week. Please give Frau Vita a big hug from me; will you?" said Gunther as he walked back to the main building for God knows what meeting.

In his room, Karl took some writing paper and a pen from the small desk and sat down, staring at the blank page, then wrote his first letter to Annie.

My Dearest Annie,

I hope this letter finds you safe with your mother in Switzerland. I cannot tell you where I am due to security restrictions. All I can say is that I am adapting well to my new surroundings.

My mother is now safely with my sister and brother-in-law in their home in Baldock.

The drive from Wien was stressful, but we made it. I am not sure if this letter will ever reach you. I pray it will arrive someday.

You can respond by sending mail to my sister's home in Baldock, Hertfordshire. The address is on the back of this letter.

I sometimes find myself wondering if we will ever see each other again. The Europe we knew and loved has and is changing so fast, and maybe it will change forever. Have you any news about your father and brothers in Wien? Things must be going downhill fast about now. If you write to me, could you include a more recent photograph of yourself? We said goodbye so quickly when I dropped you off at your parents' house that I did not ask you for one.

I would love to keep a picture of you in my wallet, so when I feel lost, I can look at it and remember our wonderful times together.

Annie, these letters are censored, so I will not say too much about our personal times. You and you alone own those memories.

My regards to your mother, and when you can get through to your father and brothers, tell them to make safe decisions.

Love always, Karl.

As he sealed the envelope, he asked himself, *Did I say too much, or did I not say enough of those words she wants to read?* Karl picked up his file, headed outside to an empty deck chair, and returned to studying. The afternoon slipped by with Karl becoming more engrossed in his studies.

"Karl, are you joining us for supper?" came a familiar voice as five of his friends came out the back door, heading for the cafeteria.

"Sure, I will," said Karl, closing his folder.

18

Baldock

Morning came early to Karl. He got himself washed, shaved, and dressed, then finished packing the belongings he would take with him for the next few days. Turning to the mirror, he adjusted his cap and tie, then walked into the hallway and out the barrack's main door.

He had arranged to meet Kitty at the front of the main building at 0830. He was early, so he sat inside the main building, reading a newspaper from the day before.

His attention was broken by the front door opening. In came Kitty, smiling as if the world was a better place than it really was.

"Are you ready, Karl? It should take us about thirty minutes to reach the station, so let's be off, shall we? Do you have your tickets, travel papers, and ID on you in a safe place?" asked Kitty like a mother packing her child off to school for the first time.

"I do, Kitty. Have you forgotten I used to run a 25,000-ton ship?" replied Karl with a certain sarcastic grin.

"Can never be too sure," replied Kitty. Karl replied to her in German.

"Oh," said Kitty, "someone has been telling you about my past life, haven't they?"

For the first ten minutes, they both said nothing, Kitty driving with both hands on the wheel and Karl looking out the car's side window.

Kitty broke the silence by asking if he was getting excited about seeing his family.

"Yes, very much so. It's not long enough, though, so I guess I will have to make the most of it." A hand came across the seat, reaching for his hand.

"This may be the only time we can talk until you come back, so let me say this without any interruptions from you, alright? You must know by now that I have fallen in love with you, Karl. I did not mean to have that happen, but it did. You have no need to worry. I will not try to stifle you in any way, but I hope we can still have some quality time together for as long as it lasts. You owe me nothing. Look, my hands are on the wheel." Kitty tried a half-hearted laugh at that.

Karl sat, thinking, *she is hurting. I must do something and do it now.* "Kitty, pull into that alleyway right now."

"What for?" Kitty acted confused at the sudden command. She put the indicator on and turned down the small alleyway, rolling to a stop. She turned off the engine just as Karl wrapped his arm around her, drawing her into a deep kiss.

She responded immediately with her mouth open and her tongue buried in his mouth. Moving back just enough to speak, Karl spoke, holding her face in his hands, "Kitty, I love you too; I had no intention of falling in love with you, but so help me God, I did. It was only yesterday that I realized this."

Kissing her again, Kitty felt that dangerous hand sliding up her skirt.

First, she thought no, but then the hold on his hand fell away, allowing him to do whatever he wanted to do, and he did.

Kissing her and gently stroking her tender wet spot, he quickly brought her to a back-arching orgasm.

Hmmm, that didn't take long, he thought as he held her tightly. "There, my love. Now, you have something to remember me by till you pick me up on Sunday," said Karl with a big smile across his face.

"I swear to God; you are the Devil," said Kitty as she rearranged her uniform.

At the station, they both looked and acted like the professional military people they were.

Karl removed his suitcase and stood by the driver's side window, which Kitty had rolled down, the engine still running.

"Have a wonderful time, Karl, then come back to me." Kitty could feel the tears welling up in her eyes.

"Will do," said Karl as he watched her pull away slowly.

"Look, Karl, only one hand on the wheel," said Kitty, trying hard to maintain a smile as she pulled back out onto the road.

Inside the station, he retrieved his ticket and military travel voucher, presenting them to the ticket agent, then walked through a tunnel to the other side of the station.

Sitting on the platform, he thought, *I've made a commitment to Kitty, and I will live up to it. If I get a return letter from Annie, I will have to tell her, even though it may break her heart. Oh, God, I hate the mess I've created.*

The train to Paddington was on time. Karl found an empty compartment to stretch out in. Before he knew it, he fell into a peaceful slumber.

Kitty drove back to the camp with a big smile on her face.

"He said it, didn't he? He loves me, and that devil gave me a going-away present to boot. The days will go by slowly till he returns. It's a good time for me to prepare for the upcoming training in Scotland. How on Earth will I keep my hands off him for four or five months? And when do I tell him I've requested a transfer on our return to Aldershot?" As she continued driving, the thought of his hand up her skirt sent a tremor down her thighs.

Karl woke as the train rattled to a stop in Paddington Station. With his suitcase in hand, he opened the carriage door and stepped onto the platform.

Inside the station, he looked for the underground's logo, a big white circle with a blue band around the edge with a wide red banner that read: Underground.

Karl had never been on an underground train before. He could not believe it was so far below ground. He purchased a ticket to King's Cross Station.

The diagrams were relatively easy to follow, so getting to King's Cross was not much of a challenge to him. To get to the right platform, he rode the long escalator down to the lower level, where he waited for the right train to come out of the dark tube.

The train ride, or as the English call it, the tube, was quite enjoyable.

The sign as they entered the stop read, King's Cross.

He exited the tube, took the escalator to street level, then went out into the station.

Each time a soldier from any branch of the service passed him, they gave him a salute, Karl returning the same. *I wish they would not keep doing that. I'm getting tired of saluting back.*

Once again, he showed his travel pass at the gate, then walked down the platform, looking for another empty compartment toward the front of the train.

Karl made himself comfortable by the window when the carriage door opened, and two Royal Air Force women climbed into the compartment.

"Made it," said the brunette to the other woman. Karl sat there, thinking, *Now, the new Karl will not start anything with these two good-looking ladies in blue.*

"Excuse me, sir. I couldn't help noticing the badge on your arm. You're one of the Free European blokes, aren't you?"

"Yes, I am," said Karl, and nothing else.

"Whoops, forgot to salute you, sir," both women said, giggling.

"That's alright. I won't hold it against you, nor will I report you. Where are you both going today?" asked Karl.

"Getting off in Ashwell. Going home for a week's leave," said the brunette.

"Both of you are from the same town?" asked Karl, trying to make conversation. "No, sir, I'm from a small village called Ashwell. Carole here is going on to the city of Cambridge to visit her family. If you don't mind me asking, where is your accent from in Europe?"

"It's Austrian, but more than that, I can't tell you." Karl was cautious about giving away information, even to these pretty young ladies in blue uniforms.

"Oh, I'm sorry for prying. It's such a pronounced accent, kind of sexy," said the brunette.

Soon, the train pulled into Letchworth Station. "The next stop is mine. Hope you ladies have a nice time on leave," said Karl as he got his suitcase down from the overhead rack.

"Pity you're not getting off in Ashwell or Cambridge. It would have been nice to have a drink with you," said Carole.

"Maybe another time. Nice spending time with you, ladies, and may I say how attractive you both are." Karl smiled at the ladies in blue.

"Baldock Station," came the cry from the platform agent. Karl climbed down onto the platform, giving a wave to the WRAF girls.

"Cor', he's a smasher," said Carole to Brenda, "would have loved to have a go at him sometime."

"Blimey, Brenda, you'd shag any bloke in uniform, wouldn't ya?" Carole asked, laughing loudly.

Karl walked to the tunnel that led under the tracks to the

front of the station. Outside, a lone taxi waited for a fare. Behind it, a small black Austin saloon was parked, a familiar Royal Airforce Officer leaning against its fender. "Ronny, so good to see you again. What a relief to be here in Baldock."

"I say, look at you, old boy, fancy army uniform and all." Ronny gave Karl a big hug and said, "The girls are so excited to have you home after all you've been through. Let's get going, shall we?"

The car was small with the two big fellows in the front seats, shoulder to shoulder. Ronny started the engine and drove down the hill to the Great North Road, turning left, the drive took all of eight minutes to reach the bungalow on Letchworth Road.

Mama and Freida stood outside, waiting as the Austin pulled into the driveway. Mama reached the car first, crying out loud, "My boy, my boy is home safe. What is this uniform you are wearing, Karl? It's not your maritime uniform. Why?"

"I'll tell you all about it inside, Mama. It makes my heart so full of joy to be holding you again," Karl said, towering over his mother.

Freida moved in next to hug her big brother, "Oh, Karl, we have been so worried about you. If it weren't for that nice Lieutenant Johnson, we would not have known what was happening with you. She has been so nice. She called us almost every day. We hope we can meet her one day."

If you only knew, thought Karl, holding them both as they walked up the pathway toward the front door.

"Called you almost every day, did she? Mama, by chance, did she talk to you in German?"

"Yes, and she speaks so clearly. It made it so easy for me to understand everything she told us."

"Those dam BIS secrets at work again," Karl said, thinking out loud.

"What is this BIS?" asked Mama.

"It stands for the British Intelligence Service, Mama," answered Ronny, walking behind, carrying Karl's suitcase.

Freida opened the front door to a wonderful, familiar aroma of Mama's cooking. "Karl, it's not quite the same as I make in Wien. Can't get the same ingredients, but thanks to Ronny, he manages to trade on the black market just like you used to do at home."

They all sat around the table, talking and laughing for the longest time. It was so good to be together again, even though it was only half the family.

Karl ate like he had never eaten before, "English food is terrible. I keep thinking about being here, eating real food. Sorry for eating the lion's share, Mama."

The phone rang. "You have a single line phone in the house?" asked Karl.

"Have to—I'm on call to the base around the clock," replied Ronny as he walked to the hall to answer it. "Karl, it's for you."

"For me? Who would be calling me here? I have only just arrived. Hello, Karl here," he said, speaking English.

"Well, sailor, how does it feel being with your family again?"

The voice on the other end was speaking in German, but Karl knew who it was. "Kitty, I can't believe you're calling me so soon," replied Karl in German.

"I wanted to make sure you arrived in one piece and to tell you how much I miss you." Kitty was back to speaking in English.

"I feel the same, Kitty. So glad to know you are feeling the same. There are things I want to say to you right now, but they will wait till I see you back at the station. By the way, how can I thank you for keeping my mother and sister abreast of how I was doing? It helped keep them from worrying."

Karl tried hard to hold back tears.

"Good night, my darling. Have a wonderful time. See you real soon."

Kitty hung up, thinking, *this has become so serious. It will compli-*

cate things for both of us moving forward, but I'll be damned. I have waited for too long to find a man like Karl. He is mine, and that's the way it's going to stay—BIS be buggered!

For the next five days, Karl and his family enjoyed their time together. The walks through the old town were fascinating.

The history that dated back to the Roman occupation bore resemblances to ruins that could be found in Vienna—and such wonderful public houses.

On the last day, Ronny and Karl stopped in at the Rose and Crown while Mama and Freida did the shopping. "This pub is a young one, only dates back to the early 1600s," explained Ronny, smiling at Karl, who was taking everything in as he looked around.

He saw four Royal Navy sailors sitting at the bar, enjoying a pint of beer.

"Home on leave?" asked Ronny.

"Yes, we are, sir. We all grew up in Baldock. Going back to our ship Saturday, the HMS *Hood*. She is in Scapa Flow, Scotland," said one of the younger sailors.

Karl looked at the sailors, then spoke, "Glad we have young men like you safeguarding our seas. One word of advice, though, and it's not to criticize your pride and enthusiasm for your ship. You should never give the location of a naval vessel even when addressed by officers such as we."

The sailors looked at each other. One replied, "Thank you, sir. You are so right. We'll be more careful in the future. Sir, I could not help but notice your shoulder badge. Are you a member of the Free European Brigade?"

"Yes, I am." All four sailors stood down from their bar stools and saluted Karl and Ronny as they left the pub, wishing them a pleasant day.

Time had run out for Karl's time in Baldock. Now, it was time to pack and head back to Aldershot before traveling to their new base in Scotland.

Mama held Karl tightly as they walked toward Ronny's little Austin car. "Karl, you are so headstrong; you are your father's son. Please, promise me you will be careful. If you can't call, have that nice Kitty keep me abreast of how you are doing. Come home soon."

Mama held onto her youngest son, not letting go till Freida intervened by saying, "Karl needs to catch his train, Mama. Be careful and safe. Karl, we will worry about you till you return to us." Freida held her mother's arm as Ronny backed the Austin out of the driveway.

19

Scotland

The journey back to Aldershot was uneventful, which was good for Karl. It gave him time to reflect on where he was going and what he would be doing in the next few months. The winter was coming, and so was the gathering storm over Europe.

The train started to slow as it approached the Aldershot Station. Karl dropped the window and was hit by a blast of cold air. Autumn had arrived early without the brief period of warm weather that happens before the doldrums of winter set in.

Looking out the window, he hoped to see the familiar face of Kitty. He was looking for a woman in a khaki uniform, but there was no one on the platform like that. What he saw was a striking woman in a fitted tweed suit with shapely legs. "Kitty," he said out loud. *God, she is a sight for sore eyes.*

The train seemed to take forever to come to a complete stop, but when it did, Karl jumped down from his compartment, half running, half walking down the platform till he stopped in front of her.

"Oh, my God, you look so fantastic. How I've missed you. Let me hold you." Karl threw his arms around Kitty before she could utter a word, her feet swept off the platform by this strong former sailor.

"My darling, Karl, how I've missed you also. I can't seem to exist without you. I love you so much." Kitty held both his arms and stood on the platform, oblivious to the other passengers walking by.

"Kitty, these few days apart have made me realize that whatever I was before you no longer matters." They walked back to the car arm in arm, both having found their life partner.

Kitty spoke as she slid behind the wheel, "Darling, you know I cannot say no to you, so let's make this pact right now. I'm driving, and you're going to behave till we get to the Inn."

"The Inn? What Inn? I thought we were going back to the camp."

Karl looked confused.

"Darling, not quite yet. I obtained an extended pass for you till 0900 tomorrow morning. Now, we can be together all night."

Kitty was feeling good about the look on Karl's face.

"This will be our first time staying together all night. How did you pull this one off?" Karl asked, not sure how she had done it.

"Just by pulling rank for once," said Kitty as she started the car.

The White Horse Inn had three rooms upstairs. The downstairs had a lounge, a dining room, and a public bar at the back of the Inn.

"We are already checked in, Karl, so let's go upstairs to drop off your suitcase, then come back down for dinner. Are you hungry?" asked Kitty.

"I hadn't thought too much about it till now, but, yes, I am."

Their room was at the end of the narrow hallway, convenient to the communal bathroom. Kitty unlocked the door, then stood back, allowing Karl to enter this beautifully decorated old room.

"Why are you standing outside, Kitty?" asked Karl.

"Are you crazy, Karl? You've been gone most of the week. If I step one foot into that room, I probably won't get out till tomorrow morning. That's why."

Hearing this, Karl threw his arms in the air, saying, "You are so right, lady. You win. Let's get some food." They went down the creaking stairway, both on a cloud of happiness.

Over dinner, Karl asked Kitty what was happening back at the camp and on what day they would all leave for Scotland.

"Things are moving quickly right now. Most of the other chaps in your old building have been shipped out already. We should be getting a new bunch in at the end of the week. At the last staff meeting, I brought up how we will address Christmas and whether any leave will be granted. You may not want to hear this, but the answer that came back was no," said Kitty.

"Kitty, I told my mother, if all goes well, I would be allowed to get some leave to spend Christmas at home with them. Can I request a special dispensation?" asked Karl, obviously saddened by this news.

"Not sure, Karl. It depends on how well we all do in training. The goal was to be fully functional as an intelligence cell by April of next year." Kitty had that commanding officer look about her as she explained the situation to Karl.

"April of next year—why so long, Kitty? Whatever will we do for all those months in the likes of Scotland?" asked Karl, obviously upset by this news.

"Damn, I'm such an idiot for starting this conversation on a night such as this one. Sorry, darling, I did not mean to take your happiness away so soon."

Karl felt foolish for bringing up the BIS.

"It's not like I'm not used to all the changes to plans and schedules. Let's block it out and enjoy the rest of the evening together; shall we? You know you will have to work overtime for this, don't you?" Karl said, now trying to get Kitty back to the lovesick lady she was at the station.

"I should have expected that, coming from you. I would say it will be a long evening. Please remember, I need some strength and focus for tomorrow." The schoolgirl look was back as she reached under the tablecloth to hold his upper thigh.

"Why, Kitty, are you anxious, or have you missed me that much?" said Karl, teasing Kitty.

"What do you think, sailor?" Kitty loved how they sparred with each other in these teasing double-meaning ways.

In the room, Karl lit the fire in the old stone fireplace, then spread the blanket from the bed in front of it. Kitty opened the wine they had purchased downstairs, placing the bottle and two glasses on the blanket. Slipping out of her blouse and skirt, she was the perfect image of a young English woman with a beautifully toned shape.

Karl took in this beautiful picture. From her overnight bag, she took a brightly colored robe and quickly put it on. *No need to wind him up quite yet*, she thought as she looked at Karl.

They lay in front of the fire, sipping their wine, and enjoying this quiet time together. Neither said much. The magic was being together in their own world, locked away from another world preparing for war.

The intense lovemaking had changed to a kinder, softer, more tender time without the animal desire they had experienced only a week before. They were in love and had all night to experience the joy of being together.

Kitty's alarm went off at 0530. She rolled over to kiss and hold Karl. "Up and at 'em, sailor. While you're getting ready, I'm going to pop around the corner to my flat to change into my military uniform; then I'll come back to pick you up. Be ready to go when I get back." Kitty was already out of bed, shivering in the cold, "Bloody hell, it's not good to get out of a warm bed with no clothes on." Kitty was feeling the chill of autumn.

Karl propped himself up on one elbow, "Think I'm going to watch you do a striptease in reverse."

"Karl, really, first thing in the morning? Didn't you get enough last night? First, in front of the fire, and again in bed, I tell you, your appetite for making love is insatiable," Kitty said this as she buttoned her blouse.

"How about a kiss before you go? You're out of bed and already dressed in less than five minutes. I didn't even get so much as a hug this morning." Karl tried to put on a spoiled brat face.

"Alright, I'm sorry. My brain is already back in military mode," replied Kitty. Walking around to Karl's side of the bed, Kitty sat down to give him a kiss when, like lightning, strong arms pulled her over onto the bed. Karl kissed her neck, which he knew would drive her crazy. "Oh, I should have known better. Let me take care of you before I leave, just to keep you quiet, you crazy Austrian."

Kitty slid the blanket down and took his erection in her hand, slowly stroking it. Then she leaned down and lowered her mouth over his throbbing erection. Karl came quickly, arching his back. "Kitty, Kitty, that's not what I had in mind," said Karl, having a hard time getting the words out.

"I know that, but this is the quickest way for me to get out of here with my clothes on." Kitty stood up, rearranged her suit, and headed for the door. Before opening it, she blew Karl a kiss, "I love you. Be ready in an hour and a half, alright?"

Karl got out of bed. Also feeling the cold, he quickly put on his shirt and trousers, grabbed his toilet kit, opened the door, then entered the bathroom next to their room. After dressing, he put his toilet kit back into his suitcase, looked around to make sure that all was accounted for, opened the room door, and locked it behind him before proceeding down the hall and the stairs.

Fred, the innkeeper, had made a roaring fire in the breakfast room. Karl walked up to warm himself. Fred greeted him with a cheerful, "Good morning, sir. Sleep well, did we?"

"Very well, thank you. Something smells nice in here," commented Karl, still warming his hands by the fire.

"How about an old English fry up?" asked Fred.

"And what is that, may I ask?" Karl was not sure what *fry up* meant.

"It's three rashers of bacon, one fried egg, fried tomatoes, baked beans, and hot buttered toast with a pot of tea, of course, to round it off," the innkeeper said with a smile.

Karl sat in front of the fire, devouring his breakfast. *I must admit, I much prefer this tea to their coffee*, thought Karl as he poured a second cup.

Kitty entered the breakfast room, now in her military uniform, her long, fair hair tied back in a bun, and wearing those ugly military-issue stockings.

"Good, you have finished your breakfast, so we can get going." Kitty could be businesslike when she had to.

"Roger, ma'am, let me get my case. Fred, thank you for a wonderful breakfast. We'll be back," said Karl as he pulled on his topcoat.

Outside, Karl opened the car door for Kitty, then walked around to the passenger side. "You know, Karl, it's not necessary to open the car door for your commanding officer." Kitty was a little too sharp for Karl.

"Well, ma'am, in that case, when we arrive at the camp, you can open your own bloody door." Karl and Kitty were having their first lovers' spat.

Heading to the camp, neither said a word until Kitty broke the ice by speaking up, "We should be there in about ten minutes."

"Good," said Karl, looking out the window.

Almost simultaneously, they both said the same thing: "Sorry."

Kitty continued by saying, "Don't be mad at me for the stupid statement I made back there. It was a foolish thing to say. Forgive me, darling; it won't happen again."

"It's okay, Kitty. We are both on edge, thinking about the transfer to Scotland. I love you anyway." Karl was feeling childish for his actions.

Kitty reached over to take Karl's hand, smiling at him as she did so, "Let's try not to be silly about small things from now on, alright, darling?"

Karl answering, said, "Agreed, honey, but I must tell you that you don't have both hands on the steering wheel." Karl was back to being mischievous.

"No, you don't, you devil. We're almost there," said Kitty with fear on her face.

Karl laughed out loud, "I knew that would get you going."

"You bugger, Karl, I never know what you are going to do. In this case, you got me good." Kitty joined in by laughing out loud, breaking the tension between them.

At the gate, the guard asked for both their ID cards, then saluted as he gave back the cards.

"Karl, I'll drop you off at the main entrance. Go back to your room and gather all your belongings. Make sure that everything is clearly labeled, leaving them on the bed. Take only what you need for the next few days. The rest will be sent on with all the other gear to our new camp in a couple of days. When you are done, go straight to the assembly area and wait there for further instructions.

"Darling, I guess you realize that, starting in a few minutes, I will not be able to hold or touch you for quite some time, so let me say this right now. Each time I look at you, you will know what I'm thinking, alright?" Kitty was getting wound up as she pulled up to the curb.

"Kitty, don't worry so much. We both knew that this was coming, and let's remember we have an important job ahead of us. Please, as much as I am flattered by your concern, it will only add to my own concerns if I see you struggling." Karl needed Kitty to stop fretting. "We are professionals. We have had our fun for a while, but now it's going to be all business, right?" Karl had switched back to the task at hand.

In his room, Karl made sure that his belongings being sent to the new camp were boxed and labeled, ready for pickup. As instructed, he placed the key in the door, leaving it open for the steward, then walked out, carrying his smaller suitcase and briefcase.

The assembly area was the large meeting room at the front of the main building. Karl placed his suitcase and raincoat on the table at the back by the doors. Looking around, he saw a few familiar faces, "Silvio, glad to see you. Who else will be with us on this training deployment?" Karl was visibly pleased to know some of his new friends would be traveling with him.

"As far as I know, it will be about eight of us from the original group and about four others from the navy," said Silvio as he looked around to look for others in their group.

"How about, Helmut, Franz, Kurt, and Gunther? Are they traveling with us today?" Karl asked.

"Yes, Karl, we are all together. The others from our barracks left to go to another location two days ago, so our group is the smallest."

Colonel Jacks entered the room, accompanied by Gunther, Clive, and Kitty. "Attention," barked Gunther as he entered.

"Gentlemen, today you will be leaving us. You will not be returning to this camp again. You are no longer persons of interest or suspicion. Today, you will leave as members of the Free European Brigade. Tomorrow, when you arrive at your new camp, the real training will start. To give you an overview of what to expect, your commanding officer, Lieutenant Johnson, will now provide you with further details." With that, Colonel Jacks sat down next to Clive.

"Thank you, Colonel. I hope you all have packed your personal belongings away and left them as instructed in your rooms. At 1130 hours, all of us will board a military bus that will

168

take us to the Aldershot Train Station. On arrival at Waterloo Station, we will transfer to King's Cross Station by chartered coaches. From there, we will be boarding an express train that will take us to Edinburgh, Scotland.

"The trip is 393 miles and will take approximately five hours. In Edinburgh, you will divide into smaller training groups, boarding military buses for the remainder of this trip. Is that clear?

"Please, make sure you are on the right bus, as the camps are a considerable distance from one another. Our new camp is located just north of *Glen Nevis*. This will take another three hours. Gentlemen, this is going to be a long day, so try to rest whenever possible."

You have no idea what a strenuous, long journey is, thought Karl as he stood listening to Kitty.

"Once you have settled in, and by the way, it's four men to a room, we will commence your training in earnest. The schedules will be given to you once we arrive."

As Kitty started to sit back down next to Clive, a question was asked in an Italian accent. "Excuse me, Lieutenant. Could you give us an idea of what the training is comprised?" asked Silvio.

"I suppose there is no harm in giving you a general overview before we leave," said Kitty, turning the briefing over to Gunther.

"Your first full day at the camp is yours to do whatever you want to do, but don't expect too much, as it will be bitterly cold and wet. My suggestion is to catch up on letter writing, relaxing, and catch up on your sleep. Lieutenant Johnson told you that each room would have four in it. This will be your training squad.

"There are five segments to this intensified training. The first will be weaponry training on weapons used by the British and its allies and weapons used by the Germans.

"The second will be hand-to-hand combat.

"The third will be radio training, which includes learning how

169

to read and send Morse code. Karl, that should be a breeze for you, so help your squad out in this area.

"The fourth will be how to survive in severe weather conditions, should you find yourself on the run from the Germans. The Highlands in Scotland can be the most taxing, the weather and lack of shelter will take you to the limits of your endurance—that's another reason we train up there. Remember, you will only be relying on what you may have in your possession, so keep that in mind.

"The fifth and final phase of your training will be how to hone your skills that could well save your life one day. Knowing your way around Europe, understanding maps and charts, and how to survive, should the need arise to hide and evade the Nazis chasing you.

"Lieutenant, do you wish to add anything else?" asked Gunther.

"Thank you, Gunther, for providing a sobering overview of what is ahead. Only one other issue, box lunches will be given to you as you board the first train and again before we board the second train," said Kitty without standing up.

With that, Gunther reminded them to be ready to board the coach at 1130 hours.

Karl decided to use this free time to go for a walk. The day was cool with intermittent clouds. The camp had a nice pathway that followed its perimeter. *Fresh air is what I need right now to clear my head. I am having a problem concentrating. I need to declutter and refocus.*

Walking with his head down, his hands behind his back, Karl appeared to have the world on his shoulders. Looking at his wristwatch, he realized he had only fifteen minutes to get back to collect his suitcase and raincoat from the meeting room and find his group.

A line had gathered in front of the two military coaches.

"If you have small cases or carry bags, place them in the overhead racks," called the corporal standing by the bus door. "If your luggage is too big to fit overhead, take it to the back of the coach to be loaded."

Karl's case was small, so he kept it with him as he entered the coach. Sitting on either side in the front seats were the four familiar commanders, one being Kitty.

As he moved back into the bus, he could see and feel her eyes on him. Karl sat next to Silvio, who had held a seat for him.

Arriving at Aldershot Station, they marched to the platform.

"I feel like cattle being led to the slaughterhouse," said Silvio, looking at the military police on either side of them.

The train ride was uneventful. Karl ate his box lunch then read a book he had acquired from one of the other Austrians in the barracks. Gunther came through the carriage carrying different-colored armbands. Standing in the middle of the carriage, so all could hear him, he said, "As you can see, we have quite a few groups traveling together today, so to make things easier for your team leaders to identify their groups, I will be passing through the carriage, handing out these armbands.

"In Edinburgh, we will divide into smaller groups going to separate locations, so make sure you stay with those wearing the same color as yours."

"Oh, that's good," remarked Silvio. "We will be like colored animals." To this, everyone nearby broke out into laughter.

King's Cross Station was a sea of army, navy, and air force personnel with lots of trains and lots of smoke covering the area above them.

"Although this country is still at peace, there is no getting away from it that they are getting ready for war. Guess you could say the likelihood of sustained peace is not likely," said Karl to Silvio in Italian, so those around them would not hear or understand.

The express train was more comfortable with compartments on one side and a corridor on the other side that ran the length of each carriage. A flexible carriage connector made it easy to walk the length of the train and to reach the small bathrooms located at the end of each carriage. The corridor was also a way to stretch your legs.

"All aboard," barked the conductor as the locomotive shuddered to life, pulling the long line of carriages out of the station.

After about an hour, Karl looked around to see who was still awake—almost no one. *I believe this is a good time to stretch my legs.* The train was traveling at a high rate of speed and rocking as it went over each expansion joint.

At the far end of the carriage, a group of navy chaps stood talking about who knows what. "Excuse me, please," said Karl politely as he squeezed behind them.

Wonder who else is in this next carriage, he thought as he crossed over the hooded coupling plate into the next compartment.

In this carriage, Karl saw mainly higher-ranking army types, so he kept on walking down the length of the carriage, passing four more compartments. In the last compartment, he saw the familiar figures of Gunther, Clive, and Kitty.

Gunther stuck his head out and said, "Karl, going for a walk; are you? Come on in. Haven't seen you since this morning."

"Thank you. I'll do that. Got tired of sitting."

"Karl, you did not tell me about your visit with your family in Baldock," said Clive, leaning forward in his seat.

"It was wonderful. I did not realize Baldock had a settlement there before the Romans and settled later by the Knights Templar. Fascinating history and wonderful, quaint pubs," Karl said, answering Clive's questions but looking out of the corner of his eye at Kitty, who was sitting with her hands in her lap and looking at Karl with a smile on her face.

"Well, gentlemen and lady, I will continue with my stroll through this train. See you at the other end." With that, Karl left, sliding the compartment door closed behind him.

Clive spoke first, "Karl has fascinated me from the first time I met him on the *Clyde Princess* in Dover. The man has an incredible talent for languages and so worldly. I instinctively knew we had to have him join us. What's your opinion, Kitty? Do you agree?"

"Clive, we are weak in operatives with multiple languages, excluding you, Gunther," answered Kitty, looking at Gunther as she spoke.

What she really thought was, *you have no idea what that man can do once he sets his mind to it.* A little excitement ran through her as she spoke.

The rest of the journey was tiring. They had arrived in Edinburgh only to find it was damp, wet, and bone-chillingly cold.

"Gentlemen, welcome to Scotland," said a grinning Gunther as he gathered his group together on the platform and made sure all their equipment and luggage was accounted for as they all left together.

The walk to the waiting coaches took about eight minutes or so. The groups now separated, saying their goodbyes to friends in other groups. On the coach going to Glen Nevis, they could spread out, as there were only sixteen in the group. The bus ride up to the camp was, to say the least, boring—lots of rolling hillside with little in the way of trees. The road was narrow, only wide enough for two vehicles to pass. Along the way, a few farms lay close to the road, their old stone buildings covered in damp moss.

A few long-haired cattle with big horns stood by old fences, not caring about the coaches driving by. "How long did they say we would be here?" asked Silvio to Karl.

"Four plus months," replied Karl, looking out over the hills.

"What the hell are we going to do with ourselves when we have time off?" asked Silvio.

"I'm sure there must be towns and villages that have pubs. Let's hope so, shall we? This ride is too depressing for me. Think I'll get some shut-eye," said Karl, looking out the coach window.

"Karl, wake up. We are turning into the camp guardhouse."
Silvio sat upright, trying to get a better look.

The military police guards entered the coach and saluted the officers. After checking the documentation provided by Clive, they were waved through.

A long, narrow road led them to another guardhouse about two miles further up. Through the gates, they could now see their new home. Even in the fading light of day, it looked bleak.

"All of you, listen up," said Major Knight, standing at the front. "Grab your belongings, then go into this building in front of us. Give the sergeant waiting for us in the cafeteria your name and service number. He will give you your room assignment. Take your belongings to the room. It's first-come, first-served on the bed allocation, so don't fight over them, alright?"

"We will have supper at 1800 hours, so you have about forty-five minutes to stow your gear," said Kitty as she also stood.

Karl gave the sergeant his information and got a room number. Down the hall, he entered room #8. "Helmut, how did you get here so quickly? I got off the coach ahead of you," asked Karl.

"So, did I," said Silvio as he entered behind Karl.

"Guess we will take these two, then." Karl looked around the room for places to stow his belongings.

"So, who is the fourth one in this room?" asked Silvio.

"I am," answered Gunther. "You're changing beds, Helmut, to the one on the back wall. I'll be taking the one you claimed."

"That doesn't seem fair, pulling rank like that," said Helmut, moving his things to the other side.

"You'll get over it, son," answered Gunther. Silvio and Karl could not hold back the laughter as they unpacked.

"Okay, you three, let's go get some of that Scottish supper, shall we? God help us to what it is," said Gunther, seeming to be in a good mood.

In the cafeteria, long benches like tables ran down the

middle with wooden chairs on both sides. Food trays were stacked up to one side of the kitchen windows. "Looks like we're first," said Gunther. "Let's grab a bench close to the kitchen window."

Soon, the others came in and found places to sit. Clive and Kitty sat at a reserved table for officers in the camp.

Too far away, thought Karl. The food was surprisingly good, a stew with added boiled potatoes and carrots.

"When you're hungry, everything is good. Let's see how we feel in a couple of days," said Helmut as he devoured a second helping.

"Gentlemen, if I can have your attention for just a few minutes," Major Knight said, standing at the front of the long tables. "Tomorrow will be your free time, so no need to rise early. If you are energetic, I plan to join the regular members of this camp in PT. You can join me if you wish. I am told they start at 0700 hours. Hope to see you all there because the following day, it will be mandatory for all of you to attend."

The disapprovals started coming at hearing this command.

"The following day, we will start training in earnest. Hope you all can keep up." Major Knight sat back down, sporting a big grin.

After supper, Karl decided to take a walk around the camp. He needed the exercise after sitting all day, "Anyone up for a walk before turning in?" asked Karl. Finding no takers, he headed out, putting on his raincoat, scarf, and gloves.

As he left by the front door, a voice behind him asked, "Mind if I walk with you, kind sir? I need to get some air as well as stretching these tired legs." It was Kitty behind him, also putting on a heavy military officer's coat.

"Not at all, ma'am. Glad to have the company," Karl answered as he held the outside door open for her. The damp air cut like a knife as the wind came at them in gusts. "Goodness, Karl, this wind is terrible. However, I now have some time alone with you, so no complaints," remarked Kitty, pulling the collar of her great-coat up in front of her face.

"Did you know beforehand how dismal this place was, Kitty?" asked Karl as he helped pull the back of her collar up.

"Yes, I did, my darling, but we were told some time ago not to discuss it till we arrived here. How are you holding up, sailor? Wish I could kiss you about now," Kitty said, looking at her Karl.

"Me too, Kitty. Let's find a secluded corner to make that kiss happen. What do you say?" Karl was smiling as he said that. Between the buildings, the narrow alleyway was lit by pole lights; however, this light did not cover the recess for the emergency door.

Karl pulled Kitty into this dark area, wrapped his arms around her, then gently kissed her. This sensation stimulated her to open her mouth and seek his tongue. Kitty broke away quickly after this brief encounter, "Must not get caught doing that again, my dearest Karl. You understand?"

Back in the alley, they walked till they arrived at the front of the building and back into the light. "Kitty, you once accused me of holding back on my past. On the coach earlier today, I decided to address this and tell you everything. Our relationship has taken on a new meaning. It's one we both want to last a lifetime. I love you so very much and knowing you feel the same makes me realize that I need to separate myself from someone I held dearly before you.

"My longtime girlfriend is now in Switzerland, safe from the black cloud hanging over Austria. I intend to write her a letter, telling her that I have fallen in love with a girl in the English Army, a senior officer to me. How do I avoid breaking someone's heart? How do I let her down, so the pain of separation is minimized? How do I say how sorry I am and that I never intended to hurt her like this? Kitty, I must do this right away. It's the right thing to do."

Karl stopped walking and faced Kitty in the half-light.

"Oh, my darling, you have no idea how that makes me feel, knowing you are prepared to forgo a relationship like you described. Like you, I have already written to Brian, my boyfriend in the navy, and told him that I could not go on and have fallen totally in love with someone else. Guess you could say right now we are heartbreakers but doing the right thing for the right reasons. Well, darling, we have arrived at my quarters, so try to have a good night, and good luck with that letter."

Kitty turned and made a casual salute to Karl, who reciprocated.

The following morning, Karl arose about 0630, feeling the cold as he left his warm bed, and headed to the communal bathroom.

Entering it, it appeared like everyone had the same idea—hot water!

After showering and having a shave, he got dressed, putting on his thick army socks and a heavy army pullover over his shirt.

"God, how can people live here in this gloomy weather? This will be a long four months."

In the cafeteria, he met up with Gunther. "What is that you're eating?" asked Karl as he looked at the bowl of grey looking something paste.

"It's Scottish porridge," answered Gunther. "Sticks to your ribs, so I'm told, and keeps the cold out." Gunther laughed at the look on Karl's face. Karl decided that he, too, would get a bowl of piping hot porridge with fresh cream and brown sugar to make it more palatable. At the table, he took a big sip of hot tea, then a mouthful of porridge. *Not bad*, he thought as he took the first spoonful.

After breakfast, he sought out Clive in his makeshift office.

The door was open, so he knocked on the frame to get Clive's attention. "Major, may I disturb you for a moment?"

"Of course. Come on in," said Clive.

"I have a question about getting a letter into Switzerland."

177

"Of course, Karl. What is it you would like help with?"

"I have an important letter that must reach a friend of mine in Bern. What I am worried about is that it may not arrive. Is there a way to get it sent through military channels or maybe by diplomatic courier service to ensure its arrival?" explained Karl as he sat facing his commanding officer.

"Karl, it's none of my business, but is this a lady you're writing to? And, by chance, does it have anything to do with Lieutenant Johnson?"

Clive spoke slowly in a softer voice and was careful how he addressed the affair he knew was going on between Karl and Kitty.

"As your friend, Karl, I know how honorable and ethical you are, so I can only imagine what that letter contains. Things like this are never easy, especially at times like these. Get me the sealed letter, and I will stamp it, 'Confidential do not open' with my signature attached. That is the least I can do for you. Now, Karl, it's going to be difficult for you two while we are here, so from time to time, I will call on you to accompany Lieutenant Johnson to certain events in Edinburgh," remarked Clive, trying to make it sound like an order.

"Is that an order, sir?" asked Karl, trying to keep the big smile off his face. "Yes, Lieutenant, it is, and I insist that you comply."

Clive tried to keep a straight face.

"Thank you, sir. Glad we had this time together." Karl came to attention, then gave Clive a correct salute.

Clive looked at Karl, then said, "Get out of here, you bloody Austrian."

Back in the recreational room, Karl found a quiet area at the back of the room. He had brought with him a tablet of writing paper, pen, and ink. Sitting in the chair, he stared at the crisp, white paper. *How do I write a letter breaking someone's heart?* He kept thinking. After three attempts, he finally wrote a letter he could live with.

My Dearest Annie,

It is with a profound feeling of guilt and a deep sense of sadness that I am writing this letter to you today. I would much prefer to do this face-to-face, but we both know that cannot happen.

The commitments we made not so long ago back in Austria, now, in retrospect, it feels like a lifetime since we said them; they are no longer valid.

I can remember us saying so much that, at the time, were honest words full of loving and caring that would transcend any war or separation.

For the rest of my life, there will always be a special place locked away in my heart with your name and memories attached.

Since arriving in England, I now have a new occupation with nothing to do with being at sea anymore. Unfortunately, I cannot say more because of security.

Annie, what I am going to tell you now was not intended to happen, but it did and cannot be reversed. I have fallen in love with an English girl I work with. It started as a silly flirtation and grew from there. I did not see it coming, but it did.

I know, when you read this, you will feel so hurt as well as betrayed, and for that, I will always carry guilt and sorrow.

All I wish now is that you meet someone else and fall in love as I did and will remember me as a loving excursion on your life's journey to lasting happiness.

Fondly and Forever,

Karl Vita.

Karl read the letter repeatedly before folding it into an envelope. *God, I hope this address Annie gave me is correct*, he thought as he walked back to Clive's office.

Luckily, the door was still open with Clive bent over a pile of documents. "Come in, Karl. I see you have your letter with you. Let me stamp it now and sign it in front of you. There, it's done."

Thanking Clive, he turned and left, his head spinning with mixed emotions. *I'm going down the hall to Kitty's office. If she is there, I can tell her that any ties with the past have been separated once and for all.* Karl's head was spinning with guilt as he was wondering, *what have I done?*

The hallway was long, with offices on one side only.

Kitty's office door was open. He knocked politely, saying, "Sorry, ma'am, may I disturb you for a moment?"

"Of course," replied Kitty, gesturing for Karl to enter and close the door behind him.

"Kitty, I have just given Clive a letter that he will send for me in a diplomatic pouch to Annie in Switzerland. I wanted you to know my commitment to you is real and forever. I love you, Kitty, very much." Karl was close to tears saying this to Kitty.

"Oh, Karl, I so wish about now that we could be normal people not wearing these damn uniforms in a home far away from these problems we are facing. Just a month or so ago, I was all military. Now, I can't wait till our new life together puts all this behind us forever. Thank you, darling, for telling me about the letter. I know how difficult that must have been for you to write. I love you, too, darling." Kitty was allowing her feminine side to show through once again.

Karl walked back to the recreational room to see who was around.

I could do with a stiff drink about now. Hope that bartender has got some good stuff back there, he thought as he made his way back.

20

The Training Commences

Zero five hundred hours came quickly with a loud "Up and at 'em" coming from Sergeant Adams, who had been assigned to their barracks.

After bathroom and breakfast were done, the squad assembled in front of the building for thirty minutes of calisthenics training.

"You blokes are like old women. Pick up the pace, or we will repeat this later today," barked the sergeant.

The constant cold winds cut like a never-ending knife against the squad's thin PT outfits. "Gentlemen, now that is behind us, let's go back and change into warmer clothes before we go to the weapons training area; shall we?"

Before dispersing the squad, he asked them to wait for him back at the parade ground, adding, "Wait here while I put on my armored suit. With you buggers behind those guns, I need to be protected." The drill sergeant was laughing at them but secretly trying to motivate them.

One of the weapons instructors lined them up into pairs, "The bloke beside you will be your training partner for the time you are here. Try not to blow off his head or mine while we are in weaponry training. Alright then, as your name is called, step forward. I will use first names only as most of your surnames are bloody hard to pronounce, not like Smith or Jones."

When it came to Karl's turn, he stepped forward, waiting for his partner, wondering who it could be.

"Gunther, please step forward, sir," ordered the sergeant.

"Gunther, you have me at a disadvantage," said Karl.

"And why is that? Surely, they gave you basic weapon training in the merchant service, didn't they?" inquired Gunther.

"Yes, but you're the one who was in the German Army. I'm sure you had lots of training on many types of weapons, did you not?"

Karl watched Gunther walk to the bench and pick up an Enfield MK 1 pistol. He disassembled it in record time before reassembling it without any hesitation, then turned to salute the sergeant before returning to the squad.

"Right, for you other blokes, on those benches, you will see a series of pistols, rifles, and machine guns. At each bench, there is a weapons specialist who will educate you on how to field strip a handgun…and here is the hard part, he will also show you how to clean it before reassembling it. When it's your turn to try, please make sure you don't have spare parts left over; if you do, please do not try to shoot that pistol. If you get that far, the instructor will then instruct you on how to load it, but before that, you will learn how to load its magazine correctly. Remember, time will not always be on your side, so reloading quickly could save your life one day. It should be very interesting to watch you buggers doing this." The instructor was having fun taking potshots at these green recruits.

"Next, you'll learn what to do when a gun is jammed and how to clear that jammed weapon safely. Should one of those weapons jam, he will show you how to safely remove the round from the chamber without shooting yourself or anyone else."

Gunther was listening to the instructor but getting aggravated at his mockery. Stepping forward, he whispered something to the sergeant.

"The captain here stripped his pistol in record time because, unlike you, he is an expert in military weapons."

The sergeant still showed signs of sarcasm toward Gunther for not waiting. "After you have successfully proven to these instructors that you can handle these pistols and rifles, we will take them over to the range and fire them. Please, I beg you, try to hit the targets and not those around you. Okay, let's commence, shall we?" The sergeant was showing much more restraint than before. What had Gunther said to him a few minutes ago?

When Karl's turn came, he took his pistol from the bench, loaded the magazine into the gun, making sure to keep the barrel facing the range, then approached the firing line.

Closing his left eye to line the sights of the pistol, he stiffened his wrists to reduce the sensation of the pistol recoiling back at him.

This action would also reduce the chance of the pistol jamming a bullet in the chamber. Squeezing the trigger slowly, he felt and heard the first round resonate with a violent left kick. "Nice first shot, sir. Now, empty the rest of that magazine into the target." The sergeant praised Karl with some additional advice on consistency.

From the end of the firing line, a loud voice yelled into a bull horn, "Gentlemen, please stop firing. Remove the magazine from your weapon, then slide back the breech into the fully open position; make sure you look down the barrel from the breech end to ensure it doesn't have a live shell in the chamber. Keep your weapon pointing toward the range, then lay it back down on the bench. When you have done that, step back behind the yellow line."

Once the firing line was secure, the sergeant instructed all the shooters to recover their targets from the poles some sixty feet away. Karl's face had a big grin on it. He had shot his first target, and all the bullet holes were reasonably close together.

Karl, feeling very accomplished, approached the instructor to show him his target. The instructor looked, then said, "Consistency in all your shots is worth more than a solitary bull's eye. Well done, sir. See you later today for the next lesson."

The drill sergeant yelled out, "All of you, gather 'round. This morning, we pushed you quite hard, and I can see from your faces that you resent being spoken to like that. All of us here are here to make sure when you finally leave us, you are prepared. The skills we teach you will make you that much better than when you arrived. So, get used to being spoken to like schoolboys because, to us, you are.

"Now, take a break back in the cafeteria for thirty-five minutes before we move on to hand-to-hand combat training." The sergeant could see that they were becoming tired.

Walking up the hill to the compound, all four squads compared their targets. "Not sure about you blokes, but I enjoyed that; I can't wait to try one of those Sten guns. When do you think we will be able to shoot one?" said Silvio.

"In about a week," came an answer from the back. Gunther spoke as if he had done this before.

"What does your target look like, Gunther? Show us—did you hit any of the bigger circles?" Silvio laughed as he teased Gunther.

Gunther was a tall man. He held his rolled-up target high above the squad, and, as if in slow motion, unraveled it to show six perfectly centered bullet holes, some in the same location, bull's eyes every one of them. "Oh, my God," Silvio was taken aback by the sight of a perfect score. "Gunther, are you just

184

having a lucky day? More likely, you were a crack marksman in the German Army, am I right?" said Silvio.

Gunther's reply was short, "Yes, I was."

Karl just kept smiling and shaking his head, "More secrets from the mysterious Gunther and the BIS."

Lunch was simple hot beef stew, rolls, and butter. The spirits were high as they compared stories.

Gunther and Karl sat at a smaller table far enough away that they could talk more openly without being overheard.

"So far this morning, we all shot six magazines of 9 mm, each with seven bullets in them. This afternoon, we will be shooting .45 caliber rounds with a much higher muzzle velocity. Let's see the reaction to the first shot fired, shall we?"

Gunther knew the drill and wanted Karl to be ready for it.

"Gunther, seeing as you pretty well know each phase of this training, let me ask you this. How long will we have weapons training?"

"Twice a day every day until you all reach a proficiency level acceptable to the instructors. Then, that level of training will continue for as much as sixteen weeks," Gunther replied.

"My God, Gunther, are we doing the same thing day after day?" asked Karl.

"By no means, Karl. Those pea shooters we played with this morning were used to give you a feel for handling a weapon. Each week, we will use different weapons, leading up to automatic rifles: English, German, Italian, American, and Russian submachine guns, and yes, even bazookas and antitank weapons.

"You will become proficient with the latest German high-velocity weapons and other shoulder weapons that are now coming online. Later, you will be instructed on the use of explosive charges and how to make effective homemade bombs. Believe you me; you are going to cover so much ground that, when you finish, you will be experts. How does that sound, my friend?" Gunther smiled at Karl's expression as he spoke.

"Why did you not tell me all this before? I know; it's a BIS secret." Karl knew the answer before Gunther could utter a single word.

All week, training continued, first PT in the mornings, followed by weaponry and classroom work, then back out to the range for more practice. The following week, the hand-to-hand combat training was taken to a new level in a heated exercise room.

Three regular army chaps, wearing military sleeveless singlets, khaki shorts, and no shoes, stood with their hands clasped behind their backs.

"Today, you blokes will continue with the art of self-defense and learn how to protect yourselves as well as others on your team. You will also learn how to silently eliminate your enemy using various methods.

"Our job is to train all of you and hopefully turn you into stealthy agents against the enemy. Over the next three months or so, we will build you up from the weaklings you are today to strong, proficient field operatives who can be effective killing machines without the use of a gun.

"Sergeant Murphy will now give you a quick demonstration of self-defense. I need two of you to step forward to help him demonstrate. You, with that grin on your face, front and center. And you, back there trying to hide, get your ass up here."

Helmut, along with Kurt, sheepishly walked to the front of the class.

"Now, what I want you to do is quickly approach Murphy and try to punch him in the stomach or face. Alright, go ahead and try."

Helmut was a strong man with a confident look as he ran onto the mat, right arm swung up high behind him.

In front of Murphy, he let his fist swing down toward Murphy's jaw. Before he knew what had happened, he was flat out on the mat, his arm in pain with Murphy's foot at his neck.

"Gentlemen, you have just seen how, with the right moves and concentration, you can overpower your enemy; be sure to remember that they have also had the same training as you.

"Now, you, over there, Sergeant Bennet will turn his back to you. I want you to quietly approach him from behind and try to swing your arm around his neck in a chokehold."

Kurt did not like the thought of doing this, but an order is an order. Waiting to one side of the mat, he took his time positioning himself for the attack. When he sensed that Sergeant Bennet was about to wonder where he was, he sprung out, wrapping his arm around the sergeant's neck, thinking he had won.

Without any warning, he found himself flying over the sergeant's side and head, landing quite hard on the mat. Sergeant Bennet gave him a hand and pulled him up, saying, "You alright, son? Never assume anything. As these demonstrations have shown you, it has nothing to do with your strength, but everything to do with speed and agility and using these moves which we will start training you."

The lead sergeant, standing in front of the squad, now had their attention. "All of you line up to start learning the basic maneuvers."

Each day the squad exercised in the morning, went to the weapons range twice each day, then trained in self-defense. Two months later, they started training on how to apply many of these moves to overcome, disarming, and when necessary, silently killing the enemy.

Christmas was rapidly approaching and everyone was asking about time off to enjoy the holiday without the strenuous daily training routine.

Most everyone at the camp did not have family in England; however, the regular contingency and the English members of the BIS did.

Clive had worked with the camp commander to release virtually all the regular army contingency, including Kitty and himself.

Those without family nearby were called upon to help by staying in camp. Gunther, as the squad spokesman, cooperated with the camp commander and Clive in making a rotational schedule, making it fair to everyone staying behind.

Karl had asked Clive if he could visit his family in Baldock. Clive could not approve this request; there was not enough time to make it happen. "It's not like I don't want to approve this request, Karl; it's more about the logistics needed to get you to Baldock. The distance and time will be against you, not to mention all the trains will be packed. The chances of you running into difficulties returning could be high. It's a full day to get there and another day to return, and that's if everything goes according to plan."

Clive was looking at the disappointment on Karl's face as he told him.

Karl saluted Clive and left his office, saddened at the response.

"Karl, one minute, there is a possible way to get you home. Give me a few hours, then come find me. Do you like flying, Karl?"

Clive was already scheming a strategy to get his friend home for Christmas.

Karl's spirits changed instantaneously when he heard this. In the recreation room, all the trainees sat around talking with Gunther, who was standing in the center of them all. "Karl, how did you make out with Major Knight?" asked Helmut, seeing Karl enter the room.

"Not sure yet, but he did say there was an option he would look into. What are you chaps planning on doing if you are to stay here?" asked Karl.

"We have just finished talking to the camp commander about getting that coach parked by the motor pool and driving it to

Edinburgh for a couple of days. He is also arranging for us to stay at a camp not too far from the city center," said a cheerful Silvio.

Karl felt better about his friends having a Christmas to look forward to and less guilty if he should leave. Finding Clive in his office, Karl sat down as Clive was finishing a telephone call.

"That's it; you are coming with us on a military transport plane leaving from Edinburgh the morning of December 24th, Christmas Eve. You have a five-day leave, so make sure you get a ride to Duxford Air Force Station to be ready to take the flight back. The first stop will be at Biggin Hill to drop off some officers along with Kitty and myself; then you'll fly on to Duxford. Looks like you will have to call Freida about a pickup," said Clive.

"Wait, Clive, my brother-in-law is stationed at Duxford. Get him the flight information," said Karl.

"Will do," answered Clive, feeling so much better at seeing his friend smiling again. "Kitty, I believe, is in the officer's lounge if you wish to share the news."

Walking to the lounge, Karl had a spring to his step.

He was going home after many long months escaping this cold, bleak place. "Close that bloody door," someone yelled as Karl entered.

"Sorry, couldn't find a window to crawl through," Karl was sarcastic to the officer with the big mouth.

He found Kitty sitting at the small bar, talking with one of the ATS girls. "Karl, come join us and meet Hazel, my roommate. How did you make out with Clive today about flying down south with the rest of us?" Kitty already had the answer.

"Good, very good. He said it would be a little cramped, but that's okay with me." Karl was now in a really good mood.

Kitty teased Karl by saying, "I did tell Major Knight that I would be receptive to sitting on your lap, so long as the pilot did not hit turbulence. Bouncing up and down on your lap would create all sorts of problems." Both girls chuckled at this remark.

Karl smiled, keeping his eyes on Kitty. "I think that would be good for both of us, don't you think, Lieutenant? May I buy you both a drink?"

"That would be so nice," Hazel said, smiling at Karl.

Kitty's roommate would have loved for things to be different between Kitty and this Austrian fellow.

21

Baldock, Home for Christmas

The night before leaving for Christmas break, the camp commander, Major Leeland, called everyone into the recreation room for eggnog and plum cake, followed by spirited conversation.

"Tonight, rank means nothing. Someone put on the gramophone with some lively swing music." The party soon got into full swing.

Hazel jumped up, walked over to Karl, and asked him to dance.

I guess one won't hurt, he thought as Hazel led him out onto the dance floor. The music changed to a nice, slow dance. Karl was feeling uncomfortable with Hazel, who was obviously loosened by one too many cocktails.

Where is Kitty? thought Karl. *I sure wish this record would end soon. This lady is holding on way too tight.*

Just as the next slow dance started, a tap on Hazel's shoulder made her turn to face Kitty, "May I cut in, Hazel, if that's all right with you, Lieutenant Vita?"

"Of course," said Karl, relieved at this intervention.

"Thanks, Kitty. I was starting to get uncomfortable with your friend."

"So, are you feeling uncomfortable right now?"

Kitty was leading him on to say something romantic to her.

"Karl, your left arm is sliding down below my waist. Although I really love it, if you want to continue, we need to go someplace else."

Is Kitty telling me she is ready for some lovemaking? thought Karl.

"We can use one of the staff cars. I still have a pass for two from earlier today. What do you say?" Kitty asked, signaling she needed time alone with Karl.

"Sounds like a plan. Guess you have a lot of pent-up energy about now," whispered Karl in Kitty's left ear.

"Well, you crazy Austrian, if I do, I can only guess what I'll be like afterward."

Kitty, deep inside, could not wait to get Karl alone all to herself.

Clive authorized the pass, saying, "I will not inquire as to your request to leave the camp. Just remember to be back no later than 2200 hours tonight, understood?"

"Thanks, Clive, you are the best." Kitty held his arm with both hands.

Karl walked to his quarters, grabbed his topcoat, and headed outside to wait for the staff car to come around the corner.

The cold night air was cutting into his face like a sharp knife, but the thought of being with Kitty numbed any thought of the cold.

Around the corner came the big Humber with Kitty at the wheel.

Karl almost jumped into the passenger seat. The cold wind was that bad. "So, where are we heading?" asked Karl as he slid across the bench seat.

"Driving back to the camp the other day, we passed a lane

with some deserted buildings at the end. I memorized how to find it again, so if all goes well, we should find it in about ten or so minutes," Kitty remarked.

"Does this car have a heater in it?" Karl looked at a round contraption under the dashboard.

"Yes, darling, open those two doors in the middle, then turn that big, round knob to blow the heat out. Might have to wait a few minutes till the temperature comes up in the engine."

"God, it's so cold. We must really be in the mood to be doing this."

Kitty was shivering at the steering wheel.

"How about I take your mind off this cold while you're driving? Is that a good idea?" Karl put his arm around Kitty's shoulders.

"And, pray, what do you have in mind, or are you suggesting that I keep my hands on the wheel to make that happen?"

"First, let me direct the heater vents at those legs of yours. That way, the heat can warm your thighs, and I'll warm my hands on your thighs after. Does that sound like a plan?" Karl loved to taunt her.

"Karl, talk less and move faster. The farm lane is coming up fast."

Kitty could feel his gentle hands stroking between her legs, and the sensation increased with every inch his hands slid higher under her garter belt.

"Feeling any warmer, my sweet Kitty?" asked Karl as his fingers found her eager, soft, warm mound.

"Thank God we are here," said a whimpering Kitty as she parked the big Humber behind the old barn. Remembering the last time, she pulled up on the hand brake!

"Kitty, let's get into the back seat. There is so much more room back there," suggested Karl as he helped her out of her uniform. The engine, still running, kept the heater going, making it comfortable for them as they climbed over the front seat in their undergarments. Their lovemaking steamed up the windows, creating a private place for just a little while. After they had spent each other's energy, they lay back in the car, having a well-deserved cigarette.

"Kitty, I am so in love with you. I want you to meet my mother and sister sometime soon. Maybe after this training is completed."

"Karl, I would love that! Something to look forward to. Do you think your mother will resent me? I am English when all is said and done," Kitty asked of Karl.

"My brother-in-law is English, so it's not like we don't already have English in the family, and you will be equally welcomed into the family." Karl now realized what he was implying.

"That sounds very much like a marriage proposal, is it?" Kitty asked, sitting up in the back seat, her arms around Karl's neck.

"Kitty, that's not how I wanted to ask you, but it's out now, so yes, it is."

"Yes, yes, yes, a million times over."

The excitement was so obvious in Kitty's voice. She had finally found the man of her dreams.

"This is the best Christmas present I will ever have. Damn it. I'm going to cut my time with my mother and sister short and head to Baldock to meet my new family. What do you say to that, sailor?" Kitty was showing her anxiousness to meet her new family.

"Are you sure about doing this?" Karl was a little concerned now that things were going much faster than he had envisioned.

Kitty felt a little chilled and reached for her topcoat, spreading it over her bare chest. "You are the man I have been waiting for so long; nothing will ever come between us other than this bloody BIS or war, should it happen."

She sat upright, turning toward Karl once again, "Does Baldock have a jeweler? We will have to get an engagement ring to make it official. A cheap one will do for now."

194

Karl was also feeling the cold, so he reached over the front seat for his raincoat. Kitty continued, "Wait one minute. I'm getting carried away here. We will have to apply to our commanding officer for permission, and that might take some time with all the bloody red tape, you being an Austrian, and me being English. However, my darling, that should not stop us. I will not wear the ring in camp until the permission is granted, and everything is above board." Kitty's mind was going a hundred miles an hour.

"Kitty, when you make up your mind to do something, it's like sailing into a force-four gale, bow on." Karl could not be happier.

In these times full of uncertainty, the clouds of war hanging over them, two young people were starting to plan their lives together, and for the moment, there were blue skies overhead.

"Now, I have a special Christmas present for you, sailor. Drop your anchor. I need it for a little while longer. Then again, it may take a while." Kitty started kissing Karl's chest all the way down. She intended to give this sailor a taste of his own medicine. "Do not move a muscle or say a thing. Remember, I am your commanding officer."

With that, she massaged his member till it was fully erect, then lowered herself onto him for the third time.

The time was now 2100 hours, time for Kitty and Karl to get dressed. Kitty brushed her hair, replaced the pins that held her hair in a bun, then turned to Karl, "Come here, you animal. Let me get you looking presentable."

They drove back through the gatehouse at approximately 2120 hours, then up the hill to the front door of Karl's quarters.

"Good night, darling, see you in the morning," said Kitty as Karl opened the door and climbed out into the bitterly cold night air of Scotland.

The following morning, the small group flying south gathered by the bus, shivering in the cold and waiting for the driver to warm up the engine and open the door.

Karl spotted Clive talking with Kitty near the front of the bus. *Oh, when that lady gets a thought in her head, she acts like a lightning bolt*, thought Karl as he approached.

"Morning, may I join you, or is this discussion not for my ears?"

"Please, do. This most certainly involves you," Clive spoke in his official capacity.

Oh, Lord, I'm in trouble now, Karl thought.

"Kitty met me earlier this morning and dropped the bomb on me. Some going away present you two have given me to digest."

Clive was now mellowing to what Kitty had told him.

"I must admit, my first thought was not the news about you two tying the knot. On the contrary, I fully expected something like this to happen, maybe not so soon. Nevertheless, now that you have told me, I could not be more pleased for both of you. However, you are both in the Intelligence Service. This could create a problem for your plans at this juncture.

"Both of you are training as field operatives with the expectation of being sent into the European theater should negotiations for peace fail completely. Have you discussed the possibility that one or both of you might never return?" Clive was trying to make them think hard about what they were planning.

Kitty responded quickly to this, saying, "I would rather have a few months, hopefully much longer, with this man than go through life never to experience the love and happiness we share right now."

Kitty reached out for Karl's hand as she said this.

"She is so right, Clive. I never thought my life would change so quickly. I guess I knew Kitty was for me from that first day I laid my eyes on her back at the camp." Karl held Kitty's hand without his gloves on.

"Well, you two, it looks like you have made up your minds, and we all know how Kitty can be when she sets her mind to something, don't we?"

"Would you mind awfully if I shared this with our fellow travelers, or should we wait till after we have returned from the Christmas holiday? It's your call," asked Clive.

"I would prefer to take this slowly, Clive. We have much to do, and right now, those chaps over there are thinking about their families and being home." Karl held Kitty's hand tightly as he said this to Clive.

"I agree. Even though I want to tell the whole world, it's better if we keep it among ourselves for right now." Kitty was beaming a radiant smile that was melting Clive's concerns.

"In that case, my lips are sealed till after Christmas. Shall we climb on board the bus before we all freeze to death?"

Clive opened the door to the coach, saying from the step, "Alright, all you buggers, let's get going, shall we?"

The journey back to Edinburgh was upbeat. Everyone was excited about returning home. The airbase they were heading to at RAF Kirknewton was located outside Edinburgh in West Lothian.

The active bomber base was on standby in the event of an attack from the East; however, today, it was quiet. Once through the guardhouse, the bus drove out to the waiting RAF, Avro Anson, in front of the last hanger on the apron. The flight line had a row of Handley Page Hampdens lined up, waiting for their next operational flight.

Two pilots, wearing sheepskin-lined leather bomber jackets, waited by the open door of the Avro Anson, the cold having no effect on them. Clive was the first to exit the bus, saluting the waiting pilots.

"Morning, sir. We're all fueled and ready for takeoff as soon as you get your people on board," said the pilot in a prep school English accent.

"Very well, they all have light luggage pieces. Shall I have them place them in the rear area of the aircraft?" asked Clive.

"Let me arrange that for you, sir. We are always concerned

about weight distribution on these smaller transports," remarked the copilot as he instructed the waiting passengers where to stow their luggage. The narrow cabin was quite low, forcing everyone to lower their heads as they entered from the rear door. Once they were seated, Clive, in his authoritative voice, yelled, "Now, chaps, I have most of you getting off in Biggin Hill with three of you going on to Duxford. Will you three raise your hands so I can see where you are sitting?"

Clive wanted to make sure. To the pilot, he said, "So, you will have these three to pick up from Duxford on the return trip, okay?"

"Excuse me, sir. There is a correction to that. There will be four returning from Duxford. I will be that fourth person." Kitty spoke up from the back of the plane.

"Oh, you have changed your plans, have you, Lieutenant, since yesterday?" Clive had a wicked smile as he questioned her.

"Major, let's say a lot has changed since yesterday, shall we?" Kitty was playing word games with Clive.

"Understood. Did you get that, Lieutenant Graves?" Clive spoke to the pilot. "Yes, I did, Major. We are ready to fire up the props. Please, buckle up, everyone."

Karl sat opposite Kitty in the last row of the cabin. This way, they could look at each other, and, when no one was looking, quickly squeeze each other's hands.

A loud, swirling sound came from the starboard engine as it slowly rotated the propellers till it coughed into life, followed by the port engine. The engine noise in the small cabin was quite loud.

These military transports had little sound insulation, so talking was taxing, to say the least.

Kitty took a pad and pen from her briefcase and wrote a note to Karl. "Darling, I will be catching the train at 0800 from Victoria Station on Boxing Day. For you European types, that is the day after Christmas Day, so I should be arriving in Baldock about 0945. Any problems call my mother's house at the telephone number below. Love you. Can't wait to be Mrs. Vita." She folded the page then passed it over to Karl. As he unfolded the page, a chill came over him like something in the future would bring an unhappy event to his life. *Please, God, no more heartache or tragedy.*

I've experienced my fair share this past year.

The change in the engine tones stirred Karl to look out the small window as the aircraft banked toward the Biggin Hill Aerodrome. On final approach, Karl reached out for Kitty's hand. In a few minutes, she, along with most of the other passengers, would be getting off, and Karl, along with the two others, would be making the short flight to Duxford.

The plane taxied for only a few minutes before the pilot made an announcement, "We will park here for a few minutes to disembark those of you who are getting off, so if you are continuing to Duxford, stay in your seats, please."

One by one, they left till it was time for Clive and Kitty to deplane. With no warning, Kitty bent over and gave Karl a big kiss, "Darling, I'll see you soon. God knows I'd rather be with you over Christmas. Boxing Day cannot come soon enough for me. I hope you feel the same."

"I'll be waiting, Kitty. I'll call you tomorrow morning." Karl felt a little embarrassed at the attention.

All the brown-coated officers standing outside were giving them a loud cheer. The secret was out, and Kitty could not give a damn.

"That's my Kitty," said Karl under his breath.

The copilot shut the cabin door, then returned to the cockpit as the pilot turned the aircraft back toward the runway. Looking over the seat, Karl could see the group walking to the entrance of the flight office, except for two. Kitty stood waving with Clive by her side.

Clive is such a good friend to Kitty and me. One day, I hope to be able to repay all his kindness. The flight to Duxford was short. After touching down, the plane taxied to the flight office, following a military Jeep that had a big red and white checkered flag waving in its slipstream.

Once the pilot shut down the two engines, he moved to the back of the aircraft, opened the cabin door, lowered the folding step, and asked the remaining three to deplane.

The temperature was so much warmer here in the South. It felt like spring, not Christmas. Karl lowered his head and stepped out into the sunshine. A voice behind the plane caught Karl's attention, "Karl, over here. So glad you made it for Christmas. Can't get used to seeing you in an English uniform."

"Ronny, you are a sight for sore eyes. Are we far from Baldock?" asked Karl.

"Once we leave the base, it will only take us about fifty minutes at the most, so we will be home before it gets dark," replied Ronny.

In the little Austin automobile, Karl waited till they were on the road before he said, "Ronny, I have something to tell you all. On Boxing Day, my future wife will be coming to Baldock to meet you all. She is a senior officer in the BIS. Her name is Kitty Johnson. Mama and Freida have both spoken to her on the phone during my interrogation, so she is not a stranger, even though they have never met her face-to-face."

"Nothing like dropping a live bomb on us at Christmas. I'm not prying, but what happened to Annie in Vienna? Does she know you are no longer interested?" Ronny was not sure how to respond to his brother-in-law's news and did not want to get into it too much before arriving home.

"Did you just say Kitty will be arriving in Baldock on Boxing Day? Are you planning to stay with us, or are you going to stay in town at the George & Dragon? I think Mama will insist that you both stay with us at the bungalow." Ronny was fishing for what plans Karl may have during his brief Christmas leave.

The signpost said, "Baldock 3 miles." They would be home in ten minutes or so. They drove through the town center, busy with last-minute Christmas shoppers.

The bungalow was located off the Letchworth Road on the north side of town. Karl recognized where he was. In his mind, he was rehearsing how to announce Kitty's arrival and their plans to become engaged. The little car turned into the driveway. As Ronny turned the engine off, the front door opened, and out came Mama and Freida with Franchot in tow.

"Karl, come here. Give your mother a big squeeze. It's been too long since you were here last. You have lost weight. Are they feeding you properly?" she asked as she reached up to hold him.

Freida and little Franchot were next, holding Karl by the neck, saying, "So good to have you home, even though it's just a few days. Let's go inside. By the way, you look flashy in your British uniform."

After some coffee and wonderful Austrian pastry, Karl stood up, looking at Ronny first. "Mama, Freida, there is some wonderful news I need to share with you both. On Boxing Day, we will have a visitor, someone you have gotten to know over the phone. And now, you'll meet face-to-face."

"That must be that nice girl, Kitty. Am I right?"

"Yes, Mama, you are right, and she is coming to meet some of her new family here in England. Hopefully, she will meet Papa and our brothers in the not-too-distant future."

"You're going to marry Kitty?" asked Freida with a wide-eyed look.

"Yes, I am. It may take a while. Our jobs do not give us much time together. I am sorry to drop this news on you like this, but it's only recently we decided, war or no war, nothing was going to stop us."

Karl was elated at telling Mama that he was all done with the girl-chasing life he had lived previously.

Hearing this, Freida went to the sideboard, opened the

drawer, removed an envelope, then walked over to Karl, saying, "Oh, my God, thank you for this news. I have been so worried about how to give you this letter. Now, it will be less painful for you to read this. About three weeks ago, we received this letter from Annie, addressed to you here in Baldock. I took the liberty of opening it just in case there was something that needed addressing immediately. I'm sorry I did that, big brother because the content was not good."

Freida handed Karl the letter, then returned to her seat next to Mama. The room was very quiet as Karl removed the letter, recognizing Annie's handwriting.

Dearest Karl,

There is no easy way to tell you this. It would have been so much easier if it could have been done in person. The times we now live in and the distance between us do not allow for this to happen.

Karl, it's been so many months since I have heard from you, so when I received your letter through the British Embassy, I was so happy for you, and it was a big relief for me. Like you, I have fallen in love with someone else living here in Bern. The people here are firmly convinced that the gathering storm here in Europe will be a long, drawn-out conflict.

The chances of us seeing each other again are extremely unlikely. Spending our lives wondering is not good for either of us, so everything is working out for the best. Karl, there is a special, private place in my heart where you will always remain my first true love.

Please, give your special lady my best for a long and fruitful life together. By the way, does she know her new life will be a constant roller coaster? Be a good boy, Karl. Don't wear her out.

My love always,

Annie

P.S. I forgot to mention, my father and brothers have left

Wien and are now with my mother and me in Bern. They left everything behind—too dangerous to stay in Austria.

Karl folded the letter and, looking down at the floor before speaking, said, "That is good news from Annie and a big burden of guilt off my shoulders. Freida, you did the right thing by opening it.

"Mama, the cake was wonderful, but I need some real food about now. What do you have for me?"

The relief Karl was feeling gave him a ravenous appetite, and Mama was the right person to ask.

"It's getting harder to buy the right things for the kitchen. I did, however, take a reasonable supply of paprika for special occasions with me when we left Wien. Give me about thirty minutes to warm up goulash, your favorite dish."

"Mama, you always know what I need, don't you?"

Later that evening, the phone rang. Ronny answered it, using his official-sounding voice, "Lieutenant Whiting here. Who is calling, please?"

A familiar voice on the other end said in a polite voice, "Hello, Ronny, this is Kitty. May I please speak to Karl?"

Kitty had butterflies in her stomach until Ronny answered, "Of course, you can. I'll get him for you. By the way, we are so pleased to hear the wonderful news about you and Karl. See you soon. Wait just one moment." Kitty let out a big sigh of relief—no war zone on the home front.

"Kitty, I knew you would not wait too long to call me. Get home alright? Have you broken the news to your mother and sister yet?"

"Everything is great here, Karl. My mother honestly is relieved to know her oldest daughter is not going to become an old age-spinster. She's still a little concerned that my future husband is from Austria. After I gave them the story about your life and career to date, including your time with the BIS, she was fine and now anxiously waiting to meet you. By the way, my sister wants to know about your brothers after I showed them your maritime picture I stole from your wallet. It's only a few hours since we said goodbye, but I have an empty feeling about now. See you in a couple of days, darling," concluded Kitty.

"Can't wait to pick you up at the station, Kitty. Bye for now. Remember how much I love you." With that, Karl returned the phone to its cradle.

Kitty sat quietly for a few minutes, thinking, *Sooner or later, I must find a way of telling him about the specialized training I am involved with and that if the political climate does not change for the better, I will be going undercover in France early next year.*

"Is everything alright with your young man?" asked Kitty's mother.

"Could not be better, Mother. Now, how about a cupper with some whiskey to start us off? Mary, where are you hiding that bottle?" Kitty said, teasing her younger sister. "Mother, what is the latest from Dad? Is he still in Gibraltar? You started to tell me earlier but did not finish."

"From his last letter, all is good, but he could not say more."

Mary returned with the whiskey bottle, and her mother brought three cups and a hot teapot. "Kitty, does this mean you will be forgoing tea in the near future for coffee?" All three started laughing.

The Christmas spirit was upon them. Little did they know, as they sat there drinking their tea, that 1938 would be the start of Herr Hitler's conquest of other countries in Europe and a new direction for Kitty that would place her in harm's way.

Christmas Eve in the Austrian tradition was enjoyable and sad for the little gathering at the bungalow.

The Vita and Whiting family members celebrated, wishing Papa and the three other brothers could be here out of harm's way.

Karl and Freida both knew from Annie's letter the extent to

which their home of Wien was becoming a dangerous city to live in.

The question was, would Papa and his sons remain safe, or should they do the same thing as Annie's father and brothers did and run?

"Karl, when Kitty arrives, you can give up your room and move in with Ronny and Franchot, and I will move in with Freida, alright?" said Mama.

"Mama, as much as we will spend the days with you, I hope you are not offended when I tell you that I have made reservations at the George & Dragon for the evenings. Kitty and I do not get to see each other often, and when we do, it's only for a few hours, so if you don't mind, that is what I would like to do." Karl was not sure about his mother's reply.

"That will be fine, Karl. We totally understand. Remember, your mother was once young and very much in love with your father. We always found quiet places to enjoy each other!" Mama was quite the lady.

"Mama, please, you're destroying my image of you and Papa," said a shocked Karl. Freida smiled and laughed, making them all remember their own hideaway times.

Christmas Day, Kitty woke to the aroma and sound of sizzling bacon, eggs, and fried tomatoes, along with thick buttered toast.

"Up you get," said Mary as she pulled the drapes back from the window in Kitty's bedroom.

From her suitcase, Kitty took two small packages wrapped in seasonal paper, put on her dressing gown and slippers, and walked downstairs, carrying her gifts under her arm. Her mother and sister were already sitting at the table.

"Mother, that smells so good. Merry Christmas, you two."

Kitty placed the two packages on the table. Her mother and sister reciprocated with their gifts as well.

"Breakfast first, then we can enjoy our presents," said Kitty.

After they had finished breakfast, they moved to the sitting room in front of the fire to open their packages. Kitty opened her sister's first to find a bottle of *L'Occitane en Provence* perfume, saying, "Oh, thank you, Mary, so very much. Hope you like yours."

Next came mother's in a larger box. She opened it to find a beautiful nightgown in pink with lace around the deeply plunging neckline. "Oh, my, this is so sexy. Mother, thank you so much."

"We need to have your young man pay attention when you wear it tomorrow night," Kitty's mother answered with a twinkle in her eye.

"Mother, you are terrible," replied Kitty. Kitty gave her Mother and Mary their gifts, a new leather purse in two-tone red and brown to replace the old one that was falling apart for her Mother.

Mary opened her gift at the same time to find a beautiful, silk scarf and a pair of soft deerskin gloves in deep red.

"Thank you, Kitty," said her mother and sister simultaneously.

"I think we have all done well. Our reservations at the King's Crown are at 12:30 p.m., or should I say 1230 hours," letting out a big laugh, "so waste no time in getting ready, you two."

Mary took charge as she placed all the packages back under the Christmas tree.

The King's Crown was a magnificent Victorian manor house converted many years ago to an upscale restaurant and country club. As they entered, Kitty noticed how nicely dressed everyone was. Then a familiar voice from behind the desk caught her attention. "Kitty, so nice to see you again. It's been a long time since I last saw you in our university days. How are you doing? Still in the army, I'm assuming?"

"You are right, Tony. And, yes, it's been some time since we took your father's car for a night drive. Won't forget that in a hurry, but then again, I was young and naïve—not the case now, I can assure you." Kitty, being her old self, put Tony on the spot. He blushed in front of Kitty's mother and sister, then excused himself.

"Kitty, you were so sarcastic to that poor chap. He didn't know where to hide his face." Mary knew her sister so well and knew Kitty would wait a lifetime to get her revenge.

"I have waited so long to put that bugger in his place. He had more arms and hands than an octopus, so today, he got a taste of a grown-up Kitty."

Lunch was wonderful, but, oh, so filling. Later, they moved to the club lounge to enjoy a glass of Maynard's Tawny Port, comfortably seated in front of the large stone fireplace with its roaring fire that gave the room a golden glow. It had been a wonderful day, concluded Kitty.

Back in Baldock, the festive mood was enjoyable, but without Papa and the boys, it cast a darkened shadow on this Christmas Day and the reasons to be joyful.

Karl broke the gloom by saying, "Mama, I bought this for you in Scotland, beautiful shoal warm gloves with a matching long scarf. Hope you enjoy them.

"And you, Freida, I thought you would appreciate this new handbag; the one you are walking around with has seen better days. There is also something else inside it.

"Ronny, being a golfer, can always use a gift of Slazenger golf balls, and, finally, for my young nephew, a fast, red wind-up car."

After handing out the gifts, Mama, Freida, and Ronny gave theirs to Karl. Sitting on the couch and the floor, they all tried on their presents.

"Karl, this shoal of Scottish wool is beautiful. This will keep me warm in the English winters. Thank you, son."

Freida reached inside her new handbag to find a beautiful gold broach in the shape of a tiger's head with bright red stones for eyes.

"Karl, this is extravagant. I love it. Thank you, big brother."

"It's your turn to open yours. It's from all of us. Hope you enjoy it as much as we had finding it," said Mama.

Karl removed the wrapping paper, then opened the box. "Oh, my God, I can't believe this...wow," was all he could say as he held up a beautiful, gold Jaeger watch. On the back, it read, "To Karl, from a proud Family Vita."

"This is too extravagant. Guess you noticed my old Jaeger needs need's some fixing I will wear it only on special occasions. Thank you; thank you," Karl said, taking off his old Jaeger for the new one.

"Now, Karl, because we have only just got your news about your proposal to Kitty, Freida, Ronny, and I talked last night after you went to bed. We want to give Kitty this, with your approval, of course," said Mama.

Karl opened the dark red leather box, then looked at Mama, tears streaming down his face, "This is your engagement ring from Papa."

"Yes, it is, son, and I have waited a long time to see you give this to a strong-minded young lady. Your father and I decided quite a few years ago that when our Casanova sailor stopped having a girl in every port, this is the ring she should wear. When your eyes wander, look at this ring on your wife's finger. It will remind you that your parents frown on that sort of thing. You, more than your brothers, are your father's son; it took me a while to tame him of his wandering eyes."

Mama sat next to her youngest son and placed her arms around his shoulders. Freida and Ronny stood behind them, all in favor of giving Mama's engagement ring to his future wife, Kitty.

This had turned out to be an emotionally charged Christmas Day.

Boxing Day dawned bright and clear, sending a clear yellow shadow across Karl's face, which woke him. *First, quietly to the bathroom, then get dressed in civilian clothes*, thought Karl, feeling the excitement of meeting Kitty at the station.

Downstairs, Mama had made coffee and was sitting by the fire in the living room. "Karl, come join me once you have poured your coffee. Let's take this quiet time to talk, something we have had little time to do. Son, is the separation from Annie and having to give up your beloved ship influencing your outlook on the new life you are making for yourself?"

Mama was being diplomatic in trying to find out if the engagement to Kitty was love on the rebound.

"No, Mama, what I do now is because we are under pressure from Herr Hitler to surrender our country. He must be stopped. As for Kitty, I can tell you right here, right now, she gives my life a new purpose. I love her so very much. If you are skirting your real question, let me say truthfully, Annie will always have a special place in my heart, but that heart is now owned by Kitty."

"It's been a long time coming. Now, go get spiffed up for your young lady. Can't be late, can you?" Mama had her doubts answered, thank God.

"Thank you, Mama. You will not be disappointed." Karl stood, then bent down to kiss his mother's cheek.

Ronny came downstairs, still in his bathrobe. "You're both up early. Looks like you're almost ready to fetch Miss Kitty. The keys to the Austin are hanging next to the front door. Are you going to check into the George & Dragon first or wait for Kitty to arrive?"

"Good point, Ronny. I think I will pick her up first, then check in before heading back here." Karl had changed his plan while talking with Ronny.

"Remember, old boy; I need to leave for the base no later than 1330 hours for my duty watch, alright?"

Even though it was Boxing Day, Ronny would be on duty till 2330 tonight, and the little Austin was his only transportation.

Karl parked the car close to the station's main entrance; he was early but could not care less. Kitty was worth waiting for.

He checked with the ticket office to confirm the train's arrival time. "It's running about five minutes or so late," replied the older gentleman behind the window.

Karl looked at his new Jaeger watch to see how long his wait would be. On the platform, Karl tried sitting on one of the benches. That lasted about eight minutes before he stood, preferring to walk the platform, his mind in turmoil. The excitement of waiting was fueled by so many memories that flashed in front of him: the trauma of leaving the *Tristian*, how the people of Wien, his father and brothers, were now bracing for the gathering storm, Annie and her new love.

So many thoughts were colliding in his head.

Take a deep breath. Gain your discipline right now. You're not a schoolboy anymore. You're a commissioned officer. Now, act like one.

Those harsh words in his head calmed him as he continued to pace the platform.

"The train from King's Cross now arriving on platform two," came an announcement over the public address. Off in the distance, Karl could see the smoke streaming from the train's smokestack.

Karl made a quick check of his light blue shirt with its patterned dark brown cravat, brown trousers, and light beige tweed sports jacket.

Must look good for Kitty, he thought, his anxiousness virtually gone.

The train slowly made its way into the station, hissing steam from the big engine, its wheels squeaking as the brakes were applied.

Like a starter's pistol going off, the carriage doors flew open, and a flood of passengers descended around Karl, all in a big hurry to get somewhere.

From the back of the train, Karl caught a glimpse of a striking woman stepping down from a compartment. She wore a fitted suit that showed off her figure so very well. Its dark blue color with white stripes complemented her complexion. Her long, fair hair flowed freely around her shoulders, taking his breath away.

It was, of course, Kitty.

Karl broke out into a fast walk, covering the distance between them in seconds. "Kitty, you're here. Oh, God, how I have missed you."

"And so have I," said Kitty as Karl swept her off the platform.

"Steady on, Karl. You're going to mess me up." Kitty really could not care less. She was back with her Karl, and that's all that mattered.

Karl picked up her suitcase and put his arm around Kitty.

"Are you ready, my love?" he asked as they walked arm in arm down through the station tunnel. "Here we are," said Karl as he opened the door to the little Austin car. "I'll put your suitcase in the back seat with mine, then a quick ride to the George & Dragon Hotel in town.

"I made reservations for us to stay there. Mama and Freida are alright with this arrangement, so long as we spend the daytime hours with them. Darling, we never get to spend many nights together, so this will be a real treat for both of us."

Karl parked the car close to the hotel. "Let's go check in. I'll get our luggage."

"Mr. and Mrs. Karl Vita checking in for three nights. Hope you have the deluxe suite I requested." Kitty looked at Karl while he signed the hotel registry. "Do you have luggage going up to the room, sir?" asked the desk clerk.

"We are alright carrying our own. Thank you."

"In that case, here are the keys to suite 107; enjoy your stay."

The wide staircase had a dramatic landing halfway up. On either side, two sets of stairs curved up to the second floor. Kitty opened the door for Karl, who was carrying the two cases.

Kitty entered the room first. Karl stopped her, "Wait up, you sweet thing. Let me go first." Stepping forward, he placed both cases to one side of the entrance and turned to Kitty, swooping her up in his arms, he then carried her over the threshold.

"Karl, you only do that when you get married, you crazy Austrian," Kitty laughed as he placed her on the bed.

"Tonight, you'll be as good as married, so let's say this will be a trial run. Now, let's get going. You have people waiting to meet you for the first time. Are you nervous?"

"Not really," replied Kitty.

The short drive to the bungalow was less than a mile, so it was just a few minutes till they turned into the driveway. Karl had hardly shut the engine off when the front door opened, and out came Karl's family.

"Kitty, you are such a beauty," said Mama in German as she held Kitty close. Next came Freida and Ronny, dressed in his RAF uniform, each taking turns to welcome Kitty with a big hug.

"So, this is the English girl who stole our Karl's heart away. Good job, Kitty. You must be a very strong woman to have pulled that off," said Freida laughing.

"Welcome! We are so happy you could change your holiday schedule to spend Boxing Day with us. Karl has been pacing the floor in anticipation of your arrival. Let's go inside, shall we?"

Mama, with her arm around Kitty's waist, went through the door, followed by the rest of the family, with Karl bringing up the rear.

"Guess I know my place in this family." A big laugh came from everyone at hearing this. Today was special, displacing the sadness they all felt for not having the rest of the family with them.

In the lounge, they all sat talking, mainly about Karl, laughing at family events, drinking coffee, and eating Mama's apple strudel.

Ronny stayed longer than he should have. Excusing himself, he bent over Kitty, giving her a kiss on the cheek before heading

to the door, "See you tomorrow. Hope they don't talk your ear
off. Save me another piece of that strudel, will you?"

The afternoon flew by. There was so much that Kitty wanted
to hear and so much that Mama and Freida wanted to know
about Kitty's life before meeting Karl.

At about six o'clock, Mama said, "Please, excuse me while I
start supper. Freida, will you help me?"

"Of course, Mama. These two have not been alone for a while,
so relax till supper is ready." With that, they both left the room,
leaving only Franchot fast asleep by the fire.

"Well, how did I do, sailor?" asked Kitty, looking to Karl for
his approval. "Wonderful, thanks for speaking German to my
mother. I could tell she appreciated that. I would venture to say
she has taken to her future daughter-in-law."

Mama prepared a traditional Austrian dish that was quickly
disposed of. "This is going to put a lot of pressure on me when I
become a Vita. You will have to teach me how to cook like this.
We all know how spoiled Karl is; don't we?" Kitty said, reaching
for Karl's hand for his approval.

Her new family was more than she could have hoped for.

"Kitty, Karl told us that while you are here in Baldock, you
two would look for an engagement ring. Is that right?" Mama
was leading up to giving Kitty her engagement ring.

"That is true; I mentioned to Karl that we should consider
buying a cheap one till we get around to setting up house. Maybe
tomorrow when the shops open again, we can go looking," Kitty
replied.

Kitty now noticed the eye play among Karl, Mama, and
Freida.

"Did I say something wrong, Mama?" asked Kitty.

"No, no, my dear. It's that I would like you to consider a
special gift from me to you, and, of course, it's with the approval
of our family, including Papa and the boys in Wien. It would
mean so much to us all and even more to Karl if you accept it."

"Karl, please give Kitty the box," Mama said, now sitting close to Kitty.

Karl reached inside his jacket on the chair and removed the leather box, then knelt on one knee in front of Kitty.

"Darling, we don't have to look for an engagement ring. Mama would like you to have hers, of course, that's if you want to wear it.

"Kitty Johnson, with my mother and sister to witness this, will you consent to becoming my wife, Mrs. Karl Vita?"

Kitty's emotions could not be contained as she put her hands in front of her face, tears of joy streaming down her cheeks, both hands shaking with excitement.

"Mama, I will be so proud to wear this family heirloom. It's such a beautiful engagement ring. Are you sure about this? And, Karl, to your proposal of marriage, yes, a thousand times yes. For once, I appear to be speechless." Kitty was beyond excited.

Karl took Kitty's hand, sliding the ring onto her finger. "Darling, looks like we will have to go to the jewelers after all, to get the ring sized, that is." At this, they all came together, laughing at Karl's sarcasm.

Kitty sat with her hand outstretched, staring at the intricacies of her new ring, her right hand holding Mama's. "My new family is so much more than I could ever hope for. Thank you for welcoming me into the family." With that, she had to stop. Tears of happiness streamed down her face, her emotions still running high.

"Karl, you said nothing at the station or when we arrived here; you are a sneaky bugger. How could you keep something like this from me?" Kitty had regained her composure.

"You could say I was trained to keep secrets by the best of the BIS, a certain Lieutenant Johnson if my memory serves me correctly."

Kitty wrapped her arms around Karl, kissing him with all the love she could muster. This was truly a memorable Christmas;

however, the new year would not be so joyous. Hearts would be broken and lives forever changed.

The time was now about nine o'clock. Karl looked at Kitty, "Guess we should think about heading out. What do you say?"

"Alright, I've had such a nice time and did not realize the time. Thank you so very much for a memorable day and evening. Mama, I can't stop looking at the ring. I will treasure it always."

Karl helped her with her coat she had carried with her from the train.

"I'll go call a taxi for you?" asked Freida.

"No, it's a nice evening. We'll enjoy the short walk. Thanks anyway," said Kitty.

Karl put his overcoat on and kissed Mama and Freida on the cheek before leading Kitty through the front door, "Thanks again for today; see you about eleven tomorrow morning. Today was wonderful."

They walked arm in arm down the driveway toward Hitchin Street and the George & Dragon Hotel.

The walk was invigoratingly cold but dry. As they strolled along the dimly lit Hitchin Street, they felt the joy of each other's company. It was so comfortable.

"Karl, this is so nice, no meetings to rush to, no grabbing an hour here and there. We have so much to look forward to, darling. Let's savor each hour and not rush anywhere for the next few days, what do you say?"

Kitty was again showing her comfort side with Karl. "Sounds good to me. Remember, though, we need to size that ring tomorrow," answered Karl.

"When we get back to the hotel, I think we should have a nice glass of sherry by that big, open fireplace. What do you say?"

Karl was not ready to call it a night, nor was he interested in making love. He wanted to have a quiet romantic evening with his lady.

Kitty stopped and turned in toward Karl, saying, "Darling, I

215

have a favor to ask you; please, don't be offended by what I'm going to ask you. It's been a long day for me. All the excitement has drained me completely. Would you mind awfully, when we finally go to bed, if we quietly hold each other till we drift off to sleep?" Kitty looked at his facial expression for approval. She was rewarded with a wonderful smile.

"That's exactly what I was thinking. I was going to suggest it over drinks, so now it looks like we are starting to read each other's minds. That is scary, how do you feel about early mornings?"

Karl loved the way Kitty laughed when excited, and this she did, squeezing him as hard as she possibly could.

"Not too early, though, and can you wait for the tea and coffee to be brought up to the room?" They were acting more like a married couple with every passing day. The winds of war would change this completely.

The George & Dragon was a happening place tonight, more so because it was Boxing Day. The sound of live music was coming from the beautifully decorated lounge with its dark wood paneling, illuminated paintings, and brocade-covered armchairs.

Karl gave their coats to the hat check lady, then took Kitty's arm, leading her to two armchairs next to the roaring fire.

A cheerful waitress came to take their cocktail order, "Two dry sherries, please. And do you have any snacks available?" asked Kitty.

This peaceful time was heaven as they stared at the fire, holding hands, and wondering about their future together. The music was glorious, and the dance floor was full of people enjoying the season. Karl took Kitty by the hand, leading her onto the dance floor. The foxtrot was the next number. Karl held Kitty tightly and guided her through the congestion. She was an excellent dancer, following his every move with smooth grace.

The band announced their last song for the evening, *I'll Be*

Seeing You, wishing everyone good wishes for the coming New Year.

"Time for us to retire to our suite, lover boy. I'm getting tired, are you?" whispered Kitty as she kissed his cheek.

"I am, Kitty. Let's pay the bill and go to our suite, shall we?"

The bed had been turned down with two hot water bottles to keep it warm. Karl went to the bathroom to clean up and change into his pajamas. When he came out, Kitty was taking off her makeup, sitting in front of the dressing table, and wearing a revealing dressing gown. "You're next, lady. Don't stay in there too long, or I may already be asleep."

"Will do, lover boy." Kitty was enjoying this comfortable time alone together.

Once under the sheets, they cuddled in the middle of the double bed, making small talk until they both fell into a deep, relaxing sleep. This is what they needed. This would be their future together, God willing.

The following morning, they were woken by a loud knock on the door, "Room service." Karl put on his pants and shirt and opened the door for the waiter to enter the room. "Morning, sir; morning, madam. Did you have a pleasant Boxing Day? Saw you out on the dance floor last night, having a nice time."

"Thank you very much. Did you get some time to celebrate as well?" asked Karl as he waited for the waiter to put the tray down and leave. "Yes, I did. Thank you for asking."

After breakfast in bed, they dressed in warm, casual clothes, then headed out of the hotel onto High Street to find the jeweler's shop. Once inside the shop, they showed the ring to the jeweler. He took a quick look, "Not a problem, madam. Should have the ring ready about three this afternoon. Will that be alright?" The shop manager was a cheerful type wearing a typical English pin-striped black suit and waistcoat.

"That will be perfect," remarked Karl as they headed for the door.

"Did you see that chap looking at your new watch?" said Kitty. "It does stand out, doesn't it?"

"Let's do some exploring of this medieval town, shall we? The book in the room said a settlement has existed here since before Roman times. Those Romans were everywhere, including Wien, weren't they?" remarked Karl.

"The big church behind the hotel has a colorful history, dating back to the times of Oliver Cromwell. He was the lord protector of the English Commonwealth and the military leader of the Roundhead movement that overthrew King Charles II in 1653. We must look inside. It's on the way to the bungalow anyway," said Kitty, looking at the history of Baldock.

After doing some sightseeing, they walked back to the bungalow for lunch. Ronny was still home, leaving at 1430 hours for his shift at the base.

After a delicious lunch, they sat in the lounge, making use of the time by discussing the current political climate in Europe.

Ronny elaborated his view to explain that England and its allies would soon reach a point that they would have to say no to Herr Hitler's demands for more territory.

Karl and Kitty were careful not to say anything about their activities in the BIS, already preparing for military conflict with Germany that could erupt into outright war within the next several years or less.

"Ronny, not to change the subject, but what are the chances of dropping us off at the jewelers in town? We must pick up Kitty's ring about three." Karl was changing the subject as well as asking for a ride.

"Not a problem, old man. It's on the way anyway," replied Ronny.

Mama, we will be back later. We're going to pick up the ring. Should not be long," said Karl as they headed for the front door.

"Mind if I join you?" said Freida. She was getting tired of being cooped up in the house so much.

"Of course not," said Kitty. "Does Mama need anything from the shops?"

Mama came out of the kitchen, asking if they could buy some more bread, adding, "Some pastries would make a nice treat for later."

Four grown adults in the small Austin car was a little tight.

"Thank God it's only a mile or so away," said Freida as Ronny backed out of the driveway. Ronny dropped them off in front of the jewelry store, kissed Freida goodbye, and drove off to the base and work.

After collecting the resized ring, the three headed for Duncan's Bakery Shop on High Street. "Freida, this is such a quaint little town; I could see Karl and I settling down here one day." Kitty looked at Karl as she was saying this. Could an Austrian city boy be content to live in a country town such as Baldock?

As they walked up High Street, Kitty asked them to wait while she bought the *News of the World* newspaper from Graham's Newsstand.

The headlines read: "*Chancellor Kurt Schuschnigg* of Austria Given an Ultimatum by *Chancellor Adolph Hitler* that Austria would become a German State and its people are, in fact, Germans."

The article went on to state that Chancellor Schuschnigg was resisting Germany's continued pressure to annex Austria, with a plea to remain a sovereign nation.

Kitty grabbed Freida and Karl, "Oh, my goodness, this is the continuation of European domination that we are so concerned about from Hitler. The Sudetenland will follow soon. The Germans have already claimed it as sovereign territory. I am so sorry for you all. Now that it's out in the open, Austria can only resist for a few short months. Karl, right now, I need to call Clive as soon as we get back to the bungalow. Let's hurry." Kitty, the jovial English girl, had changed in less than a minute back to the calculating intelligence officer she was.

"Of course. Let's also see if we can get an earlier plane back to Edinburgh; shall we?" said Karl.

Karl focused his attention on the situation in Austria. *What would happen to Papa and his brothers if the country is overrun? It was starting to get ugly.*

They made the first call to Clive, who reminded Kitty that this could be an unsecured line. "Call me from the base in Duxford. Can you get there tomorrow by mid-morning? I will redirect a plane to pick up you and Karl. Will confirm the actual time later. Stand by, will you?"

Kitty hung up the phone, then said in a controlled tone, "Mama, Freida, Karl and I must, unfortunately, return to our base in Scotland. This announcement could start the domino effect we have braced ourselves for since 1935. I'm so sorry for this abrupt ending to a wonderful two days." Kitty was back in her military mode.

Freida picked up the telephone receiver and called the base, "Lieutenant Whiting, please. This is his wife calling."

"One moment, please, while I find him," said the well-spoken Wren at the other end.

"Freida, I was just going to call you. Have you got the news about the muscle-flexing by Hitler at the Austrians?" said an excited Ronny.

"Yes, Ronny, that's why I'm calling you. Karl and Kitty are returning early to Scotland tomorrow morning. You will have to take them," said Freida with stress in her voice.

"Got a better idea. Malcom, who works for me, lives in Letchworth. He can drop off a staff car for Karl and Kitty at the hotel. That way, they can drive themselves tomorrow morning. I'll meet him at the hotel, then drive him home from there. I will have to pick him up tomorrow afternoon for our shift, so that will work out just fine. I'm coming home early, so I can spend some time with Kitty and Karl before they leave. It may be a long time before we see them again." Ronny was talking like an officer that had a mountain of a job ahead of him.

The atmosphere was solemn as they all sat around the fireplace, drinking coffee and eating pastry. Both Karl and Kitty wanted to get back to the hotel to spend some quiet time together and pack for the return trip to their base.

About 2030 hours, Kitty looked at Karl with a let's get going look.

Karl stood, "As much as we hate to leave you all, we have to get going. We need a good night's sleep. Once we return to our base, we will probably get very little. It's going to be strenuous from here on, and Ronny, your job will become chaotic as well. This, I'm sure of." Karl had also returned to his military mode.

"Mama, Freida, and Ronny thank you so much for welcoming Kitty into the family. Words cannot describe how thankful we both are for the engagement ring you have entrusted to us." Karl helped Kitty off the couch.

She, in turn, reached to Mama, kissing her cheek, then doing the same to Freida, "These few days have made me such a happy lady. I will do my best to love and take care of your precious Karl. There are no words in the English dictionary that can convey the love I have for you all.

"When all this craziness passes, as I surely hope it will, I look forward to many years of living, sharing, and loving in this family. My mother and sister are going to love you all." Kitty had tears rolling down her cheeks, saying this.

With that, Karl steered Kitty to the door. Like a flash, Kitty moved to the arm of Mama's chair and cried uncontrollably, her arms wrapped around Mama's neck, "Mama, I feel so terrible right now. I don't want to leave you. Please, write to me in German, of course, and I will do the same," said Kitty as she held onto Mama.

"In just a few days, I have found such love."

Mama patted Kitty's arm, "Don't cry, dear Kitty. My Karl will make sure that no harm comes to you. He loves you so very much. Remember what I told you. If he starts looking in the wrong direction, tell him his mother will use the wooden spoon on him." This lightened the mood, allowing Kitty to walk to Karl's side as he took her coat from the hook.

Ronny drove them to the hotel. The big Humber staff car was parked in front of the entrance, Malcom behind the wheel. "Thanks, Malc'. Give Lieutenant Johnson the car keys; then we'll be off."

Ronny turned to Kitty and Karl, "Not sure when we will see you in the future. Please, stay in touch, even if it's just a postcard. The girls will be worrying about you both from here on, so please do this, okay?" With that, Ronny and Malcolm drove off toward Duxford.

Inside the hotel lobby, Karl asked Kitty, "Do you want to have a stiff drink before we turn in? About now, I need one. I knew this would start sooner rather than later."

"Yes, Karl, let's get a large double whiskey."

In the comfortable armchairs, they sat sipping their strong drinks, talking about everything except what was really on their minds.

Kitty was contemplating telling Karl about her upcoming mission, scheduled for March, then decided she would not jeopardize its secrecy, even though it was Karl.

They lingered in the lounge for about an hour, enjoying the fire and a second glass of whiskey. Kitty stood up after finishing her drink, saying, "Let's go, sailor. We need to be fresh for tomorrow morning. There's a perfectly nice bed waiting for us upstairs, and knowing you, there's still some unfinished business to attend to." The whiskey had done its job.

As they climbed the grand staircase to their room, Karl realized this could well be the last evening they would spend like this for a long time. He was going to make the best of it by making love to Kitty.

This may be the last time they would have such privacy. Kitty would not object. She knew their times together from tomorrow on would be few and far between.

22

Back to the Base in Scotland

In uniform, they downed a quick breakfast before Kitty and Karl headed for Duxford and the plane that would fly them back to Scotland. The Royston Road had little traffic this early in the morning. Kitty drove the Humber, saying little. She was thinking about the telephone call she would make to Clive once they arrived at the airbase.

Stopping the Humber at the guardhouse, Kitty and Karl showed their identification papers and travel passes, "Thank you, Lieutenant. We were told to notify the duty officer on your arrival. Please, wait here while I notify him that you're here."

Kitty reached for Karl's hand, "Darling, once we get out of this car, things will start to happen quickly. I wanted to tell you how much you mean to me. On our arrival back on base, you probably won't see much of me. As you can imagine, I am not at liberty to divulge what knowledge I may possess, not even to you. The Germans have voiced their intentions to expand their dominance over other European countries.

"From here on, it will be our jobs in the BIS to embed

ourselves into European countries we believe they will target. Doing this will give us a conduit for information that can be sent to command for processing," explained Kitty.

"And you don't believe German agents are doing the same thing here? Hell, I could be one for all you know," said Karl, allowing his concern to show.

"My naïve sailor, we know more about you than you do," replied Kitty.

"I know that, Kitty. I was only making a point; that's all," Karl said, still on the defensive.

"Lieutenant, please follow that Jeep. They will take you to the hangar and the office that will place your call. Drive on, please," said the military police guard as he saluted, waving them on to follow the waiting Jeep.

"Well, sailor, this is it. I'll see you onboard the plane. Can you do me a favor by taking my suitcase with you? Thanks, darling," Kitty opened the staff car door, saluting the guard.

At the hangar entrance, she looked back at Karl, removing their luggage from the boot, yelling in a loud voice, "Love you, you crazy Austrian."

Karl replied, "Me too, you wild Limey."

Kitty followed the guard and disappeared into the hangar to make her call to Clive. "Kitty, thank God you called me before we connect in Biggin Hill. The plane, on arrival, will park in front of one of the hangars. It will not shut down its engines. Bill and I will be waiting inside to hand over a dossier I need you to review on the flight north. I don't want to bring too much attention to this, so bring your briefcase in with you."

"I want you to pay close attention to those pages that are marked 'KJ.' They pertain to your involvement in operation 'Next Time.'

"You need to be current, so on the plane, read up and become familiar with it the best you can. The flight and the bus ride back to base should give you enough time to familiarize yourself with the operation. Once we arrive back at the base, Bill, you, and I must be ready for a crash meeting on *'Next Time.'* Is that clear? Bill and I will keep Karl and the others occupied, so you will not be disturbed," Clive spoke quickly, trying to cover all the areas for Kitty.

"Why the mad rush preparing for this meeting?" asked Kitty with a worried tone to her voice.

"Kitty, you, as team leader, Bill, and Hazel are going into deep cover in Germany starting next month; that's why. Need I say more right now? See you in about ninety minutes!"

With that, Clive hung up the phone.

Kitty replaced the receiver, thanking the guard as she left the room and walked to the plane, the weight of her job and responsibilities now heavy on her shoulders. She stopped at the hangar door to gain her composure. How could she keep a smile on her face, knowing that next month she would be sent underground into Germany?

The vision of trying to stay concealed while carrying out their surveillance of the German military buildup sent chills down her spine. With any luck, they would not be running or hiding from a tipoff to the dreaded brown shirts or ruthless Gestapo.

What if something happens to me? What will happen to Karl?

He is going to face a similar situation when he and Gunther go undercover later in the year.

Oh, my God, life is going to be difficult from here on; get a handle on yourself. You've known this was coming for over two years now.

Karl waited by the boarding ladder to help Kitty board the aircraft. Standing behind the pilot, Kitty addressed Karl and the other passengers.

"Now, listen up. The flight to Biggin Hill will be short. On our arrival, you three are to stay on board while I join Major Knight and Captain Lowes in the hangar for a brief meeting. The pilot has been instructed to keep both engines running as our time will be short. Is that understood?" Kitty was back in full BIS mode.

The pilot came back to make sure the luggage was stowed securely behind the seats, "Would you like me to stow your briefcase for you, Lieutenant?"

"I'll keep it with me if you don't mind," replied Kitty as she strapped herself into her seat behind the pilot.

No sooner was the small Avro Anson airborne than the pilot announced, "We are on our final approach to Biggin Hill. Please, make sure your seatbelts are buckled low and tight."

On the ground, the plane taxied to the hangar, coming to a stop in front of an RAF Batman. Kitty grabbed her briefcase, then climbed down the boarding ladder already attached to the open cabin door.

An RAF officer stood outside, asking her to follow him to the hangar side door. In the enormous building, the bright lights surprised her as she walked to the familiar faces of Clive and Bill. "Kitty, so good to see you," said Clive as he saluted Kitty, followed by a heartfelt hug.

"Hold on, old man. Don't forget me on those hugs." Bill was trying to make Kitty feel less concerned than her facial expressions were showing. Kitty felt less alone now that she was with her longtime friends.

She flashed her engagement ring at them both. There was a reason for doing this so soon!

"I say, Kitty, that is a splendid looking ring. I would venture to say expensive to boot. Wouldn't you agree, Clive?" Bill held Kitty's hand as he said this.

"Will I be around long enough to wear it?" Kitty was blunt with her question.

Bill turned to the binder behind him on the table, "Once onboard, start reviewing the blue tabbed pages marked 'KJ.' We will move the other blokes to the back of the plane to give you more privacy. The excuse will be we are preparing for a training review."

"By the way, you two, this ring was Karl's mother's engagement ring. Before we leave on the mission, I need you to put it into your office safe. If anything happens to me, you must promise to return it to Karl. It's a family heirloom," said Kitty with a strange look on her face.

"Please, don't talk like that. We are not at war with Germany; hopefully, we never will be." Clive needed to get that negative feeling of doom out of Kitty's head.

"Now, let's get on board the plane, shall we? We need to congratulate your fiancé." Clive led the way, the three of them not sure how they should be feeling at this juncture.

Onboard the plane, Clive and Bill warmly shook Karl's hand, "Congratulations, old man, for making a fine English catch. Many years of happiness to you both," said Clive.

Bill followed by saying, "Hear, hear to that."

Clive regretted saying, "Many years of happiness," and Kitty was in her seat, looking up at him with tears building in her dark brown eyes.

The plane took off, and those on board tried to get some sleep, read a book, or stared out the window, watching the clouds drift past.

From the plane, they boarded the bus back to the base, no one making any small talk. The bus passed through the guarded main gate and pulled up to the main building.

One by one, they got off the bus, collecting their luggage from the compartment at the back. Kitty stood waiting for Karl to return to the front of the bus. "Karl, my dearest man, I want to find a corner to curl up and cry. It's been one of the hardest days I've ever had."

"I'm not blind, Kitty; I will not pressure you to tell me what is going on between you three. All the way back, you did not take your eyes off that binder. The tension in your eyes speaks for itself. How long do we have before you leave to go God knows where? I'm guessing it's either Germany or France. Please, no need to answer that. I respect the code of silence and secrecy we

all adhere to in the BIS. Feel like having a drink together up at
the lounge?" Karl felt Kitty needed to regain her self-confidence,
and he would make sure she did.

Karl unpacked his suitcase, then placed it under his bed.

*I'm going to stop by the dining hall to say hello to everyone before I
head down to the lounge.* He opened the door to see so many
familiar faces. "Karl, you devil, what's this we hear that you have
placed a ring on that beautiful lady Kitty's finger?" said a jovial
Helmut.

In harmony, they all cheerfully yelled out their approval.

After shaking everyone's hand, Karl left the hall and headed to
the officer's lounge. As he opened the door, he was dumbstruck
by a cheering round of congratulations by everyone there, but
where was Kitty?

From behind the wall of well-wishers came a familiar voice,
calling out in an authoritative tone, "Ladies, hands off him. He's
all mine, and this ring is all the proof I need." It was, of course,
Kitty, drink in hand, and being her cocky old self.

Thank God, thought Karl as he made his way to her, shaking
hands as he went. Kitty rose from her chair, moved a few ladies
aside, wrapped her arms around Karl's neck, and planted a juicy
kiss squarely on his lips. "There, that should seal the deal. What
do ya think, girls?" Kitty was showing signs she had one too
many.

"How many of whatever you're drinking have you had?" asked
Karl.

"Not anywhere near enough," came Kitty's reply.

Clive took the initiative by standing up on a chair to make a
toast to the newly engaged couple. With hands in the air, he
cheerfully announced in a boisterous, happy voice, "If I can have
your attention for just a few minutes?"

Nobody was paying any attention.

"Shut up, and that's an order! I have a wonderful announcement to make. In these uncertain times, we all need something to

cheer up our spirits. Thanks to these two, we all can celebrate tonight with the unofficial announcement of their engagement. Even our bloody BIS regulation book can't stop this one from happening.

"Over the Christmas holiday, they made a commitment to each other, one that will surely stand the test of time. As your commanding officer, Kitty and Karl, I am so proud of you both. Please raise your glass in congratulating them, and by the way, the next round's on me.

"Oh, before I fall off this chair, ladies, get a good look at that ring Kitty is wearing!"

As Clive climbed down, he whispered into Bill's ear, "That should clear this black cloud hanging over this bunch. What do you think?"

Clive, with Bill in tow, elbowed their way to the happy couple. "Kitty, I know we agreed to keep this quiet for a while, but honestly, with the bleak news we are getting out of Europe...well, let's say we all needed something to celebrate, and you two are making that happen. Don't concern yourselves about the damn paperwork. I'll take care of that. Now, go have fun, will you? Kitty, I'll see you in the morning, bright and chipper."

They moved to the bar for another whiskey. Karl and Kitty joined in the merrymaking till the bar closed at 2200 hours.

After saying goodnight to all their friends, Karl walked Kitty back to her quarters, "Guess you will go to bed without me tonight, honey," said Karl, holding Kitty close to him until she withdrew.

"That goes with the job, I guess. I would rather have you next to me tonight, though. Good night, darling. I'll see you later tomorrow evening. Will you miss me till then?"

Kitty was somewhat inebriated, and Karl knew it.

"Every hour of the day, Kitty, you give my life meaning. Now, get inside that building before we both freeze to death."

Karl watched until she closed the door behind her.

In his room, Karl lay on his bed, thinking about the newspaper article on Hitler's ultimatum to the Austrian government.

In the event Austria was overrun, Papa and his brothers would be trapped, their safety uncertain. Why did they stay when all seemed lost? Now, it would be too late; crossing the border would be virtually impossible. *Thank God, I got Mama, Frieda, and the baby out when I did.*

His thoughts now drifted to Kitty and the mission that would certainly put her in harm's way. *I need to ask Kitty where her ring will be securely kept while she is on assignment. I will ask her when I see her next.*

Gunther woke Karl at 0530, "Let's get ready, Karl. We are due up at the gun range at 0730 hours for further instruction on German weaponry. See you for breakfast in an hour. Glad you're back I have missed that cocky humor of yours."

Karl put on his bathrobe, gathered his toilet gear, and headed for the bathroom. Afterward, he got dressed, placed his ID card into a side pocket, then headed down to breakfast.

"Morning, Karl. Did you sleep okay, or are you nursing a hangover?" asked Helmut, speaking for all sitting at the long table.

"No, I'm fine. Good to see all your ugly mugs, even if it's this early in the morning."

The next few days went by quickly; training and more training, followed by classroom instruction on key German sites of interest.

There was extensive language training, mainly for the others in the class, with Karl and Gunther helping in this area.

Whenever they had free time, it was spent sleeping, reading manuals and other textbooks, playing cards, and catching up on even more manuals.

Karl tried to get to the lounge each night so he could be with Kitty. Even though there was no privacy, he could still be with her for a few hours.

"What are we all doing for New Year's? Any ideas?" asked Hazel to the group sitting around the coffee table.

"We are restricted to base, so I guess we will make the best of it right here in the lounge," answered Kitty.

Everyone tried to make New Year's Eve a fun time, with music from the scratchy gramophone, party hats, and a delicious spread prepared by the kitchen staff; even though everyone was restricted to base, they made it a happy New Year's Eve anyway.

Kitty and Karl managed a few brief moments and took advantage of the crowded dance floor to hold each other tightly; they both had a way of reading each other's thoughts.

The following day, a traditional holiday for most workers in England was not the case for those in the BIS; every member of the special assignment teams had deadlines to keep, working against the clock and preparing for the day they would be embedded back into strategic locations throughout Europe.

Gunther and Karl's team had been assigned to an investigation team from the Royal Navy. Their task was to gather as much data as they could on the new warships being built for the revived Kriegsmarine. The primary focus would be on Capital Ships and the expansion of the menacing U-boat Force.

England, as an island, relied heavily on its maritime fleet to supply raw materials, finished war goods, and their lifeline of food supplies. Should German warships be successful in interrupting and destroying this vital supply line, England would be starved into submission. The situation was that grave. For the next three months, they worked and trained together, preparing for the day they would return to a very different Europe.

"So, where do we start?" asked Karl to Gunther.

"Let's look at what has happened so far and what we believe will follow before we return. It is imperative we have up-to-date information on what to expect. The three operating teams will have specific duties in Germany. Our responsibility, Karl, will be to ascertain the effectiveness of their shipbuilding capabilities by posing as engineering consultants. I will have to rely on you for direction, assuming we can get close enough to see their progress. By the way, we will not have any navy personnel with us, just found that out this morning.

"The Admiralty in London is extremely concerned that we obtain information about their latest maritime technology. Helmut, you will act as our radio operator. You have the most knowledge with radios. You will receive additional training starting tomorrow morning on the equipment we will be taking. As for you, Sergio, you will be our photographer."

Sergio, hearing this, asked, "Gunther, if I'm to be the photographer, my question is, what is the equipment I will using, and who will be instructing me on using it?"

"Good question," replied Gunther.

"An RAF photographer is scheduled to arrive here in about four days with all the German camera equipment you will be using. He will instruct you and knows how to use the equipment you will be taking. By the way, you were chosen for this role because you love photography so much," concluded Gunther.

"How will we get into Germany?" asked Helmut, praying it would not be by parachute.

"Another good question," answered Gunther. "Right now, we are not totally sure. The last update I received indicated it would probably be by submarine. We have agents who will meet us at the rendezvous point off the German coast."

Karl, Sergio, and Helmut sat quietly, not wanting to interrupt Gunther; however, they all had so many questions to ask once Gunther was finished.

Gunther continued, "Once we meet up with our agent, we will travel overland to our first objective, the port city of Keil. Our first guide will get us into the general vicinity of the docks. From there, we will be on our own till we meet up with our next contact. A fellow officer in the German Army will rendezvous with us, posing as our military liaison while in the shipyard.

"Captain Herbert Werner was in my command until I defected to England. Like so many of us, he wanted nothing to do with the Nazi Party. He volunteered to remain behind to keep us updated on the latest military activities. Kurt has continuously put his life in jeopardy ever since; when we return to England, he will return with us.

"I might as well tell you now that Lieutenant Johnson, Lieutenant Bennet, and Captain Lowes are scheduled to deploy within the next two weeks. Their group is to gather information on how the German population is reacting to Hitler's military ambitions; they will stay in country for about six months, traveling around Germany until relieved by another team assigned to continue the task.

"In conjunction, they will lay the groundwork for establishing an underground resistance movement with the intention of overthrowing Hitler and his band of thugs. Are there any questions?" Gunther concluded, looking for a reaction from his team members.

"This all sounds very risky. How do they know who to trust? Someone could report them to the Gestapo. The Germans are famous for their undercover movements, are they not?" asked Karl, openly showing concern for Kitty.

Gunther realized he needed to share the latest sobering news.

"In early February, we learned about the grave situation in Austria. Hitler rejected all pleas by Austrian Chancellor Schuschnigg to remain neutral, and self-governing was out of the question. By mid-February, Hitler's constant demands and violent outrages were badgering the chancellor to convince President Wilhelm Miklas to accept the German agreement that called for the release of all Nazi sympathizers held in Austrian prisons. He wanted to lift the ban against the Austrian Nazi Party and appoint staunch Nazi supporter Dr. Arthur Seyss-Inquart as minister of war as well as minister of finance." Gunther looked at Karl as he updated the group on this painful news.

Listening to Gunther, Karl thought back to the time when he had had lunch with his old school friend Rudi Mueller, a high-ranking cabinet member in the Austrian government who encouraged him to run.

"Karl, take my advice; get out of Wien. There will be no stopping Hitler. The German Army will not be met by any resistance at the border. Have you not noticed all the Nazi flags on the sides of trucks and billboards, in restaurant windows, and the ever-growing gangs of thugs walking around waving their Swastika banners? We are beyond any hope or rescue. Soon, we will become a Nazi puppet state." Rudi Mueller was so right!

After the long, tiring day, Gunther adjourned the meeting, turning their attention to a well-deserved pint at the bar.

Walking through the door, they joined the other groups that had the same idea. Kitty spotted Karl right away, excused herself from her team members, and walked straight over. "Well, sailor, how did your day turn out?" Kitty could see the stress on his face.

She knew by that look, he had been given the time frame for her mission. "Darling, I can tell by that look on your face that you have been told of my team's deployment. It's not like we didn't know it was coming. Both of us are in dangerous careers. We can only hope we come through it in one piece and together. Now, let's enjoy whatever time we can steal till next week, shall we?" Kitty reached out for his hand, then said, "Wait right here. Let me find Clive and get his staff car keys for later. Would you like that as a nightcap?"

At the bar, they joined the merrymaking taking place. It was as if everyone was looking for an escape, even if it was just for a few hours. Clive willingly gave Kitty the car keys, "Go, have some time together; in fact, you can use that damn passion wagon any time till you depart." Clive felt sickened looking at this couple, knowing they may never see their new engagement turn into a lifelong marriage.

Karl walked hand-in-hand with Kitty to the big Humber, "I'm

starting to like this beast," he said with a smile. "Are we going to the same place as before?"

"Yes, we are. Would you prefer some other place?" Kitty tried to get him to laugh.

"No, that's fine by me," smiled Karl.

"Do you know how to drive, Karl?"

"Of course. I drove across Europe not that long ago. Does this mean you would like me to drive? I'm going to need directions on how to get there, though."

Kitty drove the car through the gatehouse, then proceeded to the main road, stopping at the first layby, "Alright, sailor, remember, we drive on the left in England. Now, slide over here."

Karl adjusted the seat while Kitty walked around to the passenger side. Karl put the car into gear. It felt strange driving on the left and changing gears with the left hand instead of the right.

Kitty sat quietly for a few minutes, then said in a mischievous tone, "Karl, keep your eyes on the road and hands on the wheel. I'll tell you when to turn down onto the farm lane."

Karl knew why Kitty wanted him to drive. His face told Kitty what she wanted to see. There would be no stopping her now. Kitty slid over the bench seat next to Karl, kissing his neck, then his left cheek, while her hand slowly moved down the front of his trousers. This touch gave Karl a sensation that immediately produced an erection.

"Kitty, what are you doing?" he said as Kitty pulled out an erect penis.

"Wow, will you look at this? That's some mast you have there, sailor. Think I'll see what I can do with this. I said, keep your hands on the wheel." Kitty was enjoying this payback from a certain Saturday last year.

Karl felt her mouth slide down his member and made a sigh of approval and pleasure, crying out, "Kitty, you are not being fair, but God, you feel so good." With that, Karl steered the car over to the side of the lane, pulling the handbrake up before shutting off the engine.

He turned to Kitty. Lifting her head toward his, he softly kissed her warm, wet lips. The black clouds of fear came flooding to the forefront in his mind, stopping his advancement on Kitty.

"Darling, what is wrong? Did I do something wrong? You are becoming so tense." Kitty had a worried look. This was not like Karl at all.

"It's not you, Kitty; it's me. In a few weeks, you will go into harm's way. I keep getting these dark visions during the nighttime hours that one of us will not be coming back. Why do we have to play such a dangerous part in this storm that keeps building? I have been running for so long that it is consuming my sense of reason." Karl was acting without the self-assurance he usually had.

Kitty, hearing this, needed to console Karl by saying, "I know how you are feeling. Like you, I get scared about our future together. What we have is so special. I would rather have this short time with you here and now than spend a lifetime trying to find you. Karl, stop this doom and gloom right now. Where is that dashing, cocky, sarcastic Austrian sailor I fell madly in love with? We both know the dangers of being in the intelligence service. We have a big job to do. Furthermore, we both know there is a strong possibility that one or both of us will not make it back alive.

"Each hour we are alone together is being stolen by the negative way you are acting right now, so snap out of it. Karl, please, for me, I beg you." Karl was holding her tightly as she poured her heart out.

"This is not the most appropriate time to mention this, while we are still talking under this dark cloud, but if something does happen to me, please make sure Mama gets my ring back and tell her how much I care for her. Karl, will you do that for me? Clive

PETER A. MOSCOVITA

has a letter I wrote the other night to her. It should be returned with the ring, okay?" asked Kitty.

Karl, listening, had turned away, looking out the car's side window into the night sky, not wanting her to see the tears rolling down his cheeks. Kitty knew she had to snap him out of this doom and gloom he had sunk into. "Oh, sailor, it looks like your mast has gone limp. Let me give it a real good reason to rise again." Kitty unbuttoned her blouse, then removed it. Next, she slid her skirt up high and removed her underwear, settling over Karl's lap, "I'm ready. Are you?"

Karl loved the way Kitty nearly always took charge. Right now, the storm was passing, and his sole intent was to enjoy this beauty straddling his lap. "You will pay for this, sweetheart. Teasing me like this has a price," whispered Karl into Kitty's ear. With that, he slid into Kitty, forgetting all else.

The two of them climaxed together, then lay back for a well-deserved cigarette. This evening was the medicine Karl and Kitty so desperately needed.

At midnight on March 11, Austrian President Miklas realized any chance for saving Austria was futile, and his own position was hopeless. As a broken leader, he turned into Hitler's puppet, making Dr. Seyss the new chancellor, replacing Chancellor Schuschnigg.

On Saturday, March 12, German soldiers in tanks and armored vehicles roared across the German-Austrian border on schedule. They met no resistance and, in places, were met like heroes. Many of Austria's seven-million ethnic Germans had their day, attaching themselves to the rising dynamic star, a son of Austria, and now the supreme leader of all Germans as well… most of them anyway.

Adolf Hitler had returned to his homeland, not as a broken artist or a nobody infantry corporal, but as the supreme leader of Germany, the Fuhrer.

When England and France received news of the invasion,

238

they did nothing, reacting just as they did when Hitler had occupied the Rhineland a few years earlier.

Clive read the telex twice to make sure he was reading it correctly, "Gwen, could you find Lieutenant Vita for me right away? Then, gather all the Europeans in the camp. Have them all report to the mess hall. Make sure they all attend; once that is done, have a general announcement made over the PA speaker for all officers on or off duty to meet me here and on the double."

Karl knocked on Clive's office door. "You wanted to see me, sir," said Karl, wondering what Clive needed.

"Please, sit down. I have just received news concerning the escalating tension in your home country of Austria. There is no easy way to tell you this. Austria has accepted capitulation instead of bloodshed in trying to resist Hitler's massive military force. Please, accept my sympathy for the pain I know this news is causing you. Would you like some time alone to call your mother in Baldock? I will leave you here while I address the camp's company. Please, excuse me." Clive could feel the sorrow coming from Karl.

One by one, all the English officers gathered in the main office area, each one wondering what had happened to call for a drastic gathering such as this. "Must be that mad bugger Hitler again. What has he been up to this time?" said one of the officers out loud.

"Silence," came a stinging command from Clive. Once everyone was accounted for, Clive stood up on the stage, his small staff behind him.

"I would like to read to you all a telex I received from the chief of staff in London. It reads: 'Earlier this morning, March 12, 1938, units of the German tank command along with armored personnel carriers crossed over the German border into Austria. There was no resistance by the Austrian military. President Miklas has been forced to resign. Before doing so, he appointed Hitler's puppet Dr. Seyss as the new chancellor. Gentlemen,

239

Austria no longer exists. It has become a German province." Clive stopped momentarily to allow everyone to process this information.

"The telex went on to say that former Chancellor Dr. Kurt Von Schuschnigg had been arrested by the Gestapo. His whereabouts are uncertain. With this latest news, we must now concern ourselves with the fate of Czechoslovakia and Sudetenland, with its three-million-plus ethnic Germans."

Kitty stood in rank with the other officers in total shock. *Oh, my God. I must find Karl. If he is not here, where is he?*

Clive spotted Kitty looking around her, "Lieutenant Johnson, may I speak with you? Karl is in my office; I briefed him first as I did not want him standing in line and hearing this dreadful news for the first time. Go to him, Kitty. He is on the phone with his mother. He will need you. Now, go." Clive proceeded to the company of Austrians and Germans waiting in the mess mall where he would repeat the announcement he had just made to the English officers.

Kitty opened the office door to see Karl sitting with his head in his hands.

"Darling, are you alright? We all got the news a few minutes ago. Did you get through to Mama and Freida?"

"Yes, I spoke to Freida. I thought it would be better for her to break this news to Mama than me on the phone. I'm okay, Kitty. It's not that we didn't expect it to happen. Papa and my brothers will be my biggest concern now that those Nazi swine have overrun Austria. I could do with a stiff whiskey about now. Let's get out of here and head over to the lounge. What do you say?"

Karl needed to be around others sharing the same grief.

"Will you be okay around everyone over there, Karl?" asked Kitty.

She knew if someone made a stupid remark, they would land on the floor. "I'm alright. I promise not to lose my temper," Karl said, assuring Kitty his temper was in check.

As they entered the lounge, a large group had, as always, formed around the bar. Seeing Karl and Kitty, they gave them space. Several of Karl's team came over carefully and politely extended their regrets for the Austrian people. *When you least expect it, people can be so thoughtful*, thought Kitty.

"Excuse me, gentlemen. May I push in next to my friend, Karl?" Gunther put his right arm around Karl's broad shoulders.

"How are you doing, friend? We will not allow this bullying to go on unchecked. It may take a while, but we will cage that bastard, Hitler."

The evening wound down. Karl walked Kitty to her quarters. At the door, Kitty said, "We only have a few days left, and darling, I may not get any quality time to be alone with you, so let's say good night and goodbye here and now. It will be for the best to do it like this. It will become too chaotic starting tomorrow. You know I'm right, don't you?" Kitty placed her hand on his cheek. Her heart was breaking, knowing she would not be there in the morning to see him.

"Yes, Kitty, I expected this and have reconciled myself to it happening. Know this, Kitty, I love you more with each passing day. Please, I beg you, do not do anything that will put you in harm's way. You have a future husband waiting for you back here. Who knows, darling? We may meet up over there. That would be something to experience." Karl was trying to lighten the mood.

"Karl, please, please walk away. I'm having a hard time holding back the tears." Karl slowly let her arm drop to her side, gently kissed her, then turned away without looking back. "I love you, sailor," came a faint whimper from Kitty as she opened the door and entered the building.

Karl would never see her again.

23

Preparing to Return to Europe

Karl tossed and turned all night long; sleep would not happen this night. He kept thinking: *Karl, you must take hold of yourself. There are people out there who are relying on you to pull your weight. Today, I will refocus on my role in Team F. Getting my confidence back may take a little more effort, though.*

After breakfast, Karl met up with Gunther in the training room, "How are you holding up, Karl? That was a shock yesterday. My blood is still boiling, thinking about that madman. This morning, I had to get up early to help Team A load their equipment before boarding the bus that will take them to the airdrome. Kitty asked me to give you this letter once she had departed." Gunther took the letter from a folder on the table, handing it over to Karl as he spoke.

"Departed? What do you mean departed? She made no mention of leaving in the morning when I said goodbye to her last night." Karl was in a state of shock at hearing this from Gunther.

Karl had been given a hammer punch by this news. "Kitty

thought it would be easier on you if there were no lingering, waiting for her departure day."

Gunther placed a hand on his friend's shoulder, trying to comfort him as best he could. Karl held back the pain he was wrestling with and said, "I hope she stays safe. Europe is far from safe right now."

In his room, Karl held the letter in his trembling hand. Lifting it close to his nose, he could still get a whiff of her perfume. Sitting on the corner of his bed, he opened the letter to find a dried-out leaf between the folds of the page. The letter read:

My dearest Karl,

As you read this letter, I am already far away from you. I can only guess how angry and hurt you must feel.

Please, forgive me, darling. The thought of all those red-eyed tears and anxious moments while waiting for my team's departure day was too painful for me to bear, so I found it easier to let you believe there were still a few days left.

If you are wondering about that dried leaf, think back to a riverbank on a sunny Saturday—on that day, you made this lady the happiest girl in the world.

That leaf you are holding has been my reminder that each day is precious, and like that leaf, lives can crumble so quickly. I pray one day we will have a lifetime to enjoy a world where all people can learn to live together in peace and harmony.

I so look forward to that time away from this military madness.

When your time comes to be deployed, remember to stay safe and come home to this lady who loves you so very much.

Our day will come, Karl. This I must believe to do this job.

With all my love,

Kitty xxx

PS: I am writing this letter at 2300 hours. Can't sleep with all that is happening.

Karl read the letter many times over, then folded it, placing it in his locked suitcase, safely stored away till another time when that leaf could be shared by two.

"Morning, chaps, am I late?" Karl tried hard to be confident.

"No, Karl, you're not. We're organizing the latest intelligence picture of Kiel that arrived earlier this morning by courier." Gunther was sorting a big pile of aerial photographs taken by an RAF reconnaissance aircraft yesterday. "Sit next to me. Here, look through this magnifying loupe and tell us what you make of that big ship in the building ways."

Gunther and Helmut could not tell what this big vessel was.

Karl took the loupe and studied many of the pictures, then, like the confident sailor he was, said, "You're looking at one of two aircraft carriers that were laid down back in 1936. I remember passing that yard in the *Tristian* when we docked in the Keil harbor. Since I saw the big keel back in August of 1936, I can see it has progressed significantly since that time.

"I would venture to say it's almost complete, and from the aerial picture, this is going to be a big aircraft carrier. If this is Kiel, it can only be the new *Graf Zeppelin*, the first of four to be ordered. As far as I know, only two have made it to the builder's yard.

"Get me real close to it, and I'm sure I will be able to assess its construction more effectively. When do we leave?" Karl had once again found his focus for the job he was chosen to undertake.

Day after day, Team F would examine the constant stream of new pictures from all over Germany. Their reports started to tell of a Germany that was breaking the international treaty established in 1919, better known as the Versailles Treaty imposed on Germany after the First World War that limited all countries involved to standards that governed the size of any newly built ship. This treaty also governed how many guns and the calibers it could have. That treaty also included the size of the army and its air corps, all of which Germany has violated without concern.

On August 14, Team F moved to the South of England to their new operating quarters in Slough, Berkshire, not too far from the castle in Great Windsor. In preparation for the conflict that was surely coming, most of the BIS was consolidated closer to London and the headquarters of the Intelligence Service.

Daily briefings painted an even bleaker picture of brutality to the Jewish community living throughout the occupied European countries. In Germany alone, more than 300,000 Jewish families had left with nothing more than a suitcase. Their rights had been stripped from them. Brutality was becoming commonplace.

Helpless Jews were set upon by gangs of brown-shirt thugs, who took great delight in beating them without mercy or fear of reprisal from the police. In Austria, these same gangs would smash shops, burn buildings, and wreck cars and trucks, in fact, anything that belonged to Jews was set upon.

"Gunther, how long are we to sit around reading of these atrocities? We must act and act now," Karl said as he became increasingly frustrated.

"We are, Karl. We are leaving in early September. I just came from a meeting held at HQ yesterday. As we all know, the Germans have been honing their military skills since late in 1936 by aiding the Spanish Revolutionary Army under the leadership of General Francisco Franco, with a military assistance program known as the Condor Legion.

"Hitler trained his air force and army personnel in the perfect training arena, the Spanish Civil War. Our general staff believes we must up our readiness at a faster pace."

Gunther knew the exact date they would leave but was restricted from telling anyone.

"As I have said before, when the hell are we leaving? Looking at pictures and reading field reports are not helping us with our mission." Karl sensed that Gunther was holding information back from the team.

"What I am permitted to tell you is that your next leave will commence this weekend. You all have a three-day pass, so make the best of it. Is that clear enough?" Gunther eyed Karl as he spoke.

"That's great news. Can I use your telephone, boss, to call my mother?" Karl was grinning at this wonderful news. It also meant they would be leaving for Europe on their return. "Gunther, do you have any news on Team A and Kitty yet?"

"Nothing solid right now other than they crossed over successfully into Germany several weeks back. From the sketchy information passed down, they are in a safe house on the outskirts of Hamburg. Sorry I can't give you more at this time." Gunther knew much more but could not run the risk of telling him, especially before their own mission.

The train slowed to a stop in Baldock Station. Freida was standing on the platform, holding young Franchot's hand. "Freida, so good to see you. It's been too long." Karl hugged his sister and nephew before heading down that familiar tunnel.

"The news coming out of Austria is bad. A few days ago, Ronny managed to get an update on what is happening in Wien. The Germans are nationalizing all the factories, ours included," said Freida, trying not to alarm Karl too much with this news.

"Any news about Papa and the boys? Are they still in Wien, or did they flee like so many others are doing?"

"Papa stayed but made the boys leave for Italy, and at this point, they are in Trieste with Mino and Fritz. Papa will be joining them any day now, once he has finished securing what valuables are still left. Our tenant farmer near Seefeld is going to bury them. Papa has arranged for Otto and his family to remain on the farm until such time as we can return home, if ever. Otto is so trustworthy, and, as you know, has worked for Papa for over twenty-five years. He will keep our things well hidden," said Freida with a concerned look on her face.

"Italy may be alright at this point, but that madman, Bruno

246

Mussolini thinks he's another Hitler, not the schoolteacher he once was. He is heading down the same road his pal Hitler is taking. Papa and our brothers should be planning their next move right now instead of later, and that move should be out of mainland Europe."

Karl paid the taxi driver and turned to address Mama's waiting arms, "Karl, my heart is so much lighter seeing you. Give your mother a big hug."

Inside the bungalow, the aroma of familiar food filled Karl's nostrils. "Mama, how I have missed your cooking. Can I see what's for dinner?" Karl laughed for the first time in weeks.

Ronny arrived home a little after six, so glad to see Karl sitting in the living room, "Karl, we are so happy you are home. Would have preferred to see Kitty, though." A big grin ran across his face.

Ronny waited till Freida left the living room to help Mama in the kitchen before continuing. "I won't ask you what's going on with the BIS, nor will I question why Kitty is not with you. Just know, we are gravely concerned for both of you. The BIS is a dangerous place to be right now. At our base, we are ramping up at an alarming pace. New aircraft are arriving daily. I can only imagine what your base is like right now.

"You chaps must be busy with all those reconnaissance pictures our boys are bringing back from the flights over Germany. No need to answer that, Karl. I understand the sensitivity; let's change the subject.

"How do you like your new base in Slough? Must be so nice being back close to a big town instead of the miles of nothing but rolling, wet hills." Ronny was now trying to get Karl to focus on anything not connected with the BIS.

"Ronny, it's so different, truly more like a functional operational base instead of that training facility in Scotland. It's so much quicker to get to Baldock now. Only took me a couple of hours instead of a whole day." Karl also was trying to guide the

conversion away from his job and the fact that Kitty was not busy
at the base but on a mission in hostile Germany.

Ronny and Karl spent more time together on this trip. He
even took Karl to the officer's club in Duxford. Karl thoroughly
enjoyed being around these flyboys; he even met a few flyers who
left Europe to become pilots in the RAF.

The time flew by, and once again, it was time to head for
Baldock Station. Ronny was on duty, so they had made their
farewells the evening before. Karl elected to walk the two miles
to the train station instead of taking a taxi.

The morning was sunny, dry, and quite warm. Baldock was
such a quaint farming community. He could see why the family
enjoyed it so. Passing by the George & Dragon, he stopped
momentarily to face the big double doors of the entrance. In his
mind, he could see Kitty coming through the door with that
contagious smile of hers. How he missed her. Turning back onto
Whitehorse Street, he walked on to the station passing the White
Horse and Engine pubs, both of which he and Kitty had enjoy
time in. Before he knew it, he was on the platform, waiting for
the train to King's Cross station in London, changing trains for
the short return ride to Slough.

24

Returning to Germany

On returning to the base, Karl was immediately called for by Gunther. "We have brought our deployment date up to tomorrow night. Take the time today to wrap up loose ends, then report back here for a mission briefing with Major Knight and Colonel Jacks. Remember him?"

"Will do, Gunther. Need to ask Clive a favor anyway." On the train earlier in the day, he had written four letters addressed to Mama.

None had dates on them. He would ask Clive to post one each month to Mama. This way, she would not worry so much or be concerned that he could be somewhere in Europe.

In his room, he packed the old brown German suitcase the BIS had supplied, took from the wardrobe the civilian grey suit and white shirt with a solid black tie, and hung them on the wardrobe door.

He took the fedora trilby hat that had a wide black band around it and placed it on the burrow along with a black belt and grey socks.

All the items in the case were from Germany, just in case he was searched while in Germany. In the briefing room, the team gathered. An army major entered, carrying an overstuffed brief-case. They all came to attention before being instructed to be seated.

"Gentlemen, at 0430 hours tomorrow morning, you will meet me in this room. I will now be issuing you with your German passports, travel cards, and security papers, along with currency in German marks. Please, take the time to review them thoroughly. We must be sure of their authenticity. Take the time also to make sure your cover name is correct and the same on each document. Any problems, see me immediately." The major then sat back down. Karl sat with Gunther, reviewing their documents. When all looked in order, he placed the package into his uniform side pocket, stood, and walked to Clive, who was sitting with the major.

"Excuse me, sir. May I have a moment of your time?" asked Karl.

"Of course. What is it you need to speak to me about? Let's go over to that empty corner, shall we?" Clive took Karl by the arm.

"Clive, would you do me a big favor by posting one of these letters each month to my mother? It will be a great comfort to her if she gets one regularly," said Karl.

"Be glad to. By the way, you know I have Kitty's engagement ring in my safe, don't you?" said Clive, waiting for the next question he fully expected from Karl.

"I know I should not be asking this, and I know you are bound to secrecy, but do you have anything you could share with me about how Kitty is doing?" Karl did not expect an honest answer but needed to ask anyway.

"Clive, you have been a wonderful friend to me from that first day in Dover. I need to thank you for all you have done for Kitty and me. One other favor I need to ask…should I not make it back, please give this last letter to Kitty for me."

Karl wanted to say so much more but knew Clive needed to return to the others in the room.

"Only if you allow me to be your best man at the wedding." Clive looked at his friend's strained face. "Now, as far as we have been told, Kitty, Hazel, and Bill are moving toward Munich. We expect another communication tomorrow. Unfortunately, you will have already left. I will add a line in the communication to Gunther. If the news is okay, that line will be, 'Your aunt is enjoying the weather.'

"Don't worry. I'll tell Gunther to expect it in the message," smiled Clive, then he walked back to the group. "Better get an early night, you lot. Rise and shine at 0330 hours sharp."

Gunther shot out of bed and shook Karl by the shoulder, "Let's get ready, Karl. Our holiday boat will be waiting for us."

"Holiday boat, what bloody boat are you talking about?" Karl was still half asleep, and his brain was not working that well this early in the morning.

"The damn submarine, you idiot," replied Gunther.

After breakfast, Team F collected their gear from their rooms. Items to be placed into storage were placed on their beds, ready to be collected after they departed. From there, they assembled outside, still a little chilly in the predawn darkness.

Clive and the base command assembled in front of the bus that would take them to the submarine waiting for them in Portsmouth.

"Gentlemen, all the hard work you have been training for, month after month, is about to pay off as well as keep you safe. This mission you are about to undertake is vitally important to ascertain the real strength of Germany's Navy and what techno-logical advantages we can expect from them.

"Our navy must be ready to take on this formidable enemy, maybe sooner rather than later. Prime Minister Neville Cham-berlain is once again back in Germany, trying to obtain a resolu-tion to commit a peaceful method to avoid military

251

confrontation. Here in the BIS, we believe it is purely a stall tactic until the Germans are fully prepared to commit their military might against Europe.

"Gentlemen, on behalf of this command, we wish you all Godspeed and safe return. God Save The King," concluded Clive, signaling the group to stand at rest after being at attention.

With that, Team F started to board the bus, shaking hands with their commanding officers as they boarded.

Karl stopped in front of Clive, shook his hand, came to attention, and saluted. "We will not let you down, sir," said Karl, then he entered the bus, sitting across from Gunther. He put his jacket against the window, trying to catch up on lost sleep.

It took most of the morning for the bus to reach the naval base in Portsmouth. Gunther reached over to wake Karl from a sound sleep. "Time for you to return to the sea, sailor. Let's go."

Karl could not believe he had slept all the way down. He had been totally exhausted by all the trauma he had faced recently.

"I'm ready," he said as he sat up straight. "Let's get this show on the road. We've been in England long enough."

The rest of the team simply looked at each other, surprised. Where had this come from?

"You heard the man, let's get this show on the road," barked Gunther.

HMS *Thorn*, a newer Royal Navy T-type submarine, lay alongside the dock. The steep gangway led to the forward part of the hull ahead of the conning tower.

"Karl, why don't you go first? You're the sailor among this group," said Gunther.

"Will do, Gunther, or should I start calling you by your mission name, Kurt?"

"Good idea. Let's all start doing that right now," replied Gunther, loud enough for all to hear.

"Permission to come on board," said Karl, saluting the officer of the deck as he stepped down onto the teak deck that covered the black painted steel casing of the hull.

"Granted, sir. Please proceed aft to the seaman waiting by the hatch. He will assist you down into the control room." Karl and the other members of Team F assembled in the tight quarters of the control room; with all the controls and red-painted valve handles, there was little room to stand upright.

"Greetings, gentlemen, and welcome aboard HMS *Thorn*. My name is Captain Timothy Aldridge. My crew and I are to deliver you to a location off the German coast near Leybuchet. A German fishing trawler will rendezvous with us two days from now a little after midnight. After transferring you and your gear, it will dock after sunrise at its fishing pier in Leybuchet.

"The captain of that trawler will give you further instructions once you are onboard the trawler. To blend in and not draw attention on and around the docks, we have been instructed to have you change into these old working clothes just before we meet up with the trawler. In the meantime, we will try to make you as comfortable as possible. Submarines are not the best when it comes to carrying passengers, so if you can remain in the designated areas assigned to you, it will make our job a little easier. We will cast off at sundown and, once clear of the break-water, will travel on the surface, then dive before dawn, so we can remain undetected. Thank you for your attention."

Captain Aldridge turned and exited the tight quarters, followed by his duty officer.

"Excuse me, Captain. May I have your permission to be on the bridge when you shove off? I'm a former seaman who has not been near salt in quite some time," asked Karl, whose mission name had been changed to Fredrick.

"So, you're the maritime fellow on board. I was wondering which one of you it was," replied the captain. "Of course, you can. It will be my pleasure to have you join me on the conning tower.

It gets a little tight up there, not like what you're used to, I'm sure. All stations report your status prior to getting underway. Engine room, report status before starting main engines."

Karl felt the steel plates of the conning tower vibrate under his shoes. After about fifteen minutes, the skipper called out to the deck crew, "Single up all dock lines."

Once that was done, the next command was, "Let go forward spring lines, let go main bowlines, let go main stern line, and let go stern spring line." The HMS *Thorn* was now free of the lines holding her to the dock.

"Engine room, both slow in reverse." The skipper was hanging over the edge as the *Thorn* moved slowly away from the dock, followed by two naval tugs. Once clear of the pier, the skipper called down the voice tube, "Engine room, all stop."

The skipper would now let the tugs turn the boat around, ready to get underway. The tug positioned at the bow moved up and slowly pushed against the submarine. Karl, watching the maneuvering, was thinking back to another time and another vessel, the *Tristian*.

The *Thorn* was turning to starboard, the tug at the bow pushing to starboard, and the one on the opposite side pushing the stern to port.

The skipper called down the voice tube, instructing the radio operator to signal the tugs to cease maneuvering. Once they pulled back, the next command was to the engine room, "All ahead one-third. Helmsman, make your heading 090 degrees."

The two tugs now took up positions on either side of the sub. Together, they passed through the breakwater and out into the English Channel. Karl felt the thrill of the deck rolling gently beneath his feet, his nostrils filling with that crisp salt air. How he had missed this. The skipper, after about half an hour, called the radio room to dispatch the tugs. "Tugs A6 and A10, the *Thorn* is clear. Thank you for your assistance."

Next, the skipper called down the voice tube to the engine room, "All ahead full, if you please."

The *Thorn* surged ahead, working up to seventeen knots, the bow wave now throwing spray back to the conning tower.

"You'll have to go below now as we are about to do a mandatory test dive. We will be under for about two hours," the skipper explained, pointing to the open hatch.

"Will do, and thank you for allowing me to join you."

"Glad we could accommodate. I could see by the look on your face that you miss your time on the sea."

Karl felt the deck start to tilt downward, and the lack of the hammering noise that came from the diesel engines was replaced by a continuous humming sound from the two electric motors.

"All compartments report," came the voice of the first officer over the PA system.

Down below, the tight confines of the control room made it difficult to move through the sub to the even tighter compartment assigned to Team F.

"Listen up," said Gunther as he lay the maps and directives for the mission on the small table. "Once we rendezvous with our trawler, we will quickly go below out of sight from what would be prying eyes until we reach the docks in *Leybuchet*. We will remain out of sight below decks, rotating two at a time to the deck in two-hour watches. This way, we will take on the appearance of being crew members.

"Our civilian clothes, equipment, and hand luggage will be wrapped in waterproof canvas bags, then placed in the bottom of the fish boxes, covered by a false bottom. Fish will then be placed on top, concealing the contents. After docking, the two assigned to the deck crew will take one box each of the fish catch into the warehouse located next to the dock.

"Once inside, you will quickly remove our things from those boxes, changing back into your civilian clothes. You will then give the two men waiting for you inside the warehouse those fishy work clothes. They will dress in those same clothes and return to the trawler, carrying the empty boxes. We will repeat this till we are all in the warehouse with our gear. Later in the day, we will squeeze into a hidden compartment in the front of the fish delivery van.

"The trip to the shop should take approximately twenty-five minutes. Once inside their garage, we will wait for our guide and vehicle to arrive. If all goes well, we will not be exposed to any watching eyes, other than during the transfer from the submarine. Are we all clear on this transfer procedure? Now, get some rest as best you can. Tomorrow will be taxing on all of us," said Gunther, looking at each one of them as he spoke.

The bunks were short as well as narrow. *How could anyone sleep in these cramped quarters for months at a time*, thought Karl as he swung his legs into the bunk.

Shortly thereafter, he heard the PA announcement, "Prepare to surface. Bridge crew, man your stations." Karl felt the deck tilt upward then level off before the hammering sound of the diesel engines returned to life.

At 0500 hours, the PA once again informed the crew that they would remain submerged till nightfall.

The skipper opened the curtain, stuck his head in, and in a jovial voice, asked, "Is everything okay with you chaps? Sorry we couldn't give you better accommodations. We will travel at five knots during the daylight hours, then surface after sundown. Our instructions are to rendezvous with the trawler around 0400 hours.

"The transfer will take place under cover of darkness, so please get some sleep. We will wake you at 0230 hours. Our cook will get you some breakfast and hot tea. Eat well as it may be the last you have for a while."

"Karl, wake up, it's almost time," whispered Helmut. Karl

quickly dressed in the smelly work clothes, made sure all his things were packed away securely in the waterproof oilskin bags, then proceeded to the small crew galley for breakfast.

"Listen up, chaps. From here on, only speak in German. Do not, I repeat, do not use English. We cannot afford a language slipup. In addition, only use your mission names. Again, a slip could easily blow your cover. To repeat, from now on, Karl's name is Fredrick; Helmut, yours is Ernst; Silvio, yours is Stefan; and mine is now Kurt.

Take a few minutes again to refresh your memories on what your surnames are, the town you came from, your place of birth, and so on. I'm assuming you have memorized all the documentation provided to you a few weeks back. Knowing these details without hesitation could be the difference between life and death. Now, eat up and be ready to move quickly once we surface.

"The mission documentation you still have in your possession will be taken from you in about thirty minutes and will return with this submarine to Portsmouth in a locked, secure BIS pouch. If you need to look at it again, take these few minutes to do so," concluded Kurt.

Each of the team sat quietly, making sure their cover stories were completely memorized, then checked that their passports, travel documents, and German identity cards were secured inside their marine jackets. From the PA came the surfacing commands, "Engine room, stand by to start both diesel engines. Deck crew to the bridge ladder. Number two, blow the main ballast tanks. Helmsman, make your ascent twenty degrees up bubble."

The captain was now ready to put the *Thorn* back on the surface.

Fredrick felt the deck tilt upward, then the sound of the diesel engines hammering back into life. The deck crew moved quickly up the ladder and out onto the deck, carrying a rope ladder. "Signalman, send the Morse Code recognition signal to the trawler."

Off in the distance, less than half a mile away, the dark shape of a fishing boat could be seen waiting quietly. The signal lamp clattered the recognition signal and received an immediate return signal.

Team F stood on the deck, watching the skiff as it approached from the trawler. In a whisper, the duty officer said, "Lower the rope ladder and prepare to grab the bow line from that approaching boat."

Kurt turned to the skipper, now down on the deck to see them off, "Thank you for the hospitality to me and my team. We appreciate all you have done to get us here."

"Good luck and stay safe. We look forward to perhaps picking you up a few months from now," replied the skipper.

Kurt said in a low voice, "Attention, permission to leave the boat." Kurt extended his hand, followed by each member of Team F.

"Permission granted," came the reply from the skipper.

One by one, the team climbed down the rope ladder and into the small boat. Last came their equipment. The sailor at the outboard motor welcomed them in German, then pushed off from HMS *Thorn*.

As they moved closer to the trawler, they heard a hissing sound coming from the submarine as it moved forward, filling the ballast tanks to return to the ocean depths. In a few moments, it was gone.

The skiff bumped against the trawler's scarred side, then the men heard, "Quickly, get on board. We cannot take a chance of being spotted. Go into the pilothouse then down the companionway to the salon."

The captain, a robust older sailor whose name was Rudi, followed them down into the dimly lit salon.

"Gentlemen, welcome to our old girl, the *Kramer Lady*. Our

return trip to Leybuchet will take about four to five hours, so if you were given the procedure, we need to have two of you on deck as soon as you can. The other two can remain here below for a few hours. We will come for you when it's time to change."

Kurt and Fredrick elected to take the last shift on deck, "Okay, off you go," said Kurt to Stefan and Ernst. "See you in two hours. Fredrick, we should get some more shut-eye while we can."

Kurt lay down on one of the bunks. In his mind, he was rolling over the intelligence information he had received while still in Slough.

When do I tell Fredrick about the last transmission BIS had received from Hazel two days before we departed Slough? thought Kurt.

The transmission read: Kitty and Bill taken into custody. Being held at Gestapo headquarters in Hamburg. It's been six days so far, no further news. Our team has moved underground into a safe house about forty kilometers from the city, awaiting revised orders. Will advise if situation changes.

How and when will I tell him? If I tell him while we are on this mission, it could jeopardize the whole operation. If I wait until we return home, assuming we get home, he will never forgive me for not telling him sooner. The teams in the field are now short two operatives; there could be a good possibility that I will be instructed to remain in Germany with the other group. What do I do if that happens? Still thinking about this problem, Kurt slowly drifted off to sleep.

"Kurt, time for our watch on deck," said Fredrick as he helped himself to a cup of coffee. In the wheelhouse, Fredrick sat in a corner behind Captain Rudi.

"How far do we still have to go?" said Kurt as he stuck his head up from down below.

"We should be dockside in about an hour and a half," Rudi answered without taking his eyes off the horizon and compass. "Time to get your stuff together in the fish boxes. We must look like it's business as usual for the *Kramer Lady.*"

The sun was making an appearance on the horizon as they

steamed into the narrow channel then slowed to make a right turn toward the pier. "Stand by your lines," called Rudi as he slowed the trawler to a stop in front of the warehouse.

Once secured, Rudi walked out onto the deck and started giving orders like any other day they came back from a night of fishing.

First off the boat were Ernst and Stefan, carrying their fish boxes on their shoulders. Inside the dimly lit warehouse, they were pulled behind a pile of boxes by the first two regular crew members.

"Quickly get your civilian clothes out of the fish boxes and give us the ones you are wearing now." The two crew members dressed in the smelly work clothes, picked up the empty fish boxes, and headed back to the boat.

Kurt and Fredrick were next, but before they left, they thanked Rudi for the chances he and his crew took in getting them back into Germany. Inside the warehouse, they made the switch with the two remaining crew members hiding behind the stacked boxes.

Over the next forty-five minutes, the fishermen carried the balance of the night's catch into the warehouse, after which they wished Team F good luck, closing the warehouse sliding doors behind them.

Quickly, they gathered their belongings, then hid behind the stored fish boxes. They would remain hidden until the delivery van arrived. About two hours later, the doors slid open, allowing the van to drive in. Two men closed the doors, then approached.

"Welcome back to Germany; we are glad to see you. Wish it could be under happier circumstances," said the older man. "We will leave in about an hour. First, you must climb into the compartment behind the cab. Sorry, it will be cramped but safe. Once we have you secured away, we will start loading the fish boxes, then depart for our shop."

The cramped compartment left little room to stretch their legs; the air was stifling and rank with stale fish odor. The drive was bumpy with many twists and turns, taking approximately forty minutes before the van came to a stop. The sound of sliding doors meant they must have arrived at their destination.

The van lurched one last time as it drove over the garage threshold. The four passengers in the cramped compartment were stiff and aching, and being so cramped made the time pass so slowly.

It seemed like it took hours for the workers to unload the van. With a gush of fresh air and light, the false wall was removed, allowing fresh air to clear the compartment.

"Thank God," said Ernst as he pulled himself out into the interior of the van. He could feel the blood rushing back into his aching legs.

Inside the storage room of the shop, they met up with the owner and brother to Rudi. Rhineholt was a big, balding man with a beer-barrel stomach. When their father died two years earlier, they continued the lucrative fish wholesale business until the National Socialist Party bullied their way into power, controlling most of the German industry and people. When this happened, the old Germany ceased to exist. The brothers would have no part of this movement, preferring instead to support the growing underground movement, helping the English to remove Herr Hitler.

These proud Germans wanted nothing to do with the Nazi Party or the National Socialist Party, which they believed would take the hardworking people of Germany on a course of eventual destruction. Most civilians in Germany were too scared to put up any resistance.

"Welcome, my friends. We are pleased to see you all. May we interest you in hot coffee and a salami sandwich? You must be hungry about now."

While they sat eating their sandwiches, Rhineholt told them about their guide, a man by the name of Bernhard.

"He will come for you after dark," said Rhineholt. "I will then take you all in my van to the nearby train station. From there, you will catch the train to Hamburg, connecting to an express train directly to Keil. Bernhard will remain with you until you arrive in Keil. However, he will remain on the train when you get off. It's better that the guides do not actually meet each other. You can never be certain of who is watching. When you get off the train, you will be met by a German Army officer, Captain Herbert Werner. Kurt, I believe you are familiar with Captain Werner. He was in the army with you. Is that right?" asked Rudi. Kurt did not respond to this question.

"Stay close to Kurt. He is the only one who can identify Captain Werner." With that, Rhineholt left the room.

The team sat, talking quietly among themselves until Rhineholt returned, leading the guide. "Gentlemen, this is your guide, Bernhard. Please, welcome him." They all shook hands, then proceeded to load the van with their luggage.

Rhineholt climbed behind the wheel of the van for the short ride to the train station. In the back of the parking area, he let them out. "God keep you safe; Germany needs your help." Rhineholt got back in the van and left by the rear entrance to the parking area.

"Alright, gentlemen, I have already purchased the tickets for both trains. Keep them handy to show the ticket collector at the entrance to the platform. Please follow me at a distance in twos, so as not to draw attention." On the platform, they waited, spread out as requested by Bernhard.

When the Hamburg train finally arrived, the platform had become crowded, a blessing in disguise. Walking down the platform, Bernhard opened a compartment door, then climbed in, followed by the team at a distance. One by one, they climbed into the compartment, not talking to each other until the doors closed, and the train got underway.

"So far, so good. Might as well get comfortable till we reach Hamburg," said Bernhard. Fredrick sat opposite Kurt by the carriage windows.

"Kurt, why did you not answer Rhineholt when he asked you if you remembered Werner from when you both were together in the German Army?"

"It's a long story that right now I would prefer not to talk about. It's alright, though. We have remained friends, even when I left for England. Herbert elected to remain in the army and in his position as the liaison officer for all outside contractors in the shipbuilding yards of Keil. Having him in this position is what will enable us to pull off this mission. Let's leave it at that, shall we?"

Kurt was showing signs of becoming a little agitated with Fredrick's line of questioning.

The train's whistle announced their arrival into the Hamburg Station as it slowed into the platform.

"Let's follow each other like we did before to the next plat- form and the express to Keil," said Kurt.

The express train was already sitting at the platform. They quickly found an empty compartment and climbed aboard. Fredrick could see Kurt's face had become stressed, "Is this upsetting you, heading back to your hometown?"

Fredrick was becoming concerned that Kurt would become unstable returning home, even though it would be only to change trains.

"I'm okay, Fredrick. Just got a little sad thinking of my family only a few kilometers from this very station we are pulling into." In another ten minutes, Kurt would be in his hometown.

"I keep wondering how they will weather the ugly changes sweeping this country when I will not be around to protect them. Don't worry about me, old friend. Both of us have similar problems; don't we?" Kurt reassured Fredrick that he would remain strong.

The sun was going down as the train neared the Keil Station. They felt the train slowing, the wheels squealing as they passed over the track couplings. Kurt stuck his head out the window, looking for a familiar face in an army officer's uniform.

"I see him," Kurt finally said. "Let's get our gear together, shall we?" Before climbing down onto the platform, Kurt turned to the guide, saying, "Bernhard, thank you for getting us here safely. We all wish you the best for the future."

Kurt shook his hand, thinking, *hope he and his family can weather the gathering storm clouds. Let's pray that they will be alright.*

As each one of them stepped down from the compartment, Bernhard gave a farewell head gesture instead of a handshake in case prying eyes were looking. Kurt led the way to where the army officer was standing. "Captain Werner, I presume. Thank you for meeting us," Kurt said, acting like it was their first meeting.

"Herr Manning, I'm assuming," said Captain Werner.

"Kurt will be fine," replied Kurt as he reached out to grip the smartly dressed captain's hand, allowing the firmness of the grip to express the pleasure at seeing each other once again.

"Is everyone in your party here? If so, follow me. Kurt, you will go with me in my staff car. You three can board the truck behind." Fredrick looked around as they all followed the captain out of the busy station to the waiting vehicles. Two uniformed drivers stood by their vehicles, coming to attention as the group approached. "Take their luggage to the truck," said Captain Werner as he climbed into the back seat of the black Mercedes Benz, followed by Kurt.

"Guess we don't count that much," said Ernst, climbing up the tailgate and into the back of the truck.

"It's a lot better than walking," replied Fredrick, climbing up behind him.

The drive took them through the busy streets of Keil, arriving at the Hotel Wendall, where they would stay for a few days before Ernst and Stefan would relocate to a safe house on the outskirts of the city. From there, Ernst would be able to relay key information supplied by Kurt and Fredrick to the BIS.

Stefan, on the other hand, would start taking pictures from a hidden compartment on a fishing boat owned by a German loyal to the overthrow of Hitler.

On selected days, they would cruise by the big naval ships high in the building scaffolds and keel blocks, the enormous propellers, keel, and rudders only partially exposed.

If the pictures taken did not provide enough detail, they would be forced to smuggle Stefan into the yard, close enough to get more detailed images. If this became necessary, it would require a tremendous amount of planning and extreme danger. Stefan knew the risk he would face if discovered. He knew he would more than likely be tortured by the dreaded Gestapo until he revealed others involved in the mission.

Kurt and Fredrick would remain at the hotel for about a week, meeting with Captain Werner in the hotel restaurant to reinforce their cover story as engineering consultants.

On the first day the three met for breakfast, Captain Werner had a leather briefcase with him, and he said, "Gentlemen, as head of security, I have managed to obtain the latest documents for the *Graf Zeppelin* at some risk to myself. If I am caught, I will more than likely be tortured, then shot as a traitor.

"After breakfast, we will go up to your room, where you can study these files more carefully over the next two days. After that, I must return them to the safe where they are kept. Do not leave the room without them. I repeat, you only have two days to study the files and take pictures. Please, always be careful."

The documentation Captain Werner provided would be vital to their cover story of being structural consultants familiar with

265

the newest construction methods being used to build the *Graf Zeppelin*.

In preparation for visiting the builder's yard, they would have to study many hours, repeatedly reviewing the specifications and construction methods, including a host of other details that would give them credence and creditability to accomplish this mission.

When the time finally came for them to meet with the management team overseeing the construction of the ship, their presentation would need to be convincing, even to the point of questioning certain methods currently being used.

They would need to project an air of expertise in the structural design of the armored decking and additional underdeck armor protecting vital machinery, the steel for which was supplied by Wotan Welch Steelworks.

Captain Werner also had the build schedule and specifications for the new super battleship *Tirpitz*, along with details on its sister battleship the *Bismarck*, now in the final stages of being fitted out in Hamburg. "Starting tomorrow, I will escort you both to the Deutsche Werke Shipyard." Captain Werner continued by adding, "Here is a list of management and engineering people scheduled to meet with you. Are you ready to take this on?

"Make sure you return that file to me in the morning before we depart. I have some thoughts I would like to share with you both. I am hoping you will see and agree with my logic. The engineers we are going to meet are experts in what they do. If you, as engineering consultants, do not give them real engineering recommendations, they will see straight through this weakness, and you will be done before we even get started. I am proposing we give them a few compelling engineering changes that will improve the building of the *Graf Zeppelin*. As I said, food for thought," concluded Werner.

Over breakfast the following morning, Fredrick voiced his thoughts on how to proceed, "Last night, I studied the plans and specifications repeatedly and found two glaring areas of the design that could bring about the loss of the ship if not immediately corrected. Allow me to take the lead when we meet. As you said, Herbert, we must be convincing," said Fredrick.

"Are you going to give them improvements that will hurt the Royal Navy? If so, we should discuss them right now," said a concerned Kurt.

"Okay, let's talk about my proposal. The first area to discuss is the thickness of the secondary armored plating directly under the armored flight deck. This plating protects the ship's vital equipment. Right now, it's only 45mm—the same as the flight deck.

"If a bomb penetrates that deck, it might also go right through that secondary armored plating. We need to encourage them to use a much heavier plating, say 60 mm. It will increase the gross tonnage but save the ship. In addition, and here is where they are totally unaware of aircraft carrier design logic, the piping for aviation fuel lines is directly between these two layers of plating, going from the port side to the starboard side without any cutoff valves in the line. The only ones are at the tanks and the fueling stations on the hangar deck. My plan will reroute those supply lines much lower down in the ship and add additional valves for cutting the supply of fuel much faster.

"On paper, these glaring problems could easily be overlooked. If you two agree with me, I believe we can be compelling, and their guard will be down from then on," concluded Fredrick.

"Wow," said Captain Werner, "where did all this come from?"

"Structural engineering is my forte. So, will you go along with my plan?" asked Fredrick, feeling pretty good about his findings.

"Well done, Fredrick," said Kurt, slapping him on the back with his approval.

The opportunity for Fredrick to get up close to these ships was exciting, even though the danger of being caught was extremely high. Being that close to Germany's first top-secret

aircraft carrier had to be a risk they were willing to take, even if
it meant capture or losing their lives to do so.

All precautions had been taken. The plan was in place. With
any luck, they would return to England with the information
they had come for, but that would not be today.

Fredrick and Kurt left the hotel just before dawn to visit the
safe house. With them, they carried the top-secret documents
Stefan needed to photograph.

They walked for about a mile to a tree-lined lane, making sure
they were not being followed. They easily found the van parked
at the rendezvous point behind a hedgerow.

"Morning, Ernst, good to see you," said Kurt as they climbed
into the back. The drive to the safe house took less than fifteen
minutes.

Turning right down a narrow lane, they saw an overgrown
farm. The house was located at the end of a row of old barns.
Once a thriving dairy distribution center, it no longer had a use.
Its rundown condition confirmed its present unwanted state.

Ernst drove the old Citroen into the barn closest to the house.
An older farmhand slid the big door closed behind them. "Welcome, gentlemen. Please follow me through the back door. It's
safer entering from the back porch," the old man said as he beckoned them to follow him. "You may call me Mulley. That's my
nickname, so pleased to meet you both."

Inside the house, they were greeted by Stefan, who was sitting
at a long table having hot coffee. "Hello, you two. How is it going
so far?" said Stefan as he rose to get some more mugs from the
sideboard.

"Stefan, why don't you bring us up to speed on your boat
photographing expeditions," asked Kurt with a to-the-point
question.

"So far, we have been out about five times. We managed to
accumulate more than two hundred images of the carrier. We
also drove to Wilhelmshaven and took another hundred or so

pictures of another new battleship. Wow, she is enormous." Stefan described many other details as he showed them the pictures of both new ships. We'll get her name from Werner before we leave the hotel. Right now, it only has a work number stenciled on the lower part of the stern on the port side. All the images so far are okay, but not the detail I was looking for. I need to get up close to get the detail we need to see. The gun turrets on the battleship would suggest she has a main battery caliber of, I'm guessing about 38 cm in four twin turrets," continued Stefan.

"My God, that's 15 inches," said Fredrick with a look of fear.

"Unfortunately, I have not had the time to magnify the images to get more defined details. We'll try to have them for you by our next meeting, assuming there will be a next time? As for the carrier, well, I can assure you she is bigger than the Treaty of Versailles allows. Then again, I believe that all new German vessels have or will exceed that provision in the treaty. The Germans don't give a damn about treaties. That is painfully clear." Stefan sat back in his chair as he concluded.

"You say you need to get closer. Let me talk to Herbert about how we can make that happen. By the way, how do you like that new miniature camera they gave you?" asked Kurt.

"I like it a lot for up-close work. However, it's useless for long-distance images. For those pictures, I reverted to the bigger, long-range unit," replied Stefan.

Over the next four-plus hours, Stefan skillfully took pictures of the pages Fredrick needed copying. Once this was done, they carefully replaced them in the original order they were removed from the files. Ernst then brought out the communication folder he had hidden behind two large bricks in the kitchen wall, giving them to Kurt to review.

"What would you like me to send back to the BIS?" said Ernst.

"Send them these design specifications and these details we have gathered so far. I expect to have much more within a couple of days. As for those original pictures, we will carry them back with us. Time to leave," said Kurt as he returned the files to his and Fredrick's briefcases.

"We will leave by another route. I will drop you off about a half a mile from a bus stop that will return you to the city. It must appear you are returning to the hotel from work," said Ernst as he led them out through the back door, once Mulley had checked the farm for spying eyes.

"Thanks, Stefan. Make sure you take extreme care developing those pictures. We will not have another opportunity to copy them. See you in a few days," said Kurt as he walked to the back door.

Ernst drove them to the bus stop by a different route, but it was still a narrow lane, much the same as the first one. "Thanks for the lift, old man," said Fredrick as they got out and started walking to the bus stop. The old bus arrived, crowded with people heading home. This was good for them as they looked the part of ordinary businessmen returning after a long day.

Back in the hotel, they headed for the bar, keeping up appearances. An attractive hostess showed them to a small booth directly behind a large group of boisterous German naval officers, who were being entertained by a group of businessmen.

Kurt motioned to Fredrick to try and listen to their conversation. After about ten or fifteen minutes, the conversation started to become more serious. One naval captain asked questions to one of the businessmen. "When you were in Japan last year, how much of the carrier fleet did they show you? You may be aware that we are still somewhat new to aircraft carrier designs and construction methods. Tomorrow, we would like you to talk more in detail about your finding as we tour the GZ. Don't want to discuss it further here in the bar for obvious reasons." The naval officer recognized that someone could overhear their discussion. "I think we should be leaving. Too much schnapps for one evening, don't you think?"

"How much of that did you get?" asked Kurt once the group had left.

"I got some of it, enough to know we may see them tomorrow at the yard. I am surprised to hear that captain admitting to not knowing enough about carrier design. We can build on that ourselves when we meet tomorrow. Between you and me, I would be more concerned about the English designs than the Japanese, though." Frederick did not have a very high opinion of the early American and Japanese carrier deck armament.

Back in their room, the two continued sifting through the mountain of data. That data had not been seen by anyone in BIS or by other agencies in England that were waiting anxiously to review copies of that data.

"When doing your research the other night, did you find anything that pertained to what type of aircraft would be used, or are they considering new designs?" asked Kurt.

"There are numerous references to aircraft in consideration. From these reports, the mix is based on modified land-based aircraft and a few new models we are totally unaware of. These lists appear to change almost weekly. I came across this list last night, which could be helpful in ascertaining the preliminary types and how many will be boarded. Here, look at this," said Frederick.

The list was laid out in columns. To the left was the name of the manufacturer, followed by what type of aircraft, and the last column listed how many aircraft would be boarded.

Messerschmitt, Fighter, BF-109, Twelve
Junkers Dive Bomber, JU-87, Twelve
Fieseler Torpedo Bomber, FI-167, Twenty

"That is a big complement of aircraft. The Messerschmitt and Junkers types are land-based aircraft that will be modified for carrier duty. Not sure about the Fieseler Torpedo Bomber. Must be a new type designed purely for carrier operations," remarked Fredrick.

"Let's go down for supper, shall we? I'm getting hungry," said Kurt as he downed the last drop of whiskey.

"Okay, that sounds good. First, let's put these files back in our briefcases. Don't want to piss off Werner." Fredrick's sarcasm came through once again. They both laughed at his dry humor.

The Deutsche Werke Shipyard

K urt and Fredrick sat in the breakfast room, waiting for Captain Werner to pick them up and escort them to the Deutsche Werke Shipyard. Captain Werner entered the breakfast room and immediately received attention from a young waitress, "Can I seat you, sir?" she asked as she approached him.

"No, thank you. I am looking for two gentlemen who said they would meet me in this room." Captain Werner stood tall in his grey and dark green uniform.

To the young waitress, he was so handsome, "Right this way, sir."

Kurt and Fredrick stood to greet their military escort.

"Good morning, gentlemen. Are you ready to leave? My car is right outside, so if you're ready, shall we get going?" Captain Werner was anxious to get this day behind him and out of the way.

"I am assuming you have all your material ready for today's meeting?" he remarked, really asking if he could retrieve his files.

"Certainly, Herr Captain, I have copies for you in this folder. Sorry, they are bulky," said Kurt as he handed over the files.

The big black Mercedes approached the guardhouse. Werner rolled down his window to flash his ID card and immediately received a salute from the guards. "Now, may I see your papers, gentlemen?" said a guard addressing Kurt and Fredrick.

"They are here to meet with the design and build groups," said Werner as he turned in the car's front seat to answer the guard.

The guard took the papers provided by Kurt and Fredrick into the guardhouse. After a few minutes, he returned, handing the papers back and snapping to attention, "Thank you, sirs. You are free to pass. Have a productive meeting."

Once inside the shipyard, they drove around a large building and down an alleyway that led to the pier. As the driver turned right, a massive structure came into view. It was the bow of the *Graf Zeppelin* towering over them. "Here she is, gentlemen. Big, is she not?" Captain Werner could see by the looks on their faces that they were beside themselves with amazement.

"My God, she is high," said Fredrick as he strained his head to look up at the flat top of the flight deck. The Mercedes pulled up to the company's main offices. The driver smartly leaped out of the car, ran around to open the front door for Captain Werner, then moved to open the rear door for Kurt and Fredrick.

"Please, follow me, gentlemen. Right this way," said Captain Werner as they walked through the glass doors into a marble lobby.

At the reception desk, Werner showed his identification card, then signed the daily security log. "Gentlemen, please show your identification, then sign in." Walking down the long corridor, Fredrick was in awe of what he could see as they passed by big glass windows that framed the design engineering departments.

Opposite the windows, they could see row after row of drafting tables and engineers hard at work at their desks.

"It bothers me to think that if all this engineering could be applied for the betterment of mankind instead of machines designed for killing, what wonderful inventions could be made," remarked Captain Werner, a proud German ashamed of the direction his country was moving into.

Eventually, they came to conference room D-12, its doors wide open. Sitting around a large oval table were six uniformed officers, representing the navy and Luftwaffe along with seven maritime engineers and designers, all casually drinking their morning coffee and talking boisterously.

"Here we are. Are you both ready? Good morning, gentlemen. Hope we did not keep you waiting too long," said Captain Werner. As they took their places at opposite ends of the conference table, Captain Werner spoke first, "For those of you who do not know me, my name is Captain Herbert Werner. I am head of security. Also, I have the responsibility for all civilian contractors and contracts that are related to this shipyard. Today, we have two engineers joining us from Hamburg. Their area of expertise is marine structural design.

"Their knowledge in this area should be of special interest to all of you gathered here. These gentlemen are current with new design practices being utilized by foreign powers for their newer aircraft carriers. So, with that said, let me introduce Herr Kurt Baumann and Herr Fredrick Bardenhewer to this meeting."

The senior naval officer stood to welcome them. "Thank you, Captain Werner, for arranging this meeting. We are looking forward to hearing from your guests about possible improvements to the new *Graf Zeppelin*. Also, I would suggest we cease with the formalities of rank and surnames. It will make the meeting flow much easier."

Herbert Werner answered right away, "That sounds like an admiral idea, sir. To start the meeting off, I would like to have Fredrick here bring you up to date on their findings on countries currently using carriers in their navies. Fredrick will also elaborate on design modifications needed to accommodate the newer aircraft specifically designed for sea-borne operations. Fredrick, would you please continue?"

Herbert beckoned to Fredrick to take over the meeting.

"Thank you, Herbert. Over the last several years, my partner and I have been gathering data on new, fast, fleet aircraft carriers. As civil marine architects, we were able to review and, on more than one occasion, see firsthand the advancements in flat-top developments in Japan as well as that of the United States.

"These new carriers are bigger than you may imagine, capable of carrying a large complement of aircraft for greater distances at higher speeds and in many cases capable of outdistancing their naval escorts. The aircraft these carriers carry can provide aerial fighter protection anywhere in the world to protect the fleet or escort convoys and attack convoys that are out of range of land-based aircraft.

"These big carriers also carry torpedo bombers, dive bombers, and a few aerial surveillance aircraft. Every one of these new aircraft carriers requires a longer flight deck to accommodate higher takeoff and landing speeds. From our observations, these newer faster aircraft come at a much higher price, considering their size and weight. The available deck space is of paramount importance for all future designs. The ability to fuel, arm, and relaunch will need to be much faster than ever before.

"The only three countries addressing these future needs are Japan, America, and England. Both Japan and America are equipping their carriers with aircraft types I mentioned earlier. The Japanese have gathered a tremendous amount of knowledge from the American designs. However, from our observations, their decks, for the most part, cannot withstand too many direct bomb hits. The aviation fuel delivery systems tend to be too close to the flight deck. This could prove to be disastrous with a direct hit.

"The English, on the other hand, design their aircraft carriers in a completely different manner. They design them from the keel up to be carriers with an emphasis on heavily-armored flight decks. In addition, they realized that sea warfare will come from air power, so they have designed well-placed anti-aircraft protection all around the ship, quite differently from the Japanese and Americans, who tend to build their carriers on naval hull designs from other ships such as battleships.

"Gentlemen, for the purpose of this meeting, I propose it may behoove us to focus on the English approach of heavily armored decks. Their ships, however, tend to be shorter than navies such as those I mentioned earlier. Many of their current aircraft are biplanes. This does not present a problem yet but will surely be a problem as newer monoplane aircraft come online. Again, let me repeat, modern Japanese and American aircraft require longer flight decks due to their higher takeoff and landing speeds.

"The English still rely on the Fairey Swordfish as their main torpedo bomber. Those biplanes can take off and land on extremely short decks. That may be acceptable at this point, but what will happen when the faster planes come online?

"For the purpose of any further discussion, I propose our focus be on improvements that can be added to the existing armored flight deck as well as the secondary armor plating over the vital equipment. The aviation storage and fuel distribution systems must be on that list as well. Should the main deck be penetrated and the pressure fuel supply lines breached, it would surely seal the fate and survival of the *Graf Zeppelin*.

"From what we have been able to ascertain so far, this first of four carriers is a match with any other navy. Herbert has been most helpful in providing us with limited information about the project. However, for us to provide meaningful engineering input, I believe we must see firsthand where the construction is to date.

"I realize it may be premature to ask for this tour. However, we can only provide meaningful direction if we are permitted to see where the build cycle is right now. I, therefore, request that all of us tour the ship before proceeding any further."

Fredrick sat down, taking a quick look for eye contact around the table. The senior naval officer had a perplexed look, "That was a quick look at the other naval carriers and possibly their shortfalls. Let me say; we are familiar with their designs and types of aircraft. I would suggest you give us a little time to review your request. Could you please wait outside while we discuss this further? Thank you."

"Not a problem," said Herbert, anxious to shepherd Kurt and Fredrick out of the room. In the hall waiting area, Herbert said in a low but angry tone to Fredrick and Kurt, "What the hell was that all about? You might as well have told them the English have windbags for aircraft and carriers that will be ineffective with the next generation of aircraft."

"Not so, Herbert. Give the English more credit for thinking this through. Have you ever heard of arresting gear to stop fast-landing aircraft extremely quickly? Not to mention their new torpedo bombers will be available later this year or early next year.

"How about the fast and deadly new fighters being tested as we stand here arguing? I have been busy learning all this before coming over from England. I told you both earlier, we need to give them something positive, or they will never get us on that ship."

"Well, I guess they are talking about that right now. Furthermore, we need to get a look at that big beast, then get as far away from Keil as we can because, if we don't, we will be behind bars within a couple of days.

"Were you two sleeping, or did you not see the eye contact going on? Right now, they believe we may know a great deal more than they do, so they will string us along. By tonight, they will be collecting background information, more than you did, Herbert. So, your neck will be on the block by tomorrow as well. When we leave tonight, you will be in civilian clothes and hiding along with the rest of us." Fredrick stopped talking, still visibly upset at the tongue lashing he just received.

Herbert looked at Kurt, then at Fredrick, "I am so sorry. I should have realized you were throwing them a bone to win their confidence and tour the ship. Kurt did tell me earlier you had a knack for leading the discussion. I will not challenge you again."

"Let's leave it at this: we are all in this hot water together. Can you get civilian clothes quickly?" asked Kurt.

"They are already in a suitcase in the boot of my car," said Herbert, now smiling.

After about thirty minutes, a uniformed guard approached them, saying, "Gentlemen, would you follow me back into the conference room?"

The atmosphere appeared much more cordial. "Gentlemen, please take a seat. We discussed your unusual request to go aboard the *Zeppelin* and are pleased to say we are all in agreement that we should start by showing you the progress so far. Now, shall we get started?" said the senior naval officer.

The walk to the construction elevator took all of twelve minutes down long, drab, green-painted hallways, down a flight of stairs, and out into the yard. There in front of them was the massive bow of the *Graf Zeppelin*.

The construction elevator was small, so only four at a time could ride up to the flight deck. Fredrick took the first ride up. Out on the enormous flight deck, he was in awe of how long and wide it was.

"So, what do you think?" said one of the design engineers, beaming with pride at what they had designed and built in this massive, new ship.

"Very impressive so far. Then again, we have been on board only a few brief minutes," said Fredrick with a sarcastic tone.

Once they had all assembled on the front of the ship, the senior officer said, "Shall we get started? Please, follow me."

For almost three hours, the group toured the ship, taking extra time and paying attention to the fabrication of the upper hangar deck. Additional time was also spent in areas where the fuel supply lines entered the hangar deck. Fredrick and Kurt made recommendations to isolate the fuel flow quickly in the event of an emergency to validate their cover story. Further, they brazenly took notes on the placement of the miles of piping. These notes would become invaluable if war should be declared. Knowing where to aim their bombs in an aerial attack would help the RAF immensely.

The truth was hard to admit. The *Graf Zeppelin* was well constructed. If she ever sailed into the Atlantic, she would be able to wreak havoc on English shipping.

Herbert now spoke, "Gentlemen, if we are done here, I recommend we adjourn for today and schedule another meeting in two days. Will that be enough time for you to prepare a meaningful report and recommendations for this group to review?"

Herbert looked directly to Kurt and Fredrick with an expression that asked, is that enough time for us to escape?

Kurt took the lead on this line of questioning, "Gentlemen, we are being tasked in a short time to compile such a report, but we will do our level best. Lots of coffee will help make this happen. What time on Wednesday are you planning to pick us up from the hotel?"

Herbert, going along with the act, answered, "How does 0930 hours sound? Gentlemen, can you make yourselves available on that Wednesday, say, at 1000 hours?"

He continued by encouraging the dialog that had been started. Herbert's parting words gave credibility and helped make today's event believable.

The challenge now would be to escape to England with all the pictures, sketches, and other documents they had gathered.

This they needed to do before the Germans caught on to this masterfully planned and executed deceptive operation.

As for Herbert, he would soon go from a highly trusted German Army officer to a traitor of the Third Reich with a price on his head, all happening in just a few short days.

2 6

Escaping to England

At the main building, they all shook hands, thanking each other for a productive first meeting with high expectations for the second.

Fredrick was thinking as he stood there, shaking hands, *it's the first and last meeting for you lot. Now, our concentration needs to be focused on running as hard as we can away from here. That damn storm is following me again.*

Walking back to the staff car, Herbert needed to tell them his plan before they reached it, "Better the driver hears nothing other than our cover story. When I drop you off at the hotel, go straight to your rooms and pack whatever you will travel with. Wait till it's dark, then leave by the back staircase. That's the trade entrance. I will contact the others and arrange for them to meet you at the same place as before, say around 2100 hours.

"In the car, I will tell you the trumped-up story loud enough for the driver to hear that we are going to one of my favorite restaurants outside of town, and you should be ready to leave at 1900 hours. My driver, hearing this, will not be surprised when I inform him that I am giving him a night off. To play it safe, I will tell him that I will use my own car for the evening, and he should return the staff car to the motor pool with instructions to have them service it the following day. I will also tell him I do not need him or the car till Wednesday morning at 0900 hours. Knowing Hans, he will be happy to have some time off."

In the car, they played out their story, the driver missing nothing that was said. At the hotel, Fredrick and Kurt thanked Captain Werner for a productive day and confirmed they would wait for him tonight at 1900 hours in front of the hotel lobby.

As the car pulled away, Fredrick turned to Kurt, "There goes an honorable German willing to do whatever it takes to make Germany proud and safe once again." With that said, they entered the hotel and climbed the stairs to their room.

"We have about three hours to kill. What say we go down and have a beer?" said Kurt.

"Sounds good to me," replied Fredrick.

In the lounge, they sat in a booth, finally able to relax for a few hours before slipping away into the darkness.

"Kurt, I must ask you a question. You may not want to answer or have no knowledge of it, but I need to know. Please, if you know, tell me the truth. Living without knowing is painful, so tell me right now."

Fredrick needed to know Kitty's fate. Was she in Germany? Or was she already back in England?

Kurt, his head lowered, slowly reached across the table, gripping Fredrick's arm. "This is the question I have been dreading to hear for so many months. I cannot give you a definitive answer, although I wish to God I could. The last contact we had was from Hazel more than two months ago, saying they were on the run and not to expect timely transmissions. Just before we left for Germany, we received a short communication from Hazel telling us that Bill and Kitty had been arrested.

"Since then, we have received nothing. Fredrick, no, wait, let me call you by your real name, Karl. It is imperative that you, as the maritime member of this group, get that information along with your observations back to the Royal Navy chaps.

"Only you can do this. When you and Herbert return to England, I, along with Helmut and Silvio, will remain here to complete the original mission in Hamburg, and, if our luck holds, other sites of naval importance. We have been instructed to meet up with Hazel and what's left of her team one week from now. Only then can we find out about Bill and Kitty."

Karl sat quietly, his darkest thoughts now out in the open, the pain hitting him harder than ever.

"Karl, I have held this from you, knowing it would hit you hard enough to cloud your focus on this mission, but now it's almost over for you." Gunther sat quietly, waiting for a response.

"I will do my best for you, Karl, whatever that may be. This, I promise you." Karl was close to breaking down, and Gunther knew it.

"Let's get out of here. You are in no condition to be seen in public. Let's go."

In his room, Karl sat at the edge of the bed, letting the wave of pain and tears flow freely. "Why does this continually happen to me?"

This quiet time alone was what Karl needed to regain his composure, refocusing all his attention on their escape that would start in less than an hour.

That night, Gunther and Karl slipped quietly out of the hotel back entrance, walking in the shadows to the rendezvous point.

Helmut flashed the van's headlights once as he saw two dark figures walking down the lane. "Pleased to see you both. Get in," said Helmut.

"We need to return to the safe house right away. Everything used to develop the pictures has been buried along with any signs of us being there. The stuff going with us is packed and ready for us to leave tonight. This afternoon, Herbert arranged through his network a plan for you, Karl, and himself to rendezvous with the HMS *Thorn* three days from now. The forged papers and travel documents are with him at the safe house. Karl, you and Herbert will be driven to the station by Mulley in Herbert's car.

"As for the three of us, we will take another route to the station in this van. Mulley's brother will ride with us. Once they have dropped us off, they will drive both vehicles to a deep-water quarry, push Herbert's car over the edge, then return to the safe house in this van, which belongs to Mulley anyway.

"Here we are. Now, let's make it fast. We only have ninety minutes to get on that train." Helmut was showing signs of anxiety with all the last-minute planning and rushing around.

Inside the house, Herbert was busy checking the documents and last-minute details. He looked so different in his civilian clothes. Karl hardly recognized him. "Thank God you are here. I was getting a little nervous watching that clock tick by. We are set, so let's get going. Gunther, here are the documents, train tickets, and travel documents for all three of you. The travel documents, should you be challenged, will take you anywhere in Germany.

"I had them ready long before you arrived here. Good thinking, don't you agree?" said Herbert as he put on his tweed jacket.

Mulley had made fresh cheese sandwiches for them to eat on the train. With both vehicles loaded, they set off in different directions toward the train station.

Pulling in, Herbert noticed two brown shirt troopers standing by the entrance. "Damn it," he said. "I hope the hat, glasses, and mustache will fool them if I'm challenged."

"Stay calm, Herbert, and act like you're concerned about missing the Hamburg Express," said Karl as he stepped out of the car.

In low voices, they said their farewells to Mulley, thanked him for his help, then headed for the entrance, passing right in front of the troopers, who could not have cared less about these two travelers.

The platform was relatively quiet. At this time of day, fewer people traveled on the express to Hamburg. After about fifteen minutes, they heard the clanging bell of the approaching express.

About fifty or so feet away, Gunther Helmut and Silvio stood nonchalantly, quietly talking.

Herbert, in a calming voice, said to Karl, "I am so sorry to hear about your fiancé, Lieutenant Johnson, and Captain Loews. I have been trying through to my contacts in Hamburg to get an update, but now that I'm on the run, I'm like all of you—in the dark."

"Thank you for trying. At this point, I am concentrating on getting back to the BIS. That's the only thing keeping me going.

"I love Kitty so much, but at this juncture, I fear the worst, and that is the hardest and most painful to accept." Karl was trying hard to hold his composure as they stood there on the platform.

Herbert and Karl found an empty compartment toward the rear of the train. Once they were seated, the carriage door opened again, and three men climbed aboard, stowed their luggage, and sat down at the opposite side of the compartment by the windows. A loud whistle and clatter of carriage bumpers signaled the departure of the express as it jerked through its initial startup motion.

On this express, there was no corridor running alongside the compartments, so once the train got underway, there was no way for others to enter the compartment or carriage.

"Okay, you three, when we arrive, walk out of the station, then look for a man standing next to a gray van. He will be leaning against the front of the mudguard reading a *Deutsch Motoren* magazine. Ask him for directions to the bus stop going to Hamburg. Thank him, walk around the corner past the bus stop and wait for him at the next corner. Make sure you do not have a tail.

"Karl and I will leave the compartment once you are on the platform and heading to the exit gate. Karl and I have about an hour to wait for our train taking us back to Leybuchet. Rhineholt will be there to pick us up, basically reversing the rendezvous with the submarine." Herbert wanted to make sure they all knew what to do once they arrived in Hamburg.

Karl slid over to Gunther, sitting on his own by the window, staring out into space. "Gunther, before parting ways in Hamburg, I need you to know this. Put in a similar position as you were put in by keeping Bill and Kitty's arrest from me, well, I need you to know I would have done the same thing as you were forced to do. Telling me sooner would have clouded my vision and probably endangered all of us on this mission.

"I wanted to tell you that it was an honor to be your partner during this dangerous mission. Thank you, my friend. I hope I have lived up to your expectations. If you do find out about what happened, promise to get word to me one way or another."

Gunther reached out and put his hand on Karl's broad shoulder. "Thank you. Hearing this has taken a big load off me. Let me also say, the honor was all mine."

"Now, I need a favor from you. If, for some reason, I don't make it back, will you make me a promise to return to Hamburg after this crisis is over? Hopefully, war will never ever erupt in Europe. When that time comes, I am asking you to try to find my family.

"If you do, give them a box that you will find in my personal things in the storage area in Slough. The address is on the outside. If they no longer live at that address, you may have to track them down. I pray daily that they are alright. Please, Karl, make me this promise. You are my closest friend and one who I can trust completely to make this happen. Let's face it; I have already trusted you with my life." Gunther cracked a weak smile as he looked into Karl's eyes.

One by one, they drifted off to sleep, exhausted after this long day's events. Karl, however, was wide awake, staring at the compartment ceiling and the blackness of night outside the window.

God, please give me strength when I finally know Kitty's fate. The thought of her being forced to endure merciless punishment... or has she already been shot as a spy?

In his head, he mulled over all these thoughts, realizing that he was now crying, tears flowing freely down his cheeks. *This pain is like nothing I have ever felt before. Right now, I must put all my thoughts aside and stay strong for these brave men around me. I cannot jeopardize their lives in any way. There will be time for my grief once we are back in England.* With that, he took a deep breath, closed the door to his pain, and hardened himself once again.

The train wheels squealed as they crossed the coupling into the Hamburg Station. "Gentlemen, this is where we must part. Karl and I wish you safety and success with your mission. Please, be careful. The tension is escalating daily," said Herbert as he put on his sports jacket. The train slowed, entering the brightly illuminated station. They all said their goodbyes, shook hands, then returned to their separate corners. They were, once again, strangers.

The train lurched to a stop. Gunther, Helmut, and Silvio got out first. As Gunther passed Karl, he said softly, "Karl, remember what I asked you to do for me. I will miss you. Hope to see you again real soon." Gunther stepped down onto the platform, joining his two fellow travelers.

Herbert turned to Karl. "Are you ready?" he said as he stepped down onto the platform.

"Right behind you," responded Karl.

By the time they reached the platform gate, Gunther and his team had vanished into the night. Now, it was just the two of them. Walking in silence, they arrived at their platform, presented their tickets to the gate attendant, then entered the platform for the last leg back to Leybuchet.

Karl finally broke the silence by suddenly saying, "Herbert, I feel strangely alone without my friends. We were together day and night for a long time. You and Gunther must have had a similar relationship, both serving in the same army unit. You know, Herbert, he always spoke so highly of you." Karl was simply making small talk to lighten the tension.

The suitcase Karl was carrying had a false bottom to it. The inside held the extensive microfilm pictures taken by Silvio of the *Graf Zeppelin* and additional microfilm of the design specifications also taken at the safe house. Karl also hid his notes and sketches in this compartment to be on the safe side.

They would now rely on Gunther and his team to collect the additional information on Hitler's new battleships and as much information as they could on the dreaded new U-boat fleet.

"I feel we should have stayed on for the remainder of the mission. Don't you agree, Herbert? We accomplished only one damn objective." Karl looked at his traveling companion with a questioning look on his face.

"Karl, Gunther was told to get you back to England and that I should accompany you there," replied Herbert. *Here we go again with those damn BIS secrets. What the hell is going on this time?* thought Karl.

The train for Leybuchet arrived on time. To their amazement, few people were waiting to board, nor did many passengers get off. "There's a lot to say for traveling on a night train," said Herbert as they walked down the length of the train, looking for an empty compartment.

Once again, they found one almost at the end of the train and climbed on board. "Let's stretch out and get some shut-eye. It's about a five-hour ride to get back to Leybuchet, and I need to get some rest," said Herbert as he stretched out.

The whistle from the engine woke Karl up at each stop and once again as it pulled into Leybuchet.

Herbert, on the other hand, slept straight through. "Herbert, time to move. We are pulling into our station," said Karl.

Herbert rolled over, rubbing his eyes, "Guess I was tired. Did you get any sleep, Karl?"

"Yes and no, each time the engine blew the whistle, it woke me up. Never was a sound sleeper. You, on the other hand, slept like a dead person," said Karl.

Climbing down from the compartment, the two walked to the exit. Karl was looking for a familiar face. Hopefully, it would be Bernhard. As they approached the gate, two brown shirt thugs stood, watching passengers as they passed through. "Keep walking, and do not look at them. Who knows who they are looking for?" Herbert was concerned, as he should be.

Outside the station, they looked for a contact or familiar face. Karl noticed a black van parked toward the end of the station with no lights on. "I'm willing to bet that's our ride," said Karl as they walked toward the parked van.

As they got closer, the passenger door opened, and out stepped Bernhard. "Quickly, get into the back. We must get out of here fast. There is something afoot with the brown shirts. They're obviously looking for someone, hopefully not you two."

The van pulled out of the station, Bernhard saying, "So pleased to see you back here safe and sound, Karl. So, this must be Captain Werner. Pleased to meet you, sir. I have been briefed about you returning with Karl to England. Germany needs more men with your convictions to save the pride of this country. Thank you also for orchestrating this mission. It could not have been pulled off without you. Right now, we are heading to a beach not far from here. The same small boat that picked you up from the sub is waiting for you at the end of the pier. It's a moonless night, so it's perfect for getting you out of here. The trawler you arrived on will pick you up about three miles offshore, then rendezvous with the submarine just before dawn."

Arriving at the seawall, Bernhard shut the headlamps off as he rolled to a stop near the stone pier. "Gentlemen go quickly. Your boat will be at the very end, waiting for you. I'm not sure if we will meet again, so please stay safe. God be with you. Goodbye."

Bernhard quietly closed the doors to the van, started the engine, and with the lights still off, disappeared into the night.

They walked briskly down the pier till they reached the end. In the dark, it was hard to see down to the water and the waiting boat. A voice whispered, "Down here, there is a ladder to the right of you. Please be careful as you step over into the boat."

"Thank you," said Karl and Herbert as they boarded then sat on the engine cover, holding their precious case of secrets closely.

After almost forty-five minutes, the fisherman slowed the boat to a crawl. As he did so, a dark shadow appeared through the darkness of the night.

As they came closer, a voice called out quietly, "Please, board quickly, and go straight below." The familiar voice was that of Skipper Rudi calling from the bridge. Moving quickly, they entered the forward cabin. Finding a place to lay down for a while was an easy task, and everywhere the aroma of fish was overpowering.

The crew quickly pulled the skiff out of the water using the stern davits. Once that was done, the *Kramer Lady*'s engine came to life, and the old trawler moved forward, gathering speed on its way out to sea.

With the coast of Germany almost over the horizon, Captain Rudi invited his passengers to get some fresh air on the bridge. "Nice to see you again, and welcome to your traveling companion, Herbert; is that correct? I must apologize for the condition of the air down below. It is a working fishing boat when all is said and done." Rudi talked over the noise from the engine, waves, and wind.

"That's alright, Skipper, we are grateful to you and your crew for risking your own safety by getting us back out to the submarine," replied Karl, the salt air clearing his nostrils and his head, even if it was for just a few hours.

He had closed the door temporarily on Kitty's fate. Somewhere deep inside of him, the hope of Kitty and Bill escaping was fading, leaving an empty, black hollow from which there was no escape.

Not today, thought Karl, *I need to hold onto a miracle for a little while longer.*

Karl shook himself out of that dark place, deciding to strike up a casual conversation with the skipper, "Being back on the sea is therapy for me right now. Being away from it makes me realize how much I truly miss it." Karl stared out over the trawler's bow and watched the sky as it slowly started its transformation to daybreak, changing from satin black to orange, then dark blue out on the distant horizon.

For a brief time, Karl allowed his mind to take him back to another time when the same picture was in his vision off the coast of Marseille. *Perhaps I should entertain the thought of returning to the sea. That's always been the place I get the most satisfaction.*

The skipper's voice snapped Karl back to the smelly fishing trawler. "I can understand feeling like that. There are stormy days when I can't wait to get off this old tub, but when the sun returns, and the water sheds its angry waves, then being out here again makes it all worthwhile. You must miss being a sailor. I see it in your face. This is the best therapy for any sad thought." The old skipper could see Karl was fighting between the love of the sea and something that was bringing him closer to the breaking point.

Rudi looked out over the bow thinking: *I wonder what drives these types to do what they do. Then again, my crew and I would be shot or worse if we were found out ferrying spies.* "Stand by to launch the skiff. We're almost at the rendezvous point." The skipper slowed the trawler until it was almost stopped.

The quiet, other than the idling engine, was suddenly broken by a loud hissing sound and water shooting from a black shadow right off their port side. It was the HMS *Thorn* returning to recover its homeward-bound passengers.

Herbert was the first to speak as they prepared to leave the trawler, "Like you, Captain, I am a German. In fact, I was an officer in the Wehrmacht until a few days ago. We share the same conviction that we are doomed by the direction being taken to destroy all that is right with Germany. Stay strong in your convictions, Captain, and to the challenges we face in the months or years it will take to remove Herr Hitler and his thugs from power. Thank you."

Karl spoke next, "Thank you for the second time, Skipper. Please continue with helping us, but please be careful on these ferry missions. It will become more dangerous for you and your crew should a war break out. You will find yourselves in a difficult position; that's for sure. Thanks again."

A crew member helped them down into the skiff, then started the small boat engine. The short ride over to the waiting submarine took only six or seven minutes. With a bump, they slid alongside the black steel hull. They both thanked the fisherman for delivering them safe and sound, then climbed up the rope ladder to the helping hands of a Royal Navy officer.

"Welcome aboard, sirs. Glad to have you back on board. The captain will greet you in the wardroom once we have submerged."

Karl was feeling safe once more. It seemed like a lifetime ago that this same submarine delivered them to the waiting *Kramer Lady*.

Inside the cramped quarters of the sub, they were escorted to the wardroom. "Gentlemen, please be seated. The captain will be with you shortly. Please, help yourselves to tea or coffee while you wait."

The sub's electric motor started that whining sound as they moved forward, followed by that hissing sound and the deck angling down to take them into the safety of the dark North Sea in the direction of England and home.

They spread out on the dark green couches that lined the cold form of the hull. Two swigs of his coffee and Karl was out cold.

"Time to wake up, old man. You have been out for almost five hours," said Herbert, gently shaking Karl's shoulder.

"What? How long have I been out?" asked Karl as he sat up to find the smiling face of Captain Aldridge sitting at the table drinking coffee.

"Welcome back to the land of the living. Glad to see you again, old man. We decided it would be better to let you get some needed sleep than waking you up to chinwag with me. Are you ready for some food and hot coffee?" asked Captain Aldridge.

"That would be wonderful. I am feeling famished about now." Karl could not miss seeing the empty plates in front of Herbert and Captain Aldridge.

"Captain Werner here has been bringing me up to speed on the German military activities and how they took advantage of the Spanish war to train their Luftwaffe, infantry, and heavy artillery. Training such as this is always so much more effective in a real war theater. Now, come and join us.

"This return trip will be much shorter as we will not be returning to Portsmouth or laying offshore as we did on the outbound trip. We are scheduled to transfer you two to a harbor tug that will rendezvous with us off Dover at dawn tomorrow morning," said Captain Aldridge as he poured himself another cup of coffee.

Karl and Herbert walked down the narrow passageway to the small cabin Karl and Gunther had used on the outbound trip.

They stretched out on the two couches, making small talk until sleep overtook them.

At 0500 hours, the watch officer woke them, telling them, when they were ready, to join some of the other officers in the wardroom for breakfast.

They both sparingly washed their hands and faces and cleaned their teeth with toothbrushes supplied by the steward.

"Good morning, gentlemen. May we join you?" asked Karl as he and Herbert found places at the end of the narrow table.

"What can I get you?" asked the steward.

"Coffee will be just fine," said Herbert. "Same for my friend here."

The first officer spoke first, "We will be transferring you in about an hour. Till then, it's best you stay here in the wardroom. The captain asked me to tell you he will be down shortly to say goodbye to you both."

The deck vibrated and angled upward as the sub slowed in readiness to break the surface. The hammering sound of the big diesel engines coming to life meant they were now on the surface. "Good morning, gentlemen. Did you get any rest last night?" asked a smiling Captain Aldridge.

"Some, thank you," replied Karl and Herbert.

"If you're ready, follow me to the control room. We need to move quickly as we will be returning to Portsmouth once you have been transferred," said the skipper as he led the way. Through the narrow, round deck hatch, they both squeezed their way through onto the wet deck. "This is where we make our farewells. Gentlemen, it has been a pleasure having you onboard. I hope our paths cross again under better circumstances." With that, the captain returned to the bridge to direct the transfer.

A navy motor-driven launch pulled alongside the submarine's hull. They climbed down the ladder into the launch. A sailor handed Karl his suitcase once they were on the launch.

The last thing Karl and Herbert did was to turn back to face

HMS *Thorn*, coming to attention and saluting Captain Aldridge in a sign of respect. The salute was returned by all on the deck crew, including the captain. The launch stood off as the submarine hissed again and slowly entered the depths. In a few minutes, it was gone.

Karl turned to Herbert, "Welcome, Captain Werner, to England, your new home." Herbert held a familiar facial expression; Karl knew the feeling of betraying his country.

"Herbert, I know what is going through your head right now. I and many others who escaped to England have had the same emotions. That feeling will never really pass. However, what we do makes it worth the pain you are feeling right now."

"Thank you, Karl. For a moment, I felt like my organized life had come to an end. Guess it's taking on a new objective, much like yours did."

"Please, be seated inside the cockpit, sirs. The trip will be quick. Should have you alongside in about an hour," said a cheerful sailor. They sat inside the cabin, looking out over the gloomy waters of Dover. This mission was almost over; only the debriefing was left.

A New Life Without Kitty
and a New Assignment

The launch approached the dock. Standing at the top of the ramp, two plain-clothed men waited in front of a familiar Humber staff car.

"Well, Herbert, you are getting a BIS welcome by the looks of it," said Karl as he stepped off the launch ahead of Herbert.

He yelled toward the launch, "Thanks, for the ride, chaps."

Climbing up the ramp, familiar friendly faces came into view. It was Clive along with Colonel Jacks. "Major Knight are you a sight for sore eyes, and so are you, Colonel Jacks. Gentlemen, it is my honor to introduce you to Captain Herbert Werner, formerly an officer of the German Wehrmacht," said Karl proudly.

Herbert came to parade attention and snapped a firm salute.

"Sirs pleased to make your acquaintance. I am requesting military asylum here in the United Kingdom and wish to extend my extensive military training to aid the Free German Brigade training here in England."

"It is we who need to thank you for such a well-executed

mission, Captain," said Colonel Jacks. "Back at the camp, we have arranged for members of the German Brigade to meet you. Two of the commanding officers have requested, if possible, to sit in on the debrief. Would either of you object to that request?" asked Colonel Jacks.

"Not at all," both answered simultaneously.

The drive back to the camp in Slough took about three hours. The traffic was, at that time of the morning, quite heavy. Karl, without warning, went into overload about the mission, surprising the others in the car. "I will need to get together with the boys in the lab on our arrival. I need to see all the pictures on 8" x 11" slides, so that we can all see what we are up against. I will also need an artist to make clearer pictures of my many sketches, and finally, I need a girl from the secretarial pool to copy all my notes as well as Gunther's notes." Karl's brain was in full-ahead mode.

"Lieutenant, slow down. Don't you think we should welcome Herbert here properly at the officer's lounge before diving into your findings?" voiced Colonel Jacks in a stern voice.

"Oh, I'm sorry, sir. I was thinking of all that has to be done ahead of our debrief tomorrow." Karl's manner continued erratically; he was outwardly displaying signs of a possible breakdown.

However, he was desperately trying to keep his thoughts from drifting toward the fate of Kitty. In his mind, he could hear Kitty saying, "Sailor, drop your anchor and stay awhile. You need to relax."

Kitty, please help me make it through the next few weeks until I can say goodbye to you in my own way, thought Karl.

Clive looked deeply into Karl's face. He could see the pain behind his intensity. *I will have to get him alone away from the camp. The truth will be hard to get across. I need to step lightly. Karl fell for Kitty in a big way. Maybe I should spare him the details and leave it at they are missing and presumed dead.*

Clive was also milling around in his mind how to diplomatically return Kitty's engagement ring along with the letter she had entrusted to him should she not return.

God, she loved him so much, but duty came first, and look where that got her. Clive excused himself, saying he had to stop by his office for a few minutes. Colonel Jacks, Herbert, and Karl continued to the lounge, the scolding from Colonel Jacks still ringing in Karl's head.

Inside, Karl spotted a few familiar faces. On one side of the lounge, a few former German military officers sat waiting for Karl and Herbert to head their way.

"Gentlemen let me introduce you to Captain Herbert Werner. Much like yourselves, he was, until recently, an officer in the Wehrmacht," announced Karl.

"Herbie, my old friend, wonderful to see you again. Heard you made it over here in one piece. It seems like a lifetime since we were all together at the academy. Come, sit next to me. We have years to catch up on," said Albert Altergott, a former major in a Panzer tank training battalion.

From across the room, Karl noticed Clive enter the lounge, obviously looking for him. "Gentlemen, sorry to break up your gathering. I need to borrow Karl; we have some business to catch up on."

Clive addressed Karl directly, "Sorry to take you away like this, old man. Let's go to my office, shall we?"

Walking across the parade ground, Karl asked Clive, "What is so pressing that you need to see me privately in your office?" asked Karl.

Clive answered, "It's better we have some privacy." Clive reached out, grasping Karl's arm in a show of friendship.

Once inside the office, Clive pointed to a chair, "Have a seat, Karl. Would you like a glass of whiskey, or would you prefer tea or coffee?" Clive was deciding how to proceed; this would not be easy.

Once Karl was seated, Clive poured two glasses of good

Scotch whiskey, giving one to Karl. He turned to his safe; opening the door, he took out a small cardboard box, placing it on the desk directly in front of Karl.

"To answer your earlier question, we need to address the facts and the realization of what has happened to Lieutenant Kitty Johnson. Up until two weeks ago, we could not obtain any information on Kitty or Bill, then unexpectedly, we received a message from Hazel, letting us know that Bill had been rescued. The prison van carrying him and Kitty to a Gestapo interrogation center was deliberately crashed into by our agents, but something went seriously wrong.

"Instead of crashing into the van to stop it, they hit it in such a way that the van rolled over several times. The three armed guards were shot in the resulting gunfight. The driver escaped, running off into the forest. Bill was pulled out of the wreck, injured but alive.

"Now, here is the hard part. Kitty was killed instantly as the van rolled over. Her head hit the side of the van, snapping her neck. Our agents took her body to a village about an hour away and managed to bury her in a Catholic cemetery under the name of Gretel Manton."

Clive slid the box with both hands toward Karl, then slowly sat back in silence, allowing Karl to open the box and review the contents.

Karl held the envelope in his hand, staring at it. He opened the box with the ring in it, allowing a tear to roll down his cheek. "Thank you, Clive. I know how difficult this must have been for you. Kitty thought the world of you, as do I. We have a job to do. We must complete the work that Kitty gave her life for. When will I return to Europe?" Karl was trying to reengage, putting his pain into the box he was now closing.

"Karl, in your present state of mind, we can't risk putting you back out into the field. We have therefore decided to keep you in a training capacity here in Slough. There will come a time when the need to return you to a field position will arise, but not right now.

"After the debriefing meeting tomorrow, you will be given a ten-day furlough. I have taken the liberty of calling your brother-in-law to let him know you will be arriving by train the day after tomorrow. Also, I have arranged for you to be driven to the station." Clive was treading carefully. As he spoke to Karl, the tension now between them was obvious.

"It appears that you and your fellow officers have made all the decisions for me. Clive, please, I beg of you, don't sideline me from field operations. You need me, and I need to be part of this operation. If I can't continue in my present capacity, then damn it, give me the opportunity to return to sea duty!"

Karl considered his options as he picked up the box and saluted Major Knight. Instead of returning to the lounge, Karl went straight to his room. Being alone right now was what he needed most.

In his room, he removed his jacket and his boots, then stretched out on the bed, his head propped up against the head-board. He held the box for a few minutes without opening it, then slowly removed the cover.

Once again, he held the envelope, fingering his name written by Kitty's hand. He opened the envelope and removed the letter, carefully unfolding it, then read the last thoughts from Kitty.

My Darling Karl,

If Clive has given you this letter, then it's safe to assume I have either been captured or worse, I have fallen in the course of my duty.

We both knew that in our profession, there would always be a high risk for something bad happening to either one of us.

Karl, my wonderful headstrong Austrian sailor, you must continue with the conviction that brought you to us at the BIS. The day that happened, it made my life a fairytale, even though it

would only be for a short time. If it had been me and not you
reading this letter, I know how I would be reacting about now.

Please, forgive me for not sharing more information with you.
The uniform we wear governs the liberties we can share, so again,
my apologies. From here on, you must continue without me.

Your life will be full and rewarding both in your career as well
as your personal life. I pray that you find someone who will wear
that beautiful ring with pride. I know I did.

Karl, have a wonderful, long life, and keep a small private
place for me in your heart.

With love always,

your Kitty

The following day, Karl rose early, had a nice hot bath and
shaved, feeling much better than the day before. He headed down
to breakfast. Due to the early hour, there were few people in the
cafeteria. Karl ate a hearty English breakfast, then headed out for
a walk around the parade grounds. The cool morning air felt so
refreshing.

Passing by the main office building, a familiar officer
approached him. It was Clive. "Good morning, Karl. How are you
feeling this morning?" he asked.

"Much better than yesterday. Thank you. I am so sorry for my
behavior yesterday. I hope you will forgive me," said Karl.

"Perfectly understandable under the circumstances. That
news would have shaken any one of us, so no apologies needed,"
said Clive as he joined Karl on his morning constitutional.

"I was thinking that, before returning from my leave, I would
like to stop to see Kitty's mother and sister. What are your
thoughts on doing that?" asked Karl.

"Admiral idea, Karl. I met her once when she came to visit
Kitty. Her sister is very nice as well. We need to make sure she
will be home when you visit. Tomorrow give me the date you
expect to visit her, and I will make the call. Have you considered

your options yet?" Clive was still being careful and unsure of his friend's frame of mind.

"I have. May I take the time on my leave to make sure? You must know I want to return to field operations, don't you? I could never survive behind a desk."

Karl was trying to impress Clive enough so that what he had said last night would no longer apply. The two walked on till they arrived at the building were the debrief would take place.

"Do you have everything you need for the meeting?" asked Clive, stepping forward to open the door.

"Yes, this will surprise our naval friends. You will see!" Herbert had already arrived and was sitting on the side, waiting to be invited to the table. The room was occupied by six naval officers, eight naval architects, and two secretaries, all sitting around a large, oval table.

"Gentlemen and ladies, please join me in welcoming Captain Herbert Werner, formerly of the German Wehrmacht, and Lieutenant Karl Vita, former first officer on the German merchant service. Vita, by the way, is now a member of the BIS. We look forward to the same happening to Captain Werner very soon. Yesterday morning, these officers arrived back in England. Today, they will share their findings from that mission with this panel.

"Today's topic is the status of the German naval aircraft carrier development. Karl Vita, other than being a successful merchant officer, was previously trained as a marine architect, so he is in an excellent position to speak about what was shared and seen. So, with that brief introduction, let me turn this meeting over to Lieutenant Vita."

Clive sat down next to Colonel Jacks, turning to face the charts already mounted on the easel at the head of the room.

"Thank you, Major Knight, for the introduction. Captain Werner here should be the one we thank for making all the arrangements to access the new aircraft carrier, the *Graf Zeppelin.*

Again, thanks to the captain, we have copies of almost all the design specifications and most of the performance projections.

"At the time of our first meeting, there remained some speculation as to how many and what type of aircraft would be shipped onboard. This direction appeared to be driven by development coming from the Americans as well as the Japanese, both having extensive success in this area. It was also of interest that they did not put much stock in the directions being used by the Royal Navy. I believe the term used was *'nice small carriers with string bag aircraft.'* Time will take that smile from their faces; I suppose.

"Now, my first impression, by any measure, was the sheer size of this very large vessel. Let me now provide you with all the data and photographs we managed to bring back with us. Herbert, if you would be so kind as to distribute the data sheets for everyone to follow along."

Over the next four hours, Karl and Herbert went into extensive detail on every aspect of this first of four carriers ordered by the German Navy. However, Karl emphasized this was the only one being built so far. No other information could be gleaned about when and where the other three would be laid down.

"But when will work start on the other three?" asked one of the naval officers.

"No one seems to know," came the reply from Herbert.

The meeting concluded by Clive thanking Karl and Herbert, adding that a team was still in Germany, gathering intelligence on the new German super battleships and heavy cruisers presently berthed in Hamburg, Wilhelmshaven, and Bremen. Another team is also undercover collecting development and building information on U-Boat production."

The senior naval officer stood, thanking Karl and Herbert for going into harm's way, a job well done.

Outside, the warm sunshine bathed the small group that had gathered in the parking lot.

Herbert was the first to speak, "Karl, tomorrow you leave for a long-overdue leave, and I will be traveling to Aldershot to take on my new role as an intelligence instructor. I'm not sure if we will meet again. I sincerely hope we do. Let's leave it by making a commitment to being comrades forever." Herbert shook Karl's hand as well as grasping his arm with the other.

Finally, he stepped back and saluted in respect to the small group.

Karl reciprocated, then took Herbert's arm, saying, "Herbert, this war, when it comes, and we all know it will come, needs so many more like you. Please, stay safe and remain in touch, my friend." With that, Herbert joined the naval members as they walked toward the waiting staff cars.

"Well, Karl, shall we have a cocktail before we have dinner? I decided, tomorrow morning, I will take you to the station myself. Ronny will be waiting for you on your arrival," Clive remarked as he led the way to the lounge, feeling so much better about Karl's disposition.

Tomorrow, he would be back with his family in Baldock. *I hope this time at home with his family will be the medicine he needs to reset, refocus, and return ready to be the field agent we trained him to be. One can only hope.*

2 8

Returning to Baldock

They arrived at the station a little early, so there was time to get a hot cup of tea before they parted. "You do have the box and the letter to your mother from Kitty with you, Karl?" asked Clive.

"Yes, I do. This letter Kitty gave you to keep is the reason I am feeling better about what we are doing. I'm sure Kitty would not mind me sharing it with you before I leave." Karl reached over, giving the letter to Clive.

"Are you sure about this?" remarked Clive as he removed it from the envelope.

Karl sipped his hot tea while Clive read the letter, after which he slowly returned it to the envelope, saying nothing for a few minutes.

"I think Kitty has a way of making this insanity understandable, and from the look on your face, you are almost back from that dark place you had fallen into. All that I said the other day was probably premature. I did not consider that you were still in so much pain, and that was clouding your vision, so I am truly sorry for those hasty remarks. When you return to us, I believe that after that presentation, you will be much in demand as a key agent," concluded Clive.

"I gave you that letter to read because it applies to all of us who operate in harm's way. Thank you, Clive, for saying that. They are announcing the arrival of my train, so thanks for the lift and spending this time with me. I think we have said what had to be said. See you in ten days."

Karl gathered his things, placed his cap to one side of his head, smiled, then saluted his friend, Major Clive Knight.

He walked out of the café. His swagger was almost back.

"We put our caps on straight in the British Army," a laughing Clive yelled out loud. Clive got a big chuckle out of watching Karl walk away.

An answer came back from Karl. Without turning, he yelled, "I'm not English. I'm a bloody Austrian." His laughter was contagious as he kept walking.

Karl enjoyed his time with Kitty's mother and sister. They had afternoon tea with buttered scones coated with homemade jam. Before leaving, Kitty's mother gave him a picture of Kitty from when she graduated as a first lieutenant.

"She was so proud that day and looked so smart in her uniform. Her life was short, but she lived every day to the fullest. You made the last months the best for her, and for that, we thank you."

Both mother and daughter hugged Karl as he was leaving.

"Please, write to us when you can, and please take care of yourself," Kitty's sister said as she closed the front door behind her.

"I will, and please drop me a line also when you can."

At the station, Karl stood on the platform, staring at Kitty's picture in his hand. "The train for Cambridge with stops in

Welwyn Garden City, Hitchin, Baldock, and Ashwell, now ready for boarding on platform six," came the announcement over the PA system.

The train, with its big smoking engine, slowed to a stop. Karl looked down the length of the train, hoping to see a smart, well dressed English lady walking through the steam and smoke, but that did not happen…just a few disembarking passengers heading who knows where.

He found a compartment and climbed aboard for the short trip to Baldock. Ronny met him at the station. "What say we stop for a pint at the George before we make it home?" asked Ronny.

"Now, that's a wonderful idea," replied Karl. Walking into the lobby, Karl could feel Kitty's presence. *It will be like this*, he thought, *every place we went together, so I will embrace the feeling!*

"Ronny, tomorrow, I want to go to Lloyds Bank to open an account. What time do they open?"

"Banker's hours in England are usually from 1000 to 1530 hours," replied Ronny, smiling at Karl.

"Are you kidding? That's like a half-day," replied Karl.

"As I said, banker's hours." Ronny got a big rise out of Karl's reaction. "How long do we have you for?" asked Ronny.

"About ten days. It will be so nice to be a civilian, even if it is just for a short while," Karl answered in delight at being just that, a civilian.

Sitting at the bar, Ronny gingerly approached the situation with any new information on Kitty. "Karl, it goes without saying that we are heartbroken and extremely worried about not knowing Kitty's whereabouts."

Karl took a large swig of beer, then looked at Ronny squarely in the eyes, "You can stop worrying about where she is because she is dead. She got killed in an ambush some time back. I, myself, only received the news several days ago. That's why I need to open a safe deposit box to keep her ring safe unless Mama would like to put into her own safe deposit box."

"Oh, my God, Karl, I am so sorry to hear this tragic news. Mama and Freida will be so upset to hear this." Ronny placed his hand over Karl's as he replied to the news.

Arriving at the bungalow, spirits were high. Mama had her youngest son home again. Being surrounded by her daughter, son-in-law, and grandson gave her a great deal of happiness, even though she lived each day in fear of hearing about Papa, her three other sons, and grandson Fritz.

They were in a dangerous place with no way of getting information to her. "Karl, you are home. How long do we have you for this time? And do you have any information about Kitty?" asked Mama.

"Mama give me a big hug. You're throwing all sorts of questions at me before I'm even in the house." Karl needed a few more minutes before giving Mama the answer to her question about Kitty.

"I'm so sorry. The excitement of seeing you again has turned me into a raving lunatic. Please, forgive me," said Mama, feeling a little embarrassed.

"The good news is I'm home for a nice, long, ten-day visit. Unfortunately, I have some bad news about Kitty. Mama, she is dead. I did not have time to tell you as I only received that news two days ago."

Karl knew this would upset Mama very much. In the short time she had gotten to know Kitty, she had as much adopted her as her own daughter.

"Oh, no, my God, are you sure? Could there be a mistake? My poor Karl, how you must be hurting. I'm so sorry. I can't believe this."

Mama was openly distraught by this unwelcome surprise.

"Where are Freida and Franchot?" asked Karl, trying to break the tension.

"They're up in the field. Franchot likes to feed the big draft horse up there with carrots. They should be home in about forty-five minutes," replied Mama, still holding onto her son.

"I am going to walk up to the field with Ronny to meet my sister and nephew. Do you mind? I will be back soon. I hope you have a nice dinner planned for tonight." Karl was still trying to overcome the Kitty situation.

Reaching the field, he saw Franchot and Frieda sitting on the fence, the big cart horse enjoying being fed carrots.

"Look, Mama, it's Uncle Karl and Daddy," said Franchot, jumping down and running over to hug his uncle.

"Why don't we take a little walk and get Tug to follow us with those carrots?" said Ronny to Franchot, wanting to give Karl time alone with Freida to share the terrible news about Kitty. The reaction was the same: total surprise, plenty of tears, and regrets for the time they would never have together as sisters-in-law.

Over the following week, Karl spent many hours walking the streets of Baldock, reliving the happy hours he had spent with Kitty not so long ago.

He opened the bank account at *Lloyds*, getting his safe deposit box and placing the ring inside, along with a large envelope with cash and other documents he would not need for quite a while.

The key, he gave to Mama for safe-keeping, making sure she knew, if she needed to, she could use the money in the box.

The rest of the time, he spent around the bungalow. He was getting himself ready for what lay ahead. One night, he and Ronny, over a glass of beer, talked about the latest attempts by Prime Minister Neville Chamberlain to appease Hitler in a meeting in Munich but returning to England with a useless non-aggression treaty, claiming, "Peace in our time."

"What a waste of time and humiliation for the English people. Who is kidding whom? By next year, we will be at war with Germany. Everyone in the armed forces knows it except that spineless Chamberlain. They must all be laughing in Germany right now." Ronny was very angry as he said this.

Ronny continued, "We keep giving in to Hitler's demands, Austria, Sudetenland in Czechoslovakia, his constant bullying and pressuring Poland for its principal port of Danzig, which we both know is already a free port run by a puppet administration for Nazi Germany. Hitler insists it will soon become a part of Germany. Watch out, Poland. He has plans to take the rest of your country over by force, if necessary.

"Karl, if he makes an outright attack on Poland, England, along with France, will not stand by. Ideally, we will declare war on Germany. Left unchecked, he will keep recklessly overrunning Europe until he has it all. The British cabinet has a mutual assistance plan they are pursuing in the first quarter of next year with Poland and endorsed by France. If it were me, I would have it already signed, but then again, I'm not a politician." Ronny again showed his frustration with the British Government.

That following storm is getting close to becoming a catastrophic storm, thought Karl as he listened to Ronny. In one way, this conversation fueled Karl's conviction to stay and be active in the BIS.

The enjoyable week passed quickly. Being with the family was the medicine Karl needed; however, his time was now up. It was time to say goodbye until the next time, whenever that would be, if ever.

Mama, Freida, and Franchot accompanied Karl to Baldock Station. Ronny drove them all in the big staff car. Mama's parting words were to the point, "Son, please be safe doing whatever they have you involved in. Promise me that, will you?"

"Mama, I will take every precaution, but I can't promise you anything. It's the nature of the job I do."

Out on the platform, they all waited for the arrival of the smoking beast that would take Karl away for who knew how long.

"Here comes the train, Mama. Why don't you leave now? It

311

will be easier for all of us if you do." Karl could feel the tension building.

Standing around was not making it any better. They quickly hugged, kissed, and blew more kisses as they walked back down the platform. Karl felt relieved; he wanted to say so much more.

On the train, Karl reflected on the course of events that had brought him to this point in his hectic life: his life growing up in Vienna, the fun times as a merchant navy cadet, his rapid climb to become the first officer of the *Tristian*, the beautiful, intelligent women who had left lasting impressions on him forever.

Now, he began his new life and career as a British intelligence officer.

Arriving at the station in Slough, Karl could see Clive standing with another person. *Wonder who that is?*

The train came to a full stop, banging the bumpers as it did so. Stepping down onto the platform, Karl turned, momentarily looking into the smoke and steam, imagining the trim figure of a striking English lady emerging. That did not happen, nor did Karl expect it to.

Walking closer to Clive's position, Karl kept his vision on the bent-over image of the man wearing a trilby hat that covered most of his face. As he drew closer, he stopped in disbelief, "I can't believe it. Bill is that you?" gasped Karl, seeing his old friend.

"When Clive told me, he was heading to the station to pick you up, I said I had to come, even though walking for me is still a big problem."

Bill held Karl tightly by the arm as he spoke. "This is wonderful; the three of us back together once again." Bill was elated at this reunion, his face now beaming with a broad smile.

Karl held onto his friend Bill, saying, "Chaps, do you realize it was you two who first met me on the *Clyde Princess* in Dover, and look at all that has happened since then. We are still alive, including you, Bill. Guess we have come full circle, so to speak. I think we should celebrate at the nearest pub. What do you say?"

The three friends walked slowly down the platform, allowing for Bill's limp. This friendship would transcend all the hurdles of the *following storm*, friends forever. The storm was far from over.

EPILOGUE

The year 1938 would not come to a happy ending. On October 15, the German troops occupied the Sudetenland without any resistance from the alleged allies.

November 9 and 10, the Kristallnacht, the night of broken glass, set a black cloud over the fate of the German and Austrian Jews.

In those two days and nights, the Nazis destroyed more than one thousand shops and synagogues, arrested more than thirty thousand, and brutally killed many more.

On January 5, 1939, Poland, as predicted, under extreme pressure from Hitler, returned the seaport of Danzig to the Germans.

In that same year, England moved forward with the British and Polish Mutual Assistance Treaty, which came a little late to be of any use.

It did, however, trigger the start of World War Two, when the Germans invaded Poland on September 1st. Karl would go on to be a vital part of the British Intelligence Service, operating undercover in many parts of Europe.

His predictions on the German naval buildup were uncannily accurate. His knowledge of other maritime activities became key in strategic planning for the allies. In his personal life, he would meet other ladies, some of whom were English military types, but no lasting loves.

Kitty still had his heart.

THE END

ABOUT THE AUTHOR

In his formative life living in
England, Peter Moscovita enjoyed
extensive European travel with his
parents. Those summer vacations
planted a seed in him to experience
new lands beyond the boundaries
of Europe.

In 1966, he made that desire a
reality, emigrating to the United
States as a Design Engineer,
working mainly in aerospace and
finally in medical instrumentation.

In 1982, he married his wife,
Martine. The new couple shared
many similar interests, including the love of traveling, sailing,
cruising, culinary food groups, reading, and world history.

1986, he joined with two fellow engineers to start up their
own medical instrumentation company. It allowed Peter and
Martine the opportunity to continue their love of traveling,
experiencing new lands around the world.

In 2010, the decision was made to successfully sell the
company for a new life in retirement. The love of travel now had
no boundaries, so in 2011, the couple packed up their boat and
headed south from their home in Rhode Island, arriving in Sara-
sota, Florida, in November of that year.

Since that time, they have continued traveling and enjoying
their new lifestyle as residents of Lakewood Ranch, Florida.

Made in the USA
Coppell, TX
06 September 2021

61922064R00184